A BODY OF FORENSIC EVIDENCE

The morgue was quiet.

It almost seemed as if, somehow, this humiliating experience would be over for the girl in a few minutes, she would sit up, jump down from the table, put her clothes back on, and leave. But her body was ashen, the color of death, and she would not.

"I understand we have some bite marks. You think they *are* bites?" Pinchus asked.

"No question." Peter kept photographing. "I think I can get an impression on one of them. It looks pretty deep."

The stone was hard in less than five minutes. Peter lifted the apparatus gingerly from the skin. He turned it over, studied the contours in the rubber.

"Well?" Onasis asked.

"Here's your killer."

DEADLY
IMPRESSION

▼

DENNIS ASEN

▲

BANTAM BOOKS

New York • Toronto • London
Sydney • Auckland

Deadly Impression

A Bantam Book/September 1996

ISBN 0-553-57515-5

Published simultaneously in the United States and Canada

Bantam Books are published by Bantam Books, a division of Bantam
Doubleday Dell Publishing Group, Inc. Its trademark, consisting of the
words "Bantam Books" and the portrayal of a rooster, is Registered in
U.S. Patent and Trademark Office and in other countries. Marca
Registrada. Bantam Books, 1540 Broadway, New York, New York
10036.

PRINTED IN THE UNITED STATES OF AMERICA

OPM   0 9 8 7 6 5 4 3 2 1

To Nancy, my lovely wife — biggest fan and best friend. You shared this dream and never let it die even when I had my doubts. And for Lisa, Lee and Shelby. Also in memory of my Dad, the real Fox, and inspiration for this book.

There are those who deserve to be acknowledged.

First and foremost, Bob Silverstein, who discovered this story's potential and who invested more time and energy than I had a right to expect. Beyond teacher and agent, his friendship is truly my fortune.

Next, Dr. Isidore Mihalakis, forensic pathologist, for his knowledge and expertise. So, too, the Coroner's offices of Lehigh and Northampton counties for the privilege of working with them.

Likewise, a word of gratitude to Casey Alenson Blaine, my editor at Bantam, for her dedication and hard work.

And finally to so many others, too numerous to mention, who guided me along the way. You know who you are — and I thank you one and all.

DEADLY
IMPRESSION

PART
ONE

1

Pinchus wasn't that smart. Hardly anyone ever was. And those who were mostly did not draw notice to themselves. That was why they could slip through the world like shadows, gardening it to their desire.

As he did.

Pinchus pissed him off: People who got heaped with credit they didn't deserve, by others who were even dumber, always pissed him off.

Especially cops. Cops were dumb. He'd proved that before. He'd prove it again—with this cop, Pinchus, and the false humility that had oozed out of him like slime during the television interview.

He lay in bed on his back, hands moving idly, fingertips trailing across his chest, down the flatness of his belly. The plan was still vague, but he didn't worry about that. The essence was what he enjoyed, what pleasured him. The logistics would come: They were the rules of the game—fascinating, needful of attention—but not the prize, where the pleasure was.

He thought about this prize.

And the ends of his lips lifted in a little smile as he imagined the scene, saw fleeting bits and pieces of it.

He didn't have a painter's imagination; he had more of a photographer's memory. He let the hazy half-formed images of his imagination fall away in favor of the sharper, detailed images of memory.

He lay in bed, remembering—how she looked, how it *would* be.

Her pretty oval face framed with sleep-tousled

chestnut hair. Lips full and winecolored, the kind that scarcely ever needed enhancing, parted now in a welcoming half smile, her eyelids batting as she came awake, blinking to consciousness.

His hands slid lightly down the flatness of his belly to his loins.

But he wasn't who her dream had led her to expect to find, and she had wakened to a world she could not have imagined when she went to bed.

Her eyes, lovely to behold, blue he knew, but their color unreadable in the dim light that filtered through the curtains drawn across the nighttime window, widened in incomprehension, in the utter inability to understand the information coming through them into her mind. Then, though it seemed impossible, they widened even further as she did begin to realize where she was and what she was seeing, and then her jaw dropped, her mouth gaped, and she began to scream.

He lifted his hips a little, placed his hands inside the waistband and pushed his shorts down his thighs. And then, reembracing the fantasy in his mind, he stroked his hardened shaft with one hand, and gently, rhythmically, pulsed his cupped testicles with the other.

In a quick careful movement, one that she could see, he placed his knife into the cavity of her mouth, the tip pricking into the rear of her upper palate and the part nearest the haft pressing down slightly on her tongue, and he said, quietly and very calmly: "If you scream, I will kill you. Piece by piece. I'll start by cutting out your tongue."

Outside, thunder boomed.

In the end, what brought him the final, short, intense rush to ecstasy was a stunningly vivid image: not only the sight, but the feel, the smell, the sound. . . .

Her back was graceful, beautifully curved from neck to lumbar and swelling rise of buttocks, her spine in a bit of relief now because of the tension in her. His fingers digging into her shoulders, his straightened

*arms raising his torso up off her, her hair draggled and
sweat-soaked now, her head turned to the side, half off
the pillow, eyes squeezed shut, mouth twisted open, her
breath rasping, body rocking as he pounded into her,
the bedsprings squeaking, the headboard striking
against the wall, cotton sheets, fading perfume, sweat,
private pungencies, he was driving, driving in where he
was sure no one had ever driven into her before, where
she had never thought anyone would, and he was driving . . .*

And he shuddered, and convulsed, and convulsed
again, and lifted his hips off the bed, squeezing himself.

Afterward, he lay with his arms loose at his side,
the tiniest of smiles on his lips, his eyes closed, breathing deeply and steadily, as some people breathe after
yoga or running, when their heartbeat has returned to
normal again, endorphins washing through his brain,
his mind clear of thought, his body sinking down into
peaceful sleep.

2

The late-Sunday-afternoon press conference was only half over, but Pinchus had had enough.

"Gentlemen," he said. "Ladies. There's nothing more I can tell you. You've been kinder to me than I deserve. I'd like to help you, but I'm afraid I can't, and I do have an engagement. Captain Schwenk knows more about this person and his background than I do. I'm sure he can help you."

Not only could Schwenk help them, he was nearly salivating for the chance. Pinchus hated to be the one to give it to him, but it was the easiest way out.

"Lieutenant," said a young man with the university paper—

Jesus, the *university*? Everybody was here but the First Baptist Church *Community Bulletin*.

"—would you say he might have picked his next victim from the campus if he hadn't been caught?"

Pinchus was on his feet and already making his way out from around the table, where the mayor had been sitting on one side of him and Schwenk on the other. He paused.

"No. There's nothing in his history to suggest that. His victims were pretty much targets of opportunity."

Flashbulbs popped, television lights followed him as he made his way out of the room. He wished they'd gone right to Schwenk, who was in his natural element before a camera and always happiest there.

"One more, Lieutenant—"

"Give us a thumbs-up, Seymour."

"Nice going, Loot."

Carmen Suarez, a feature writer for the *Ledger*, arched an eyebrow at him as he passed her chair: a great mane of black hair, slightly oriental cast to her eyes, olive skin. A looker. Smart. Straight-shooter, too. One of the few journalists Pinchus really liked. (He remembered long ago when there weren't any journalists; when they were called reporters.)

"Hot engagement?" she said, rising.

The rest of the press had turned their attention to Schwenk, who had taken the microphone.

"Depends on whether you're free or not."

She laughed, walking to the door with him.

"Seriously," he said.

She gauged him, saw that he *wasn't* serious, but that he wasn't happy either. "Kate?" she asked.

"Yeah. We're not doing so well."

"You've been through hard times together before."

Pinchus nodded. "But this time," he said gloomily, "I don't know."

She stopped at the door to the hall. "Okay if I call you at home late tonight?"

"Give some couples' counseling?"

"Maybe. If you give me some inside stuff on Terranova."

"That's what I like about you, Carmen. You're all heart."

"Okay?"

"Okay," he answered.

He went out of the room and down the wide curving marble stairs to the first floor of the city hall building, nodding to the uniforms on post, and out into the parking lot. He got into his five-year-old Cutlass Supreme and started off, glad of the fresh air that flowed through the two open windows playing with strands of his longish, graying hair.

They weren't bad most of the time, the press, but in a case like this they came plunging down like vultures, squabbling and croaking, each one wanting to tear off a bigger piece than the others.

Pinchus wondered if that quality wasn't intensified by the city's unconscious fear that it was really still just a small town in comparison to its nearest and legendary neighbors. Philadelphia lay only half an hour's drive, south and east. New York was just a little over an hour and a half away, north and east. Through the nineteenth century, Hamilton, Pennsylvania, *had* been a small town. It was born of textiles, grew with steel, and made money. By the twenties, lent a certain intellectual prestige by its well-endowed and thriving university, but with its rural surroundings still quite picturesque and inviting, it had become a popular summer area for the privileged from New York and Philadelphia.

In the late forties, fifties, and sixties, it exploded. It became a kind of urban suburbia, attracting industrial and high-tech corporations. People migrated from both of its sophisticated neighbors and moved to Hamilton to live, commuting to their work in New York and Philadelphia. Upscale malls arose. Quaint restaurants opened. Local history was exploited and made charming.

Now, as the new century approached, Hamilton was a modern American city of 250,000. Proudly, it called itself the "Little Apple." Being a city also meant that it had its share of problems, including violent crime. But sometimes, fearing in its heart that it was still just a small town, Hamilton would seize opportunities—triumphal or obscene—and try to prove that it was just as vivid, vital, and substantial as its overshadowing neighbors.

It was a quality that Pinchus did not hold against the city. In fact, it was part of its appeal. He liked Hamilton. He liked being a cop here. He liked doing what he could do to make it an even nicer place to live, for himself and everyone else.

Pinchus put the press conference out of his mind,

driving west on Tamarack Avenue through town, then turned north onto Fifteenth Street, heading toward the Hillcrest Community Home. He had a standing appointment there every Sunday at six, had had it for nearly fifteen years; he called on the rare occasions he couldn't make it.

Seymour Pinchus was nearly fifty-five years old. He still had his hair, but it was growing finer and it broke more easily than it once had. He had a full face with a large nose and soft brown eyes that gave him a kind appearance. Mostly he was kind. When he needed not to be, he wasn't. He was five-feet-ten-inches tall and just a little overweight. For years, he had been just a little overweight. And for nearly as many years, he'd been saying he was going to start a diet soon.

Pinchus had been in homicide nearly twenty-five years. He didn't like seeing murdered people, but he liked catching the people who had murdered them. He'd always liked that—even loved it, sometimes even thought it was what he lived for. It still bothered him when he couldn't catch them, as sometimes he couldn't, but that was part of the job and he'd learned to accept it. At fifty-four, Pinchus knew how not to lose sleep over the ones that got away. Most of the time. At fifty-four, he was amazed by the fact that he *was* fifty-four. Not that he felt he should be younger, but that he had actually lived that many years. At twenty-five, after surviving a knife wound when he was working a patrol car, he'd become convinced he was going to die early.

Before he was thirty. Then, before he was thirty-five. Forty . . .

It was almost a running joke in homicide, like his diet: any day now.

His mother had threatened to sit *shiva* when he told his parents he was going to join the police department. Jewish boys from good Jewish families did not become policemen. They became doctors, lawyers, psychotherapists, dentists. At the least, accountants. She sustained her disapproval for years but came around in time, even became proud of what he did, kept a scrapbook of his achievements. Loved to hear him called the Fox.

He didn't. He hated it.

He *wasn't* smart like a fox. He was just a good cop who happened to pay attention to details, to notice things, to be—as Kate liked to say—*present*. That and a couple of breaks in the right place at the right time equalled the Fox. Finding Dale Terranova, the Riverside Killer, was a matter of both those two elements: being present and being lucky.

He was halfway to Hillcrest when he got a call on his radio. "Pinchus," he answered.

It was a crash and burn. Two dead: the driver, and someone else who had been in the trunk, tied up. Autopsy at 6 A.M. tomorrow. Pinchus had been assigned. He acknowledged. He sighed. He was tired. He was glad Sam would be back from vacation tomorrow—though not early enough to make the autopsy. More than the help, Pinchus was looking forward to the company. No doubt, Sam would hear about the Terranova affair on the news.

It bothered him, the way murders were handled in the media. The impact of the event was lost. Generally, the victims had families, which were only passingly acknowledged, their pain and anguish scarcely recognized, never assuaged. To lose someone close was devastating, the most horrible trial anyone could undergo. Pinchus knew this from his own experience. He knew the terror of the night when all was awesomely still, the overwhelming grief, the fear that you can't go on, the even greater fear that you probably will.

In time, and not much time at all, the media would forget the Riverside Killer. But for the families of the victims, Dale Terranova would haunt and hurt them for the rest of their lives.

For them, Seymour Pinchus grieved.

"Was she raped?"

"What kind of weapon did he use?"

"Cut into how many parts?"

That was what they wanted to know, wanted to hear.

"How does it feel to be a hero?"

I wouldn't know, Pinchus said in his mind.

All *he* had ever felt like was late.

Had the victims been able, they would have screamed: "Where were you two hours ago?" "Six hours ago?" "A week?"

It was the nature of the job. He always got there too late. Often his work saved other people—at least he liked to think it did, future victims—but those people would remain forever faceless and unknown to him. Not like the ones for whom he was too late. He could never quite forget any of them. Sometimes, in his mind, he said to a particular face that swam up before him: I'm sorry I couldn't have gotten there earlier. I'm sorry.

Rose Fitapaldi was in a good mood.

"I saw you on TV," she shouted when he entered. "Channel Six. You looked very good. Very handsome. Kate didn't come?"

Pinchus stooped over Rose's chair and kissed her. He also turned on her hearing aid, through the control in her lap.

"Thank you," he said. "They say the camera adds ten pounds. Did I look ten pounds heavier?"

"No," she said at near normal volume now that she could hear again. "You looked five pounds over-weight, which you are."

"I'm going on a diet soon." Pinchus furrowed his forehead.

"At my sweet sixteen party."

Rose Fitapaldi had lived at Hillcrest Community Home for almost as long as Pinchus had been coming to see her. She wasn't really as old as she looked or pretended to be, but she was bent and ravaged by rheumatoid arthritis, and, to the eye, was hardly distinguishable from the other, older residents in the nursing home.

"Shall we?" Pinchus pulled her walker around and moved to help her up.

"Get your goddamn hands off," she said testily. "I can manage myself."

"How would it look if, God forbid, you fell and broke a leg? The papers would have a field day! 'Celebrated Detective Looks On While Older Friend Fractures Femur.' I'm only thinking of myself."

She relented. "Well, if it will protect you."

He helped her up.

"I don't want to be late," she said, swinging the walker forward and stepping up into it. "Everyone else probably saw you on TV too—since there's not much to do here but watch—and I want to bask in some of your glory."

"Glory is in the mind of the beholder."

"Wherever they keep it is fine with me."

They left her room and began making their way down the hall to the commissary, where Sunday evening dinner was about to be served.

"Where's Kate? This is the weekend she usually comes with you."

Pinchus made a vague gesture. "Next time maybe."

"She's not an easy woman," Rose said. "But you're not an easy man either."

"I'm a nice guy, though."

"And she's a nice woman. That and a marriage license, maybe you could live happily ever after. But then maybe not. What do I know?"

Dinner was bland turkey with a stuffing that was cold. Alternate weekends it was fairly tasteless roast beef with a gravy that was cold. There was a really good apple pie, though (as there almost always was), and the server brought Pinchus a hunk of cheddar cheese to put on top of it without being asked.

They lingered over coffee so Rose could show him
f to her friends and to their Sunday guests.

Pinchus didn't mind. She seemed to get such a kick
it of it.

It was a struggle for Rose to return to her room.
ie was exhausted when Pinchus got her settled into
er chair.

"You know," he said, "if we got you a wheelchair,
would be easier for you here. And I could take you
it to places. We could go to a nice restaurant on Sun-
iys or—"

"Don't start again, Seymour." Rose paused, still
orking for breath after her trip. "People look at you
fferent when you're in a chair, like you're pathetic.
id enough I have to use the walker. Bad enough I
ive to live here. Don't go making it worse."

"Whatever you say."

"Damn right. Did you see the look on Irma
idderman's face when she saw you showed up, that
>u left your television show to see me? Her son the
g deal surgeon couldn't make it again."

They chatted. About Rose's canasta scores of the
evious week, how the cuttings in the solarium were
>ing, a little about Dale Terranova.

Rose Fitapaldi's world was largely limited to Hill-
est; her personal part of it was a modest room with
firm chair, a single bed, a little writing desk, and a
iair for a visitor. She'd gotten hold of some pleasant
llow curtains Pinchus had put up for her, along with
couple of bookshelves. Against the wall was a little
moire that held Rose's collection of tiny crystal ani-
ials, the only true touch of individuality she chose to
<press here.

They were interrupted by a tentative knock.
Rose?"

"Alice! Come in, come in, dear. Seymour, this is my
ew friend Alice from the university. Alice Schaeffer.
lice, this is the very famous lieutenant Seymour
inchus I already told you all about."

"And whom I've seen a lot of on television the last two days."

Pinchus was silent—almost entranced.

"Well? Seymour?" Rose prompted.

Pinchus realized he was staring at Alice Schaeffe. She was probably the most beautiful woman he ha ever seen in his life. Possibly the most beautiful woma in the world.

Alice was smiling at him. Clearly, she had lor since gotten used to being stared at and dealt with goodnaturedly.

"Uh, hi." Pinchus said. "There'll be less of m soon. I'm going on a diet."

Alice laughed. Her teeth were perfectly white an straight. Her lips were like pomegranates, whatever th hell a pomegranate was. He thought he remembere something like that from the Song of Solomon. sounded wonderful. He saw the faintest pulse of a vei beneath the flawless skin of her throat. He wanted kiss it. He did not think he had felt anything quite lil that since he was sixteen years old.

"You look fine exactly the way you are," she sai

And he knew she meant that, and loved her eve more for it.

"You solved a big one," she said, tucking a lor strand of chestnut hair behind her ear.

"We got lucky," he demurred.

"He solved a big one," Rose boasted. "He solv all the big ones."

"I just came by to drop off this book you wante Rose. I have to get back to the library."

Seymour looked at the book. It was a large volun on bonsai trees, with color plates. "My newest pa sion," Rose said. "We're growing them in the solariun I'm going to give you a bonsai Christmas tree f Christmas."

"Bonsai Chanukah bush for Chanukah."

Rose made a face. "Bonsai pagan Yule log."

"Got to go," Alice interrupted. "Nice to meet you, Lieutenant."

"Seymour."

"Seymour."

"Thank you, Alice," Rose said. "You're a love. Seymour, why don't you walk Alice back, it's only a couple of blocks to the university. Get to know each other a little. I'm tired anyway. I think I'm going to go to sleep."

"Sure—if you don't mind," Pinchus said, looking at Alice.

"I don't mind at all. But I wouldn't want to bother you."

"Not a bother," Seymour said sincerely. "A pleasure."

Alice smiled.

There was a chill in the night air. Alice turned up the collar of her blazer against it.

"That was some case you broke," she said. "It's the talk of the campus."

"It wasn't much."

"Come on, you needn't be modest with me."

"Really?"

She cocked her head. "Well, a bit, seeing as how we just met." She smiled.

"Actually, I was telling the truth. It wasn't much of a challenge. Just digging and luck. Most police work is like that. We get more credit than we deserve. People want to think we're smarter than we are. I think it makes them feel safe."

"So how *did* you do it?"

"If I told you, I'd spoil it, like a magician showing you how a trick works."

She winked. "Don't hold out on me now."

"I don't know if I could even if I wanted to." Pinchus reached into his breast pocket and took out a notepad.

They had arrived at the edge of the campus.

Pinchus put his hand on Alice's elbow and steered her across the street to the opposite corner, where a sodium lamp cast a wide circle of light. He wrote something on the top sheet of the pad, then pulled out the sheet beneath it and handed it to Alice.

"What does that say?" he asked.

She looked at both sides. "Nothing. This isn't the one you wrote on."

"Correct. Give it back." He wrote on the paper and returned it to her. "Now what does it say."

" 'Knock, Knock,' " she said, reading.

"What else?"

"Nothing."

"Look carefully."

"Still nothing." She smiled, puzzled and interested.

"Hold it slantwise to the light. Look for an indentation made by the pen when I wrote on the previous page."

Alice did. "Oh, I see it now. You wrote the word Be. . . . ?" She pursed her lips. "Be . . . Beware."

"Right."

"Why? What's the significance of that?"

"Always beware when someone knocks," Pinchus said sententiously. "Especially when you're young and innocent."

"A little less young than I used to be, certainly much less innocent."

"As are we all, alas. Nevertheless, a little wariness never hurts. But that wasn't my point. What happened was that we got a letter from the killer telling us where we'd find his most recent victim. It was the first of three murders he planned here. He'd already killed three in Boston, then three in New York. Maybe he was working his way south."

"Yecchh!" Alice gave a theatrical shudder.

"The note didn't say. But it did say, 'One down, two to go.' I kept looking at it. And then I saw, very faintly, beneath some of the writing, the indentation of what turned out to be a telephone number that he had written on the page on top of this one."

"You're kidding!"

"No. He was dumb. Most criminals are. And we got lucky. The number was a Detroit number, a small pharmaceutical house. We got the records of calls to that number and matched one to a hotel room here. And staying in that hotel room was Dale Terranova, a drug detail man for a large supply house. He was doing a little business on the side with the Detroit outfit. His territory was the Northeast. And the last two areas—"

"—he canvassed were Boston and New York," Alice finished.

"Bingo. The rest was easy."

Pinchus gently nudged her and they continued walking.

"You sound almost disappointed."

"Not that we got him. God, no. I'm grateful we stopped him when we did. But sometimes—don't take this the wrong way—sometimes I long for a challenge."

"This wasn't?"

"All I did was notice."

Carved in a flat sandstone rock that stood on a wooden tripod in the living room of his little house was the word NOTICE. The work had been done by one of the apprentice stonecarvers working on the Cathedral of Saint John the Divine up in New York. Kate had gotten it for him for his last birthday. Doing that, Kate had said—being quiet and noticing, truly *noticing*—was a form of meditation. The thought of Kate brought Pinchus mixed emotions: longing, sorrow, anger. Others he couldn't identify.

"Was it something I said?" Alice inquired. "Or didn't?"

"Pardon?"

"You got gloomy."

"Oh. Sorry. How do you know Rose?"

"From a research project. On metabolism and age. I'm working on my doctorate, in biology." Alice tucked her hands in her jacket pockets. "I met her two weeks ago. We got on famously."

"Good for both of you. She doesn't make friends easily."

"I gathered. It's sad she's so alone. She doesn't have any family at all?"

"She had a son once. She grieves silently. We all have our private *shver harts*."

"*Shver harts?*"

"Yiddish. It means sadness or misery, of the highest order."

"I don't."

"Don't what?"

"Have any *shver harts*."

Pinchus laughed. "It should only be."

"What happened to her son?"

"Ah." There was a long pause. He said, "He was a detective. Vince Fitapaldi. Nicest guy you'd ever want to meet. He and his partner got a call on a robbery in progress. It wasn't their call, they were homicide, but they took it anyway. They were only a block away. When they got there, his partner wanted to wait for backup, but Vince wanted to go in, told his partner to cover the side exit. Something went wrong inside. The gunman came out with Vince, using him as a shield, holding a pistol to his head. The other cop dropped into a combat crouch, aiming, and froze there. Vince yelled, 'Shoot him! Shoot the bastard!' as the guy hustled him toward a car. His partner didn't move, afraid he'd hit Vince. But if he *didn't* fire, the gunman might kill Vince. 'Shoot him!' Vince shouted. 'Don't let him get away.' His partner cocked his gun. The robber got the car door open. Vince's partner didn't move. 'Shoot him, I tell you, or I'm dead!' Vince pleaded. His partner psyched himself up to take the shot. . . ."

"And?"

Pinchus wet his lips. "But he couldn't do it. He stood there dead-still like a goddamn coward unable to accept the responsibility for his accuracy, of taking the chance. The gunman got into the car with Vince, took off, stopped about fifty feet away, and shot Vince through the head. Blew his brains out through the open passenger window, then dumped him out and kept going."

There was silence.

"Vince Fitapaldi was your friend, wasn't he?"

"Yes. He was."

"And he was your partner?"

"How'd you know?"

"Because it was hard for you to tell me."

Pinchus nodded. "What else?"

"You called his partner a goddamn coward. You wouldn't have said that about someone else."

"You'd make an okay detective."

"You make a lousy coward. You can't blame yourself. You didn't know that guy would kill Vince."

"But I was wrong, and he did."

Alice considered Pinchus with her compassionate blue eyes. "Rose says you've been coming by nearly every Sunday for years. Don't you think you've paid off any blame you had?"

"No. That can't be paid. But that's not why I come. It's why I started, but not why I do it now. I do it because she's all alone. And I know what that's like."

"What happened to the guy who killed Vince?"

"It was a very long shot. But it was like I had all the time in the world, like everything was in slow motion. There was nothing that could disturb me. I stood in the street, took aim, and squeezed the shot off. It went through the back window and through the back of his head and out between his eyes and then out through the windshield. It was a textbook-perfect shot. The only thing was, I made it too late."

They had come to the library, a brightly lit three-story building of stone and glass. They stood at the foot of the short flight of stairs leading up to its entrance.

"Lieutenant Pinchus?" Alice said.

"Yes?"

"I have a fiancé. He doesn't live here and I don't see him as often as I'd like, but I do have one. I wanted you to know that."

"Yes," Pinchus said, a bit surprised. Actually he was flattered.

"Give this thing up, will you?"

He nodded. "I almost have."

"You know what's keeping you from finishing it?"

"What?"

"The little touch of self-pity you have."

"Oooomph!" Pinchus made a sound as if he'd been hit in the belly.

"Which is not attractive in an otherwise extremely nice and appealing man." Alice rose up on her toes, gave him a little kiss on the lips. "Bye," she said, and started up the stairs.

Pinchus watcher her go. This time, he thought, I'm about twenty-five years too late.

When Pinchus got back to the modest, pleasant old house he owned on the southern edge of town—an area that had once been country, now absorbed by the city, but where there were still streams and tiny patches of woods—the blinking light on his answering machine told him he had received only one message.

So much for the wages of fame.

He had anticipated Carmen's call, but not this early. It was from Diane.

"You were dashing and wonderful," she said. "But then I expect nothing else from you. Peter was a little pouty that he didn't get mentioned in any of the reports, but he'll get over it. We love you. Congratulations, congratulations."

Pinchus smiled. He loved Diane. Still, he wished Kate had called, or even Daniel—and he was more glad than he was willing to admit that at least Diane had.

The night was awfully quiet sometimes.

3

He was sitting at the kitchen table with a cup of bouillon. From the living room, he could hear Pinchus's voice on the Sunday evening newscast.

Jesus, he had come almost to hate Pinchus—a man who had never done him any harm.

He had formulated the last of the details. Slowly, he rehearsed them in his mind. His brow wrinkled as he concentrated, trying to picture it all. This time, when he reached the final moments, there was only a little pleasure—more anticipation, like an athlete moving forward to compete.

The timing had to be perfect.

The opportunity would present itself tomorrow. At latest, Tuesday.

He finished his mental rehearsal. In the living room, the channel was changed, a movie began. He sipped his broth. He pictured the small box he had prepared, the implements inside. These images were palpable, easier for him to conjure than the scenes he had rehearsed because they already existed.

Pinchus would never catch him. No one ever had. No one ever would. It was a world of fools.

4

Peter Roberts reached out sluggishly from beneath the blanket and picked up the phone on the second ring. He opened an eye. The numbers on the clock-radio said 6:30.

"Hello," he said, voice raspy.

"Peter, it's Seymour. Sorry to wake you."

"I've been up for hours."

Pinchus chuckled. "We've got a real doozy here. Two of them, actually. Car crash. Burn jobs. Possible homicide with one. Hell, maybe both. How soon can you get to the morgue?"

Peter calculated. He'd have to call Nina, tell her to reschedule the morning appointments. Not easy. Mondays were rough. There would be some very unhappy patients. Well, she'd have to deal with it.

"Eight," he said.

"Good. We truly need you on this one. Incidentally, you get a nice mention for your Riverside ID in this morning's *Ledger.* A front-pager by Carmen Suarez. Kiss the kids for me."

They said good-bye. Peter put the receiver back on the hook.

Beside him, Diane stretched, yawned. She sat up. "Who was that?"

"Seymour. They've got another case."

"Already? My God."

"Not like the Keller girl."

The Keller girl—Dale Terranova's victim—had been cut into pieces. Which rotted for a week before they were found. At the morgue, a technician had put her severed head into a white enameled pan for Peter to work on. Peter had had to clean some maggots out of the mouth that the technician had missed.

"Small favors," Diane said. She yawned again. "Might as well get up. Another half hour isn't going to help." She rose and headed for the bathroom.

"Seymour says I'm in the *Ledger* ... front page. You'd think they'd at least have fucking *mentioned* me on TV."

Diane stopped at the bathroom door. "Is it really that important to you?"

"A little credit where credit is due doesn't hurt. Besides," he added defensively, "it's good for business."

Diane nodded. She went into the bathroom.

Peter got up, stripped off his shorts and T-shirt. The shower went on in the bathroom. He heard the beat of water against the fiberglass wall of the enclosure, then heard it interrupted as his wife stepped into the spray. He listened to it pulse as she moved, as she changed positions. He grew excited and for a moment considered joining her there: slippery wet bodies in the gathering steaminess.

But he really didn't have time, and the kids were probably already up anyway and would come banging on the door if at least one of them didn't appear downstairs soon. He resigned himself, put on a pair of pants and slippers, and headed downstairs.

He would tell Heinemann about this unexpected flare of lust for his wife. Undoubtedly, Heinemann would be pleased. "Good, good. Less anger at her," he would say, or something like that. Peter didn't really believe he *was* angry with Diane.

The staircase leading down to the kitchen was to the right of the master bedroom. The staircase leading down to the foyer—and the living room off the foyer— was at the opposite end of the hall.

The house was old, built around the turn of the century, and big, with fourteen rooms and three staircases, though one of the latter was sealed off now. Some of the rooms were small, even tiny, but the ceilings were high and figured with plaster work, the woodwork good, and the floors and windows sound. Peter was proud that he'd been able to buy this house for his family, proud of the renovations he'd paid for: He and Diane had had two of the upper six bedrooms joined to make a single large master bedroom, miles of plumbing ripped out and replaced, a skylight installed over the foyer, and the wiring redone. Peter had found period leaded glass for the study. And they had sealed up the old service staircase.

Off the kitchen, in a utility room that gave access to the garage, a plasterboard panel was nailed to studding behind the washing machine. Behind the panel was the service staircase, a narrow affair actually embedded in the wall that led to an upstairs room that had once been a maid's quarters. That room now belong to Melanie, the Robertses' twelve-year-old daughter. The entrance was similarly sealed off in Melanie's room, much to her dismay; she would have loved to use the stairwell as a secret chamber.

"Rats," Peter had said.

"Spiders," Diane had said.

"Dark and musty."

Melanie hadn't believed them, but after a few months she stopped pleading for them to open it up.

Peter hopped down the last step into the kitchen. "Hi, guys."

In the breakfast nook, Melanie and Paul were eating cold cereal. They were watching a small color television set. Wile E. Coyote was chasing the Road Runner on the screen.

"*BeepBeep!*" sang the Road Runner, zooming past Wile E. Coyote's clutching hands.

"I said, 'Morning guys!'" Peter called, more loudly.

Melanie said, "Morning."

Paul, half her age, waved.

Neither turned from the television.

Despite the half-hearted reception, Peter stood beaming at them. He loved them more than he had ever loved anything—or anyone—else in his life. Even more than he had ever loved Diane, although he did love her.

Heinemann had said that one of the reasons he was angry at Diane was because he felt she had drawn away from him in favor of the children. Now and then Heinemann got something right, and Peter supposed the therapy was helping, but all things considered, he didn't think Heinemann was all that bright. Peter *might* have wanted more time alone with Diane before they had Melanie, but he had no regrets.

Peter had no regrets about anything. He had never seen much point in regret.

Melanie had freckles and dimples and long brown hair that she often wore tied with a bow. She was pretty and mischievous. She did well at school, but nowhere near what Peter felt was her potential. As he himself hadn't. She could be selfish, sometimes not polite—again like him, although he had learned to conceal that over the years.

Paul was almost the opposite: perpetually good-natured and generous. His smooth light brown hair was cut bowl style, and bangs hid his forehead. He had green eyes, like his mother. Neither of them looked like Peter.

Peter was six-feet-two-inches tall, had thick curly black hair, which was just starting to gray, and small brown eyes. Pleasant, but not memorable features. A good build, though: defined muscles, strong legs. He worked out and was proud of his build.

Peter went to the front of the house and got the morning paper from the porch. By the time he was back in the kitchen, he'd read the paragraph that mentioned him twice.

"I'm in the paper," he said to the kids.

They didn't hear him. The Road Runner had placed Wile E. Coyote's dynamite under Wile E.'s own vantage point.

"*BeepBeep!*" The Road Runner went racing by.

Wile E. Coyote shoved the plunger down—and blew himself up.

The kids laughed hilariously.

"That's wonderful, Dad," Peter said to himself. "Congratulations."

"Thank you," he said to himself.

"You're welcome," he said to himself.

He set a pot of coffee on, pulled a stool to the counter, and spread the paper out. He had read the whole article and finished a cup of coffee by the time Diane appeared. She was in a bathrobe, hair wet. She said hello to the kids, who gave her the same perfunctory acknowledgment they'd given Peter.

"Nice?" she inquired of Peter, pointing to the newspaper.

"Pretty good." He read her the paragraph: "Prominent local dentist . . . forensic consultant to the police . . . careful reconstruction of victim's dental profile though victim had been brutalized about the head and several teeth were missing . . . matched to dental records of Trudy Keller, a runaway from Scranton."

Diane playfully pinched his cheek. "Congratulations."

"Thank you. Most of it's about Seymour—a regular Pennsylvania Sherlock Holmes."

Diane smiled but didn't respond. She started cutting oranges into slices for the kids. "Want eggs?" she asked Peter.

"I don't have time," Peter replied. "I have to be at the hospital at eight. Got to call Nina."

"It's only ten to seven," Diane pointed out. "Let me make you something."

"I still have to shower and get dressed. I don't feel like eating when I'm rushed like this."

"So you're just going to have coffee again? And

rush around and probably end up skipping lunch too. It's just not healthy. Two? Over easy? Bacon and an English muffin with them?"

"I don't want any eggs!" Peter said slowly and clearly. "I'll just have some cereal."

"You're impossible." Diane slammed a box of cereal down on the counter. "Kids, enough now. Upstairs. Time to get dressed. . . . I *mean* it." She clapped her hands. "Chop, chop!"

Melanie and Paul both recognized the annoyance in her voice, slid out of the nook, and started upstairs without protest.

Diane went to get a bowl, spoon, and milk for Peter. Peter enjoyed the irritation on her face. It made her even prettier.

"I'm perfectly capable of getting my own stuff." he said.

"Fine," she said. "I'll help the kids, then. Will you be home for dinner?"

"Probably," he lied. "I can't say for sure. I'll have to see how everything turns out. I'll let you know either way."

Diane stood looking at him. "Peter . . . is something wrong?"

'Wrong? No. Why?"

"You seem preoccupied, almost brooding sometimes. We haven't been making love as much as we used to. Sometimes you even get short with Melanie and Paul."

Peter made a gesture as if shooing something away. He smiled, shook his head. "It's your imagination. I've been working hard. And, I'm still trying to figure out if I can open another practice, maybe over in Calder Lake. I'll try to pay more attention."

She nodded.

Half an hour later, Peter was back in the kitchen, showered, shaved, and dressed. He was feeling buoyant, almost exhilarated: Two bodies were waiting.

Diane was putting the children's snacks into their lunch boxes. The children were still upstairs. "How are you guys doing?" she called up to them. "Bus in twelve minutes."

Peter gave her a deliberate hug, kissed her on the lips. "Got to run," he said. "I love you."

"I love you," she said.

"Don't forget to call the plumber."

"Anything else I can do for you?" She slipped a thigh between his legs, pressed it into his groin.

"We'll talk about that when I get home," he said, smiling.

Her expression told him that was not what she had wanted to hear.

It took Peter minutes to weave his way out of the winding, heavily treed streets of the community in which he lived. Normally he turned left on Polk Avenue, toward his office. Today, he turned right and headed for Hamilton General Hospital. Twenty minutes later, he was in the parking lot behind the hospital, the trunk of his car open, taking out a sheaf of folders and a small black case.

He entered the hospital at 8:05 and showed his pass to a guard at the staff entrance. He walked down a long corridor past administrative offices and testing labs, through a set of swinging doors marked AUTHORIZED PERSONNEL ONLY, and headed toward a pair of elevators. The door to one of them opened just as he arrived. An attendant wheeled out a pale old woman on a gurney. The old woman was wrapped in hospital sheets, looking almost like a mummy. A glucose bottle hung from a pole attached to the gurney, a plastic tube trailing down and into a Heplock valve inserted into her forearm and taped to her chalky skin. She looked worn down by time, worn down by pain, fear. Her helplessness fascinated Peter. When he realized he was staring, he looked away.

After the gurney had cleared, Peter stepped into the elevator and rode it to the subbasement. He got out and went around the corner, past an area labeled PASTORAL CARE, through a set of swinging doors, past a room marked ANTI-CONTAMINATION: ISOLATION. He caught a glimpse through the wire-reinforced window in the door of workers in hospital blues wearing latex gloves, surgical masks over their mouths, light blue plastic caps over their hair. Further on, empty wheel chairs and stretchers stood along the wall.

The morgue was at the end of the hall. Peter stopped outside its door, stood and breathed deeply a couple of times, calming himself. Then he opened the door and went through it. It closed behind him with a *ch-hunk*.

On both sides of the walkway, from top to bottom, were the doors of refrigerated slab compartments. Each was numbered and had a polished stainless steel handle. Red cardboard tags hung from some of the handles, indicating that those compartments were occupied.

The autopsy room was directly ahead.

Peter had done his first job for the coroner's office six years ago, identifying the remains of three people killed in a small plane that had gone down in a lake and hadn't been found until months afterward. By that time, there wasn't enough left of the bodies to tell who had been who. Peter made the identifications by comparing postmortem dental exams with antemortem X-rays and records.

It was the medical examiner, Dr. Thomas Onasis, who'd requested forensic dental help, and it was Lieutenant Seymour Pinchus, Diane's uncle, who had recommended Peter. Yet one more reason to be both grateful to and resentful of Seymour Pinchus, who, Peter suspected, occupied the topmost seat in Diane's pantheon of People to Adore.

Mostly Peter was called to identify a charred or

badly decomposed body. Often, all he had to do was to confirm or deny a tentative identification that had already been made. Now and then, he was asked to corroborate other forensic conclusions: Once he'd had to examine the mouth and larynx of a dead four-year-old boy to confirm whether or not the injures to the oral cavity were consistent with child abuse. Unfortunately, they were. Peter never minded working with adult bodies; in fact, the process even thrilled him. But he didn't like seeing dead children. The few times he'd had to examine one, he was depressed for days.

Peter liked being an insider to this kind of police work. As a dental student in Philadelphia, he'd done an independent-study project at the city medical examiner's office. He had immensely enjoyed watching the pathologist work, watching him put together the pieces of the puzzle to determine the sometimes elusive cause of death.

Death fascinated Peter.

"And what do you think lies behind that?" Dr. Heinemann had probed.

Sometimes Dr. Heinemann pissed him off.

In his student days, Peter used to discuss the pathologist's cases with his father, who was also a dentist and who was nearly as interested in them as he was. It was ironic that the first time Peter ever employed forensics himself, it was when his father died.

Peter had been only two years out of dental school when he got the call. The call made him want to throw up. He drove into Philadelphia that same afternoon. At the airport he met his brother, Joseph, who'd flown in from Chicago, and together they went to the morgue to identify the body, to spare their mother the task. He remembered standing in the viewing room: small, empty, a sheet of glass on the opposite wall covered with a curtain. The need for identification was only a formality. The senior Roberts had crumpled from a heart attack at a bank and was dead within minutes.

Someone unseen on the other side pulled back the curtain. And there on a gurney lay Harold Roberts with his mouth twisted open in a grimace. What Peter saw first was not his father's face but the gold bridge in the upper rear of his father's mouth, the one he'd looked at for his father a year earlier when his father thought he might be having trouble with it.

"Yes," he said, before his eyes even moved to his father's face. "Yes, that's him."

Tears slipped down his cheeks. He had put his palm to the glass, as if to shut his father's mouth for him, to smooth back his hair, to comfort him.

Now, walking into the autopsy room, Peter shook his head against the memory. The smell hit him immediately. He had never gotten used to that first encounter: the odor of burned or rotting flesh, open bowel, exposed and sectioned organs.

Two long stainless steel tables stood in the center of the room. Both occupied. Dr. Thomas Onasis and his assistant Kristina stood on either side of the nearest one, working on a fire-blackened corpse. Kristina had her back to Peter. Next to her stood Pinchus. On the other side, next to Onasis, was a tall young man Peter didn't recognize. They all wore hospital gowns.

"Two tables, no waiting," Kristina had said the first time Peter saw the autopsy room.

The tables had bare metal surfaces with dozens of small holes, which drained away the blood and other fluids that spilled out of a body during an autopsy. The fluids were collected in angled pans that emptied into a sink at the head of each table. Each sink was fitted with a hose for washing down the corpse.

Directly above the tables hung hooded bright lights that could be drawn down close. On a cart off to the side were scales for weighing organs. Wall shelves and glass-fronted cabinets held specimen containers, instruments, rubber gloves, gowns, and other equipment. A microphone dangled from a wire above each table, for the medical examiner to record his findings as he worked.

The limbs of the body Onasis was working on were twisted, badly fractured. The exposed ends of bone had been blackened by fire. The intense heat of the fire had caused all the muscle tissue in the body to shrivel, making the body curl in on itself.

Onasis was a short middle-aged man with thick, black-rimmed glasses. He was intensely focused on the corpse. Kristina was in her late twenties, with big shoulders, and a pretty smile. She wore her hair short and had a direct manner. Peter sometimes wondered if she was a lesbian. The tall young man was lean, serious.

Between Kristina and Pinchus, Peter could see a red cavern in the middle of the crusted black flesh, where Onasis had entered the chest and abdominal cavity. The internal organs, unaffected by the fire, gleamed beneath a separated layer of bright yellow body fat, which had only partly melted. Onasis was fumbling through the inner folds of the stomach.

"Well, at least we know what his last meal was. Rice. And, uh-huh, a little chicken . . . some broccoli."

"Maybe he's Chinese," the tall young man said.

Peter saw Pinchus look up to see if the young man was kidding.

"Hi, Peter," Dr. Onasis said raising his eyes for the first time. "Suit up and come over."

Pinchus and Kristina acknowledged Peter. Kristina introduced the tall young man as Brian, a resident.

"Guess Peter shoots your theory to hell," Onasis said to Kristina.

"Meaning?" asked Kristina.

"Look at his hair. And he's not black."

"Guy has a little patch of hair on his head that didn't burn cause of the way he was lying," Pinchus explained to Peter. "It's curly and frizzy. Kristina said he was black."

"Never assume," Onasis said. "Always rely on your facts."

Peter got into a gown, mask, gloves.

"Tell me what you see," Onasis said to him. "Any cusps of Carabelli?"

The cusp of Carabelli was a fifth pointed projection found on the back molars of blacks, usually pronounced.

Peter held the corpse's mouth open with gloved hands. "Nope. Also, no two-cusped mandibular first premolars, no three-cusped lower second premolars. Those are commonly found in blacks, too. . . . He's not oriental either."

"How do you know?" Brian asked. "He's the right size."

"In orientals, the incisors generally have a shovel-shaped appearance. Take a look. These are anything but shovel-shaped."

"So he's white," Kristina announced. Then, as she saw Pinchus about to say something, she added, "or Hispanic."

"No." Pinchus shook his head. "Just not black or oriental. Could be Eskimo, though, or Indian—East Indian or American Indian—or something else. Unless you have more rule-outs, Peter?"

"Actually, Eskimos and American Indians also exhibit shovel-shaped incisors."

Pinchus shrugged. "So much for *my* knowledge of anthropology."

Onasis laughed.

"Maybe we'll do better on her." Kristina nodded at the other table.

Peter looked closely at that table for the first time. "Jesus! What happened?"

The body was only a little burned, but was split in half into an upper and lower torso. Both pieces, which were facing downward, were wrapped in black plastic garbage bags held in place with twine. Here and there the plastic had melted and fused with skin. From the top portion, some of the deceased's head protruded. Long black hair was visible. A tear in the lower half revealed calves in fishnet stockings, a high-heeled pump still strapped to one foot.

"The well-done one here was the driver." Pinchus turned and pointed. "He ran off the road and hit a tree. The car went up in flames. That—" he nodded at the other table "—was found in the trunk."

"We could have a case of double suicide here," Kristina offered.

"You're on a roll," Onasis remarked.

The doors through which Peter had entered swung open, and Louis Trane, the coroner, appeared. Trane had red hair and a bushy red moustache. He said hello to everyone. "We don't have anything on either of these two yet," he told Peter. "Be fastidious documenting your postmort. We may have to rely on it for future comparisons."

"What I'd like to do is cut out the jaws when Tom is done," Peter said, "if no one has any objections. I'll X-ray them in my office. That way, if we get any antemortem records, we'll have a solid reference."

"Fine with me." Trane looked over to Onasis.

Trane had no medical training. He ran the forensic, or legal, part of the investigation. Onasis directed the pathological work.

"No objection here," Onasis agreed.

"Seymour," said Trane, "did you hear that the car was stolen?"

"Yup. Jersey. Montclair."

"The owner never reported it. He said he didn't realize it was missing till we got in touch with him."

"I know. I'm betting on him for the slice job."

"Why?"

Pinchus gestured toward the second table. "Well, she looks to be at least three days old. Even *I* can tell that without Tom's help. But the driver is fresh. What

I think is the owner kills the young lady, cuts her in two so he can get her into his trunk. But before he can dispose of the body, his car gets stolen." Pinchus paused, noticing everyone's attention. He then continued.

"So what's he going to do? Report it to the police? Not likely. He waits, hoping that whoever stole the car finds the body in the trunk and gets rid of it for him. He knows the thief won't go to the police. Or, if he gets too nervous, he changes his mind and reports the car gone. He hopes that if the police ever do find the car, and the body's still in the trunk, they figure the thief for the killer."

"What I think," Trane said, "is that nailing Terranova has gone to your head. I talked to the guy myself. He's pure Mary."

"He's what?" asked Peter.

"He's gay," answered Pinchus. "Exaggeratedly gay."

"One hundred percent," Trane emphasized. "I can't see him hurting a fly, let alone killing and cutting up a woman."

"Never assume," Kristina said somberly. "Always rely on your facts."

Trane raised his eyebrows.

"My assistant is being sarcastic," Onasis smiled.

"Oh."

"Besides," Kristina said, "who says that's a woman over there?"

"Who says the pope lives in Rome?" Brian responded.

Kristina didn't seem to think that was funny and Brian was disappointed. It was clear that he found her attractive.

When most of the autopsy was finished, Peter made a chart of the corpse's mouth.

"You can take the jaws after we do the brain," Onasis said.

"Good."

Kristina lifted the corpse's head and slipped a block under the neck, which supported the head. She took up a scalpel, positioned it on the scalp at the apex of the right ear, then cut directly across to the apex of the left ear. She peeled the scalp forward, exposing the front half of the skull, then repeated the action, exposing the rest of the skull. She reached for a small electric oscilating saw with a rounded blade, then looked at Onasis.

He nodded.

Kristina turned the saw on. It whined shrilly. She touched the whirling blade to the top of the corpse's skull, on the right side, pressed down, and began to cut. The whine lowered in pitch as the motor torqued down. The blade buzzed in the skull. Bony dust rose into the air. Kristina turned the saw off, set it aside and picked up an instrument that looked like a little crowbar. She inserted one end of it into the cut surface of the bone, at the side. She tapped the other end with a mallet, twisted, and the skull cap came off. Light straw-colored cerebral fluid rushed out of the head and flowed over the supporting block and down to the table, where it disappeared into the drain holes. Onasis peered at the exposed brain.

"Okay," he said, giving Kristina permission to remove it.

Kristina slipped the gloved fingers of her left hand between the brain and the rear of the skull and lifted the brain gently. With her right hand, she took up a pair of blunt-tipped scissors and slid them under the brain. She snipped the brain stem. Then she lifted the organ out, weighed it, and placed it on a dissecting table for Onasis.

"Thank you." Onasis made ready to cut the brain into cross-sections. "Would you give Peter a hand with the jaws, please?"

Brian stood close to Onasis, to observe the brain dissection. Pinchus watched Kristina and Peter.

First they cut the upper lips and cheeks away from

the underlying bone. Then Kristina used the saw to cut through the bone above the upper teeth from left to right, passing through the sinuses. Peter inserted the little pry bar into this cut. He twisted the bar. The upper jaw came off into his waiting hand, with all the teeth intact. Then they cut away the flesh around the lower jaw. They severed the tendons and ligaments that held the mandible in place. That done, Peter was able simply to lift it free.

Kristina took both jaws. "How do you want these wrapped?"

"In anything that can be sealed and that will keep the odor from escaping."

"I'm out of Tupperware. You'll have to settle for a specimen container." She put the jaws into one. "By the way, you were supposed to bring me a toothbrush. Did you forget?"

Peter reached beneath the blue gown into the pocket of his shirt and took out a wrapped new brush. "Red was what you requested, I believe."

Pinchus shook his head. "I don't believe you two."

Peter took some pleasure in having discomfited Pinchus.

"Doesn't what we're doing remind you of the importance of brushing?" Kristina said.

Pinchus made a face.

"I use a toothbrush to scrub the smaller instruments when I'm cleaning up. I guess I *could* recycle them, though. Waste not, want not."

"You are a disturbed person," Pinchus said.

Kristina smiled brightly at him.

"Kris, you want to close up over there?" Onasis asked. "I'm about ready to start on the next one."

Kristina used the hose to clean debris from the body, fitted a large curved needle with a heavy-gauge cord, and then with quick, strong movements, sewed the body closed. She tied down each stitch.

Brian said, "Back in Iowa, we had this drive-in movie theater that featured nothing but horror movies.

Once I was half-tanked and went to this triple feature: *Chain Saw Massacre, Happy Harry Hatchet,* and something else about guillotines. Actually, they were pretty great."

Kristina shuddered. "They were, huh? I can't stand those films myself. All that blood and shit. They make me sick."

Pinchus gave her a look.

"Really. I'm serious!"

They gathered around the second table. Onasis cut the twine from around the lower torso and peeled the plastic away. It turned out not to be a full lower torso, but only a pair of legs, severed just below where they would have joined the hips.

"Nice stockings," Brian said.

"Nice shoes, too," added Kristina.

At Onasis's direction, Kristina and Brian each picked up a leg to carry to a work bench.

"What do you say," Kristina said, nudging Brian as they went, "want to do a menage? I was always a leg woman myself."

Brian looked thoroughly unhappy.

Onasis removed the plastic from the upper portion of the body. The body was slender, with a naked, gracefully curved back. Blue bikini panties covered rounded buttocks. The panties were bloodstained. Onasis dictated his preliminary observations into the hanging microphone. With Kristina's help, he turned the corpse over. The corpse's face was peaceful: long-lashed eyelids closed, bow mouth relaxed. Her naked breasts were of moderate size, set high, saucered now against her chest.

"A real waste," Onasis commented. "Well, let's see what the bastard did to her."

He pulled the panties down from her hips slowly, almost as a lover might. There was a tensing around the table as the dark pubic hair came into view. . . .

Suddenly Pinchus emitted an explosive laugh. "So that's what the bastard did to her!"

"Never assume," Kristina said gravely. "Always rely on your facts."

They were staring at the remnants of a recently amputated penis and what appeared to be part of a scrotal sac.

5

Today was the day. He'd known it from the moment he awoke.

Pinchus would get the case. He knew that too. This didn't bother him at all, regardless of how clever the detective was thought to be. In fact, he was relying on it. Were Pinchus *not* to get the case, then nothing would be proved, there wouldn't be any fun—beyond the deed itself. For the game to be worth playing at all, they had to throw the best they had at him.

6

Alice Schaeffer finished cutting the split ends of her hair—a frequent task, given its length (but Mark loved it, so she was loath to cut it short)—ran a brush through it a few times, then walked out of the bathroom through the living room and into the small bedroom.

She took off her robe and tossed it on the bed, opened a dresser drawer and fumbled through her panties, picked a plain white cotton pair. The satin ones, the frilly ones, were for weekends with Mark. Or occasionally, during the week just for the hell of it, when she was feeling sexy.

Which she wasn't at the moment, although she might well have been: It had been two weeks since she'd seen Mark. Last weekend, when normally he would have come down from New York where he was in third-year law at Columbia, he'd been dragooned to help with orientation for first-year students. This Friday, he'd called at the last minute, with a flu.

"So I'll come up to visit you," she had said. "We'll spend the weekend in bed. I'll take care of you. It'll be fun."

"I don't want to pass this on to you."

"I have the immune system of a bull elephant."

"I'm serious," he said.

"So am I."

"Alice. Please. I feel like shit. Not only that, but remember, *I* have a roommate to contend with."

She was disappointed. She told him so.

"Listen," he said. "I'll rest. I'll get better. I'll make

it up to you next weekend, I swear. I'll wine and dine you. I'll bring you chocolates. I'll sing you love songs."

What she had wanted was love making, not love songs. Now, Monday morning, she wasn't feeling sexy so much as frustrated. That, and her annoyance with Mark for not letting her come up to New York to take care of him accounted for the flirting she'd done with Lieutenant Pinchus last night. Well, accounted for *most* of it. (And it *was* flirting, though she hadn't been able to admit that to herself—guiltily—until later.)

Seymour Pinchus was a very easy man to be with. A comforting man, a capable, confident man with a kind of quiet animal energy. An attractive man, though—my God—he had to be as old as her father.

Well, tough patooties. Alice had no intentions of judging herself or trying to analyze her feelings.

She did, though, consider for a moment putting on a pair of thong-briefs, the ones with the little coral cache-sex. But almost instantly she felt guilty for even having thought it, and didn't.

She suppressed a powerful urge to call Mark. She had called him three times over Saturday and Sunday. Though she never really doubted his story, the fact that he'd been there each time made her feel a little better. Now, she just wanted to tell him that she loved him. But she knew he'd be annoyed, and she couldn't blame him. She'd wait for him to call today. If he didn't, she could call him tomorrow night. She felt a rush of tenderness for Mark.

Alice put on a long gray peasant skirt and light green sweater. She hung her head back and flicked her fingers through her hair, evening out its fall over her shoulders. She glanced at her watch: 8:40. Twenty minutes to get to the lab on the third floor of the Whitman Building.

Alice lived four blocks from the university—one flight up on top of a laundromat that was part of a strip of commercial storefronts. The apartment was small and not in the greatest condition, and her father was always trying to persuade her to move. ("We'll be *happy* to cover more rent, sweetheart. We *want* to.") But she'd painted the place and brightened it up with curtains, throw rugs, and half a dozen house plants, which were thriving, and didn't intend to move. The apartment rented for $275 a month, a steal. That, along with her teaching fellowship, and the weekly $50 she was still willing to take from her parents—reluctantly, but graciously—enabled her to get by.

Her parents would have given her more, but she knew they'd had to borrow to get her through undergraduate school. She didn't want to take any more from them. She knew they loved her very much. And she loved them very much too.

Alice checked the thermometer she'd mounted outside the living room window, got a lightweight navy-colored jacket out of the closet, put it on, and slung the strap of her purse over her shoulder. She gathered up a notebook and a couple of books that were lying on the couch and left, pulling the door shut behind her. It clicked, locking automatically.

She descended the narrow flight of rickety steps and exited to the street. The air was crisp, the morning clear and gorgeous. She covered the distance to the campus and then to Whitman Hall with a springy step. The lab was high-ceilinged with tall windows—in need of washing—that looked out over an oak and a couple of maples that were still green but that would be turning in a couple of weeks.

Two of her twelve students were already there, getting their cats from the storage closet in the rear. Alice hated the smell of formaldehyde. But it went with the territory.

Most of the lab work for Mammalian Anatomy 2 involved the detailed dissection of a cat over the semester. This course was for advanced students, generally seniors, and most of them would go on to professional schools in medicine and dentistry. Or, as Alice had, to higher degrees in biology.

Alice sat at her desk and scanned the outline for the current exercise as the rest of her class arrived. It was a couple of minutes past nine by the time they had all retrieved their cats and were at their assigned workstations.

"Good morning," Alice announced. She came around her desk and leaned back, her arms extended behind her, palms resting on the desk's surface. "Today, we're going to be studying the abdominal muscles and external genitalia. You can find the dissection directions on pages thirty-three to thirty-nine in your manuals. As usual, you're to locate and identify in your specimens all the parts listed in heavy type.

"I want to remind you that I'll be giving a review of everything we've done to date a week from today, next Monday. Two weeks from today, you'll have your first practical exam. Any questions?"

There were a few, which she answered.

"Good, let's get started then. If you need help, please ask for it. You'll only hurt yourself if you don't. Mostly, I'll be walking around to observe and assist you. If I'm at my desk, feel free to interrupt."

The students went to work. Alice made her first circuit of them, pausing to say a personal word now and then, offer a compliment, a suggestion.

Each cat was pinned down on its back, spread-eagled, atop a paraffin base inside dissection trays. The eyes were open, as was the mouth. The students had already made various shallow, flaying cuts in the upper torsos, revealing the musculature. Deeper cuts had opened the thoracic cavities. Red and blue dyes had been injected by the supply house through slits in the throats and inner thighs to make the arteries and veins stand out from the organs and surrounding internal tissues.

Typically, most of the students had named their cats. They made jokes about them, sometimes nervously. In any lab there was always at least one Felix and one Sylvester; this time there was also a Felicia and Sylvestrix.

Without close supervision, only a few of the students would execute their dissections to the demanding level called for by the text. The work was tedious and the bulk of lab time was spent cutting rather than identifying. Because of that, Alice made a point of going over the identifications with them at the end of each lab, using one of the better dissection jobs of the day to illustrate.

Alice had finished all of her assignments that were due for today and most of Tuesday's over the weekend. She was looking forward to relaxing with Kathy and Janet and Richie at Faulkner's tonight. For a moment, she regretted that she hadn't gone home to spend the weekend with her parents. But at the time, she'd been happier sulking in her apartment and feeling sorry for herself.

At the far end of the room, David Harper stuck his hand up. He waved it frantically.

Alice was not happy. But she left the student she'd been observing and walked around the table toward David.

In the first lab session of the semester, David had said to his table partner in a voice loud enough to be overheard, "Now there is one teacher whose pet I certainly would not mind being." And over the next couple of weeks he'd given her a few archly smoldering looks. Alice had let it go. She was used to this kind of thing. Still, David had a manner about him that discomfited her. At the end of last Thursday's lecture, he had said—again loudly enough so that she could not help but hear it—"Oh, our professor looks good enough to eat today. And would I love to do just that." Alice had slammed a book down and glared at him, kept it up until he'd backed down, ducking his head and busying himself with readying his notes.

Alice had simmered for an hour afterward, but had given it up, deciding he was probably just a dork who somehow thought he was coming on to her. Who knows? Hit on the apparently manless good-looking lab instructor and maybe you'll get lucky. Thing was, he was good-looking enough himself, and seemed smart enough despite his crudity, and she wondered why he didn't focus his attention on any of the ample number of clearly available coeds on the campus.

"Do you need help with something?" Alice asked in a deliberately neutral tone.

"Actually—to my surprise—yes," he replied.

He gave her a big, friendly smile. David Harper was a bit under six feet. He had dark brown eyes—intense eyes, she saw now that she looked at them more closely—and good cheekbones, a strong chin. He wore his brown hair at a moderate length, parted on the left. He was dressed in a tan Champion sweatshirt and jeans, good loafers.

"I can't seem to locate the rectus abdominous muscle," he said.

That's odd, she wanted to say, I thought every asshole would know where that is.

Instead, she kept a poker face, studied his cat for a moment, then said, "It would help if you employed more finesse in your dissection. Your cuts are much too deep. You've slashed through several of the muscles you're supposed to be studying. The manual talks about teasing away layers of tissue. You have butchered that cat."

"Listen, Alice—"

"*What?*" Alice's voice cracked like a whip.

The click of instruments in the lab stopped. Conversations ceased.

Alice was aware that everyone had turned to look at them. David knew it too.

"With all due respect, Alice—"

"What did you call me?"

"Alice. That is your name, isn't it?"

"*Ms. Schaeffer* to you."

David was silent a moment. "All right. With all

due respect, Ms. Schaeffer, I did the best I could. I have a thing about cats. I can't help it. I hate them. Not hate, I mean it's more like a phobia. I can't stand them. They make my skin crawl. This lab is not easy for me. I've been trying, but I haven't been very successful. But I promise you, when the practical comes, I'll know my stuff. Maybe not from my own dissection, but from studying other people's. You can check on my record or just wait for your first test—I'm not a screw off."

He appeared sincere. Alice softened a bit.

"If you can't do the work because of some personal difficulty," she explained, "I'll take that into consideration. But if you're malingering, I will not be happy."

"That's fair enough. Thank you. Now that we've cleared that up, are you by any chance free for a drink Saturday night?"

Jesus!

There was laughter.

Alice stared hard at David. "We need to speak after class," she said slowly. "I will give you an opportunity to explain why I should not expel you from this course."

She turned away from him.

David said nothing more through the remainder of the lab. The few times Alice glanced covertly in his direction, he seemed intent on his work. There was a touch of unpleasant energy in the air, but otherwise all went smoothly. At eleven-thirty, Alice began her review. At eleven-forty-five, she was done with it. The students spent the remaining five minutes cleaning up. They unpinned their cats and wrapped them in heavy plastic bags, carried the trays and packaged cats back to the storage locker.

David was with another student who had come in from the hall. David gathered up his books and started to leave with him.

"Mr. Harper," Alice called out with authority, "we are scheduled to talk."

David stopped, cocked his head. "Wait here," he said to his friend. "Ms. Schaeffer wants to straighten out my fear of pussies." He walked over to Alice. "So, *are* you free this Saturday?"

"Are you simply an ass, Mr. Harper? Or are you suicidal?"

"Neither. I just think you are stunningly beautiful and I would like to go out with you."

"First: No. Second: I am your professor; you will show me the same respect you show your other professors. Third: At the next inappropriate remark from you, I will dismiss you from this class with a failing grade. I will also file a formal grievance against you with the dean's office."

David looked past her as she spoke.

"Have I been clear?" she asked.

"Yes, ma'am. I . . . apologize." He did not say the words easily.

"As you should."

"You know, I wasn't putting you on—I really *am* afraid of cats."

"Good day, Mr. Harper."

Leaving the Whitman Building, Alice literally bumped into Dr. Miles Hawthorne as she came around the piece of steel sculpture at the end of the walkway. She knocked his briefcase out of his hand.

"Oh! I'm sorry." She picked it up before he could, handed it back.

"No harm."

Hawthorne was dressed in slacks and a corduroy jacket, a shirt with tiny checks, and a fabric tie. He was a good-looking man with black-silver hair, one of the department's more distinguished lecturers. He was in his early forties, but laugh lines around his eyes made him seem a little older than he actually was. His usual expression was one of geniality.

"Actually, I was hoping to find you here," he admitted. "But you appear distracted. It can wait."

"No. That's all right. I was just thinking about the run-in I had last period with one of my students. But I'm fine, really. What's on your mind?"

"What happened?"

"It wasn't all that serious. I'm probably overreacting. Do you know a student named David Harper?"

"David," Hawthorne said with a sigh. "What did he do this time?"

Alice told him.

"Not a paragon of savoir faire," Hawthorne said. "I agree. He's harmless, though—and a very good student. He wasn't kidding when he said he'd handle the practical. He'd be holding close to a four-point if he weren't so arrogant and if he didn't try to get out of what he considers drudge work. He sometimes pushes an instructor in the beginning, to see how much he can get away with. He usually settles down once you put him in his place." Hawthorne smiled. "And he *does* have good taste," he said, with a little nod in her direction.

"Thank you. On both counts. Now, what was it that you wanted?"

"I need help grading papers this semester. It would be a steady thing, for the full term, and I'm willing to pay the going rate plus ten percent—for inducement purposes."

"I'm flattered you thought of me. I'd be happy to do it, if I can work out my own hours."

"Absolutely. Then we have a deal?"

"Yes, Dr. Hawthorne."

"Miles. We'll be working together. Colleagues should be on a first-name basis."

"Miles."

Hawthorne took a leather notepad and a silver pen from his breast pocket. "I should have your home number. Might as well give me your address too."

"Doesn't the school pay assistants directly?"

"For the record. And if I need you in a pinch or have any questions." He smiled diffidently.

She gave them to him. "My answering machine's broken," she said. "I probably won't be getting a new one till next month."

Hawthorne wrote out his own for her. "I'm looking forward to this," he said, "and to getting to know you better. I'll have the first batch of papers for you by the middle of next week."

He reached out his hand. She accepted it.

He gave her hand a little squeeze. "Talk to you next week, then. Thank you, Alice. Bye for now."

Hawthorne continued on toward the Whitman Building. Alice walked off in the opposite direction. She *was* flattered that Hawthorne had asked her—he had a reputation for being willing to work with only the best. And the extra money would be more than welcome. She looked back over her shoulder.

And saw Hawthorne staring back at her.

He smiled, gave her a little wave.

She returned the wave, smiling uncertainly.

7

Sam Milano was in the squad room by the time Pinchus got there, after the autopsy. Pinchus poured himself a cup of coffee and sat down at his own desk, across from Sam. "Good to see you."

"Good to be back."

"Really?"

"The last few days," Sam said, "Billy and Tommy got poison ivy, Helen went stir crazy, and the fish stopped biting. Plus, it got hot. Plus, Hoochie tangled with a porcupine and the vet cost me a fortune."

Sam had been on vacation in the Delaware Water Gap. Pinchus had missed him. Sam Milano was a thirteen-year veteran, six as Pinchus's partner. They worked well together. They liked each other, were good company for each other.

"How was the rest of it?"

"Pretty good. Congratulations on shutting down Terranova. The Fox strikes again."

Pinchus gave him a baleful look.

"You don't want them to keep calling you that, stop solving notorious cases."

"I've tried," Pinchus said shrugging. "I can't. I'm addicted."

"Maybe you should start a twelve-step program— Freak-Catchers Anonymous or something. I heard you were at the morgue. Anything for us?"

Pinchus gave him the details.

"Chicks with dicks," Sam said.

"What?"

"That's what they call them. And she-males. It's a scene. They advertise on the cable sex channels in the big cities—she-males, chicks with dicks."

"How do you know this stuff?"

"It's important to stay abreast, so to speak."

"Sometimes you make me feel old."

Sam scratched his head. "What's that old saying? Shoes fitting? Something like that."

"No. Foot, mouth, I think."

Sam looked at his watch. "Want to grab a burger at Benny's?"

Pinchus almost said yes. But suddenly, a chasm opened in him and he toppled into it—realized he had been teetering on the edge of it for days. He felt lonely, unbearably lonely. And what he craved, needed, was not company but love.

"Tomorrow," he said. "I'm sorry. I wanted to. But there's something that came up I have to see about. Wanna get a beer when we're done?"

"Sure," said Sam.

Pinchus left the station. He drove to Kate's. He just assumed she would be there. He needed her to be there.

Kate lived west of the city in a little town called Daleyville. Daleyville didn't have much money. There were three auto-parts stores along its short main thoroughfare. Kate owned a frame house on a couple of wooded acres off a narrow road, with a small barn behind it that was her workshop. Her silver Tercel was in the drive, but Pinchus saw right away that her truck wasn't out by the barn. Still, he wouldn't accept that she wasn't there. He reasoned that the truck might be in the garage for repairs, that she could have loaned it to someone. He pulled in behind the Tercel.

He went to the barn first, looked in the window next to the closed double doors. No lights were on, no movement. There was no sound of a power tool. He knocked anyway.

He waited almost a full minute, then turned back to the house. The stone Jizo, about a foot-and-a-half tall, looked out at him from beneath a rhododendron bush.

"So?" he said, raising his hands.

The Jizo, a benevolent and protective wandering Buddhist monk, simply smiled back.

Pinchus went around to the front, onto the porch, and rang the bell. The house remained silent.

Pinchus sat down on the porch, his feet resting two stairs below. The yard between the house and the asphalt road a hundred feet away was well kept. There were flowers around the front of the house, some stone and moss arrangements fitted into dipping contours of the land. A big Douglas fir towered to the right. In riotous contrast, the land across the road was overgrown with high brush and crowded, second-growth trees. Tangled vines wound through the trees.

Pinchus tried not to think about anything. Or to feel much. But what if she wasn't on a job—out on a renovation, hanging doors, setting cabinetry somewhere—what if she was with another man? She'd been that route before. Not with him, but still. . . . God, he didn't want to lose her.

He wasn't being rational. He crushed the thought. After a few minutes he almost wished he still smoked, was glad there weren't any cigarettes in the car. He might have gone and got one.

Uncomfortable, he turned to one of the meditation exercises Kate had taught him—simple, conscious breathing. He paid attention to his breath as it went in . . . filling his lungs . . . as it came back out. As it went in . . .

Pinchus was certain that he was not very good at these things. Yet when he looked at his watch, what seemed two or three minutes later, he found that more than fifteen minutes had passed. He probed himself, something else he had never done before he met Kate:

He looked within, just looked, to see what he was feeling.

The terrible loneliness was gone. There was sadness, and some yearning, but the loneliness was gone.

He stayed another quarter hour, hoping Kate would come, but not needing her to anymore, and taking some comfort from letting himself be aware of her presence, her life: It was in the land, the feel of wooden porch beneath him, emanating from the house behind him.

And then it was time to go. He'd stayed as long as he reasonably could. He got up and went to his car. As he was opening the door, Kate came down the road in her big blue Chevy pickup truck and turned into the drive. She pulled up alongside his car and parked.

She got out. "Well. Hi."

"Hi," he said.

Kate was wearing a gray pullover, jeans, and ankle-high work boots. She was tall, only a couple of inches beneath Pinchus's nearly six-foot height, and had shoulder-length light brown hair. There were spots of natural color high on her cheeks. She had a full mouth and a good figure. She was forty-six years old. She and Pinchus had been lovers for almost a year and a half.

Kate waited, standing by her truck.

Waiting was a detective's trick, letting someone grow so uncomfortable in the silence that he would start talking, saying things maybe he hadn't planned on, just to break the silence. But with Kate it wasn't a trick. If she didn't have anything she needed or wanted to say, she was comfortable remaining silent, and just as comfortable if the other person did too.

"I was missing you."

She gave him a little smile. "I was missing you, too."

"Were you?"

"Mm-hhm."

"I thought you might call, with all the news coverage and stuff."

"I thought you were brooding. I thought you didn't want to talk to me."

"Well, I was," he said. "And I didn't. At least part of me was and didn't. Another part really wanted to hear your voice."

"Good."

He opened his arms. She hesitated for a moment, but stepped into them. They held each other, not tightly.

"Why is it," Pinchus wondered, "that when a man doesn't want to make a commitment, people call it a fear of intimacy. But if a woman doesn't want to commit, they say she's being independent, autonomous, and living her own life."

"The times you live in," she said. "Besides, it's not that I don't want to make a commitment—it's that I don't want to make the kind of commitment *you* want me to make."

"Mmmmm," he said, not wanting to reignite trouble.

They were quiet again.

She leaned back and looked at him. "I *was* happy for you. And I'm glad that man won't be able to hurt anyone anymore."

"Me too. Thank you. . . . I have to get back. I was just leaving when you pulled in."

"I saw."

"I was here the better part of forty-five minutes."

She nodded.

He kissed her lightly on the lips. Then he got into his car. They looked at each other through the open window.

After a few moments she said, "Would you like to come to dinner tomorrow?"

"Yes."

"Seven-thirty," she said.

"Seven-thirty. I will." He put the car in gear. "Bye."

"Bye." She waved.

He backed out of the drive, shifted, and started off.

Driving, Pinchus felt more peaceful than he had at any other time in the last several weeks, since things had begun to grow difficult between him and Kate. He didn't think they had resolved anything this afternoon, but at least he knew that—for now, anyway—they were not going to go their separate ways.

He had met Kate on April ninth almost a year and a half ago. He'd been interviewing her as a possible witness to the flight of a getaway car in a robbery-homicide. He had responded to her almost instantly: sexually, emotionally. He remembered that it was April ninth because that was the date on which his daughter had died, twenty-one years earlier. He had been acutely aware of April ninth for the next twenty-one years. The last thing he had ever expected to penetrate the pain and grief he still felt on that day would be attraction to a woman.

Melissa had been diagnosed a month after her fifth birthday. Acute leukemia. Pinchus also had a son, Daniel, who was an infant then, but it was Melissa who was his joy and chief delight. He was stunned. Sharon was stunned.

For the first time since he was a small child himself, Seymour Pinchus had become truly afraid.

It was the last time, too, for afterward nothing ever again meant as much to him.

Despite the fear, he had believed during Melissa's illness that everything would work out all right. God wouldn't let his little girl die. Not *his* little girl. And he had kept believing that almost to the very end, when Melissa herself made it impossible for him to continue that way. Each day of those final two weeks he had brought her a new doll at the hospital, somehow thinking that these vital representations of life would shield and protect her and make it impossible for her to die. He would tell her a little story about each of them, everything this one was going to do for her to make her strong again. But she stopped believing what he said: her body wouldn't let her anymore.

"Daddy. I'm scared. I'm so scared."

"I know, baby," he said, holding her and rocking her. "But you don't have to be, you're going to be all right. Your dollies will protect you."

And he would have given his life to make that true. He would have taken the life of everyone he had ever known to make that true.

He and Sharon were called at two in the morning to come to the hospital. Melissa's condition was deteriorating rapidly. When they got to her bedside she was awake, crying quietly. She clung to Pinchus, needing him much more than she did her mother, which was something Sharon was never quite able to forgive him for.

"Daddy, I'm *so* scared."

This time he simply said, "It's all right to be scared, honey." And he held her, as tears slipped down his own cheeks.

Suddenly she stopped crying and asked, "Does it start all over again?"

"Does what start all over again?"

"When you die. Does the whole thing start all over again, and you get born again?"

"I like to think it does," he answered. "In fact, I'm sure it does, baby. But I wouldn't worry about that. You're going to be fine."

They needed blood from him for her.

"I have to go downstairs so I can give some of my blood to make you well," he said. "I'll be back very soon." He kissed her on the forehead and left.

He was directed to the second floor. He lay on a table for ten minutes, frustrated that it was taking so long for them to get a technician. Finally the technician did come, put the needle into Pinchus's arm expertly, with scarcely a trace of discomfort, and began to draw the blood.

Barely thirty seconds had passed when the resident they'd met in Melissa's room appeared at the door.

"John," he said to the technician, "that won't be necessary." He came into the room reluctantly and stood at Pinchus's side.

Pinchus was already shaking his head from side to side, denying what didn't have to be said.

"I'm sorry," the resident said softly. "I'm very sorry."

Afterward, Pinchus had buried himself in his work. His career became his life. Sharon gave him time, but not forever. He wasn't there to be a father to Daniel. He wasn't there to be a husband to her. She left him, taking Daniel, a year later.

For a while, Pinchus tried: with Daniel on weekends; with Sharon over the phone, at a few dinners, on a vacation they took together. But it just didn't work. It was too painful, too hard. All that allowed him to escape the agony, the riving grief was his work, and he clung to it like a drowning man to a lifeline.

Sharon moved away, to Connecticut.

Pinchus wrote to Daniel now and then. He sent him birthday presents. He called him at intervals, but even that stopped in time, because neither knew what to say to the other.

And then, at Daniel's graduation from high school, he had told Pinchus he wanted to be a cop, startling his father, shaking him out of the long sleep he had been in over his son.

And Pinchus tried again, feeling pain once more over one of his children, but this time hope too, and then joy, and then he was nearly overwhelmed by the love that came pouring forth through the opened floodgates of his heart.

He had a son.

It was that unfamiliar richness, that reawakening of himself, that had made him ready to the possibility of someone like Kate, whom he had met two years after Daniel entered the John Jay College of Criminal Justice in New York.

Pinchus and Daniel were close now. They talked on the phone four or five times a month. They saw each other with some frequency. And next weekend, for Pinchus's fifty-fifth birthday, Daniel was coming down from New York to take him out to dinner.

"Amazing," Pinchus said to himself as he pulled into the parking lot behind the station. When he'd turned fifty, there had been no son in his life. There had been no Kate in his life. And he had not thought he would live to see fifty-five; nor had he cared all that much then whether he did.

Walking toward the station, Pinchus felt a sudden chill as the sun disappeared behind a gathering bank of dark clouds. He shivered involuntarily.

Fifty-five, yes, he thought. But I'll never live to see sixty. For an instant he felt sad—because now it was different and he *wanted* to see sixty, and many years beyond that.

He shook his head, breaking the melancholy. He laughed at himself: Old, morbid ways of thinking did not die easily.

He entered the station.

8

After leaving the Whitman Building, Alice walked a little out of her way, past Roosevelt Auditorium, enjoying the sun on her face, and across a grassy swath with a high stone wall to the left and a row of campus buildings to the right. It was Alice's favorite area on campus: quieter and more peaceful than the large quad. On the other side of the wall, the town side, there were maples and oak trees. Alice was impatient for the leaves to start changing. When they did, this whole area became aflame in color, and she loved the crunching sounds of her feet trampling in the dry leaves. In the spring, flowers were planted along the wall.

Alice passed through a gate, leaving the confines of the university. The area immediately beyond the university was composed of older homes—many a bit run-down, some converted into small apartments for students—and stores and businesses that largely catered to students: a movie house, a bowling alley, a couple of delis, a used text-book store, a small supermarket.

Alice stopped at a coffee shop for a cup of tea and a tuna fish salad. Then she walked through a neighborhood that became ever more residential, with kids riding bikes in the streets, the houses bright and freshly painted. She turned east, passed a little park filled with mothers with infants and toddlers and a couple of people throwing Frisbees for their dogs, and arrived at the Hillcrest Community Home.

Some of the residents were taking the sun, sitting

on benches in the modest grounds around the home. Rose Fitapaldi was not among them. Rose, Alice had learned quickly, went outside only under duress.

When Alice reached Rose's room, which was at the end of a hall on the first floor, she found the old woman fretful and agitated.

"I just don't know what to do," Rose cried. She was sitting on her bed wringing a handkerchief. "It's gone. Simply gone."

"What is?" Alice asked. "Calm down, Rose. There's nothing wrong we can't fix."

The day Alice met Rose, she had greeted Rose in a condescending tone that developed unconsciously during her interviews with three older and senile women in a row—"And how are we today?"

"Go to hell," Rose had growled.

Alice was jarred out of her abstraction. "What?"

"Go to hell," Rose repeated, this time slowly and clearly.

Alice had studied her a moment, then looked around at the sterile, sparely furnished interview room, which was painted a dull institutional green, and spread her arms wide to indicate not only the room but the rest of the of the building too.

"I would say that we're pretty much there already," she declared.

Immediately she regretted that. But Mrs. Fitapaldi brightened, then grinned.

"I think I'm gonna like you," the old lady said. "Even if you *are* so young and pretty you ought to be horsewhipped for even coming in here to remind us all of what we'll never be again." Rose narrowed her eyes and peered at Alice. "Hell, in your case, what we never even *were*."

Within fifteen minutes, they were fast friends.

Now, sitting on her bed wringing her handkerchief, Rose recounted: "My bear. I had it out this morning, it was on my night table. Just before you came I was taking a nap. I had an awful dream, a nightmare, and I woke flailing my arms around, and I knocked it off the table."

"What bear?"

"*That* bear." Rose pointed.

Behind the night table, on the floor, was a scattering of tiny glass fragments.

"It was very fragile. It was one of a kind."

"Let me clean it up for you." Alice took a tissue from her purse, tore a page out of her notebook. She used the tissue to sweep the glass fragments onto the paper, which served as a dustpan. "Maybe we can replace it with something equally unusual."

"It wouldn't be the same. Frank gave that bear to me, forty-two years ago. We were on our honeymoon. Just the two of us in a cabin on a lake in the Ozarks."

"It wouldn't be the same," Alice agreed. "You're right. But we'll find something just as unique that will embody the *spirit* of it."

"You're a dear," Rose said, feeling a little better. "I would have liked my Vinnie to have married someone like you. Only you're too smart to have married someone like him. I mean, not because there was anything wrong with him—only that you're too *intelligent*. Vinnie was a wonderful boy, but not the kind of man you need. Speaking of that, did you hear from Mark today?"

Alice looked at Rose suspiciously. Rose was trying to sound casual and innocent.

"No. I'm going to speak to him tonight."

"I'm taking a chance here," Rose confessed. "But what the hell. Life's too short. He's no good for you, Alice."

Alice laughed. "You've never even met him."

"I know what I'm talking about."

"He loves me, Rose. Very much. And I love him very much."

"So where *was* Mr. Loving this weekend? And last weekend?"

"He has a flu this weekend. He was tied up last weekend."

"The dream I had earlier," Rose began. "The one that upset me—I was crying over you. Some man hurt you. Mark is not telling you the truth. Something is going on. I know. Sometimes with a dream, you just know. You should break this engagement to Mark."

"I know what's going on *here*, Rose: You're just worried that when Mark and I get married, I'll forget all about you. That's why you dreamed what you did. Well, it's not going to happen. I will always have time for you. I will always stay in close touch."

"No, you won't. You'll abandon me." Rose bit her lower lip.

"Biting the lower lip is too much," Alice stated. "You'd be more convincing without it. I don't do blackmail, Rose."

Rose shrugged her thin shoulders. "Well, who can blame an old lady for trying?"

Alice went and got them some tea. They chatted for half an hour. At the end, Alice said, "Mark will be here next weekend, Rose. Guaranteed. I'll bring him to meet you. You'll see for yourself that we can all coexist happily."

"I really *did* have a bad dream about you," Rose maintained.

"You're sweet to care. But you'll see."

"You'll come again before next weekend?"

"Tomorrow."

"Really?"

"Promise."

9

Sam was out. He'd been called to look over a crime scene where an elderly man had been found dead. He had left a message on Pinchus's desk saying that Daniel had telephoned and asked Pinchus to return the call.

Pinchus was pleased. He called back immediately, got Daniel's answering machine.

Pinchus busied himself with work. He tried not to think about when Daniel might call but wasn't entirely successful.

The phone rang about four.

"Hi, Dad," Daniel said.

"Hi, Daniel." Pinchus felt a flush of well-being.

They were just finishing their conversation when Sam came back to the squad room. Sam gave Pinchus a wave, sat down at his own desk, which was across from Pinchus's—the back of each butting up against the other—and began writing up a report.

A light on Pinchus's phone lit up indicating that another call was coming in. The automatic switching system transferred it to Sam's phone. Sam took it, exchanged a few words with whoever was on the other end, then pulled a pad over and began writing on it. He asked questions, jotted down the answers.

Pinchus ended his conversation with Daniel. He put the phone back in its cradle. He stared at it pensively. He laced his fingers behind his head, leaned back in his chair, and looked at the ceiling. After a few minutes, he got up and went for a cup of coffee for himself and Sam, Sam's with a little milk and a tea-spoon of sugar.

Sam was just ending his own call when Pinchus walked back, a ceramic up in each hand.

"That was Daniel," Pinchus said. He handed Sam one of the cups, then sat down behind his own desk, brow furrowed.

"Uh-huh?"

"I think maybe he's making up for those years we were apart. I think maybe he saved up all the *tsuris* I missed so he could give it to me in one lump."

"He having some trouble?"

"I wish. No. I think it's more like someone else is."

Sam raised his eyebrows.

"I told you about Daniel coming out to stay with me this weekend?" Pinchus asked.

"A couple of times. So?"

"So, it's my birthday. And I think he just delivered his present," Pinchus said sadly.

"Happy nearly-your-birthday. What did your son get you that appears to fill you with such delight?"

"It seems he's been seeing this girl for a while. He likes her very much, he says. He wants to bring her along this weekend."

"These things happen, Seymour. Even among children who idolize their parents. *I* think it's nice."

"They moved in together a few days ago," Pinchus said gravely.

"That's not so bad. Things are different than they were when you were that age."

"That's not the problem. Daniel think she's pregnant."

"Aha. Well—*mazel tov*, Grandpa!"

"Thank you. His mother's gonna kill me."

"I thought it was *him* that knocked his girlfriend up. Look at it this way: You'll have your own little family here, a place to go for Sunday dinner. Did you talk to Foster about Daniel coming to work here after he graduates?"

"Yeah. He said sure. If I want, he'll even put Daniel here in homicide with us."

"I guess he feels he owes you. Even more after Terranova."

"Daniel apologized for that, for not calling about Terranova. He said he meant to, but that he and Susan got busy with the move; it slipped his mind. Kids."

"Jesus Christ, Seymour—you should forgive the expression—you sound like a bad joke about a Jewish parent."

"Well I *am* a Jewish parent," Pinchus said defensively. "And, in that vein, I *would* like him here. But he expressed some doubt recently. He doesn't want to ride my coattails. Well, there's a few more months left—who knows?"

"Who ever does?"

Sam went down to the vending machine in the little lunchroom on the first floor to get them something to eat. He returned with a chocolate doughnut for himself and a piece of soggy apple pie for Pinchus, both wrapped in plastic. Pinchus tried to pay him. Sam waved him off.

"My treat to you, for having solved another case—this time in less than a day, and without hardly trying."

"Which means?"

"The chick with the dick. That was Trane on the phone while you were talking with Daniel. After you left this morning, they managed to pull prints from Jane Doe the John Doe. He had a criminal record. Light shit: mostly petty theft, possession. He also had, Onasis discovered, a bullet in the brain. A .22 short. Onasis almost missed it first time around. Dinky little entrance wound in the back of the head with no blood. Turns out Jane/John had the same address as the guy who owned the car. The car owner broke down when the Jersey police confronted him. There was a lover's quarrel. Our guy freaked and shot our gal—that is, our gal the other guy. Then he cuts him in half, packages him up, and stuffs him in the trunk of the car. Then the car gets stolen—just like you said—before he can get rid of the body. We haven't made the thief yet. Maybe we will, maybe we won't, but the case is closed so far as the homicide goes. Trane thinks you are the craftiest man on the face of the earth."

"You'd have called it the same way if you'd have been there, wouldn't you?"

Sam nodded. "But I am not the Fox," he said.

10

Alice went over to Beresford Street near the old Moravian church after she left Hillcrest. It was a pricey, touristy area with brick sidewalks and neocolonial storefronts, but there were a number of gift and notions shops, and their stock was good.

She found what she wanted in Friedman's: Fine Things for Friends & Family. Amid the silver, fabrics, ceramics, mirrors, copper, and stone, she found a handblown glass bear. A koala bear that was beautiful, delicate, and utterly irresistible. It was perfect. She knew so the instant she spied it.

It was also expensive—seventy-five dollars.

She vacillated only a moment. She had the money in her account. And there *would* be money coming in from the work she'd be doing for Hawthorne.

She decided: This was what she *wanted* to do. She picked the bear up, feeling a rush of pleasure, and started toward the cash register at the front. She thought briefly about looking for something inexpensive for Mark, but there wasn't anything like that in here and besides, she was spending more than she could really afford already. She wondered if Mark had been well enough to attend classes today. She'd find out tonight at six, the time they customarily spoke on Mondays.

There were four people in line at the cash register. Absentmindedly, Alice gazed at a display of Lladro and Royal Copenhagen figurines on freestanding shelving. An older woman in a linen suit was reaching out to touch one. In the aisle behind her, a stock clerk with a hand truck clipped the corner of the shelving as he passed. Three figurines came crashing down, shattering on the tile floor. Heads turned.

A short man came out from behind the cash register. He was nearly bald, with a fringe of gray hair. His cheeks were flushed. He started bouncing up and down on the balls of his feet.

"Madam," he yelled. "Do you know what you have just done?"

"But I only—" the woman began.

The man threw his arms wide. "This must be paid for! That's six hundred dollars worth of porcelain scrap on the floor." He stabbed a finger at the woman, who was clearly flustered and intimidated. "This must be paid for!"

Either this was Mr. Friedman and his store was losing money, Alice thought, or this was someone who worked for Mr. Friedman and who had already screwed up and was in danger of losing his job.

"Sir," the woman said, trying not to cry, "I barely touched the piece. I don't think I could have caused that."

"Madam, you were the only person around. These didn't fall by themselves." The man clearly felt in control now.

"Well, I just don't understand." The woman shook her head and began to cry.

"Tony," the man called to the stock clerk, who was now two aisles away, unloading boxes from his hand truck, "clean this mess up. Save the tags on these items so we can sort out the price."

Alice watched in astonishment as Tony got a broom and began to sweep up without a word. He was a young man, early twenties, about five feet ten. He had long dark hair that needed washing, a muscular build. He looked familiar to Alice, but she couldn't place him. Then she remembered: She had seen him once at Hillcrest, in a custodian's uniform.

"Mr. Friedman?" Alice said to the short man.

"No. He won't be in till later. I'm Mr. O'Malley."

"That woman had nothing to do what happened. I saw the whole thing. Your stock clerk hit the display with that thing he was pushing, with the boxes on it. That caused the figures to fall. This woman just happened to be reaching for one of them when it happened. She's not responsible. Maybe your stock clerk didn't realize what happened."

"She's full of shit!" Tony protested. "I was nowhere near that display."

"Watch your mouth," O'Malley warned.

"Mr. O'Malley, I am telling you exactly what I saw," Alice fixed her blue eyes on Tony. "And I will swear to that in court, in an affidavit, to Mr. Friedman, or in any other way that is necessary."

The woman in the linen suit took her hand. "Thank you, dear."

"You gonna believe her over me?" Tony asked indignantly.

O'Malley looked unhappy. He went behind the display, followed by Alice and the older woman. Tony remained in front, glowering.

"There," Alice pointed.

O'Malley bent, probed a fresh gouge on the side of a box with his finger. He straightened up, looked over at the hand truck Tony had been wheeling. He walked back around the display.

"You're fired," he told Tony. "Get your coat and get out."

"Over a lousy goddamn accident?"

"No. For not owning up to it when I blamed this woman, and then for lying about it."

"Fuck you!"

"I suggest you leave without a scene. I don't want to have to call the police." O'Malley turned to the older woman. "I'm deeply sorry, madam."

The woman had regained her composure. "You should be. I would like a business card, please. And I would like to know what time Mr. Friedman will be available. I want to discuss this with him."

O'Malley looked as if he wanted to protest, but didn't. Instead, he apologized again, wrote out some hours on a business card, and gave it to her.

"Thank you for having the courage to speak up," the woman said to Alice as she pushed open the door. She left.

"Mr. O'Malley," Tony pleaded, "I need this job to help get through school."

"You should have thought of that before."

"What about the back pay I got coming?"

"What about the broken figures? Take it up with Mr. Friedman if you want. You'll be lucky if he doesn't want you to pay for what you broke."

Tony slammed a fist against his thigh. "Son of a bitch!"

He went to the back of the store, reappeared a moment later with a denim jacket slung over his shoulder, and stalked out.

Alice lingered a few minutes in Friedman's before she left. When she stepped onto the sidewalk, she looked up and down it, and was relieved not to see Tony. She started home. Half a block later, Tony appeared from a doorway. He was at her side before she knew what was happening.

"You satisfied you got me fired, bitch? Why didn't you mind your own fucking business?"

Alice was shaken. But she was also aware that there were many people on the street, and she probably wasn't in any real danger. "It's a matter of integrity," she said, despite a desire just to ignore him. "I couldn't stand by and let someone innocent get hurt."

"Integrity, shit! You don't know shit about my situation. I really needed that job."

Alice stopped walking. "If you don't leave me, and right now, I'm going to scream for help."

Tony's nostrils flared. The tendons in his neck tensed. He backed away a step, then another. "Don't think I don't know who you are. I've seen you at the Home."

That he recognized her alarmed Alice.

"You say anything to the people there about this, you're dead meat."

Alice stared at him.

"Goddamn meddling cunt!" Tony turned and marched off in the opposite direction.

A man and woman who had stopped a few feet away to watch walked up to her. The man was wearing a brown suede jacket. "Are you all right?"

"Yes," Alice nodded. "Thank you."

"You sure?" the woman asked. "Would you like us to walk with you a ways?"

"Thank you. That's very kind. But I'm fine."

All three of them looked off in the direction Tony had gone. The back of his head could be seen, a block off. He was drawing away, striding rapidly.

Alice acquiesced to walking two blocks with the couple. Then she thanked them, parted from them, and went into a clothing store called the Side Stitch. She browsed, taking her mind off the unpleasantness with Tony, and daydreamed about winter coats she could not afford. She felt relaxed by the time she went out to the street again half an hour later.

Back in her own neighborhood, she was on Decker nearing Sixth Street, where she lived, when someone called to her from across the street:

"Professor Schaeffer! Wait up."

She turned, trying to place the student's face as he crossed the street. He was of medium height, had close-cropped sandy-colored hair.

"You're David Harper's friend." She suddenly remembered him from the lab this morning.

"Partly right. I'm *Barry* Harper, David's cousin. Actually, we're more like brothers. We pretty much grew up together. Do you mind if I walk with you a bit?"

"What's on your mind, Mr. Harper?"

He looked uncomfortable. "I want to apologize for David's behavior. See, David has some problems, but basically he's harmless. He was only ten when his parents died. They were killed in a car crash. That's when he came to live with us. He's had a lot of counseling over the years. He's very bright, maybe even a genius."

"I'm sorry he's had a rough time, but there's a limit to what I can tolerate in my class."

"Absolutely. I understand. You won't have any more problems with him. But"—he looked uncomfortable again—"just in case you do, I'd be grateful if you'd get in touch with me before you file any complaints. I'm sure I can help. I'm in Lincoln Dorm."

"You must care for him very much," Alice remarked.

Barry grinned. In a stagy voice, he said, "He ain't heavy. He's my brother."

Alice laughed. "I'll call you if I need to, Mr. Harper."

"Thank you. Thanks a lot."

Barry gave her a smile, then a wink, which puzzled her.

"Bye, Ms. Schaeffer."

The rest of Alice's afternoon was uneventful. She had a four-thirty biochem class of her own, after which she walked back home. It had grown colder. The sky was dark. There was the sound of distant thunder. Alice balanced her books under her left arm and put her hands in her jacket pockets. Her right hand touched something unfamiliar. She took the object out, immediately recognized it as the koala bear from Friedman's. In the excitement there, she had forgotten to pay for it, must have slipped it into her pocket when the commotion started. She'd stop by tomorrow.

Alice reached her building, waved through the plate glass of the laundromat window at Martaha, the Syrian woman who owned it, then went inside and walked up the long narrow flight of stairs to the second-floor landing and her door.

Inside, she dropped her books on the couch, took the bear from her jacket pocket, dropped the jacket on top of the books, then brought the bear into the bedroom and put it on the night table, next to the framed picture of Mark. On the other side of the bed, atop a twin to this night table, was a picture of her parents—in a frame of real silver, which had belonged to her grandmother.

She removed her skirt and top, changed into jeans and a sweater. She sat on the bed and put on cotton socks and sneakers. It was nearly six. Mark would be calling soon. At eight, she was due at Faulkner's.

She went into the kitchen. The front of the refrigerator was festooned with notes, newspaper cutouts, and store coupons. Some were fixed in place with magnets, others with tape: faculty meeting Friday, dental appointment in three weeks, meat loaf recipe, two rolls of Bounty towels for the price of one. . . .

There was leftover chicken in a plastic storage bag. She cut up a cucumber and a tomato and shredded some romaine lettuce. She put a pot of minute rice on, sautéed some mushrooms to add to the rice. It was all done in less than fifteen minutes. She poured herself a glass of seltzer, then took her dinner into the living room and set it on the coffee table in front of the couch. She put a Judy Collins tape into the player, then sat down to eat.

At six-thirty, she turned off the tape and turned on the television to watch the news. Mark still hadn't called.

At seven, she decided to hell with it, she wasn't going to stand on principle, and called him.

Mark's roommate picked up on the second ring.

"Hello, Johnny? This is Alice. Is Mark there?"

"Uh, no, he's not, Alice."

"Is he going to be home soon?"

"I don't know. I haven't seen him all afternoon. I'll leave a note telling him you called. So long, Al—"

"Johnny, *wait*. Don't hang up."

"Yes?"

Alice felt a little foolish. "I mean, how's he feeling? After being sick all weekend."

"He got up this morning and felt all right," Johnny offered. "He wasn't in Biz Law this afternoon, but he's got a test on Wednesday and he told me he might cut to study in the library. He probably lost track of time. He's probably on the way back now. Or will be soon. I'll tell him to call."

"Tell him to make it after ten-thirty. I'll be out till then. Unless he gets in within the next half hour. Okay?"

"No problem. Good talking to you, Alice."

Alice made some tea and waited till seven-thirty. Where the hell was Mark? He had to know that she was concerned about him. Jealous, she suddenly thought. My God, I'm not hurt, or even truly worried—what I am is jealous.

Yes, and stupidly. Mark was probably in the library cramming for a test.

No sense speculating. Might as well forget about it for now and have a good time.

She put on her navy jacket again, picked up her bag, and left the apartment for Faulkner's.

11

Faulkner's was a century-
old university bar: dark wooden beams, a stone fireplace that held real wood fires in the winter, booths,
wooden tables with gingham tablecloths, old coal-
mining tools on the walls. The jukebox was in the rear
and the music was loud. In a corner, stood a pinball
machine. Pinball machines were making a comeback
and this was a vintage fifties' model. Top score for the
week won a bottle of wine. The place was crowded
and noisy, and just what Alice was in the mood for.

Alice spied Kathy as she entered. Kathy was at the
near end of the bar holding a glass of beer and chatting
with Ed, the bartender. Ed was huge. He had flowing
blond hair. He looked like a Viking.

Last year, Kathy had held the fellowship that Alice
had now. She had since been taken on to the faculty as
an associate professor. Kathy was Alice's height. She
was attractive, in a plump, cuddly kind of way. When
she and Alice were out together, they drew a lot of attention from men, which they fielded in a manner that
was friendly but without interest: Alice had Mark,
Kathy was seeing Gary, an intern at Saint Bonaventure's Hospital.

Alice caught Kathy's eye. Kathy came over, kissed
her on the cheek, and guided her to the rear, where
Janet and Richie had a table. Janet was finishing a burger and fries, Richie a plate of lasagna.

Richie had been named Alice's alternate for her fellowship, which meant that he would step in for her if
she were unable to complete the year. Richie was tall,

slim, and had thinning blond hair. People liked him well enough, but he was shy and limited most of his social contact to this little group. Janet was short, a little chunky; she'd been a competition wrestler in high school. Janet and Richie were in the same graduate curriculum as Alice.

Janet ordered another pitcher of beer for them.

They caught each other up on what had happened in their lives over the past few days, then wandered into what developed, in only a few minutes, into a heated debate on the ethics of gene-splicing.

"So this time you get a Frankenstein's monster on the loose, only there's nothing in the whole world that can stop it!" Richie said. "Nothing! That's what you want? That's the change-of-the-millennium gift you want to give to your kids?" Richie had had a lot to drink. His gaze, directed at Kathy, was fierce.

"I don't think we should sit around with our thumb up our ass because we don't have the guts to take the next step," Kathy said. "If everyone had always thought the way you do, we'd all still be living in caves gnawing on meat bones and painting our bodies blue!"

"But we're not! And the reason isn't because they were able to cut and paste their chromosomes," Richie retorted hotly.

"Natural selection? Spouting a little Darwinism, are we?" Kathy said sarcastically. "You missed the point. Come back into the twentieth century, *asshole*."

"You can be a real bitch at times."

"Screw you."

"That's your answer for everything," Richie shouted.

Janet put two fingers in her mouth and whistled shrilly. Conversation died around them. People turned to look.

"Time out," Janet said. "Time fucking out."

The noise of the bar picked up again.

"The match is over," Janet announced. "I declare it

a draw. But no more, not one more word. I did not come out tonight to listen to an argument. I came out to have a good time."

"Hear, hear," Alice cried.

Kathy and Richie breathed heavily, glaring at each other, but then agreed. Shortly, the passions of the previous minutes were forgotten. The four of them were laughing again, Richie loudly.

Alice told them about the incident at Friedman's, about finding the koala bear unpaid for in her pocket when she returned home.

"You go home tonight, you're going to find that O'Malley guy has got the cops waiting to bust you for shoplifting," Janet said.

"And Richie will corroborate," Kathy teased. "He'll tell them you confessed to us. Then he takes over your fellowship."

"Oh, no," Richie said with great earnestness. "I could never do anything like that. I completely and utterly adore you, Alice."

It was apparent to all three women that Richie meant this. An embarrassed silence settled over the table.

"No more beer for you," Janet said, giving him an out. "Not, anyway, unless you're willing to adore Kathy and me too."

"It's a deal," Richie happily agreed. He chuckled, and poured himself another glass.

They had drunk three pitchers since Alice arrived, and Alice wasn't drinking much at all.

Kathy, who was nearly as tipsy as Richie, was looking toward the middle of the bar. She snorted, a little sound of contempt.

"Yeah?" Janet raised an eyebrow.

"Horny Hawthorne: lecher—excuse me—*lecturer* extraordinaire."

Dr. Miles Hawthorne was at the bar, one foot on the brass rail, elbow leaning on the bar itself, deep in conversation with a woman Alice didn't know but whom she recognized as a professor in the history department.

"Horny Hawthorne?" Alice asked, surprised at Kathy's comment.

"Bastard." Kathy was looking at Hawthorne over the rim of her glass.

"Why don't you shut up and leave the man alone?" Richie suggested.

"He just hired me to grade papers for him," Alice told the group.

"You'll be lucky if that's all he asks you to grade."

"That's enough mouth from you, Kathy," Richie said, pointing a finger at her. "Hawthorne is a fine man. I'm not going to sit here and let you run him down."

Alice now noticed Hawthorne staring at her from across the room. He gave her a friendly nod, and then he continued with his conversation.

"Just because you're teacher's pet doesn't mean you have to act like his lap dog," Kathy said arching one eyebrow in Ritchie's direction.

"Fuck you, Kathy. Which was probably what he didn't do and that's why you're pissed at him."

"In his dreams, baby boy. And in yours."

"Fuck you all. You're all alike. Goddamn genital bigots." Richie got up abruptly, threw some money on the table, then stormed out.

"Well," Kathy said, half-apologetically, "hard to recapture a happy mood after that."

Janet blinked, looked at Alice, then at Kathy. "I've never seen Richie so angry."

"You were a little hard on him," Alice told Kathy.

"We've been harder on each other in the past and been able to laugh it off. You remember when he said he adores you? Well, I think he does. And I think he somehow feels threatened by having you and Hawthorne work so closely together. By defending Hawthorne, he protects his interest in you by denying the kind of guy Hawthorne is."

"You changed your field to psychology?" Janet asked.

"You're way off," Alice said. "First: Richie *doesn't* adore me. He might have for that moment, but he was drunk. There was nothing more to it. Second: Your analysis of Richie's motivation for defending Hawthorne is wrong. Hawthorne is Richie's mentor, almost a father figure. Richie would defend him against any kind of attack."

"Oh, yeah? Tell me: Did Richie know earlier that Hawthorne had offered you the job?"

"Yes. I told him in class late this afternoon. But that doesn't—"

"And did you realize that Richie was drunk before he even showed up here tonight?"

"No."

"I rest my case. What do *you* think, Janet?"

"I think Richie ought not to drink so much. And I think you ought to recognize it when he does and cut him some slack."

"I guess." Kathy was silent a moment, then sighed.

They tried to rally their mood over the next half hour but weren't very successful, and since thunder was rumbling outside and it sounded as if the storm would move in earlier than expected, they paid their tab and left. Outside, Janet said good night and left Alice and Kathy for the dorm in which she lived.

Alice and Kathy walked off in the opposite direction.

"You know," Kathy said, "I really do have to talk to you about Hawthorne."

"Don't start again, Kathy."

"No, really. But I wanted to wait till we were alone."

Alice heard the seriousness of Kathy's tone. "All right. What?"

"It's true, what I said about Hawthorne. I had the same job last year he just gave you, remember?"

"Yes. I'd forgotten."

"I wish I could. Richie was wrong: It's not that he wouldn't fuck me, it's that he *did* fuck me—and then fucked me over. Dumped me. After three weeks. For some visiting little Filipino pussy in the poly-sci department. He's very discreet, our professor Hawthorne, but he really is a lecher extraordinaire. Keep your legs crossed, sister."

"Kathy, I'm *engaged*."

"He's a very determined guy."

"I'm sorry for what happened to you. Thank you for telling me. I appreciate it."

"I'm a big girl. And, hey, what else is sisterhood for?"

They said good-bye at the corner of Vine and Sixth Street. Lightning illuminated the night. There was a clap of thunder. The first raindrops began to fall. They hugged quickly, then Kathy hurried up Vine, and Alice turned right onto Sixth to walk the final two blocks to her own apartment.

12

He waited in the dark, breathing slowly, quietly. Time was suspended. He had no sense of it passing, no sense of it not passing. He was like a spider on a web—still, but aware.

13

The street was quiet for 10 P.M., only a few people out. Even the diner on the corner seemed subdued, just two students sitting at the counter over a cup of coffee, the vinyl booths empty. The waitress had her elbows on the counter and was reading a newspaper.

The laundromat, which closed at nine-thirty on weeknights, was dark, a metal grate drawn down over its window, the door padlocked. Alice entered her building, thinking of what Kathy had told her about Hawthorne. Should she tell Hawthorne that something had come up and she couldn't work for him after all? Or just ignore it and see what happened? She had no reason to doubt Kathy, but she realized that she was, after all, getting only Kathy's side of things.

"Damn," Alice said, entering the vestibule. The overhead light on the landing above was burned out.

She squinted in the gloom, the hall faintly illuminated by what little light filtered in from the frosted skylight over the landing. She got her keys out of her purse, located the one to her apartment by feel. She started up the narrow stairwell, one hand against a wall to orient herself.

Maybe there was a grain of truth in what Richie had said—maybe Kathy was the one who'd done the pursuing rather than Hawthorne. Maybe *she* had seduced *him*, and then, if he'd thought better of it and decided not to continue with her, she had become angry. It was possible. Hawthorne was attractive. Famous. Alice knew of at least two of her classmates who had crushes on him.

Ah, well. No use trying to think through it tonight. Better to sleep on it, decide in the morning what to do, if anything.

Alice located the lock with her fingers, managed the key into the slot. She unlocked the door and went in. She tossed her purse to where she knew the couch was, heard it land there. She took her jacket off, tossed it after her purse, then crossed the living room in darkness and entered the bedroom, switching on the lamp on the night table. She closed the blinds, came back around the bed and sat down on it. She picked up the koala bear from the night table. She turned it over in her hands, smiling, thinking of Rose Fitapaldi, then set it down on the coverlet. She crossed one leg over the other, untied her sneaker, and took it off, then her sock. She took off her other sneaker and sock, stood, unbuttoned her jeans and slipped them down her legs, stepped out of them.

She looked at the clock on the night table. It was 10:15. She wondered if Mark had tried to call. Goddamn, she was going to buy a new answering machine tomorrow regardless of what she decided to do about Hawthorne, even if she didn't bring in any extra money. Enough of this already.

For a moment, she almost picked up the phone to call Mark. But she had done enough calling. More wouldn't be cool, and he'd tell her so. Wait. Till midnight anyway. If he hadn't called by then, she'd be justified. But he probably would. She'd told Johnny she wouldn't be home till ten-thirty. Mark was probably there waiting.

She bent, picked up her jeans, and tossed them through the open door into the dark living room. She tossed her socks after them, to be picked up on her way to the bathroom, where the hamper was. She took off her sweater, folded it, and laid it on the top of the dresser. She unhooked her bra, slid the straps from her shoulders, folded one cup inside the other and put the bra on top of her sweater.

She admired herself in the mirror. Great tits, she mouthed silently to her own image. She winked at her image, which winked back.

Then she went to the closet, pulled back the sliding door, and reached inside for her robe.

She was grabbed suddenly from behind—hard—by an arm that went round her throat and jerked her backward against a body. A gloved hand clamped over her mouth.

In one terrifying moment, Alice's eyes widened, and her legs went weak, as she sucked air through flaring nostrils.

"You scream," said a harsh low voice above her left ear, "I'll kill you. Understand?"

Alice remained frozen.

The man wrenched her head back. *"Understand?"*

Through her nose, Alice managed to get out: "Mm-hmm." The sound was high-pitched, throttled.

"Good girl."

The man touched his lips to the nape of her neck, once, lightly.

"Give me a hard time," he said, "I'm gonna hurt you. Real bad. Remember that. Remember it good."

For some reason, the most horrifying thing was not the brush of his lips or even the meaning of his words: It was the heat of his breath flowing on her naked skin.

"Now we're going over to the bed," he said.

Oh my God, Alice thought. Oh my sweet Jesus.

She could tell that he was taller than she, strong, and that he was wearing surgical gloves. She could smell the latex, feel it over her mouth.

Clumsily, he walked her to the bed, pushed her down on it, on her stomach. Her head was cocked obliquely against the covers, facing the nightstand.

Oh no, no. . . .

He freed her throat, took his hand from her

mouth. His weight lifted from her, but he kept his hand on her shoulder and dug his fingers into her flesh.

"Just there. Just like that. Keep your eyes closed."

"I'd like to talk with you," Alice said quietly, trying to keep her voice steady. "I'd like to talk with you about this."

He swung his hand up from her shoulder and hit the side of her face with the back of it. "Shut up!"

Alice stifled the scream welling up inside her. She knew now that there was no way to prevent this. She would remain quiet and do what he told her to do.

"Lie still."

She did.

He was gone a moment. Then she felt his presence again. She heard a rustling, like a cardboard box being opened. There was a moment's silence, then a metallic *click*. She shuddered. She knew that sound. She had heard it in movies, heard it as a teenager when one of her boyfriends showed off: the sound of a switchblade knife opening.

"Remember," the man said in that raspy, artificial voice, "you don't scream, you stay alive."

She felt cold steel touch her back, just below her left shoulder blade. She stifled a cry when the point pricked her. He drew the blade down, slitting skin. She bit her lip to keep from screaming. The horror, as he made small cuts, was worse than the pain, which was only a stinging. Alice felt blood flowing across her skin. Despite herself, she moaned.

Instantly her attacker grabbed her hair and yanked her head up from the bed. He slashed at her hair, cutting off a handful of it. He shoved the hair up against her face. She squeezed her eyes shut.

"I'm not fucking around," he said. He threw her hair aside. "Keep your mouth *shut*."

His weight shifted. She heard a scrape from the box. Then she felt him bending over her.

Suddenly, Alice felt a sharp pinching pain below

the base of her neck. But then, just as suddenly, the pain ceased.

"Shit!"

The man's weight moved again as she felt him shift closer still, his hot breath on her skin. Then the pinching returned, but lower this time, and more brutal—a vising pain.

She gasped.

And it happened again, lower.

"Ahh-uhhhh!" she cried.

And then the pain, the pressure, stopped. Immediately the area began to ache.

"Now," he said. "Now we're going to make you naked."

She felt the flat of the blade move under the waistband of her panties, slide over her buttock.

She grimaced, eyes squeezed shut, tried to pray, couldn't remember any prayers.

He cut her panties open, cut through the elastic at the leg holes.

God. God.

"Sweet ass," he whispered lustfully. "Very, very sweet."

Tears welled in Alice's eyes.

She heard him unbuckle his pants, pull the zipper down. She heard fabric sliding against flesh.

The tip of his hard penis touched her anus.

"Oh no," she whimpered, barely audible.

He tried to push into her. He couldn't. It hurt.

"Come on, cunt," he said. "Loosen up. Come on—let me in goddamn it!"

She tried, but she couldn't. She was too frightened. Her body wouldn't obey her.

"Fuck," he said. "Fuck!"

The mattress shifted, there was pause, and then he was pricking the flesh of her anus with the point of the knife. She screamed. He hit her. And then the pricking stopped. She could feel blood running from the little cuts. She felt him shove himself deep into her, his weight coming down on her back.

She reached out. Her right hand clutched the coverlet and bunched it up. Her left fell on the little glass koala bear. She closed her hand around the bear, clinging to it as if it might save her. She pressed her face into the coverlet to muffle her cries as he drove into her, and drove into her again, and again.

She felt as if she were being split apart.

She groaned. Her head lifted up from the bed. In the glass that covered the photograph of her parents, she caught, reflected, the first glimpse of her attacker. He wore a dark long-sleeve T-shirt. He had a ski mask over his head, with holes for his eyes, his nose and mouth.

She looked at the images of her parents, who were smiling at her. Help me, she thought. Oh please help me.

She focused on the ski mask. Something about it. Yes. That he was wearing one. That he had taken care to hide his identity. That meant he would leave her when he was done. That he had told her the truth—she would be safe as long as she submitted.

But it went on and on. He sodomized her for what seemed forever, without spending himself.

Come, she begged silently. Please come. And then leave me. I can't bear this any longer.

As if in answer, he pulled out of her. She gasped with the abruptness of it. He lifted himself a little, seized her by the shoulder, and pulled her over onto her back. She looked into his eyes, but as soon as she did, squeezed her own eyes shut again.

He straddled her, began to fondle her breasts.

"You don't look so prim and proper now, Alice, do you?"

Alice?

Oh God, he knew her. Or maybe, she thought, he saw my name on something in the apartment.

"Wonder what your mom and dad over there would say if they could see you like this, getting your tits played with, getting fucked. Bet you've done a lot of fucking in this bed. Not like this, though. Bet nobody's ever fucked you like this, in the ass. Bet I'm the first. . . . Tell me. I'm the first, aren't I?" He twisted her breast. "Tell me!"

"You're the first!" she whimpered.

"I knew it. Yeah, I knew it."

He separated her legs roughly with his hands, then inserted himself into her vagina.

"Sweet cunt, sweet cunt," he said, rocking into her.

She offered just enough resistance to try to move him to orgasm.

"Oh, that's good. You're liking this. I can tell you're liking this."

And then he came, grunting and shoving.

She had never felt dirtier in her life.

He slumped on her.

"That was real good," he said. He patted her hair.

He lay quietly atop her for several long moments.

Then he put a hand on her throat.

She opened her eyes in alarm.

He got up on his knees, pulling her arms down and pinning them beneath his knees. He put one hand across her mouth. With the other, he took hold of the top of the ski mask and slowly pulled it off, revealing himself to her.

Suddenly Alice knew she was going to die. She urinated over the coverlet.

The hand that had pulled off the mask came down to join the other one on her throat, began to squeeze. And he leaned forward, bearing down, squeezing.

The phone began to ring.

And bucking futilely, Alice began to die.

14

Pinchus pulled slowly to the curb in front of the apartment house on Sixth Street. Sam Milano, whom he had picked up on the way, sat beside him. Two patrol cars were on the scene already, their twirling lights splashing the buildings on either side with intermittent swaths of red and blue. There were two unmarked cars, too. The thunder and violent rains of the earlier night had stopped, but a steady drizzle was coming down.

Pinchus got out of his Olds. His breath misted in the cold damp air. He pulled up the collar of his trench coat. Sam moved to lock the doors as he exited from the other side.

"Don't bother." Pinchus shrugged. "They steal the car, I don't want to have to fix the lock or replace the window when I get it back."

"I like a man who thinks ahead." Sam yawned. "I hope this won't be an all-nighter." He hunched up against the drizzle. "To think, only forty-five minutes ago I was fast asleep."

"What time is it now?"

"One-fifteen."

"Vacation made you soft."

"What were you doing when the call came in—pushups?"

"Sleeping," Pinchus said.

Sam laughed.

They went into the building, through the door beside the laundromat and held it open.

Pinchus took a Mini-Mag flashlight out of his

jacket pocket, squatted down and examined the door latch. "Outer lock doesn't work. Looks like it hasn't for a while." He grunted as he pushed himself erect.

"Any details on the vic?" Sam asked as they climbed the narrow stairs.

"Nope. Female. Raped and murdered. Thane is being extra cautious, though. He called Onasis to the scene. He doesn't usually do that. That's all they had for me. What else is new?"

What light there was in the hall came through an open door at the landing. Murmuring voices drifted out too. Pinchus noted a ceiling fixture at the top of the stairs with an unshaded bulb in it. The bulb was not lit.

"What do you bet?" he said pointing to the bulb.

"Not a plug nickel."

Pinchus stood on his toes, grasped the naked lightbulb with his fingers, and gave it a clockwise turn. On the second turn, the light went on, illuminating the landing.

"Convenient."

"In the dark, you wouldn't see the jimmy marks on the door," Sam said.

Pinchus shined his light on the door lock.

Sam bent over and peered at it. "You'd think people would know better. Probably took the perp all of two-and-a-half seconds to get in."

"Three," Pinchus pressed. "Harder to do in the dark."

"Who says he turned the light off before he did it?"

"Point," Pinchus acknowledged.

They entered the apartment. Flashbulbs popped in the bedroom as a photographer worked. Pinchus could see Trane in there, the coroner, standing with his arms crossed. He could also see the legs and naked pubic region of the victim on the bed. Out in the living room, where he and Sam were, two plainclothes officers from the crime lab were making a careful survey of the

apartment. In the corner, a pair of uniforms were talking to a distraught young man and woman.

One of the uniforms—black, female, looking too
slight and young to Pinchus to be a cop—detached
herself and came over to Pinchus and Sam. "Officer
Collins, Lieutenant. I was the one who took the call."

Pinchus nodded. "We've met before. The Thompson shootings."

Leon Thompson was a fifteen-year-old who'd been
pegging shots from a .22 caliber rifle at motorists on
the throughway. One had hit a woman in the eye, who
had lost control of her car and been killed in the crash.
Which had made it homicide.

Collins was clearly flattered that Pinchus remembered her. "Yes," she said. She looked at Sam, indicating that she recalled him, too. "Sergeant."

"So run it down for me," Pinchus asked. "What
happened here?"

"We're not really sure. The victim was twenty-five,
lived alone. She's a graduate student—*was*. Taught
part-time at the university. Really brutal. I've never
seen anything like it."

"They're all brutal," Pinchus said abstractedly. He
was looking at the bedroom door. An eerie feeling had
come over him.

"This is rape, Lieutenant. I bet the fucker sexually
mutilated her, too."

Pinchus swung his gaze back to Collins. "Onasis
say that?"

"No, but . . ."

"So you got some kind of inside track on that because you're a woman? What you look like is a cop,
Collins. Act like one."

"Yes, *sir*."

After a moment Pinchus said, "You never saw one
like this before, huh?"

"No," Collins admitted, reluctantly.

"Uh-huh. Well, I hope you never get to like them
any better than you do now. Just that you learn to

handle yourself better. That's what makes a really good cop. A good detective."

She was less angry, but it would still take her time to cool down completely. "Dr. Onasis can give you a better idea about how and when. He went out to get something to eat. He should be back soon."

Pinchus was looking at the bedroom door again.

Sam gestured to the couple. "Them?"

"The woman's a friend of the victim. She and her companion discovered the body."

There was a moment of silence.

"Seymour?"

Pinchus looked at Sam.

"You want to talk to 'em now?" Sam asked.

Pinchus glanced at the couple. "Yes. Sorry." He looked back at Collins. "Is there anything else you can tell me?"

"Like I said, Dr. Onasis'll have to give you the rest."

Pinchus looked around the living room, studying it.

Collins started back toward the couple. "Anyway," she muttered, "I'm sure the great Fox'll have it all figured out by breakfast."

"Collins!"

Collins swung around, startled by the intensity of Pinchus's voice.

"Get the fuck back here," Pinchus said.

She swallowed hard and walked quickly back.

"That Fox shit is just that—" Pinchus said angrily, "shit. I'm not that good. *No one* is. So—"

Sam touched his arm. "Seymour," he said quietly, "take it easy."

Pinchus drew in a breath. "So just ease off, Collins. You ease off, and I'll ease off. We're both on the same side. We both want the motherfucker that did this caught. Okay?"

"Okay," she nodded, solemn-faced.

Collins went over to the couple.

"That Fox stuff," Pinchus said to Sam. "It puts the pressure on."

"Don't listen to it. You okay to do 'em now?"

"Yeah."

They walked over to the couple.

Pinchus introduced himself and Sam.

"I understand you discovered the body. I know this is very upsetting for you, but I'd appreciate it if you could help us out here, if you'll tell us everything you know about the situation, as calmly and accurately as you can."

The woman was Katherine Bollinger, an associate professor of biology at the university. Her eyes were puffy and red from crying. The man, a couple of years older, was Gary Markovics, an intern at Saint Bonaventure's Hospital. Markovics kept a protective arm around Kathy.

"I was out earlier with Alice at Faulkner's," Kathy said.

"Alice?" A pit opened in Pinchus's stomach. It was real. What he'd felt but hadn't let himself consciously admit.

"Yes. Alice Schaeffer."

He worked to keep anything from showing.

Late. I am too late again! Oh God, Alice. *I'm sorry*.

He asked, "Were you alone with her, or were there others present?"

Sam was taking notes.

"Janet Cooper and Richie Zimmer were with us. But Richie left earlier."

Under Pinchus's questioning, Kathy described the evening in detail.

"I had second thoughts about what I'd told her about Professor Hawthorne. So when I got home, I decided to call her."

"Why second thoughts? Was it true, what you told her?"

"Yes, but that didn't mean it necessarily had anything to do with her. She needed the money.

Forewarned, she could probably handle anything that came up. I don't know, I just felt I should talk to her some more. But there was no answer."

"What time was this?"

"Ten-thirty. Maybe a little after. I remember because I thought she'd probably be on the phone with Mark."

"Mark?"

Pinchus got what information Kathy had on Mark, including that he had been unable to visit Alice these last two weekends.

"Why did you think she'd be on the phone with Mark?"

"She was expecting him to call around then. She hadn't been able to reach him earlier. When she didn't answer, I figured I must have dialed the wrong number. So I called again. I tried up until eleven o'clock. Nothing. No busy signal or anything else. It just kept ringing and ringing. At eleven, that's when I called Gary at the hospital. He was getting off his shift. I told him I thought something was wrong."

She started to cry again.

Markovics drew her in closer. Pinchus gave her his handkerchief.

"Gary told me not to jump to conclusions. He said it was probably just trouble with the phone or something like that."

"How many times would you say you dialed her between ten-thirty and eleven?" Pinchus was intent.

"I don't know. A lot. I tried every couple of minutes."

"And you never once got a busy signal?"

"No."

"What time did you get here?"

She looked to Markovics.

"About eleven-thirty," he recalled.

"Did you hear the phone ring at any time since you've been here?"

"No," Kathy replied.

Markovics nodded, agreeing.

"Interesting," Pinchus said.

Kathy looked horrified. "You don't think that Mark—"

"I don't know anything and I don't think anything. Yet. I'm just trying to put a picture together. So Gary came by from the hospital and picked you up?"

"Yes. I said I wanted him to."

"And you both came here."

"Yes. We knocked. Alice didn't answer."

"How was the outside stairway when you came up—before you got to the landing and knocked?"

"What do you mean?"

"Just close your eyes and picture it. Tell me what you see."

"It was dark," Markovics said, an instant before Kathy did.

"No light at all?"

"No."

"So you knocked, and Alice didn't answer. Then what?"

"Gary tried the door. It wasn't locked. It opened when he turned the knob. That's when I knew something terrible had happened!" Kathy broke down.

Sam led her to the couch and sat down with her. Officer Collins got her a glass of water from the kitchen. Pinchus stayed with Markovics.

"Sergeant Milano will finish taking her statement. Why don't you go on? Tell me what you did after you found the door unlocked."

"That's when I got spooked, too," Markovics said. "I told Kathy to wait outside. But she came in behind me. It was dark, but there was a light on in the bedroom. I walked toward the door, and then—then I saw her legs. I didn't know what I should do, and I started to say, 'Alice?' but Kathy pushed by me and went in. And then—then she was screaming. I ran in behind her, and there was Alice lying on the bed naked and not moving with her eyes open. I saw blood."

Markovics shook his head at the memory. "I grabbed Kathy and turned her around so her back was to the bed and I said, 'Just stay here, don't move. I'm going to check her for a pulse,' and I did, though I could tell from looking at her that she was dead, that somebody had killed her."

"And then I thought, 'Oh, shit, the guy might still be in the apartment,' so I grabbed Kathy and ran out with her. We went down the stairs right into the diner on the corner. I called the police from there. Officer Collins and the other cop showed up in about five minutes. I don't know. Maybe it was three minutes. It seemed like forever and right away at the same time. That's pretty much it."

On the couch, Kathy had calmed down, though she was still sniffling and blowing her nose. She wiped tears from her cheeks with the back of her hand. Sam had taken the rest of her statement. There was no reason for her or Gary to stay any longer. Pinchus told them to go home and get some sleep, he'd be in touch. In the meantime, if either of them remembered anything else he wanted them to call him or Sam. He and Sam gave them cards.

"I'm sorry you had to see this," Pinchus said, placing a hand momentarily on Kathy's shoulder. "I wish you hadn't. I wish your friend was still alive."

"Thank you." Kathy wiped her eyes.

They started to leave.

"Oh, one last thing," Pinchus called them back. "Kathy, what was Alice wearing at Faulkner's."

Kathy looked up trying to remember. "She was wearing jeans and a mauve sweater. Sneakers, I think. She had her navy blue jacket. Why? Is that important?"

"Maybe. Maybe not. I don't know."

Kathy and Gary left. They said they didn't need anyone to drive them home.

It was time. Pinchus didn't want it to be, but it was. He went into the bedroom.

Trane was there. So was a uniform. A guy from the crime lab was poking about in the carpet. The photographer had finished and gone.

Pinchus stood beside the bed looking down. Alice was on her back, naked. Her arms were at her sides. Her head was turned a little, angled up toward the headboard. Her eyes were open. Her chestnut hair was spread out around her head. Her legs were parted; there was blood on the coverlet between them. There were bruises around her throat and neck.

She had been so vibrant yesterday, so filled with life. Now she was a sack of meat.

"Pretty girl," said Trane.

"Are they done in here?" Pinchus asked.

"With her. We're waiting for the meat wagon. Then we'll bag her up and send her down to the morgue."

"What about the room?"

"I'm finished with the furniture," the crime-scene guy said from his squat on the floor. "Haven't done the closets or the insides of the drawers yet."

Pinchus went to the phone on the night table and picked it up. "Nice clear dial tone," he said to Sam, who had come in behind him.

Tom Onasis entered the room. "Hi, Seymour."

"Hi, Tom."

"Pretty nasty one here."

"It stinks," Pinchus said. "What you and I do stinks."

Onasis raised his eyebrows. Sam gave him a look that said, Who knows?

"So what have we got?" Pinchus asked.

"Cause of death, probably strangulation. Rape almost certain. Anal and vaginal. Time of death, somewhere between ten and eleven. There are light cuts below her left shoulder blade, but no stab wounds. You want to look for a very sharp knife or a razor. There are also what might be bite marks on the upper portion of her back. If they *are* bite marks, they'll be important. She had some kind of glass bear clutched in her left hand. Maybe she was trying to tell us who the killer was with it. I don't know. Figuring that out is your department. I gave the bear to the lab men. Any more details, you'll have to wait till the autopsy."

"Tomorrow morning?"

"Tomorrow afternoon. Three o'clock."

Pinchus nodded.

The men from the morgue arrived. They unrolled a long heavy plastic bag onto the bed beside Alice, lifted her—one by her shoulders, the other by her ankles—and slung her onto the bag. The one nearest her head leaned and positioned her arms at her sides. Then they zippered the bag closed, strapped it to a stretcher and took it away.

Pinchus stood quietly a moment. Then he began to look about the bedroom, taking his time. He made careful entries in his notebook. He went into the bathroom, looked it over. He went into the living room, opened the closet door and glanced through its interior. He went into the kitchen. Sam, meanwhile, made his own rounds of the apartment.

Sam finished before Pinchus. He leaned against the doorframe into the hall and smoked as he waited for Pinchus.

When Pinchus was satisfied, he directed technicians from the crime lab to note certain articles he wanted brought to his office when they were finished with them. Then he left with Sam.

Officer Collins and her partner sat in the living room waiting for the men from the crime lab to finish up. It was their responsibility to stay until everyone was done here, and then to padlock the apartment and seal it off with notice that it was a crime scene.

The phone on the end table in the living room rang.

Collins looked at her partner, who looked back at her. She picked up the phone.

"Hello?"

"Collins? That you?"

"Yes. Uh, Lieutenant Pinchus?"

"Right. Just making sure the phone works both ways. Thanks for your help. Good night."

"Good night, Lieutenant."

"Who was that?" her partner asked.

"The great motherfucking Fox," Collins said. But this time there was some grudging respect in her voice.

PART
TWO

▲

PART
TWO

15

Peter Roberts pulled with unrelenting force, moving his hand slightly to one side, then slightly to the other, and back again. Blood began to flow, first a trickle, then a gush. Peter's knuckles were white, his forearm knotted. Feeling a release, he executed a rotating twist. There was a cracking of bone . . . then tissue tore, blood came pouring out, and with a final effort Peter pulled the tooth free.

He held it in the tips of the stainless steel forceps for Elmer Parker to see. "Looks like this one wanted to stay put."

Bright early sunlight streamed into the operatory through one window. Peter had closed the blinds over the other to keep the sun out of Elmer's eyes.

Peter put the tooth on the steel tray in front of Elmer: Elmer liked to save his teeth. He wiped a clot of blood from the new socket in Elmer's mouth, then took up a second piece of sterile gauze, folded it, and pressed it against the socket, stemming the flow of blood.

"Bite down on this for the next few minutes," Peter instructed.

"Mmm-hmm," Elmer said around the gauze. "Good job."

Peter left the operatory. Sallie, who had assisted him, followed. When they were out of earshot, she asked, "How many does that make for him?"

"Five in the last year. He never comes to get them fixed. Only extracted. If he had an ingrown nail, he'd probably get his finger amputated."

Sallie giggled.

Peter liked Sallie: liked the way she laughed at his jokes, liked looking down her shirt when she bent over a patient.

"Dr. Roberts," Nina called from the front desk, "Kristina from the morgue on line one. You want to take it?"

"I'll pick up in three."

Adrenaline surged through him. He went to the last of the three operatories in the suite, where there was no patient waiting. He shut the door behind him, sat on a stool, and lifted the phone. "Dr. Roberts," he said.

"Hi, doc. Kristina. We got a murdered woman here. We know who she is, that's not the problem. What is, is she was raped and has these marks on her Dr. Onasis thinks are bite marks. He wants you to take a look. He says this could be first-class evidence."

"I can get away from here in an hour."

"Relax. They're not doing the autopsy till three. Dr. Onasis is beat. He called me in the middle of the night to make sure I got you early. He especially wants you here."

"Three o'clock is fine. Who's the victim?"

"Name of Alice Schaeffer. She taught at the university."

Peter was silent a moment. Then he said, "Boy, I don't hear from you guys for months, then all of sudden it's three in a row."

"Maybe it's the silly season. Incidentally, yesterday's case—John Doe and John/Jane Doe. Did you X-ray the jaws yet?"

"No. Why?"

"You don't need to do Jane's jaws. We got her ID'd." Kristina told him what had happened. "You can bring hers back this afternoon. We still don't know who the driver was, so go ahead with his."

"That was amazingly fast."

"We're good. Well, Pinchus is anyway. He called it. Don't forget my Tupperware."

"I won't." Peter hung up and went out to the desk. "Nina, I have to be out of here by two-forty. Do whatever you need to free me up, okay?"

"You're going to the morgue on another case?"

Peter enjoyed the admiration in her voice. "Yes."

Nina gave a mock shiver. "It's getting scary around here." She opened a Rolodex. "I'll get Dr. Cohen to cover."

Jeff Cohen was Peter's associate. Tuesday was normally a day off for him.

"By the way," Nina said. "Dr. Cohen said he'd help you X-ray those jaws if you want."

"Tell him thanks, but it's not necessary. I only have to do one set."

"Open the windows when you do."

It had taken three days to get rid of the lingering odor last time.

"I will."

"Are you going to bring jaws back from this one, too?"

"No. This is a bite-mark case. Someone raped and murdered a young woman. He left his teeth marks in her flesh."

"Ugh! Do they know who the poor thing was?"

"An Alice Schaeffer or something," Peter said casually.

"We treated an Alice Schaeffer just last month! Remember?"

"No."

"Sure you do. Pretty girl, from the university?"

Peter shook his head.

"Odd." Her tone was a little arch. "You usually remember the pretty ones. You were, as I recall, ogling her."

He smiled. "Was I?"

"Anyway," Nina continued, "it's a common name.

I'd hate to think it was the same one. I hope they get the bastard."

"So do I," Peter said.

At two, Jeff Cohen helped Peter collect what he'd need at the morgue. Cohen called off the list:

"Blank charts . . . impression material, mixing pad, spatula . . . marker, celluloid squares, chip blower . . . dental stone . . . mixing bowl . . . mirror, explorer . . . camera, film . . . ruler, calipers. Good. Looks like everything. Wait, we forgot staples."

"Right. Need staples. Thanks, Jeff."

Peter was on the way out when he stopped at the open door. He turned. "Jesus, I forgot to call Diane. Nina, could you . . . ?"

"Sure. I'll tell her where you are and that you'll be late again."

"Thanks. Tell her I'll call her from the hospital as soon as I can." He shut the door behind him.

Nina was reaching for the phone when it rang. It was Diane.

"You just missed him," Nina said. "Literally—he went out two seconds ago."

"Can you call him back?"

"I probably shouldn't. He's on the way to the morgue. They have another case. . . . Someone got raped and murdered last night. The killer bit her."

"That's horrible!"

"She might even have been one of our patients," Nina disclosed. "Peter said he'd call you from the morgue. He didn't think he'd be home till late."

"Nothing new in that. But I guess I should look on the bright side: Since he X-rayed those jaws last night, he won't have to put in another night this week."

"He didn't do that last night."

"No?"

Nina made a quick, unhappy face. She thought a

moment, then said, "I think he was working on back-logged paperwork last night. There's a ton of it here."

"Probably," Diane said.

"But he only has to do one set of jaws now. So you should have him home for most of the week."

"Yes," Diane replied evenly. "I should."

After they hung up, Nina rolled her eyes.

The morgue was quiet.

The naked body of Alice Schaeffer lay on the steel autopsy table. Even like this, she was astonishingly beautiful. Looking at her, Pinchus felt something stir within him—he crushed it, violently. He looked away, shook his head.

He looked back. It almost seemed as if, somehow, this humiliating experience would be over for the girl in a few minutes, she would sit up, jump down from the table, put her clothes back on, and leave. But her body was ashen, the color of death, and she would not.

Moreover, she would be butchered and violated and reduced to parts in the next few hours. Pinchus did not want to watch that.

When Pinchus told Sam about meeting Alice, the effect she'd had on him, Sam had asked, "You want off the case? Is it bothering you?"

"No," Pinchus had said. "I very much want *on* it. Just tell me if you see me getting out of line. Like maybe I was with Collins."

"Sure," Sam promised. "Fact, I'll enjoy it."

Onasis began the external examination, dictating his observations into the overhead microphone: "We have a young Caucasian female in her early twenties. She is well nourished with reddish-brown hair and blue eyes. . . ."

Pinchus signaled to Peter. Peter, who was staring at Alice, didn't see him at first. When Pinchus did catch Peter's eye, he motioned him to the side. Peter joined him.

"She was very pretty," Peter admitted. "I can't believe people can do things like that."

"They can, and do ... all the time. And there's nothing you or I or anyone else can do about it except to stop them from ever doing it again. I hope you can help us."

"I'll do everything I can."

"I understand we have some bite marks."

"On her back. At least that's what Kristina told me."

"I guess this is especially eerie for you."

Peter lifted his eyebrows, questioning.

"Her being one of your patients," Pinchus pointed out. "She was, wasn't she?"

"Yes. Nina reminded me this morning. I only treated her once. I hardly remember. How did you know?"

Pinchus smiled. "It's my job. You didn't remember someone who looked like that? Boy, I'd remember her for the rest of my life."

"I get kids from the university all the time," Peter shrugged. "Besides, I'm married to your niece, who, you will recall, is no mean looker herself, and with whom I am hopelessly and forever in love."

"Nice girl, Diane. It's good that you make her happy."

"I try," Peter nodded.

They went back to the table. There was a blackboard on the wall with Alice Schaeffer's name printed in big capitals. Beneath her name, it said: AGE: 25. Beneath that: HOMICIDE. This was followed by approximate time of death and a final notation, 245-96, the autopsy number.

Onasis finished the frontal side of his external exam. Kristina helped him turn Alice's body onto its stomach. Kristina was uncharacteristically silent this afternoon.

Onasis wiped his gloves with a towel. "Peter, get some pictures before I continue. The blood's pooled to her back. That gives us nice, clear contrast in the bruised areas. It'll start pooling down to her front soon and we may lose some contrast."

"Right."

Peter took up his camera. He placed a small plastic ruler alongside the marks and began shooting. He varied the angle and distance.

"The lab can calibrate to size," Peter said, with some excitement. "We can blow the prints up and get a one-to-one relationship with the actual size of the bite."

"You think they *are* bites?" Pinchus asked.

"No question." Peter kept shooting. "Jesus, I think I can get an impression on one of them. I hardly ever get a chance to do that. It looks pretty deep. Actually, both the bottom two look deep. The high one, up near her neck, is kind of faint."

"What do you make of that?"

"I don't get you," Peter replied with uncertainty.

"If he's biting viciously enough to pierce the skin in two places, isn't it odd that he doesn't do it in the third?"

"Maybe that's where he started." Peter was circling the table, shooting. "Maybe she moved. Could be several reasons."

"Mm-hm," Pinchus said.

Peter went through three rolls of film. He asked Onasis, "Should I try for an impression?"

"Let me swab for a saliva specimen first."

Kristina brought Onasis three sterile swabs. Onasis dipped them into sterile saline solution. One at a time, he stroked them over the deeper marks. The third swab he stroked over her thigh, as a control. Kristina sealed the swabs separately into sterile test tubes, labeled each.

"I'd like to study the area," Pinchus requested. "Okay, Tom?"

"Go ahead. I'll finish the dorsal exam."

Pinchus got out an old pocket magnifying glass,

one he'd had since he was a teenager. The frame was taped where it had broken. He walked around the upper portion of the table, crouching, leaning, examining the marks from different angles.

Peter was busy laying out his impression materials.

Onasis, who was examining Alice's buttocks, paused in dictating his observations to say, "Hey, Seymour, did you make anything out of that figurine we found in her hand?"

"Haven't given it any thought yet. Sam and I spent the morning making appointments to talk with people. I understand you met her parents when they came in to ID her. We're supposed to see them this evening."

"I don't think they'll be much help," Onasis warned. "They're basket cases. The father's worse than the mother. . . . Kristina, give me a hand and spread her legs, I want to see what the anus looks like."

"Where's that resident, Brian, today?" Pinchus asked.

"Don't need him with just the one here. Oh, Christ!"

"What?" Pinchus came down to the other end of the table. Sam was there a moment later along with Roberts.

"Sonofabitch!" Kristina was staring, wide-eyed.

Onasis cleared his throat, then began dictating again: "Brutal tearing and bruising of the anus and rectal muscle. Unquestionably sodomized. Lacerations." He bent close, brows furrowing, and gently spread the anus with his gloved fingers. "Shallow puncture wounds in the anus. Two on the left wall, two in the posterior wall. Maybe three millimeters each in length, and about that deep. More like little pricks than cuts or stabs."

Onasis flushed saline solution from a syringe into the rectum, then retrieved it—as he had done with the vagina—on the chance he could get a sperm sample for DNA profiling. He repeated the procedure twice more, had Kristina label the specimens.

"Are you done with the bite marks?" he asked Pinchus.

"Yes."

"Anything helpful?"

"Not that I'm aware of yet. There's some fine powder around the highest one. Might be something, might not."

Sam went to look at the mark. "Talcum powder?"

"That's usually white, isn't it? This looks kind of yellowish."

"Let's get some." Onasis rolled the tip of a cotton swab around the mark, put the swab into a test tube. "Doesn't look like enough for the lab to analyze. But who knows?"

"Peter," Pinchus called, "have the police lab develop your film. Tell them to make a set of the prints for me, too."

"I will."

Peter rolled a cart up to the autopsy table. He put his forensic bag on it, opened the bag, prepared equipment.

"Can you tell anything at all from what you've seen so far?" Onasis asked Pinchus.

"Oh, yes," Kristina cut in. "She had the bad luck to run into a real scumbag." Kristina threw up her hands in frustration, anger. "I mean, how can he tell anything from this?"

"I can tell that the killer knew her," Pinchus offered. "And that she knew the killer."

"Yeah? How?"

"I'll let you know when I'm absolutely certain. Now I'm only pretty sure. But there is one thing I *can* tell you for certain now."

"What?"

"The killer was definitely a man."

For a moment, Kristina looked as if she would become furious. But she laughed instead. "I guess that's why I'm just a body schlepper and you're a great detective—your tremendous deductive powers."

Pinchus smiled, and was glad of the opportunity.

"I'm ready," Peter announced.

Onasis gave him a go-ahead. The rest gathered round to watch.

Peter placed a small celluloid square, about the size and thickness of a playing card, over the deepest of the bite marks. He traced the outline of the mark onto the square, then repeated the procedure on the other two marks. Next, he squeezed a line of dark blue gel from a tube onto a mixing board. From a second tube, he squeezed a line of yellow gel alongside the first. He mixed the two until they formed a uniform green mound, then gathered the mound up with a small spatula and smoothed it over the deepest bite. With the chip blower—a long, curved tube with a rubber bulb at one end—he squeezed bursts of air onto the gel to spread it evenly and eliminate trapped bubbles.

When the gel was tacky, Peter placed loose staples into its surface, prongs upright. When it had become rubbery and dry to the touch, he mixed water and yellow dental stone—which was like plaster of Paris, but much harder when it set—in a rubber bowl, and after it had thickened, poured it over the green rubber.

"Now we wait," he said. "The stone hardens around the staples. It gives us a base."

The stone was hard in less than five minutes. Peter placed his fingertips around its edges, lifted the apparatus gingerly from the skin. He turned it over, studied the contours in the rubber.

"Well?" Onasis asked.

"Here's your killer," Peter said, with satisfaction. "The marks of his teeth, anyway."

"What do you do with those?" Kristina asked.

"I make models of the bite marks. Then, when the police find a suspect, I take an impression of his mouth and make models of his teeth. If the models of the suspect's teeth fit into the models of the bite mark, we have our killer. But first we need a suspect. These aren't any good without one."

"A detail for the Fox and his friend." Trane winked at Pinchus. "Just a detail."

"Your lips to God's ears," Pinchus replied, trying not to be annoyed.

"I want to try for an impression from the next mark too," Peter told Onasis. "There isn't enough penetration on the top one. Before I do, though, I'd like to call my wife. I want to tell her I'll be going back to the office to pour the casts and make the counter-models tonight." In addition, at the end of the autopsy, Roberts would have to dissect away one of the bite mark areas. It would be preserved for evidence and study.

"Take your time." Onasis shrugged. "Kristina, would you run out for coffee? Seymour's buying."

"I guess it *is* my turn," Pinchus confessed. He dug a battered leather wallet out of his pocket, gave Kristina a bill. "But Sam and I can't stay. Give me a call when you have a positive on the cause of death, Tom."

"We'll have that as soon as we dissect her throat. I'm sure her hyoid bone is broken. The tiny hemor-rhages in the eyes give it away, too. Assume it's death by strangulation. I'll call you otherwise."

"Never assume," Pinchus said. "Always rely on your facts. A wise old medical examiner told me that."

"Wise, anyway. All right. I'll call you either way."

Pinchus and Sam left. In the hall, Sam said. "I'm glad we got out before he started to open her."

"Yes. This one, I just didn't want to see." Pinchus breathed, worked his shoulders. "Ah, well. What the fuck? It's just another corpse."

"Be a help if you could convince yourself of that."

"I will. But for now, let's start looking for the slimeball that made her that way."

17

Peter used the phone in a small office adjacent to the morgue. The office had green walls, a steel desk, a metal chair with thin padding, and two filing cabinets. It was lit in a hard, sterile way by an overhead fluorescent bulb.

Peter knew Diane wouldn't receive the news well. Working two nights in a row was taboo, no matter how important the task. He was right.

"What I'll do," Diane said with exaggerated cheeriness, "is put a photograph of you at the head of the table. That way, the kids will remember they have a father."

"You always overreact," Peter said, annoyed.

"Do I? I'm so sorry, darling." It was clear that she was not.

"This is important, Diane. For Seymour. For the city. For this poor girl's family. For us, too: This is the kind of thing that gets me publicity. Publicity means business. And business is how I bought the house we live in and how I'm going to pay for the kids' college tuition. I don't work a lot of nights, or have to travel—like a lot of other women's husbands."

"You have a point," she admitted.

He smiled to himself.

But then her tone sharpened. "So since you didn't X-ray those jaws last night, where the hell were you till quarter to twelve?"

"Excuse me?"

"You heard me. Where the fuck were you last night? Nina spilled the beans. You didn't work on that other case last night, so now I'm supposed to believe you have to work on this one tonight?"

"Look, Diane. You can believe what you want. The truth is, I have a *lot* of work to take care of. Last night I just didn't feel like dealing with stinking, decomposing jaws. And there wasn't any rush. You can check with your *uncle* on that." Peter put a nasty tone to the words. "So I took care of some other stuff instead. Look, people are waiting for me here. I don't want to get into this now. If you're up when I get home, we'll talk then. If you doubt my whereabouts, I can bring a note from Seymour if you like."

"Don't bother, Peter. Do what you want, you always have. Just try not to make it too late this time, since I plan to sleep in for a change. You can get the kids off to school."

"Fine," Peter said.

"Fine," Diane said. "Good-bye."

"Good-bye."

Peter was relieved when he hung up. She'd shaken him, but he thought he'd handled it well enough.

Diane sat with the phone to her ear several seconds after the final click. She reached over to hang up wondering if she *had* overreacted. She had tried not to over the years.

Diane believed that Peter *was* telling the truth and began to feel foolish. She was tempted to call back—even reached for the phone again—but then thought better of it. She had already played her hand. At the very least, it would be nice sleeping late for a change.

18

It was a little after five-thirty by the time Pinchus and Sam returned to the station. Pinchus had called Kate earlier, when it became apparent he wouldn't be able to make dinner. She told him she'd keep something warm, to come anytime before midnight. Otherwise, they'd talk tomorrow. Sam stopped to get snacks from the vending machine. Pinchus went upstairs to make a pot of coffee.

On his way, Pinchus passed Captain Alex Schwenk, the commanding officer of the station, who was coming down. They nodded to each other—long past the point of having anything to say unless circumstances made it necessary. Their dislike of each other dated back nearly to the start of their careers.

Although Schwenk was the titular captain, it was generally assumed that Pinchus ran homicide, and a good deal of the rest of the station as well. Schwenk rarely took a personal part in investigations these days, and whenever problems arose, people usually turned to Pinchus first.

"Sure he keeps his hands off," Sam had said to Pinchus. "How would he look up against you? It's okay for us common troops to follow in your shadow, but not him. He's scared shitless they'll force him out and make you captain. You got to watch yourself around him, Seymour. He'll bury your ass if he ever gets the chance."

Pinchus knew that. He also knew things Sam didn't. What Pinchus and Schwenk had was an armed truce. So long as neither stepped seriously on the other's toes, each let the other be.

Schwenk was a year younger than Pinchus, more socially facile and vastly better at politicking than Pinchus would ever be or want to be. When they were young patrol officers, Pinchus had been out in the street working his butt off while Schwenk had been in all the right places, kissing the butts of all the right dignitaries and superior officers. Schwenk had gotten what he wanted.

But that was a long time ago. Times change, and dignitaries and superior officers with them. Schwenk's status was no longer as secure as it had once been.

Schwenk walked with a limp; slight, but noticeable. Department folklore had it that he'd been injured in the line of duty when young. What had really happened was that he'd fallen over a log on a hunting trip and shot himself in the ankle. Schwenk never said anything to foster the myth, but neither did he say anything to disabuse people of it. Pinchus, one of the few oldtimers, knew the truth. He had held his silence, only to realize that Schwenk had come to hate him even more for that, maybe even feared that Pinchus was simply biding his time.

On his part, Pinchus disliked Schwenk for what he saw as the man's ineptitude, laziness, and dishonesty. He was also convinced that Schwenk was anti-Semitic.

"He's looking for a Jew to burn," Pinchus had once said to Sam. "And how many Jews do you see around here?"

In the squad room, Pinchus threw out the stale coffee and made a fresh pot. Leaving it to brew, he went to his desk. There was a Post-It message on his phone: Ken and Lenore Schaeffer would be here at six. He looked at his watch: twenty minutes. He listened to the Mr. Coffee burbling.

Want to win a chess game? Get your opponent emotionally involved.

He was already emotionally involved. Distance, that's what he needed to establish.

He put his head in his hands and took a long, deep breath. He let his eyes lose focus. He followed his breath . . . in . . . out . . . in . . .

And he saw Melissa saying, "Daddy, I'm *so* scared."

With a final gurgle, the Mr. Coffee went silent. Pinchus looked up and saw the ready light on.

Sam was walking toward the desk.

Pinchus rubbed his face roughly, as if he were tired, and wiped away the tears that had formed.

"No apple pie," Sam said. "I got you Twinkies. Okay?"

"I only eat the pie because it's here. You really shouldn't eat apple pie without a wedge of cheddar cheese on it."

Pinchus got them coffee. They sat down at their desks, facing each other.

"Something's been bothering me since we left the morgue," Sam said, pulling apart the Twinkies' plastic wrapping.

"What?"

"You're good, but no one's that good—how can you tell Alice Schaeffer knew her killer? Why couldn't it be just some guy who broke in, was going to toss the place, and she surprised him?"

"Not only do I think he knew her, I think he had his face covered, too."

"I am not going to play Watson here. Give."

"Well, if you accept the fact that she knew her attacker—which you don't yet, but humor me—then he *must* have had his face covered. Because she didn't have any defensive wounds. Alice was not a stupid girl. If she knew him, and recognized him, she would have realized he would probably end up killing her to keep her from identifying him."

"So she'd have fought back."

"Right. And that would have left marks—of a kind

that weren't present. That indicates she thought she could survive the ordeal if she submitted. Since we've granted that the rapist was indeed known to her, then obviously she wasn't able to recognize him. Thus a disguise or a mask."

"'*We*' have not granted anything. You still haven't proved he was known to her."

"There was too much planning for him not to be. Careful planning suggests a planned outcome. We know the guy didn't follow her home: He got there first, jimmied the door. Then he unscrewed the bulb at the top of the stairs to hide that, relocked the door after he was in. He didn't trash the apartment, which he would have if burglary had been the motive. Instead, he waited for her to get back. He stayed hidden, watched her while she got undressed. I'd say he was in the living room closet. All this suggests that Alice, specifically, was his target."

"What's to say he didn't get there just before she did, jump her when she got into the bedroom, and rip her clothes off or force her to take them off?"

"The order of things. When was the last time you saw a rape victim who had her socks ripped off? Alice's jeans and socks were lying in the living room."

"So he threw them in there during the attack."

Pinchus rose, put a notepad on the floor several feet from his desk. He sat down again, removed his shoes, and slipped off his socks. He held one of his socks, looked at Sam.

"If I order you to take your clothes off, and you do, you drop them at your feet, right next to the bed. If I tear them off you and throw them aside—" Pinchus threw his first sock, keeping his gaze on Sam, then the second, "where do they land? Say the pad is her jeans."

He looked over at the pad. The socks were several feet away from it, and from each other, too.

"Try it a hundred times. I bet you never get them

once in the order they were in in the living room—socks neatly together, just about on top of the jeans."

"He grabbed her in the living room," Sam said. "Made her take them off there."

"Then took her into the bedroom, had her remove her sweater and bra and fold them, and put them on top of the dresser? I don't think so. She doesn't know anyone's there. She's in the bedroom getting undressed. She takes her jeans and socks off, tosses them together into the living room, toward the bathroom. She takes her sweater off, folds it, sets it down. Meanwhile, the killer's in the living room closet. He's got the door cracked open, having a good time watching. When she takes her bra off, it's too much for him. He busts out just as she sets the bra down and grabs her."

"Maybe," Sam allowed.

"To cap it off," Pinchus continued, "we have these cuts on her back—the *cuts*, not the bites. I think maybe they make two letters: *A* and *S*. Hard to tell with the blood crusted around them, but I think that's what they are."

"Okay," Sam conceded. "Let's go with it—*AS*. All we know from that is that he carved her initials in her back—Alice Schaeffer. He could have found the name in the apartment. Got if off the mailbox."

Pinchus and Sam often played devil's advocate for each other: It helped them think better.

"Possible," Pinchus acknowledged. "But I doubt it." He closed his eyes. "There was no name on the mailbox. There was nothing in plain sight in the apartment that had her name on it."

"He took it with him when he left."

"Could have," Pinchus allowed. "You think he did?"

"No."

"Me neither. The act was too well planned. The guy was careful not to leave any clues. He does his best to thoroughly violate her. He even carves her initials into her back. He's telling us something with that. This was no random murder. She knew him, he knew her. This was murder with a cause."

"The initials," Sam wondered. "If they *are* initials, why not they're his initials or something else connected with him. Like an artist signing his work. Or maybe it's a challenge to us."

Pinchus thought. "Yes," he said. "Ah. This isn't going to be easy."

Two quick little rings sounded from the telephone, the intercom signal. Pinchus picked up the receiver. "Right. Thanks." He looked over at Sam. "The Schaeffers are on their way up."

19

The detectives swept Twinkie crumbs from their desks. Sam got fresh cups of coffee.

The Schaeffers arrived. Ken Schaeffer was a man of about fifty. He had pepper-gray hair that receded from his forehead, wore glasses, and was dressed in a black suit. He was haggard. Lenore Schaeffer was in her late forties, but still a knockout. It was clear where Alice had gotten her looks: Lenore Schaeffer had the same luxurious hair, the same cheekbones, lips. She moved with more certainty than her husband did.

Sam brought chairs for them.

Pinchus offered to get them coffee, sodas.

"No, nothing, thank you," Lenore Schaeffer shook her head.

Her husband reached for her hand.

"I'm Lieutenant Seymour Pinchus and this is Sergeant Sam Milano," Pinchus told them. "I'm deeply saddened about what happened to your daughter."

"Thank you," said Lenore Schaeffer.

"We'll try to be brief. I know how painful the loss of a loved one can be. I know what you must be feeling."

"How the hell could you?" Ken Schaeffer replied angrily.

"I lost a daughter myself once."

Ken Schaeffer looked at his wife, swallowed, and turned back to Pinchus.

"I'm sorry. It's just that . . ."

"No apology necessary. It was a long time ago."

Sam moved in to provide some psychological space between Schaeffer and Pinchus. "Our information says Alice was your only child. Is that right?"

Tears rolled down Ken Schaeffer's cheeks. He couldn't speak.

"Yes," Lenore Schaeffer responded.

Pinchus felt a wave of gratitude that he had Daniel. "Do you know anyone who might have wanted to harm your daughter?"

Both Schaeffers shook their heads.

"Did Alice ever tell you she was having a problem with anyone?"

"Everyone loved her," Ken Schaeffer stated. "I can't believe anyone would do this to my baby."

Lenore Schaeffer put a hand on his shoulder.

Pinchus showed them the glass koala bear that had been found in Alice's hand. "Does this mean anything to you?"

Ken Schaeffer exploded. "What the hell does that have to do with anything!"

"I'm sorry. It may not be related to Alice's death at all. We found it in . . . close proximity to her. We have to check these things out. Your daughter was engaged, I understand."

"Yes."

"How was her relationship with her fiancé?"

"Surely you don't think Mark had anything to do with this," Lenore Schaeffer said excitedly. "He loved Alice very much. The relationship was nearly perfect. We couldn't have asked for a better son-in-law. And now, now . . ." She gestured vaguely.

Despite Lenore Schaeffer's collected appearance, it was becoming clear that she was no more able to think clearly at this point than was her husband. After a few more questions, Pinchus thanked them and ended the interview. He escorted them out.

When he returned, Sam said to him, "The only thing I wonder is why, in a nearly perfect relationship, her fiancé doesn't return her phone calls."

"We must talk to this boy, Sam."

"Indeed we must."

Dr. Miles Hawthorne didn't arrive at the station until nearly seven, twenty minutes late. He was wearing a sandstone cotton car coat over a tweed jacket. He took the coat off, apologizing for his lateness and casually sat down.

The next interview was scheduled for ten minutes from now. Pinchus got right to the point.

"Dr. Hawthorne, do you know any reason why anyone would rape and murder Alice Schaeffer?"

"No," Hawthorne said, as he uncrossed his legs and leaned forward. "From what I understand, she was an extremely well liked young woman. This is a terrible, terrible thing."

"She was one of your students, wasn't she?"

"Not currently. Last year. And once, maybe twice, earlier, I don't recall precisely." Hawthorne took a pipe from his jacket. "All right if I smoke?"

"If it makes you more comfortable." Pinchus didn't like this man. He saw no reason to coddle him, perhaps even some gain in pressing him.

"I'm not uncomfortable," Hawthorne explained, smiling. "It's simply that I enjoy a pipe. I'd be happy to refrain if it bothers either of you."

Not so easy, this guy. Pinchus elected to remain silent. Sam followed his lead.

Hawthorne filled his pipe, tamped it, lit it. The bouquet was pleasant.

"What was your relationship with Alice?" Pinchus asked.

"None, really. Teacher-student once. Currently, we were colleagues in a way. Alice had a teaching fellowship. She taught in the same department I do."

Sam asked, "Nothing more, huh?"

Hawthorne turned to Sam. "No. Just the nor—"

Pinchus cut him off. "Didn't you just hire her to work for you?"

Hawthorne swung his head back. "You must be remarkable detectives. That was only yesterday afternoon. Yes. Grading papers." He drew on his pipe and exhaled. He looked directly into Pinchus's eyes. "You don't think I had anything to do with this, do you?"

"Where were you between ten o'clock and twelve midnight last night?"

"You *do*. Perhaps you're not so remarkable after all."

"I'm waiting, Professor."

"I was at Faulkner's Pub last night. You can find people to corroborate that."

"You were at Faulkner's from six to approximately nine P.M. I asked you where you were between ten and midnight."

"I was home in bed. I teach an early class on Tuesday."

"Can your wife verify that?" Pinchus asked. "And the time you came home?"

"Less impressive by the moment. I have no wife, Detective. I'm divorced—three years now. I guess you'll have to take my word for it."

"I'd love to take your word for it. But the thing is, it's not only up to me. My partner here has a problem with something he dug up this morning. Sam is a suspicious guy, makes tons of extra work for me. Seems you've got a weakness for tits and ass. Seems that's why your wife divorced you. Seems there was some kind of flap last year when you were guest-lecturing up at Rutgers. How'd that go, Sam?"

"What they told me," Sam said to Pinchus, "was that our professor Hawthorne here propositioned some undergrad who got pissed, and that he used his 'wife' and the damage it would do to his marriage to keep her from filing a complaint."

"Course we all know that couldn't be true," Pinchus said to Hawthorne. "Because you don't have a wife."

Hawthorne sighed. "I don't know where you get

your information, but I suggest you check the veracity of your sources. Do you have an ashtray?"

Sam got him one.

Hawthorne took a silver tool from his pocket, dug what remained of the tobacco plug out of his pipe, and tamped the embers out. He smiled at them. "Since you obviously consider me a suspect, I prefer not to answer any more questions without my attorney present."

"We don't necessarily consider you anything right now," Sam admitted.

"But it's your right to handle this any way you see fit," Pinchus added. "You're free to go if you wish."

Hawthorne stood, slipped into his car coat. "Gentlemen." He nodded and left.

They looked after him.

"So I cause you tons of extra work, eh?" Sam said.

"But I love you anyway."

"A real slimeball, isn't he?"

"Without a doubt."

Katherine Bollinger was early. She had brought Janet Cooper with her.

"I hope you don't mind," she said. "I need the moral support—*really* need it now." She glanced back at the door.

"Did you run into Hawthorne?" Pinchus asked, alarmed.

"Yes."

"Jesus," Janet cried. "The look he gave you was like a nuclear meltdown."

"Damn." Pinchus gritted his teeth. "I'm sorry. We should have taken him out another way."

"It's all right," Kathy said. "I can't avoid him forever. And he knows I'd have to tell you about him, in light of what happened."

"What a piece of dirt," Janet declared.

"You told her?" Pinchus said, indicating Janet.

"Yes. Was that all right?"

"It's all right. But I have to ask you both to keep

this to yourselves from here in. It can only get in the way otherwise."

"You think *he* killed Alice?" Janet squeaked.

"We don't suspect *anyone* yet. Is that clear?"

It was.

Pinchus asked a couple of innocuous questions to put them at ease while Sam got a glass of water for Kathy, a cup of coffee for Janet.

Then he said, "It's important to keep a completely open mind about this. Now, holding that thought, do either of you know why anyone might want to hurt Alice? Someone holding a grudge against her, for example. Did she ever mention she had a problem with anyone? Or complain of improper advances someone might have made toward her?" On the last question, he saw something flicker in both Kathy and Janet. "Yes?"

"As a matter of fact," Kathy answered, "she did have a weird experience with one of her students yesterday. The guy kind of creeped her out right from the beginning—little sexual innuendoes, heavy looks, that kind of thing. Yesterday, he gave her a real hard time in class, then right after, he asked her out. A very strange guy."

"She give you a name?"

"Harper. Donald Harper."

"*David* Harper," Janet corrected.

"Oh. Yes. David Harper."

"A student?" Pinchus asked. "Classmate?"

"One of her students," Kathy said. "She asked me if I'd ever taught him. When I said no, she said she hoped I never did. Supposedly some kind of genius type. And supposedly some kind of screwed-up background. He's got a cousin on campus who interceded with Alice on David's behalf. Actually, the cousin sounded a little weird himself."

"How?"

"Alice thought he was just, you know, kind of odd. She thought he might have been following her around, or waiting for her, trying to meet her so he could explain his cousin. He told her it was important for her to know."

"What's his name?"

Kathy wrinkled her forehead. "I don't remember."

"Barry?" Pinchus asked.

"Yes! That was it. How did you know?"

Among the articles from Alice's purse had been a slip of paper that said *Barry Harper—Lincoln Dorm*. Instead of answering, Pinchus asked: "What else did Alice say happened in class? Give me as much detail as you can."

"There wasn't much else, at least not that she told me. 'Remarks rude, and remarks lewd'—that's the way she put it. And some idiot story he told her about being afraid of cats so he could get out of having to do a dissection. Nothing else."

Pinchus asked Janet, "Were you thinking of David Harper too when you reacted to that question?"

"No. I was thinking about Richie. Richie Zimmer."

"Oh, no." Kathy shook her head vigorously. "Richie can be an asshole sometimes, but he'd never dream of hurting Alice."

"I'd like to be the judge of that," Pinchus cautioned. "This Richie, Janet, he was at the bar with you last night, right?"

"Right. But he left before we did. He was very angry. He was drunk. He'd gotten into an argument with Kathy. He was angry with her, angry with women in general, I think." She paused, glancing quickly at Kathy. "And then there's this thing he's always had for Alice. He's carried a torch for her ever since I've known him. When she got engaged, he got depressed for weeks. Last night, when Kathy told Alice she'd be lucky if papers were all Hawthorne asked her to grade, Richie went nuts. That's when he stormed out."

"Is that how you remember it?" Pinchus asked Kathy.

"Yes. But I don't think there's anything to it."

"You're not helping us by trying to do our job," Pinchus pointed out. "Please, don't make judgments. Don't try to decide what's important, what isn't, who did it, or who didn't. Okay? Please. Now . . . how about anyone else? Like Alice's fiancé. So far as you know, did she have a good relationship with him?"

"Absolutely," Kathy nodded.

"No problems at all?"

"Only that she wanted to be with him more," Janet added.

"Is there anything else you can remember that might help us? No matter how unlikely it might seem."

Both women were quiet for a few moments.

Kathy shook her head.

"Wait, that reminds me," Janet said suddenly, pointing to the glass koala bear, which was still on Pinchus' desk. "The bear, Kathy, the bear."

"That's right," Kathy said, remembering.

"Alice was at Friedman's yesterday—the store on Beresford Street. She was buying a bear like that. There was an incident with one of the employees." Janet related the story. "Alice was going to stop back and pay for the bear today."

Pinchus did not tell them this was the same bear, or where it had been found. "Do either of you know the name of this guy?"

They didn't.

Sam was writing notes.

"Poor Mrs. Fitapaldi," Janet mumbled.

"Mrs. Fitapaldi?" Pinchus asked.

"An old lady in a nursing home. The bear was a gift for her. Alice was her friend. The poor woman must have been devastated by the news."

She had been. Pinchus had driven out to tell her himself this morning, not wanting her to hear it on the news. She had collapsed against him, weeping. He had stayed with her as long as he could, called a nurse to sit with her when he had to leave. Now, he was annoyed with himself for having missed the possible connection of the bear to Rose Fitapaldi's collection, slender as that was.

He grieved: for Alice, for Rose Fitapaldi, for himself.

I will catch this bastard, he vowed. I will catch him if it is the last thing I ever do. For a moment he felt chilled, as if by a premonition that it would be just that.

"You know," Kathy recalled, "that guy from Friedman's works part-time at the nursing home. I remember Alice saying she hoped she wouldn't run into him there."

Sam wrote in his notebook.

Neither woman could come up with anything else.

"If you do, please call. Right away." He gave a card to each of them. So did Sam.

"Will you catch whoever did this?" Kathy asked.

Pinchus hesitated. He never promised anyone a result. "Yes," he said.

"Even if you don't," Janet commented. "He'll pay. One way or another. If not in this lifetime, then the next. And if there aren't any other lifetimes, then he'll burn in hell. I believe that. It's the only thing that's keeping me going." She started to cry.

Pinchus handed her a box of tissues.

She blew her nose.

"Do you believe that?" she asked.

"I'd like to," Pinchus said softly.

Sam escorted the young women out. When he returned, Pinchus was leaning back in his chair, playing with a paper clip.

Sam sat down at his own desk. He put his feet up on the corner. "Got a lot to sort through here."

"Yup," Pinchus said, twisting the paperclip.

"What are you thinking?"

"I'm thinking that as much as I don't want to, and you probably don't want to either, we better get started tonight."

"Aw, Seymour. We were up most of last night. I didn't even see the kids this morning."

"I know. I was supposed to have dinner with Kate."

"Oh? Things looking up again?"

"Maybe."

"*Mazel tov.*"

Just then, Pinchus noticed Captain Schwenk glancing curiously into the squad room from an outer hallway. When their eyes met, Schwenk turned away and continued on.

"We're not the only ones working late, Sam," Pinchus said, as he pointed to the door.

Sam caught a glimpse of a shadowy figure limp away. "Ah, I see."

"I bet he's afraid we may not solve this one for a while."

"Or maybe he's afraid *you* already have."

Pinchus laughed. "Tell you what. It's only quarter to eight. You leave right now, you might be able to get to Friedman's before it closes. Talk to Friedman about this guy that got fired. Talk to the other guy too, this O'Malley. You get there too late, forget it, go back in the morning. How's that?"

"Good. Thanks."

"Either way, find the guy tomorrow and question him. Also this Richie Zimmer."

"You going to take the Harper cousins?"

"Yup. Tonight if I can. Tomorrow morning if I can't. I'll do Mark Donaldson too."

Alice's parents had told them Mark would be arriving tonight, had given them the name of the motel in which he'd be staying.

"Jesus, Seymour, you'll have to take your own notes."

"I know. Command decisions are not without consequence."

Pinchus liked to question everyone involved in a

case as soon as possible. The longer the wait, the more details were forgotten. And it was in the details that the answer often lay. This time, Pinchus wanted the answer very much. Almost, he thought, *needed* the answer.

20

He undressed her slowly, savoring the process, resisting the urgency, the desire to tear her clothes off and plunge into her.

This was forbidden. Wrong. Terrible.

And it thrilled him. God.

When she was naked he took his own clothes off, lay next to her, rolled half onto her, wedged his thigh between hers. He kissed her deeply.

They stroked and kissed each other. He licked her. She caressed his features with her mouth. He nipped at her throat. She clutched his buttocks. He drove into her powerfully, unconquerable. She bucked, thrashed, rose to meet him.

"My God," he began moaning. "My God . . . my God . . ."

She started to make sharp little whimpering sounds. They rose in intensity. The intervals between them shortened. Then she cried out: "Oh! Oh! Oh! It's so good, so good!"

And he released himself—"Y-es! Ah!"—and they clutched at each other, quivering, and then fell back, holding each other, breathing deeply and hoarsely.

"Oh God, that was *so* good," Terri whispered.

"Yes. Incredible. I'd forgotten how good it could be."

Terri giggled.

"The thing is," he said, "it's true."

"I love you," she said.

He didn't say anything, just hugged her close to him.

Terri didn't press him. She figured it was part of the overhead of being involved with a married man. She had met Peter Roberts six months ago, in the Post and Carriage where she had begun working as a waitress. He came in once or twice a week for lunch, sometimes a quick dinner when he was working late. It had started harmlessly enough, a little bantering, a little light flirting; the kind of thing she did with many of her regular customers, particularly the friendlier ones. Even more particularly, the good-looking ones. And why not? She was young (twenty-six was *still* young), blond (*natural* as Peter had been delighted to discover the first time he pulled her panties down), and single (married at eighteen, beaten for three years, divorced at twenty-one).

After her divorce, Terri had intended never to get seriously involved with a man again. And she hadn't, until she met Peter. Never, never, under any circumstances, would she have considered getting involved with one who was married. And she never had, until Peter.

Four months ago, in the restaurant, she asked Peter if he'd mind a professional question. She was worried about a tooth. He said he couldn't tell anything without examining it. She said she was getting off soon. He said his office was closed, but it was only a couple of blocks away and he'd be happy to open it up, take a look at the tooth. She demurred. He insisted.

"I'll go open it now," he'd said. "Meet me there . . . when?"

"My shift ends in half an hour."

He left.

Still not believing what she was doing, Terri went to Mr. Mellankamp, the shift supervisor, and said she was sick, she had to go home. She had lied to Peter: Her shift wasn't scheduled to end for another two hours.

The problem was minor—a chipped tooth that had

been irritating her cheek. Peter ground down the sharp edge. It didn't even need a filling.

They started to talk. He got them sodas from the small refrigerator in the back office. They laughed at each other's jokes.

An hour later, they were making love on the carpeted floor of the office. An hour after that, giddy, and lustful, they did it again, with Terri lying in one of his dental chairs.

Even that night, when she returned to her apartment alone and Peter went home to his wife, she had known it was a no-win situation. Still, she didn't care. She was happier than she'd been since she was seventeen, and felt nearly as silly.

Peter had told her this was the first time he'd ever been unfaithful to his wife. She had no reason to disbelieve him. He had told her they couldn't do it again. But by the time he was kissing her good-night, they had already agreed to meet the following afternoon, during his lunch break, at her place.

And he had never again said they couldn't do this again.

Now, lying in his arms and stroking the hair on his chest, she said, "How long can you stay?"

"I have to leave soon," he said gently.

"A little more?"

"Fifteen minutes. I wish I could spend the night. But I can't."

"I know. I'd just like it, that's all."

He kissed the top of her head.

"Oh, well. Maybe next time."

"Maybe next time."

"Back in a sec'." She got up and headed toward the bathroom.

Peter admired her body as she went, the graceful curve of her back, the taut roundness of her buttocks, the length of her legs.

He was a lucky man.

He was also—his lust now spent—a man who was

beginning to feel guilty, even though he was trying not to. And fretful. He sat up and started gathering his clothes. He hoped he could get home before eleven; it had been nearly midnight last night. Diane was already suspicious. There was a limit to how much time he could account for.

"Peter!" Terri cried from the bathroom. "How could you?"

"How could I what?"

She came out and marched over to him, pointing to her neck. "This! How am I supposed to go to work with a hickey? Do you know the kind of razzing I'll get from the other girls, from my regulars? What got into you to want to bite me like that?"

"You weren't complaining at the time."

"That's true," she admitted.

"In fact, you enjoyed it."

She pulled his face into her belly, roughed his hair. "A gentleman wouldn't bring that up."

"But an enamored lover would."

"You're sweet. But you did get carried away."

"Wear a turtleneck," he suggested.

"I can't. I have to wear my uniform. How would *you* like it," she mentioned, mischievously, "if I gave you one of those to bring home to your wife." She bent over.

Peter scuttled away on the mattress. "Don't even kid around!"

"Just a little bitty one? You could say, 'Honey, guess what? One of my patients literally jumped out the chair when I turned the drill on, and look what happened.' Or better yet, you could just wear a turtleneck to bed."

"You're right," he conceded. "I'm sorry. But you *did* like it."

"I liked it, you bastard. And you liked doing it. Well, a little makeup and maybe it won't be so noticeable."

Peter was unhappy with Terri's remark that he had

liked doing it. Heinemann had confronted him with what the psychiatrist called a "minor element of sadism" in him, suggesting that perhaps on a repressed level, it was one of the reasons he had been attracted to dentistry. Heinemann had even speculated that, manifesting as a kind of necrophilia, it explained his fascination with the morgue.

Thinking of it, Peter became annoyed with Heinemann all over again. He decided it was time to end the therapy. He didn't think it was doing him much good anymore.

Terry went back to the bathroom to wash up. Peter got dressed. Terri came out in a blue silk dressing gown, tied lightly. Her hair was brushed. The gown lay softly against the curve of her breasts. Her nipples were visible in outline. She looked beautiful.

She slipped her arms around Peter, held him. She said, "So what are we going to do, Peter? Who's going to win? Your wife or me?"

"I don't know." He sighed. "I guess things can't go on this way much longer."

"You're going to have to tell her, Peter."

"I know."

"When?"

"Soon," he answered.

"So who wins, who loses?" She leaned back and looked at him. It was clear that she didn't really expect him to reply.

"We all win," he responded. "No matter what happens. We'll all end up with whatever is best for us."

"I'm afraid we're all going to lose."

"I have to go," he told her.

"I know," she said.

Peter was relieved to get out of Terri's apartment and into the hall, to hear the lock click behind him. He didn't wait for the elevator, which was slow. He took the fire stairs down to the ground level.

The night air felt good, helped him clear his head.

Driving home, though, he became uncomfortable again: What in God's name was he doing? He had an ideal life—money, a thriving career, a beautiful wife who loved him, kids he was nutty about. Why was he jeopardizing all that?

He had to break the affair off. He had to do it no matter how powerfully the passion flowed in him. But he didn't know if he could.

21

Pinchus parked in the north lot, on the opposite side of the campus from Lincoln Dorm. He wanted to walk, take time to formulate questions for David and Barry Harper.

The night was bright with a three-quarter moon. The sky was clear and starry. Students strolled about. Some of the classroom buildings were lit.

Crossing the center quad, Pinchus looked west toward Adams Hall, one of the older buildings on the campus: gray stone, leaded windows, ivy. There was a light on in what used to be the office of the dean of students, and maybe still was. Pinchus didn't know the name of the present dean, or even how long he or she had held the office.

Twelve years, Harris Daniels had been dean of students. And twelve years ago, Harris Daniels had committed suicide in the ground-floor office of Adams Hall. Pinchus, who was a sergeant then, had been sent out to take a look around, a routine homicide procedure in the case of suicides.

The dean's office had been functional then but was still being worked on. The rooms in Adams Hall were small. Harris Daniels had requested a larger office than the existing one. Since the university prized him and other schools were actively wooing him, the administration had acceded. Workmen had removed a wall to expand the office into the storage area adjacent to it, which had once housed grounds-maintenance equipment, but which had been filled for years with nothing but boxes of files. A set of heavy double doors opened from the storage room onto the quad.

Pinchus remembered how Daniels's office had looked when he first saw it: an incongruous mix of Daniels's furnishings—leather chairs, wood bookcases, brass—with painters' equipment and carpenters' tools stored in a corner, and framing studs stacked neatly at the foot of the double doors, which were going to be sealed over.

At the far end of the room, Harris Daniels was slumped over his large mahogany desk. There was a gun in his right hand. Blood and brain tissue mixed with tiny splinters of bone were splattered across the desk in a kind of halo. There was a pool of blood around Daniels's head, blood in his lap, blood on the carpet around his chair.

The bullet had entered his right temple, creating a small hole with singed hair around it, a little above and in front of his ear. It had exited through the left orbit, shattering bone, blowing out the eyeball. A glistening band of white tissue hung from the empty socket, the remnant of the optic nerve.

Not pretty, but not as bad as others Pinchus had seen. Especially those that involved a shotgun. They were real messes.

Pinchus stood looking at what appeared to be a neat open-and-shut suicide: Campus security had broken into the office after a distressed call from Daniels's wife. The doors and windows had been locked from the inside. A typed note lying on the left corner of the desk said:

> It hurts. It just hurts all the time now. I have tried, God knows I have, but I can't cope with it anymore. Forgive me.

Harris Daniels's initials, in pen, were at the bottom.

It was nine A.M., Sunday. The bells of the campus chapel were pealing. Pinchus, still a smoker back then, lit a cigarette and began nosing about. By the time he put the cigarette out, he was convinced that someone other than Harris Daniels had shot Harris Daniels.

But he couldn't prove it.

Two days later, he was puzzled and frustrated and still had not filed his report. Alex Schwenk, who had been newly elevated to captain, ordered him to. Pinchus balked. Finally, it came to Schwenk bellowing at Pinchus in a voice that was heard through the door by half the personnel in the station.

"How the fuck can you possibly say it was murder?" Schwenk roared. "The guy had a history of depressive episodes. He was seeing a shrink. His wife said he'd been getting worse all week. The forensic pathologist says powder burns and projectile trajectory are consistent with suicide. Everything was locked from the inside. The campus guys had to break in. What the fuck do you want—a fucking *videotape*?"

"That would be helpful," Pinchus had replied.

Pinchus couldn't give it up. He knew in his gut Daniels hadn't shot himself. The evidence slight, almost nonexistent, but it was there nonetheless: Beneath the note Daniels supposedly left, Pinchus had found a tiny droplet of blood. The implication was clear. If Daniels had committed suicide, he would have set the note down before he pulled the trigger. And if he had done that, then how had this little speck of blood gotten under the note? On the other hand, the speck was so fine that someone placing the note there after Daniels was dead might not have noticed it.

It was not impossible, Pinchus supposed, for the muzzle blast to have lifted the note ever so slightly—enough to allow the droplet to strike the desktop before the note settled back down again—but he found that highly improbable. This got him thinking about the note itself. Why had it been typed? It would have been simpler just to scrawl it out.

Something, he was pretty sure, was rotten here.

If it was murder, how had the killer gotten in and

out? Everything had been locked from the inside. And what were the desperate circumstances?

Motives were strong emotions: hate, greed, lust. The desperate circumstances, as Pinchus liked to think of them, were the driving forces—the configuration of time and event, the surrounding situation—that transformed motive into action.

Two days later, Pinchus believed he had the desperate circumstances, and—though he still couldn't prove anything—the killer.

Not only was Harris Daniels a talented dean, he was a talented investor as well: Over twenty-five years, he had managed to parlay a small inheritance into nearly $2 million. His wife, Kendall, was his third wife, and twenty years younger than he. It was discreetly rumored on campus that Harris Daniels had caught Kendall Daniels in *flagrante* with an associate math professor and had threatened divorce.

Further, Saturday night, the night of Harris Daniels's death, Kendall Daniels had been at a neighborhood party alone. According to her, Harris hadn't felt up to socializing, had thought he'd try to get some work done in his office. During the party, Kendall had retired to a room in the host's home with a headache. No one had seen her for an hour—a period which coincided with the approximate time of Harris Daniel's death.

Kendall Daniels had had enough of a chance to slip out of the house, drive to the university, kill her husband, and return. She had motive: money. There were desperate circumstances: loss of lifestyle compounded with no hope of support due to divorce on grounds of infidelity. And she had a ready-made setup in her husband's known depression.

Getting into Daniels's office had been easy: She knocked, he opened the door. But how had she gotten out, leaving the door and windows locked from the inside?

Schwenk gave Pinchus till the following morning to get his report in or face disciplinary charges.

Pinchus returned to the dean's office. He felt certain the old double doors had to be the answer. They were the only point of access without an internal lock, secured from the outside by a chain pulled tight around the stems of the two large knobs and fixed with a heavy padlock.

Pinchus examined the lock again, confirming what he had found the first time—that it was so badly rusted it could not be opened, not by key, not by pick tools. Still, this had to be the access point. So . . .

At seven P.M., Pinchus had Kendall Daniels in his office. He'd asked Junior Gibney, another detective, and Laura Patterson, a plainclothes officer from Vice, to serve as witnesses for him.

Everyone was smiles and empathy for the widow. Pinchus got her some water. He propped himself up on the corner of his desk, one leg hooked over the other, and said:

"Why'd you kill your husband, Mrs. Daniels?"

"What?" Kendall Daniels's jaw dropped. "This is insane!"

Risking everything—including his job—Pinchus arrested her for the murder of Harris Daniels and read her rights.

"I can't believe this," Kendall said. "My husband shot himself. Why are you doing this to me?"

Even Junior Gibney looked worried.

Pinchus walked Kendall Daniels through the killing, step by step, ending with her back at the party.

Kendall's shock gave way to anger. "Lieutenant, I remind you that my husband locked himself into his office. Men had to *break down* the door to reach him."

"What you did, Mrs. Daniels, was leave through those old chained doors—which you opened after you shot your husband—then locked them up again."

"Have you been drinking Lieutenant?"

Pinchus pressed forward, improvising where he had to, gambling that he'd come close enough even if he didn't get it exactly right.

"Those big knobs on the doors," he said. "When you turn their base counter-clockwise, while holding the knob fixed, what you do is loosen the stem. Turn it far enough, you can pull the stem out. With the stem out, the chain falls slack and the doors can be opened. Reposition the chain, screw the stem back in, and you've got locked doors again, with the padlock still untouched, still ungiving. Evidently your husband discovered that and mentioned it to you, probably in passing, as a curiosity. Unfortunately for you, he also told a colleague, who informed me of it this afternoon."

This was an outright fabrication.

"The problem with that fanciful tale," Kendall Daniels's tone was icy, "is that if a friend of my husband's knew about the knobs—assuming what you say about them is true—then others could have known, too. And if my husband *was* murdered, then anyone could have done it. *Except* me. More than forty people can testify that I was at a party till quite late."

"But none of them can testify to having seen you during the hour you claim to have been resting because of a headache."

"That is not surprising," Kendall Daniels argued, "since the very point of resting is to lie down away from people."

"And if it weren't for the eyewitness we have who saw you just outside those double doors at ten forty-five—when you were allegedly resting in a guest bedroom at the Halsteads's—you probably would have gotten away with it."

"With all due lack of respect, Lieutenant: bullshit. You have no eyewitness."

Pinchus braced his hands on his knees and bent forward, smiling broadly. "Then how in hell, Kendall, would I know that you were wearing a red scoop-necked dress with a string of pearls? My witness has a very good eye for clothes."

"You sonofabitch!" Kendall Daniels screamed. She shot from her chair and tried for Pinchus's face with her nails, was grabbed by Laura Patterson. "You god-damned sonofabitch! Why couldn't you have left it alone! It *could* have happened that way. I set it up fucking perfectly! Why couldn't you goddamn leave it alone like everybody else!"

She didn't realize until half an hour later that all Pinchus had had to do in order to know what she was wearing that night was ask anyone who'd been at the party, which was exactly what he had done.

It was the Harris Daniels case that prompted the first person to call him the Fox—a twenty-two-year-old stringer for the *Hamilton Ledger*.

Feeling more than the dozen years older than he actually was now, and a bit winded from the climb up to the fourth floor of Lincoln Dormitory, Pinchus knocked on the door of 4-B.

"It's open. Come on in, Wayne," a voice called.

Pinchus opened the door. "Sorry, I'm not Wayne. Lieutenant Seymour Pinchus. From Homicide." He displayed his badge. "May I come in anyway?"

"Sure." A pleasant-looking young man with short sandy-colored hair was sitting at a computer on a desk by the far wall. "I thought you were the guy who's bringing me over a book on Mesopotamia."

"That would make you Barry Harper," Pinchus concluded.

"How does that follow? You're right, but I don't see how."

"David's a biology major. Barry's a history major. Mesopotamia goes with history."

"It does—but that I am therefore Barry does not follow absolutely."

"It does follow probably, though. And when the

odds are right, I take a shot. I hit more often than I miss."

Barry smiled. "What can I do for you?"

"Big place," Pinchus said, looking around. There were three different doors leading to rooms off this one, which was obviously the living room as well as a study room.

"It's a small suite," Barry said. "It was meant for four, but one dropped out and another flunked out, leaving David and me lords of all you survey."

There was no sign of college frivolity here: no pennants, no beer mugs, no centerfolds tacked to the wall. What there was, were books—all over the place—and piles of complex-looking journals that would intimidate anyone other than the most scholarly. Pinchus scanned a few titles: The materials were about evenly divided between the humanities and the hard sciences.

"May I sit down?" Pinchus asked.

"Sure." Barry typed something quickly on his keyboard. A screensaver came up on the CRT. He turned to Pinchus, who was on the couch, and waited.

"You probably know this already," Pinchus began, "but a young woman from the school was murdered last night. An Alice Schaeffer."

"It's all over the campus," Barry commented.

"She was one of David's instructors. I believe you knew her, too."

"If you mean did I ever meet her, yes. Yesterday as a matter of fact. After David's morning lab with her. And then I ran into her near Heller's Bookstore yesterday afternoon."

"Don't take this the wrong way, Barry, but I have to ask some routine questions here. It's my understanding that David did not get along well with Ms. Schaeffer. Is that true?"

"I wouldn't really say that. David comes off kind of odd sometimes. He's very intelligent, probably a genius, but he's not the most emotionally mature guy you've ever met. And frankly, he tries to get by with as little effort as he can. Because of his brains, he usually pulls it off. He didn't mean anything with Ms. Schaeffer. He was just being David."

"He's your cousin, right?" Pinchus had his notebook out.

"Right."

"Older or younger?"

"Younger. I'm twenty-four. David is twenty. I lost some school time because of . . . well, I just did. And David skipped a couple of grades. That's why we're both seniors. I kind of try and look out for David. Sort of like an older brother."

"I have reason to believe that your meeting with Ms. Schaeffer outside Heller's wasn't chance, that you had a purpose in seeking her out."

"That's half true, half not. The meeting *was* coincidental, but I did take advantage of it to talk to her about David, which I had intended to do anyway."

Pinchus nodded. "Yes. I did some checking. Apparently you told her that David has had psychological problems, that he lost his parents in an accident several years ago."

"Wow—I can't believe how much you found out. Well, again, what you just said is half true, half not. I mean, that *is* what I told her, but what I told her is only half true. David did lose his father in an automobile accident when he was ten. His mother fell apart, from what I remember and what my parents told me. David was her only child and she'd given birth to him when she was old, in her forties. My father and David's father were brothers.

"Anyway, David's mother started drinking a lot. She ended up making an arrangement with my parents for David to come live with us until she could get a handle on things. I was an only child, too, so it was like I got a younger brother. David's mother did pull things together, but everyone just sort of agreed that David was better off with us, so that's the way it stayed. For a while, anyway."

Barry took a deep breath, held it for a couple of seconds, then released it. He began talking again, this time slower, with a more serious tone.

"Four years ago, that changed. Both my parents died. David's mother took David and me in—the reverse of what had happened before. David and I seem sort of fated to be more brothers than cousins. The change was harder for David than it was for me. He was four years younger, and in a way it was like he'd lost his parents a second time. He had a tough time dealing with it. So that's what I mean when I say that what I told Ms. Schaeffer was half true. It was easier to say that his parents were killed in an accident. It makes the same essential point, but it's simpler."

"Lot of grief for you guys," Pinchus said, writing. "I'm sorry you had to go through that. If you don't mind my asking, how did your parents die?"

"They were murdered," Barry said, without any visible emotion. "Beaten to death. The killer, or killers, were never caught. I'm told that happens frequently, that killers aren't caught. But you would know that better than I."

"It happens. My job is to make sure it happens less frequently. I'm sorry for your loss."

"Thank you."

Barry seemed oddly detached from the subject, Pinchus noted. "Barry," he said, "Alice Schaeffer had a piece of paper in her bag with your name and your dorm on it. Can you tell me why she'd have that?"

"Certainly. I told her. I wanted her to know where she could reach me, that she had some recourse if David acted up again. She probably wrote it down."

"Good-looking woman, wasn't she?"

"Very."

"And maybe you were a little interested in her."

"I'm only human," Barry said with a half-smile.

"Where were you last night?"

"I've been waiting for you to ask that. David and I had a hamburger at Faulkner's around six-thirty. We left there about seven-thirty. I came back here to work on a paper."

"Did you go out again at all?"

"No."

"Where was David?"

"He went down to the basement to play video games and some pinball. He's a freak for those. But he discovered he'd left his wallet at Faulkner's, so he went back to get it."

"And when did he return?"

"I don't know. He didn't come up here. I figured he went straight to the basement again. I was beat. I fell asleep at my desk. The last I remember, it was around ten. Later, David woke me up so I could get into bed, but I have no idea what time that was."

"Do you know where David is now?"

"In the basement. He's a *real* game freak."

"That can be an expensive habit, can't it?"

"Not when you're as good as David is. He can play for half an hour on a quarter. He's truly amazing."

22

On the first floor, Pinchus located the basement stairs, then went down them. To the right, were a pair of swinging doors with glass panels. He could see washers and driers through the panels. Clothes were spinning in some of the driers. A *chunk-chunk* came from one of the washing machines. A girl was folding laundry at a table. To the left was a padlocked door marked STORAGE. A short hall led directly ahead to another locked door marked BOILER, then took a left and a few feet later opened into a sizeable room with a Ping-Pong table and more than a dozen arcade games. The room was lit by fluorescent ceiling lights. A pair of vending machines stood against the wall: snacks, sodas.

Before a pinball machine midway down one wall was a boy of about Pinchus's height. He was slim, had short dark hair, wore jeans and a denim shirt. The pinball game was called Rocket Express. Lights were flashing from it, bells going off, whistles and buzzers sounding. The boy's head was bent forward, eyes fixed on the playing field. He stood lightly on the balls of his feet, weaving and bending with the rhythm of the play.

Pinchus walked over to him and stood to the side, watching. The boy paid no attention to Pinchus. The score mounted:

815,000 . . .
875,000 . . .
910,000 . . .

At 985,000, the boy missed a paddle shot. The metal ball flew through a side gate and disappeared.

"Shit!" he yelled.

The machine flashed GAME OVER.

"I'm sorry if I broke your concentration," Pinchus apologized. "You would have had a million."

"I'd have had a million if I hadn't already passed it three times."

"That's amazing. Are you David Harper?"

"There is general agreement on that. What can I do for you?"

"I'm Lieutenant Seymour Pinchus from Homicide." Pinchus showed David his badge. "I'm investigating the death of Alice Schaeffer."

"She was some piece of work. That was a great loss."

"Yes. A great loss. I understand she was one of your instructors."

"Uh-huh. Mammalian Anatomy. So?"

"So, tell me how you got along with her."

"We got along fine. She wasn't the brightest instructor in the world, but for this school she was better than most. Actually, I think she kind of liked me." David smiled. "But I guess I'll never know for sure now."

"Tell you the truth, David, I've heard just the opposite: that she thought you were an ass, that she was annoyed with you.

"Come on, Lieutenant. You're talking about Monday's lab. I was just kidding around with her. She knew that. You've been listening to some bad gossip."

"Could be. Mind telling me where you were last night?"

"My, we are serious, aren't we? Sure. I was upstairs in my suite."

"From when?"

"Oh, I'd say from about eleven o'clock on."

"What about before that?"

"I was down here playing pinball."

"Alone?"

"Alone. Monday night's usually a study night. Most people are partied out."

"You weren't?"

"I'm never partied out."

"Don't need to study like the others?"

"No. Not like the others."

"Your cousin Barry tells me you were at Faulkner's last night."

"That's right. From about six-thirty to seven-thirty. We ate there."

"Then you came back to the dorm and discovered that your wallet was missing, right?"

"No. Barry wanted to study. I didn't want to sit around and watch him. So I came down here to play the machines. I'd known my wallet was missing since yesterday afternoon. Somebody had called and left a message with Barry that he found it. I was supposed to meet him at Market Square at nine o'clock. He said he worked near there. So I played here for about an hour, then went to get my wallet. But nobody showed up. Or called again. Whoever it was was jerking me around for some reason. Who knows?" David shrugged.

"So at nine o'clock you're at Market Square. Then what?"

"I waited till ten, then came back here. I played some more games, went upstairs about eleven."

"Barry told me you left your wallet at the pub, that you went right back for it."

David shrugged again. "Barry can be a flake sometimes. He knew I'd lost it earlier—he was the one who gave me the message."

"When you got back upstairs, is that when you woke Barry so he could get into bed?"

"I didn't wake Barry until two. When I first got there, he wasn't in the suite. Maybe he was down the hall talking to someone. I don't know. I went to bed. I woke up later, came out to the living room, and found him asleep over his books at his desk."

"Didn't that strike you as odd—you leave him because he wants to study, yet when you come back at eleven, he's not there, and then later he's sleeping at his desk?"

"No. He was probably just taking a break. Anyway, like I told you, Barry's a flake. Half the time he doesn't remember what he's doing."

Pinchus finished writing, closed his notebook, put it back in his breast pocket. "That'll do for now. Thank you." He gave David his card. "Either I or my partner will be in touch. We'll want to talk to you and Barry together, clear up some of these discrepancies."

"Sure thing."

"Good night then."

"Good night."

Pinchus started out.

"Oh. Lieutenant?"

Pinchus stopped. "Yes?"

"You got a quarter on you?" David patted his pockets, then lifted his hands, palms up, with a smile.

23

Sam Milano should have been finished for the night, wanted to be finished. But he felt compelled to make one more stop. At Friedman's, he'd gotten the name of the fired stockclerk: Tony Scampolla. He'd also learned that Scampolla had a gig tonight at the Blue Nightingale, a small coffeehouse on the west side.

Get 'em while they're hot, Pinchus had said more than once, even when your ass is dragging.

Sam drove over to the Blue Nightingale. It wasn't the best part of town: old single-family houses now broken into apartments, junk cars, a biker bar, a community action storefront center, potheads on the streets.

A sandwich board outside the Blue Nightingale said, NOW APPEARING: ANTHONY SCAMPOLLA—ORIGINAL SONGS.

Anthony Scampolla, Sam noted: AS. As he entered the coffeehouse, he also noted that a paste-on beneath the menu mounted on the outside wall said, CLOSED MONDAYS.

The Blue Nightingale was a little bigger than it looked from the outside. It was lit by muted bulbs in wall sconces. On the tables, candles burned in bowls. Behind a counter stood a big silver espresso machine. To the right was a pastry case. A blackboard on the wall listed sandwiches and salads.

A young man was sitting on a stool on the small stage in front, framed in yellowish light. He was playing a guitar and singing. From the description he had been given, Sam recognized the boy as Scampolla.

Sam took a table, ordered a decaffeinated cappucino and a napoleon. There were maybe twenty people in the place. The kid had a nice voice, Sam could tell that much. He didn't know if the songs were any good or not. His own taste ran more to Verdi, Donizetti. He didn't know much about this kind of music. Folk rock, he thought it was called.

When Scampolla finished his set, Sam followed him backstage. He accosted Scampolla at the dressing room door, with his badge out.

"Tony Scampolla?"

"Oh, don't tell me fucking Friedman called you guys. I can't believe it." Tony yanked open the door to the dressing room. "Yeah, come on in."

"This has nothing to do with Mr. Friedman." Sam followed Tony in, leaned against the wall as the young man sat down, kicked off his loafers, and picked up a cup of murky-looking coffee. "I'm Sergeant Sam Milano from Homicide."

"Homicide?"

"Right. I'd like to ask you a couple of questions."

"About what?"

"I'm investigating the murder of Alice Schaeffer," Sam said, looking for a reaction.

"Who's she?" he asked, furrowing his brow. "I don't know any Alice Schaeffer."

"The woman who got you fired yesterday."

"Jesus."

"She was killed in her apartment last night."

"Look, man. I was pissed off she got me fired and I'm still pissed. But I'm sorry she's dead—and I didn't have squat to do with it."

"You'd seen her before, hadn't you? At the Hillcrest nursing home?"

"So?" Scampolla said defensively.

"So tell me where you were last night."

"Here, there. Around."

"Do better."

"I don't know, damn it! I was freaked, losing that job. I needed it, you know? So I just got in my car and started driving. Trying to drive it out. Anyway . . . well, fuck it, man: I got stoned. I got stoned out of my gourd. I don't know where I went or what I did. I remember being in some bar in Appleton, or maybe Birch Hill, trying to pick up some blond chick, but that's all I remember.

"I woke up late this morning in my car, off the side of I-78, about sixty miles from here. I got back just a couple of hours ago. I washed up, changed, got it together to come and perform."

"Not too good a story," Sam remarked.

"Maybe not. But I'll tell you—the shape I was in, it was hard enough just driving the fucking car. You come here about a hit and run, maybe you got a case against me. But as far as planning a murder, no."

Sam studied him for a moment, long enough to cause Tony to shift and shift again in his chair. Then he set a card down on the counter next to Tony. "For now, that's where we'll leave it. But what I want you to do, Tony, is think about last night real hard. Because you're going to have to come up with someone who can remember having seen you. *Capisce?*"

Tony looked at the card. "I'm serious. I really didn't kill anybody. I got a temper, but I'm not a violent guy. I'm not."

"That'd be good for all of us, Tony. Try and come up with someone."

Tony nodded.

"Got another set tonight?" Sam asked.

"Yeah, half an hour."

"You got a good voice," Sam admitted. "I liked the song about the hayloft."

"Thanks."

"You're welcome. Give me a call soon, Tony. 'Night."

24

It was close to eleven when Pinchus got to Kate's.

He was too tired to worry about how the night would go. He just wanted to see her.

She had dinner warm.

"You didn't eat?" he asked.

"I snacked. I didn't mind waiting."

Pinchus was touched, as he often was with her. He loved Kate. He wanted her to come live with him. Or for him to come live with her. He didn't care which. That had become the problem between them: He wanted more than she did.

She had made a ginger chick-pea dish, which she served over white basmati rice. It was very good. Afterward she brewed tea in a stoneware pot and served it in small handleless cups that went with the pot. The tea was good. They sat around the table in the small dining room drinking it. She'd had a fire earlier in the stone fireplace in the living room. He could see the fireplace from where he sat. All that was left of the fire were dying embers, but they were still radiating a heat he could feel.

"God," he said, stretching, "this is the first time I've really relaxed, first time I've felt good all day. Thank you."

She smiled.

"So . . . how've you been?" he asked.

Up until yesterday, they hadn't seen each other or talked on the phone for three weeks.

"Good," she replied. "I'm busy through November

and I've got bids out on three other jobs. Tonight was the first fire"—she nodded toward the living room—"and I'm looking forward to the fall, the leaves changing. I took a three-day weekend at Kripalu, worked out some stiffness. And, I have missed you. But I said that to you yesterday."

"I'm glad to hear it again. As I said yesterday, I've missed you."

They were both silent for a while. He was always amazed at how comfortable she could be in silence.

She motioned toward the living room. "Would you like to go enjoy the last of the fire?"

He said he would. Kate pushed at the embers with a poker, stirring them into small flames and shimmering heat. She put cushions on the floor and they lay down before the fireplace. He held her, not very tightly, and they looked at the fire. She stroked his arm, in a comforting, nonsexual way.

As the time passed midnight and the fire was nearly out, he asked, "Are you going to ask me to stay?"

She shifted to look at him. "Do you want me to?"

"Yes. Very much."

She turned back to the fire. A minute or two passed. "Can you leave the subject alone?"

"I think so."

"No. You have to tell me you can. I don't want to go through it again. I don't want to talk about it."

Kate was forty-six years old. She'd been married at twenty, to a pharmacist. They loved each other with nearly unabated intensity for ten years. Then her husband dropped dead of a heart attack playing tennis. Dead at thirty-three; Kate a widow at thirty. They had not been able to have children, which was a disappointment. They were Catholics and both had wanted children, but Kate was sterile. When her husband died, Kate hated God. Then she lost even that comfort, for she stopped believing in God.

For the next few years, she felt dead. She didn't

care what happened to her, and some bad stuff had, mostly with men. At thirty-eight, she started to do yoga, and changes began. Now she liked her life, had liked it more and more each of the last several years. She wasn't eager to alter it. Two years ago, she went to Japan and meditated in a Zen monastery for a month. She had almost gone again this summer.

It was the thought of being without her for so long that had prompted Pinchus to start pushing to have more of her. And it was her need to protect her hard-regained balance, along with her discomfort over the nature of his work, and fear that if she let herself love him without reserve he might be taken from her, that caused her to resist. In the end, there were some frightful scenes.

"I can do that," he promised.

"Then stay with me. I would like you to."

Kate's bedroom was on the second floor. A big window looked out over the field in the back, part of the pond. The moon was bright, and its light flooded into the bedroom.

They made love in the moonlight. It was sweet to Pinchus, as sweet as he ever hoped it could be. They lay quietly afterward, stroking each other slowly with some tenderness.

After a while, he said, "This case has really got to me."

He told Kate some about it. Not all, but enough so that she could gain a sense of it.

"It makes me feel old," he confided. "It makes me feel mortal. It makes me feel helpless. And it just plain makes me sad as hell. I want to cry."

"You can," she said. "People cry."

"I don't," he lied. "Besides, death is an illusion. Isn't that what the Buddhists say?"

"There's a story about a Zen master," she told him. "One day a disciple came to the master's hut and found him weeping inconsolably. Shocked, the disciple asked what was wrong. 'My son has died,' the master sobbed. 'But, master,' the disciple said, 'you have taught us that all death is an illusion.' 'It is,' wept the master, 'and the death of one's child is the most painful illusion of them all.'"

"That's the story, huh?"

"Yes."

"It's an okay story."

Pinchus began to cry. He had done that before, a long time ago, but alone, in private, and bitterly. He had never grieved for Melissa with such complete sadness, and never, ever in front of anyone else.

Kate didn't try to comfort him, only offered her hand for him to hold. And when it was over, she didn't ask him if he felt better. Pinchus was grateful she didn't. He didn't think "better" was the way he felt. Cleaner, maybe. A kind of clean emptiness where something that needed to be gotten rid of had been gotten rid of.

After a while he mentioned, "There's something I need to tell you. Something that happened this afternoon at the morgue."

She waited.

"She was lying on the table when I came in, lying on her back. Alice Schaeffer. She was naked. This incredibly beautiful girl was lying there naked. Her body was as beautiful as her face. And, and looking at her . . . for an instant I forgot where I was, I was just looking at a beautiful girl who was naked, and I started to get aroused. My God!"

Carefully, Kate asked, "What do you think about that?"

"It's not what I think, it's what I feel—like a goddamn *freak*, like some fucking disgusting animal, like the motherfucker who killed her."

"Seymour."

"That's what it feels like, Kate. I can't help it. What does it feel like to *you*?"

Kate was silent a moment. "Disturbing," she admitted. "Because I see it as the result of the kind of disconnection—the *disunion*—the brutality that your work forces on you."

"Great," Pinchus said. "That's a big help."

Kate withdrew her hand and pursed her lips together.

"I'm sorry, it's just that this really got to me."

"Then maybe you can just accept that. You don't have to do anything about it. Seymour, look at me."

He did.

"Did you kill her?"

"No."

"Are you an animal, really?"

"No."

"Just let it be then. There was nothing wrong with what you felt in the morgue. And there is nothing wrong with what you feel now about what you felt then. There is nothing wrong, my love."

He rested his head against her breast.

"Is there more you want to tell me?"

"No," he answered.

"Let's sleep then. I'm tired. So are you. I'd like to get up with the dawn. I'll let you sleep a little later."

They went to sleep. In her sleep she snuggled into him. He held her, and she let him.

25

"*Bang, bang!* Yaahhh! Master of the Universe lives! You'll never take me alive! *Paching, pachew!*"

Shouting at what Peter Roberts thought had to be the top of his lungs, Paul was alternately climbing up on his parents' bed and jumping off it.

Peter rubbed his eyes. The clock-radio read 6:18 A.M. "Paul," Peter said, "do you know how to be a little quiet?"

"No, but I know how to be a little noisy," Paul said gleefully.

"Give us a break, Paul. It isn't even light yet. Go back to bed or be quiet so I can get back to sleep."

From behind the footboard, Melanie poked her head up. "Dad," she whispered, "Mom said you're supposed to get us ready for school today. You better get moving, we're hungry."

"Yeah, we want breakfast," Paul bellowed.

Peter glanced over his shoulder at Diane. Diane yawned without opening her eyes, rolled over away from him. She wasn't going to give him a reprieve.

"Okay, okay. Both of you go downstairs. I'll be down in a couple of minutes."

Paul and Melanie scooted out. Peter forced himself to swing his legs out of bed and put his feet on the floor. He sat on the edge of the bed. Diane continued to feign sleep. Peter didn't know whether he was amused or annoyed at her.

Melanie called up the stairs.

"Coming," Peter said. He got up, slipped on pants,

a shirt, and a pair of moccasins, and went down to the kitchen.

"You guys get the milk and bowls," he yawned. "I'll get the cereal."

"I want something different this morning." Melanie glanced over at Paul.

"Me too."

"Practically every morning of your life you eat cereal, but today you want something different?"

"Right," both children said in unison.

Peter shook his head. He opened the freezer. "How about some nice waffles? Or maybe a fresh but frozen croissant?"

"I want pancakes," Paul whined.

"Pancakes?"

"Yeah, Dad, pancakes."

Peter fumbled around in the freezer. "I don't see any pancakes here. Have a waffle. They're just like pancakes, only with ridges."

"Pancakes!" Paul demanded.

Peter turned to Melanie. "Do you know how to make pancakes?"

"Sure, Dad. They're easy. But I really think I need three dollars to make them."

Peter looked shocked. "Extortion? My own kid is extorting me?"

"Yup."

"No way. . . . Would you take a buck?"

"Get serious, Dad. It's a bargain at three. That *does* include yours and mine as well as Paul's."

"Deal." Peter opened the kitchen drawer where he and Diane kept change and some small bills. He took out three dollars for Melanie.

"You want coffee?" Melanie asked.

"How much?"

"Dad! What do you think I am? Coffee's on me."

"Fine," Peter said. "And I know what you are."

Melanie giggled.

Peter got the *Ledger* from the front porch. He sat

at the counter reading it while Melanie fixed breakfast. There were two separate articles about the Schaeffer killing. He was mentioned in each, got good play in the main one. He was pleased.

Melanie put the pancakes on plates. She brought them to the breakfast nook while Peter got butter and syrup for them. He sat with his children, eating.

"Hey, Dad," Melanie swallowed before continuing. "I heard that you looked at a dead girl some guy bit. *Gross.*"

"Yeah, *gross,*" Paul said.

"Where'd you hear that?"

"Mom was talking about it on the phone. Paul heard her, too."

Peter had never discussed his forensic work with his children. Melanie was old enough to understand, but he wasn't sure about Paul. He wondered how much the boy already knew. "Paul, do you know what Daddy does for the police sometimes?"

"Well, I know that sometimes you look at dead people's teeth."

"Do you know why I do that?"

"To see if they should have been brushing better?"

Melanie burst out laughing, spitting milk from her mouth.

Paul looked offended.

Peter couldn't help smiling himself. "Good guess," he said with as straight a face as he could manage. "But actually, it's to help the police identify the dead people when the police don't know who they are."

Paul nodded. He didn't seem interested in knowing any more, so Peter didn't say any more. They finished breakfast. Peter gave Melanie an additional dollar to pick out Paul's clothes for him and help him get dressed. Peter stayed downstairs and cleaned up the kitchen.

"Pretty good," he said, eyeballing them when they returned. "Fed, dressed, and ready for the bus. We're doing okay."

"What about lunch?" Melanie asked.

"Lunch?"

"Mom usually packs us lunch. So you have to do that . . . Unless . . ."

"Unless what?"

"Unless you want us to buy lunch today?"

Peter sighed. "How much?"

"Five dollars should do it. For an extra two, I'll make sure Paul gets *exactly* what he wants on his tray."

"Here's ten. But bring me change. Or else."

"Change and a full accounting," Melanie promised.

Peter took them out to the corner to catch the bus. He kissed them good-bye before they got on, waved to them as the bus pulled away. He returned to the house feeling good. He liked having had the morning with Melanie and Paul. It was nice to feel normal for a change.

As he got inside, the phone on the mail table in the foyer rang. He picked it up. "Hello?"

"Hi, Peter."

"Seymour." He waited.

"We're lining up some people: suspects, possible suspects. If you can handle it today, I thought we'd send 'em over so you can take impressions, see if we can get a match."

"Sure. How many do you have?"

"Three, so far. We'll have more by this afternoon, I think. I'm having Officer Collins pick them up and bring them to your office."

"Perfect. I'm off every other Wednesday, and this is it."

"I hate to have to spoil your day off."

"Not a problem. Actually, it works out better this way. Have Collins bring the first one around noon and we'll go from there."

"Will do. Thanks, Peter."

"You're welcome."

Peter put the phone back in its cradle and went upstairs. Diane was sitting up in bed. She looked especially beautiful this morning, her wide green eyes looking at him with affection, a little smile on her lips.

"I know what I did was maybe a bit nasty," she said. "But you deserved it. I've missed you."

"I've missed you too."

She lifted the sheet invitingly.

Peter hesitated. "That was Seymour on the phone."

"I don't want to hear about Seymour. I want to hear you growl."

"He needs me to make models of suspects' teeth from that murder yesterday."

"When?"

"Today, unfortunately."

"Peter! It's your day off!"

"I know. I'm sorry. I really am."

"I'll tell you what. . . . You come here and play with me awhile before you go. I won't complain, not one little bit." She slipped her nightgown down from her shoulders, smiling.

Peter felt a surge of desire. Powerful desire. But he had to see Terri this morning. He had decided—spontaneously, as he watched the bus pull away with Melanie and Paul—that he had to end this thing with Terri, had to end it today; and now he also had to be at his office by noon to meet Collins.

"I can't tell you how much I want you," he said, truthfully. "More than anything else in the world at this moment. But I can't be with you now, honey. I have to get over to the police department as soon as possible. I'll make it up to you tonight."

"Are you going to be late again?"

"I swear to you: I will be home by eight no matter what happens. And as soon as the kids are in bed, I will do my best, my absolute best, to totally fry your nervous system."

Diane crossed her arms over her breasts. She assumed a pouting expression, half-feigned, half-serious.

"You know what this sounds like, Peter? It sounds like you're having an affair or something. So what's her name?"

Peter froze.

Diane looked at him quizzically. Then, slowly, her mouth opened.

Blood was pounding in Peter's ears, heating up his face. He felt himself falling into an abyss.

"Terri, Diane. Her name is Terri."

26

It was nine-fifteen. Seymour Pinchus knocked softly on the door of room 108 of the Blue Ridge Motel. There was a rustling within. The door opened slightly. A young man in a bathrobe peered out. "Yes?"

"Mark Donaldson?"

"Yes. May I help you?"

Mark had blue eyes, strong features, a strong jaw. His hair was blond and a little curly. He looked like what Pinchus thought a competitor in the ancient Olympic games in Greece would look like. This morning, Mark also looked haggard.

"Mark, I'm Lieutenant Pinchus from Homicide." Pinchus showed his badge. "May I come in? I need to talk to you about the death of your fiancée, Alice Schaeffer. I know it's been painful. I'll be brief."

Mark opened the door. "Come in."

The television was on but without sound. Mark turned it off and seated himself in one of the two small club chairs. Pinchus took the other. Mark had a cup of coffee on the table between the two chairs. "There's enough for another cup," he said. "One of those little brewing units in the bathroom. Can I make you some?"

"No, thank you. Mark, I'm terribly sorry for what has happened," Pinchus said gently. "I offer you my deep condolence."

Mark nodded.

"I hope I haven't come too early," Pinchus apologized. "I didn't call first for fear of waking you up. I figured I'd just come over, knock lightly, and if you weren't up, come back later."

"That's quite all right, Lieutenant. What is it that you want to say?"

"Well, more like ask than say. Do you know of anyone who had any reason to hurt Alice? Anyone at all? Take your time."

"No, Lieutenant. Alice got on with everyone. She was very positive, very upbeat. If she *did* have a problem with someone, she never mentioned it to me."

"You're in law school, right? Columbia University?"

"Yes. I'm a third-year student."

"Very nice. I have a son who's in school in New York . . . John Jay College of Criminal Justice. Wants to be a detective."

"You must be proud of him."

"I am. Like your parents must be of you. It's a parental privilege."

"I guess that's true."

"When was the last time you spoke to Alice, Mark?"

"Over the weekend. I don't remember exactly which day."

"Not on Monday?"

"No."

"You're sure?"

"Yes. Why?"

"I was under the impression she was expecting a call from you on Monday."

"Oh. Yes. She left a message with my roommate, but I got in too late to call. Is that important?"

"It could be. Now, I have to ask you a difficult question. I hope you understand that I have to ask it."

Pinchus noticed Mark stiffen slightly.

"All right."

"Mark, how did you spend Monday night?"

Mark looked away. "I can't tell you."

"Son, you have to. I know this is painful, but you

need to tell me the truth, all of it. Otherwise, you become a suspect in your own fiancée's murder."

"I know the law, Lieutenant. I am not *obligated* to answer. And I am not your son."

Pinchus nodded. "True on both counts. You're a bright guy, Mark. You're probably going to be a fine attorney. But right now, you're acting like a schmuck. Son, you *want* to tell me where you were . . . because if you don't, I am going to kick your ass all the way up to New York and then back again, and I'm going to do it in perfectly legal ways. So tell me where you were."

Mark looked miserable. He stared down at his coffee. "I was with another girl," he said, voice barely audible. "I met her a month ago at a party. She knew I was getting married, but she didn't care. She said, 'Hell, you're not married yet!' We started seeing each other. This past weekend, I told Alice I was sick and couldn't visit. My roommate was gone. This girl spent the weekend with me. Alice called a couple of times, but I always made sure to answer the phone. When my roommate got back Monday, I filled him in, told him to cover for me. I was taking this girl home to Connecticut, where she lives. Johnny—that's my roommate—didn't want to lie to Alice. He hoped she wouldn't call. But she did. I didn't get home from Connecticut till it was too late to call her back."

Pinchus waited.

"That's the truth," Mark said. "All of it."

Pinchus said nothing.

"I'm not proud of myself, but I'm not as slimy as you might think. That first time, okay, I acted like a prick. I was half-tanked. That's an explanation, not an excuse. And then, oh shit, I don't know, I started to fall for this girl. It got confusing. I didn't know what to do. I was going to call the engagement off next week, tell Alice I couldn't go through with it."

Pinchus looked at Mark, his expression neutral.

Mark shifted uncomfortably. "You can see why I didn't want to tell you where I was. Look, maybe I'm a real shit. I don't know. But irrespective of that, please don't say anything to Alice's parents about this. They're good people. It would be an unnecessary blow. Especially for her father. He's taking it very hard."

Pinchus continued to wait. But Mark offered nothing more. "I can't promise you anything," Pinchus explained. "You know that. But if you're telling the truth, and if it makes no difference in the case, I'll do my best. Give me the name and address of the girl you were with."

"No way! I'm sorry, Lieutenant, but I'm not going to get her involved."

"Then you have no alibi."

"I told you where I was!" Mark said in frustration.

"Mark, this plays one of two ways: Either you account for your time in a way that can be substantiated, or you become a prime suspect. It shouldn't require a law degree to see that."

Mark said, "I have to stand by my statement."

"Have it your way. For now."

Before he left, Pinchus asked Mark if he would agree to having Peter Roberts make an impression of his teeth, expecting him to decline, asking simply to get the request on record. But Mark surprised him. He said fine, he would make himself available this afternoon.

Gai vais. Go figure.

27

Sam Milano hadn't been able to find anyone on campus who'd seen Richie Zimmer since Monday night. Neither, it appeared, had Richie attended any of his classes today. Twice Sam had gone to Richie's dormitory and knocked on his door, without response. None of the students he'd spoken to on that floor knew where Richie might be.

It was past noon. Sam was hungry. He drove over to the student union building and got a cheeseburger, fries, and a milkshake to go. Then he drove back to Richie's dorm and parked across the street from it, keeping a casual eye out for Richie as he ate.

When he finished eating, Sam got out of his car and went into the dorm to try a final time, on the slight chance Richie had returned while Sam was off buying lunch. The next move would be to get the address and phone number of Richie's parents from the dean's office, go back to the station, and call them.

But Richie opened the door on the second knock.

The boy was a mess: unshaven, thinning hair in need of washing, eyes bloodshot, clothes rumpled.

Sam introduced himself, invited himself in. Richie's small room was crowded with electronic equipment. The bed was unmade. Richie sat down on it; Sam remained standing.

"Where've you been?" Sam asked.

"Home. At my parents. I just got back about half an hour ago. I got really fucked up when I heard about Alice on the news Tuesday. I—"

"Alice?"

"That's why you're here, isn't it?"

Sam nodded.

"Like I said, I went home. I only live an hour from here. But it didn't make me feel any better. It made me feel worse, actually. So I came back. I still can't believe it. Not Alice."

"I understand you were with Alice Monday night."

"Yes. At Faulkner's. There were a couple of other people there, too."

"What time did you leave her?"

"I didn't leave her. I left Faulkner's. About eight-thirty. I don't know exactly."

"Where did you go after that?"

"Why? Am I a suspect?" Richie said, as he stood and threw his arms up. "Sergeant, I really *liked* that girl. I could *never* have done anything to hurt her."

"Calm down, Richie. All I asked is where you went after you left the pub. I have to ask these questions. They're routine."

"Okay. Yes. I understand. I went to a fraternity party. Some undergraduates. Actually, I went *back* to it. I had started off there before I went to the pub. I don't usually go to that kind of party, but a kid I've been tutoring won an award. The party was in his honor. He asked me to come. I hadn't had a very good time at Faulkner's. I needed some cheering up. So I went back. A lot of people must have seen me there."

"What time did you leave the party?"

"Midnight, I think. I don't know. I was pretty drunk. I had a terrible hangover the next morning. I was in the bathroom splashing water on my face trying to come to when I heard the news about Alice on the radio. I threw my guts up. I must have heaved for five minutes straight. Afterward, I just fell apart. That's when I decided to go home."

"Where was this party?"

"Delta Phi. Corner of Fifth and Lombard. The kid who invited me is Ken Laufer. He's a junior, a biology major."

Sam finished writing, closed his notebook. "Thanks, Richie. That'll be all for now. Listen, this kind of thing is always hard. No one gets through unscathed. Take it easy. Get some rest."

"Thank you, Sergeant. I will."

"Good."

"Did you see her? Alice?"

"Yes, I did, Richie."

Richie started to cry. "How . . . how did she . . . No, I don't want to know."

"She looked at rest."

Richie nodded. He smiled at Sam through his tears. "She was some good-looking girl, wasn't she, Sergeant?"

"Yes, Richie. She was. Take care of yourself."

28

Peter Roberts parked behind Terri's building. He didn't want to be doing this, but still, he hoped she was home. He didn't know if he could muster the courage again.

Diane hadn't cried, though he was sure she'd been on the verge more than once. She had insisted he tell her the whole story. And he had, though without details—certainly not that he had often fantasized about her, Diane, when he was with Terri. He wanted desperately for Diane to know that he loved her. But he understood that she would not perceive his fantasies of her as evidence of that.

He had hated himself while he confessed. He felt cheap, worthless.

When he finished, he stood with his head hanging, looking at the carpet. And then—for all his shame and self-loathing—he was aware that she was sitting in bed with her breasts exposed, and he became passionately aroused, wanted to take her.

Diane was silent several moments. Then she said, with careful enunciation: "You motherfucking sonofabitch. You stinking, lowlife piece of garbage. You pile of human shit."

He was shocked. He had never heard her speak like that.

"Why?" she asked.

He lifted his hands helplessly.

Her eyes were furious. "I will not cry," she said. "That would indicate that somehow I cared. Please get out of the house."

"Diane, we need to talk."

"We will talk tonight. If I am here. I don't know whether I will be."

"I love you, Diane! Please."

"I do not at this moment love you. I do not love you at all."

She had pulled her nightgown back up and closed it over her breasts. She had gotten out of bed, gone to the bathroom door. Without turning, she had said, "I will be in here for five minutes. Please be gone from the house by the time I come out."

Now, waiting at Terri's door, Peter felt sick. He felt as if he were fading away, disappearing.

"Yes, who is it?" Terri called.

"It's Peter, can I come in?"

The two locks on the door clicked as Terri opened them. She was barefoot, clad only in a long football jersey. She smiled brightly.

"Peter! What a nice surprise. But your timing isn't too good. I was just having breakfast. I woke up late and have to get to the restaurant in forty-five minutes. Come into the kitchen. Sit with me and have a cup of coffee."

Peter followed her in, sat down at the small table. "Terri, we need to talk."

Terri poured a glass of orange juice for herself from a large pitcher. "Want some?"

"No."

"Oh, sure you do. Come on." Terri poured him a glass.

"Terri—"

"And you'll have some eggs too, right?" She jumped to the refrigerator, pulled the door open, yanked out a carton of eggs.

"Terri. We have to talk."

She threw the carton of eggs into the sink and slammed the refrigerator door closed. "No, we don't, goddamn it! I'm going to make you breakfast, and you're going to tell me jokes, and I'm going to call the restaurant and say I'm going to be late, and we're going into the bedroom and make love, and we're not going to talk. We're not going to talk! Do you understand!" Tears were running down her cheeks.

"I spoke to Diane this morning," Peter began.

"Good," Terri said. "That means we don't have to hide everything anymore. No more sneaking around in the dark. No more making love to me and then leaving right away, leaving me to sleep alone. That's good, isn't it, Peter? Isn't that good?"

"Diane took it pretty hard."

"She won, Peter, didn't she? Your goddamn wife won!"

Peter got up and moved to hold Terri. She backed away.

"I care for you very much," he confessed. "But I also love my wife. I didn't expect anything like this. Neither did you. We didn't think we'd come to feel about each other the way we have. I'm sorry. But I'm not sorry for having . . . loved you. If I weren't married, or if I didn't love Diane so much, things would be different.

"Shit," Terri said. "Shit, shit, shit."

"I'm sorry."

"Fuck you, Peter."

Peter could think of nothing to say.

"Ah," Terri said. "Ah. Oh, hell. I just never expected to fall in love with you, that's all."

All Peter could do was repeat, "I'm sorry."

"Me too, Peter. Me too."

"Diane didn't win. She lost. And I lost. And you lost. Just like you said you were afraid would happen."

"It's nice to be right," Terri said with a weak smile. "I don't blame you, Peter. It's just that it hurts. You know something? I even feel compassion for Diane. I can actually relate to how it must be for her. She must feel cheated, like I do. I used to think I hated her. I wanted you that much. But now I feel bad for her. I feel bad that I caused her pain. You know, she doesn't think so now, but she's lucky in a way: She's got a husband who obviously loves her. There's something to be said for that. I hope you told her you loved her."

"I did. I don't think she believes it. Maybe she never will again."

"Do you think it would help if I talked to her? I feel responsible. God, that would be painful for both of us, but I'm the only one who knows that you really *do* love her."

"No, Terri. It wouldn't work. It would make things worse."

"I guess. I think I want to help, but maybe it's only a guilty conscience."

"No—you *do* want to help. It's one of the reasons I . . . care for you." He put his hands on her shoulders. She let him draw her in and hold her lightly. After several moments, he said, "I have to go, Terri. I have to meet the police at my office."

She disengaged. "I have to get moving myself. There's just one more thing. If you don't want me to get in between you and your wife—Christ, I guess it's a little late for that—but if you don't want me to try to help, there's something I have to do at least for myself."

"What's that?" Peter asked.

Terry took his face in her hands and looked at him lovingly.

"This," she said.

She picked up the pitcher of orange juice and poured out its entire contents over his head.

29

When Sam Milano got back to the office that afternoon, he found Pinchus eating a big piece of apple pie with a slab of cheddar cheese on top of it.

"New vending machines downstairs?" Sam asked.

"It should only be. The machine ran out of the god-awful pie it stocks. I found this new deli three blocks from here, Sanford's. I will never buy my pie from anyone but them again."

"What about your diet?"

"I will definitely begin this weekend. If you promise never to ask me about my diet again, I will give you the piece I brought from Sanford's for you."

"Has it got cheese on it?"

"There is no other way to eat apple pie."

"Well, maybe half," Sam said.

"Fine." Pinchus reached into his desk drawer and produced a second piece of pie. "I will eat what you don't."

Sam shook his head.

"It's not next week yet," Pinchus pointed out. "Tom Onasis called. Says death was indeed due to strangulation. Lab tests are negative on saliva, negative on semen."

"All that effort, the poor bastard didn't even get to come."

"Not necessarily."

"No semen stains on the sheets or anywhere else, right?"

"Could have used a condom," Pinchus noted.

"These are perilous times. Not to mention the risk of leaving evidence."

"Of course," Sam nodded.

"I'm just saying we shouldn't jump to conclusions. Tom thinks the cut marks on her back may be the initials *AS*, same as hers."

"You tell him you figured that yesterday, before they cleaned the body up?"

Pinchus shrugged. "Let him have it. He came to it on his own. So, how'd you make out?"

"Not bad. I got to Friedman's before it closed, got the stock clerk's name, Tony Scampolla. After that, did I go home? No. I pushed my tired body onward. Scampolla's a musician. He's playing at a coffeehouse on the west side, the Blue Nightingale. So I went to see him. You know how he's billed? Anthony Scampolla—*AS*. Nice? Also, the coffeehouse is closed Mondays. Monday night, you will recall, being the time of the murder."

"Nice. Where does he say he was at the time of the murder?"

"He says he can't remember much. Claims he was high. All he knows for sure, he says, is that he woke up in the morning in his car, off the side of I-78. He says he was in a couple of bars, around Appleton, Birch Hill, but he can't remember their names."

"Interesting."

"More than that, I think."

"Still too early for me. I'm not nuts about revenge as a motive. Getting fired? Maybe he wants to kill her on the spot, when his initial anger is high, but not later, after he's cooled down."

"He acted like he didn't know who Alice was until I told him she was the one who'd got him fired. Even then, he said zip about having seen her at Hillcrest. Prima facie, I like him for the job."

"Time and opportunity aren't good," Pinchus argued. "He meets this girl in the afternoon, and by late evening kills her? That gives him only a couple of hours to find out who she is, where she lives, what her schedule is, to case the place, plan the job, and so on and so on."

"*If* we assume that your original premise is correct—that the killer knew her, that it was a well-planned attack."

"True. And for now, I'm still going with it. Did you get to Richie Zimmer?"

"This morning. I don't see any point wasting time with him. Guy's afraid of his own shadow. And he has a good alibi. He was at a fraternity party. Got there well before the murder, left long after."

"Lots of booze and drugs at these parties sometimes. Wouldn't be too hard to slip away, come back with no one being the wiser. He doesn't sound particularly stable. And apparently he was upset over Alice working for Hawthorne. Do we know anything about his background, like maybe a history of violent behavior when intoxicated?"

"Believe me, the guy's a pussy. If I'd had a Valium, I would have given it to him. I don't put much stock in Janet Cooper's theory."

"You tell him we want permission to take an impression of his teeth?"

"I didn't think it was necessary. But I'll tell Collins to put his name on the list if you think we should."

"I do."

"When she contacts him, the kid is going to shit or keel over from a heart attack."

"He'll survive. Scampolla?"

"I gave his name to Collins this morning. How'd you make out with Donaldson and the Harpers?"

"Our Mr. Donaldson alleges he was with another girl over the weekend and most of Monday. Surprise, surprise: the loving fiancé. He says he was going to call the wedding off. Alice didn't know yet. Anyway, he says, he drove this other girl back to Connecticut on

Monday and didn't return to New York until late. That, he says, is why he never called Alice Monday night. The problem is, he wouldn't tell me the girl's name. So for now, he has no alibi. But it seems far-fetched to think he'd kill Alice just to get out of marrying her. Unless of course, there's more story to be told, like maybe Alice had something on him. We'll get the new girlfriend's name when we need it, if there is a girlfriend. So with him, we have opportunity—as long as his Connecticut friend remains anonymous—and someone who knows Alice, her apartment, and her schedule."

"The Harpers?"

"David Harper is an oddball. There's some talk that he's a genius. Maybe. Maybe not. I know *he* likes to think so. And he had opportunity. According to a story Barry tells, David was out trying to find his lost wallet at Faulkner's. Barry says he fell asleep around ten o'clock, was awakened by David sometime after that. Time unknown.

"Then there's David's version: According to *him*, Barry knew that he'd gone to Market Square to get the wallet. But whoever was supposed to have it never showed up. David says he got back at eleven, but Barry was gone. David says he went to bed, woke up at two, and found Barry asleep over his books in the living room.

"Depending on who you believe, each had the opportunity. Actually, neither of them has an alibi. I can't quite figure this: David could have matched his story to Barry's and still look no better or worse than he does now. There's no need for him to lie. But Barry is more believable than David. And if *Barry* was lying, he'd know I'd discover that as soon as I talked to David.

"I wouldn't put it past David to fictionalize just for the hell of it, to jerk my chain. *One* of them is lying. Maybe both of them are. As to what the desperate circumstances might be for them, or even a motive for that matter, I have no idea."

"They're cousins, right?"

"Yes. First cousins. But more like brothers." Pinchus related what Barry had told him about their childhood, including the murder of Barry's parents.

"Bizarre," Sam said.

"Barry says that's why he told some of it to Alice. He wanted her to understand David, maybe cut him a little slack. That leaves us with Hawthorne. What do you think about him?"

"I think he probably made advances to Alice, like he did with Kathy Bollinger. I think Alice probably rejected him. That puts him on my list."

"Doesn't seem like his style."

"Who do you like for it?"

"I don't have a favorite," Pinchus said unhappily. "It could be any of them—or none of them. My gut tells me it *is* one of these six, but I just don't know."

"Let's do motive," Sam said. "Richie Zimmer: lost love and jealousy. Tony Scampolla: revenge. Mark Donaldson: not wanting to marry her, maybe fear she'd reveal something damaging about him. The Harper boys: good old-fashioned lust. Finally, Miles Hawthorne: because she spurned him and because he's a perv."

Pinchus wrote down the suspects' names on a yellow pad, leaving spaces for motive and desperate circumstances. He gave the pad to Sam.

"You go first," offered Pinchus. "I won the last one."

"You won the last three."

"I'm modest."

"And proud of your humility."

Picking the murderer was a game they played. The loser bought the winner dinner at any restaurant the winner wished to eat in. If neither won, they still went out, but split the bill.

Sam put his initials after Anthony Scampolla's name. Pinchus chose David Harper. Sam picked Mark Donaldson. Pinchus took Richie Zimmer. Sam took Miles Hawthorne. Pinchus was left with Barry Harper.

"So now what?" Sam asked.

"Now we relax. We wait for Peter to call us tonight and tell us who did it."

"You really think we'll wrap this by tonight?"

"Unless Collins can't get everyone to Peter today . . . or unless, God forbid, the killer isn't one of these. That reminds me, you'd better tell Collins to add Richie Zimmer to the list."

"Actually, I think I'll go find Richie. If Collins shows up out of the blue and asks him to consent to go with her to have impressions made of his teeth, he'll freak."

"Whatever you think."

"You'll be here?"

"Yes."

"I'll be back in a while." Sam rose, but paused. "You know, Seymour, I've been thinking—Peter Roberts is in an awfully powerful position. He decides who the murderer is, and we're obliged to believe him."

"We're the ones who have to provide him the suspects," Pinchus said. "If he gets a match, you can bet any defense lawyer in the state will have his own experts examine the impressions. If there's no match, we're back to the beginning. You have some kind of reservation about Peter?"

"I was only making an observation," Sam said carefully.

Pinchus nodded.

Sam left.

After a few moments, Pinchus opened the file that contained the photocopies of the items that had been fixed to the door of Alice's refrigerator. He found the item he was looking for on the third page: a card from Dr. Peter Roberts's office noting that Alice had an appointment with him next month.

Pinchus rubbed his chin with a finger. He didn't know what he thought about that. He didn't know that he *wanted* to think anything about it.

30

Diane Roberts spent most of the day feeling wounded and angry. She hated Peter, or at least thought she did.

Diane was a good-looking woman. Over the course of her marriage, more than a few men had let her know—and sometimes not very subtly—that they would be delighted to bed her. She'd been tempted once or twice. But she loved her husband very much and would never have betrayed his trust.

Why hadn't Peter felt the same way? Obviously, she thought, he didn't love her. She wondered if he ever had. Certainly the affair explained his distance over the past few months, the falling off of their lovemaking. Maybe it explained the cancelled checks to Dr. Frederick Heinemann she'd discovered when she opened one of her husband's personal bank statements, thinking it was hers. Heinemann, she'd learned through discreet inquiry, was a psychoanalyst. She had never asked Peter about him, thinking that in time he would tell her about whatever was hurting or confusing him. She regretted now that she hadn't.

She tried to distract herself, tried cleaning the house. But she couldn't stop her mind from engaging in hurt and hurtful dialogue with Peter, couldn't block out the sudden, searingly painful images of him in naked embrace with another woman. Several times during the day, she sat down and cried. Once, she kicked at a chair cursing.

In the early afternoon, she went into the study. She took a heavy photo album from the bookcase cabinet and sat on the floor with it. After a moment, she opened it.

Lies, lies—all those happy photographs: Peter with his arm around her; the four of them splashing in the surf; Peter kissing her at their anniversary party.

She moved quickly through the more recent pages back to the older ones. There she began to linger, smiling and crying at the same time. She looked at photos of Melanie as a young child, Paul as a baby. Then Melanie as a baby, before Paul was born. She moved further back, to the thirteen-year-old wedding pictures, when she was twenty-four and he twenty-five and they had been deliriously in love. She thought her heart would break. She almost wished she had never met Peter Roberts.

She had been Diane Saperstein then, twenty-one years old, home from school for the summer and living with her parents in the large house with its rolling landscaped grounds in Ardmore, a well-to-do suburb outside of Philadelphia. Her father, William Saperstein, owned a company that manufactured surgical instruments and small medical devices. Her mother, Ellen, Seymour Pinchus's older sister, was active in raising money for charities.

Diane had been lounging on a recliner beside the family pool in the spacious backyard, screened off from the neighboring houses by tall hedges, when she first saw Peter Roberts. Peter appeared from around the side of the house wearing the uniform of the pool maintenance service the Sapersteins used, carrying a plastic bucket of filter powder.

He was tall, muscular, dark-haired, and very good-looking. Diane had responded to her first sight of him with something that was nearly an animal hunger—which had never happened to her before.

She said hello.

He said hello back and smiled in a kind of reticent way she found hugely appealing. But he didn't say anything more and he went about his work with quiet efficiency. She thought he cast a covert glance at her once or twice, but wasn't sure. She did, though, make a point of walking slowly out on the diving board once, pausing before she dove into the water, so he could get a better look at her if he wished.

Normally, the pool service came every ten days. Peter reappeared a week later. Then five days later. The third time he arrived, Diane was home alone. It was a hot day. She said to him, "I'd invite you in for a dip, but I guess you don't have a suit with you."

"I've got one on under my pants," Peter answered. Then, shyly, he said, "I was kind of hoping you'd ask me in."

Diane winked at him. "Pretty sure of yourself, aren't you?"

"No, not really," Peter said quickly.

Diane laughed.

His name was Peter Roberts, Diane learned. His father was a dentist with a practice in what Diane knew to be a fairly poor part of town. Peter had just finished his senior year at Temple and was working over the summer to help pay for dental school, which he was going to enter in the fall.

They began dating—on the sly, since Diane wasn't sure how her parents would react to Peter's background. They were sensitive to social standing. The night of their fourth date, Diane's parents were out when Peter brought her back home, and they wouldn't be returning till very late. They went skinny dipping, and then—dripping wet, on the manicured grass in moonlight, in the warm cricket-chirping night—they made love together for the first time.

That was the night Diane knew she had fallen in love with Peter Roberts.

By summer's end, William and Ellen Saperstein had grown suspicious of Diane's odd comings and goings, her reluctance to talk about her social life. So neither was surprised when, a week before Diane was to return to school for her senior year, she announced that she wanted to invite a young man to dinner. What did surprise them was Peter Roberts's appearance at the appointed hour: They had met Peter during the course of the summer in his role as their pool maintenance man and had never had an inkling that he was also playing another role in their family. And what surprised all of them was that William and Ellen were fairly taken with Peter by the time the evening ended. They called Diane off to the side and told her so before she went out of the house with Peter to walk him to his car and kiss him good night.

Three years later, a week before Peter began his final year of dental school, Peter Roberts and Diane Saperstein were married.

Unfortunately, they did not live happily ever after. They lived happily for thirteen years, until this morning when Diane, mostly jokingly, had asked: "So what's her name?"

Diane was brought out of her reverie by a noise at the front door—a knock? She looked at her watch. It was a little after three. The children's school bus had arrived early, she guessed.

But when she opened the door, there was no one there, only an envelope lying on the mat. The envelope had her name on it. Diane looked up and down the street but didn't see anyone. She picked the envelope up, closed the door, and went into the living room. She sat down and opened the envelope. Inside was a letter written in flowery unfamiliar script.

Dear Diane,

You don't know me, but I know a lot about you. By all rights, we should hate each other. You see, I'm the woman your husband was having an affair with. My name is Terri. I know it must be uncomfortable reading this, but please hear me out. I needed to tell you how lucky you are. I'm sure you don't feel that way now, but you are indeed lucky. For the short time that I was seeing Peter, I thought I despised you. My reasons were selfish. I wanted Peter for myself. Then when Peter said he could no longer see me because he loved his wife, I hated you even more. I hated you, but I never met you. Doesn't make a lot of sense.

The truth is, I don't really hate you at all. If anything, I envy you. You have a husband who truly loves you. You have to trust me on that. I know what it's like to have it the other way around. I was briefly married to a man who used to come home at night and abuse me. He would torment me physically, emotionally, and sexually. Finally I left him. I have seen all kinds of men treat their wives in all kinds of different ways. Where I work, men come in all the time and talk degradingly about their wives. Their wives are supposed to be the women they love, but instead they just belittle them. There are only a few who talk lovingly about their spouses. I think those women are lucky.

I know what Peter did to you was inexcusable and nothing he can do may ever make up for it, but you have to believe that he loves you deeply. You can see it in his eyes when he talks about you. And when it came down for Peter to decide between you or me, I knew deep down you would win. You have always been the winner. Forgive him.

To have someone who truly loves you is rare. If nothing else, you have at least that. Why did he do what he did? We all make mistakes. And we all, I hope, have the capacity to forgive. If I didn't believe what I am telling you, I wouldn't be telling it to you.

Like I said, I don't hate you. Now I hope you can find it in your heart not to hate me. I owe you an enormous apology. What I did was terrible, but can you blame me? You have someone special. Someone who loves you very much. I hope you can see that. Diane, you won. Please don't lose now by default. Losing is the worst pain.

Terri

Diane folded the letter and put it back in the envelope.

She looked at the envelope.

"You little cunt," she said.

Then she said, "Bless you. Bless you."

31

It was growing dark outside when Sam got back to the office.

Pinchus asked, "How did Zimmer take the news? Is he still on this planet?"

"Actually, he surprised me," Sam said. "He was very calm. What I did was I told him I wanted him to know that personally I didn't suspect him at all. It was just that the quickest, best way to clear his name was to do this. He consented. He also gave me a list he'd drawn up of people who'd seen him at the party Monday night, and two signed statements from friends who swear they were with him practically every minute till he left at midnight."

Sam gave the documents to Pinchus, who scanned them. "Doth he protest too much, you think?" asked Pinchus.

"Nah. I think he's just very earnest and very shaken. Collins should be bringing him over to Roberts's office about now. She'll call after she's ferried the last of them."

"Good." Pinchus looked at his watch. "What do you say we get dinner?"

Sam was agreeable. They ate Italian, were back in the office at seven-thirty.

Collins hadn't called yet.

Pinchus unwrapped the portion of the piece of apple pie from Sanford's that Sam hadn't eaten earlier. He got a plastic fork out of his drawer.

"If Daniel's taking you out to dinner this weekend, how are you going to start your new diet?"

Pinchus swallowed, cut off another forkful. "He can't afford very much. I'm destined to eat light."

Pinchus's phone rang. He shoved the pie aside, picked up the receiver. "Detective Pinchus."

"Hi, Seymour." It was Kate.

For an instant, Pinchus was disappointed. But then he was happy. "Hi, Kate."

Sam gave him a thumbs-up sign, went and busied himself elsewhere.

"How are you guys doing?" Kate asked.

"Okay. We're waiting to hear that everybody's had an impression taken. Peter agreed to stay late and do the comparisons tonight. He wasn't happy about that at all, but I pushed him. With any luck, we'll have our man in a couple of hours."

"I hope you do—for your sake and the girl's sake. Mostly I just wanted to check in, and to tell you I was happy you were here last night."

"Thank you. I was, too."

"If we can take things slow, I'd like to do it again. Soon."

"We can take them slow. Slow as you want."

"That's probably slower than *you* want, but faster than you think *I* want."

Pinchus laughed.

"Call me tomorrow?" she asked.

"Yes."

It was easier for Pinchus to wait after he had talked with Kate. For a while, he followed his breath, meditating. But then he began to grow impatient again.

Officer Collins showed up at eight-thirty.

"Ooops," she said. "From the looks of you two, I guess I should have called. Sorry."

"It's okay," Pinchus said. "All finished?"

"Yes. Hawthorne was the last one. I had to pick him up after a class. He wasn't a happy man."

"Tough," Pinchus quickly replied.

"I don't think he likes his women to wear guns," Sam suggested.

Collins said, "Dr. Roberts estimates it will take at least another hour and probably a bit more till he knows whether there's a match. He wears a weird cologne, you know? Smells just like orange juice."

"Never noticed." Pinchus shrugged. "Listen, Collins. Thank you for everything you did today. I know you put in a long one."

Collins smiled. "You're welcome."

Collins left. Pinchus told Sam he might as well go home; there was no sense both of them hanging around.

"Not on your life," Sam said.

The time passed slowly. By ten, Peter still hadn't called. By ten-fifteen, Sam was asleep in his chair. He began to snore. Finally, at ten-forty, the phone rang. Pinchus snatched it up.

Across from him, Sam woke. He stretched, yawned, blinked at Pinchus. Pinchus spoke briefly. He said good-bye and set the receiver back down.

"You're smiling," Sam noted.

"Yes, I am." Pinchus said, "I am smiling because I just found out who killed Alice Schaeffer."

PART
THREE

32

Lieutenant Seymour Pinchus and Sergeant Sam Milano sped through the night in Pinchus's Oldsmobile, followed by two patrol cars.

"I can't believe I have to buy you dinner again," Sam said. "I would've bet anything it was Tony."

"You did bet," Pinchus reminded him. "A meal."

"With you, that's tantamount to anything."

"I'll be on my diet. You'll get off easy."

Pinchus turned off Decker onto Sixth Street. A moment later, he slowed, involuntarily, as they passed the building in which Alice Schaeffer had lived.

Sam noticed, glanced over at the building. "Hard to believe this all began only forty-eight hours ago."

"Seems like a month," Pinchus said.

The Schaeffers had taken Alice's body back home with them this afternoon.

"You going to go to the service?" Sam asked.

The Schaeffers lived three hours away.

"No. I said my good-byes already."

Pinchus turned again, onto the university campus. The patrol cars followed. No flashing lights, Pinchus had said. No sirens. He didn't want to alert his prey.

Sam leaned forward, turned to Pinchus. "We've been working together what, six years now?"

"About that. Why, had enough?"

"No. I'm serious. I want to ask. . . . You ever get nervous just before you bust a perp?"

"Ever? Always. I'm nervous right now."

"Me too. I get nervous every time."

"I think it would be weird if you didn't. We deal

with people who kill people. I wonder how the bust will go down. Nice and easy? Or is this maybe . . . is this maybe the time I buy it."

"Seymour, you are never going to buy it. You, despite your annual prediction of imminent demise, are going to live to be a grumpy old man who sits around complaining that nobody brings his grandchildren to visit him enough."

"You arrange that, I'll be grateful."

Pinchus parked in the lot behind Lincoln Dormitory. The patrol cars pulled in alongside. Pinchus assigned one officer to the rear entrance of the building, another to the side entrance—which gave access to the basement—and a third to the front. Then he and Sam went in and climbed up to the fourth floor, followed by the remaining uniform.

At the fourth-floor landing, they started down the hall. While they were still several feet away, the door to the Harpers's room opened and Barry Harper stepped into the corridor. He turned back to lock the door without noticing them.

Pinchus lunged and seized Barry from behind, clamped a hand over his mouth and pulled him back from the door. Sam and the patrolman had their guns out.

Barry's eyes were wide with fear.

"No one's going to hurt you, Barry," Pinchus said in a low voice. "This is Lieutenant Pinchus. Is David in there?"

Barry shook his head no.

"Check it," Pinchus said to Sam, pulling Barry out of a possible line of fire.

Sam and the patrolman positioned themselves on either side of the door. Sam nodded. They burst through the door into the room.

"Police!" Pinchus heard Sam yell. "David Harper, if you're in here, announce your location and stand with your hands over your head! Fuck with us, we're going to blow your fucking brains all over the wall!"

Pinchus heard Sam and the patrolman banging open doors. Two minutes later, they emerged, holstering their weapons.

"Not there," Sam shrugged.

Pinchus released Barry.

"Oh my God!" Barry cried. "Oh my God! What's *happening*?"

Pinchus said, "We have reason to believe David killed Alice Schaeffer."

"No!" Barry shouted. "David wouldn't do anything like that! He *couldn't* do anything like that!"

"Either way, we have to talk to him. It would be in both your best interests if you tell us where he is."

"Believe me, I understand that, but I have no idea where he is. Honest!"

"If you withhold information," Pinchus warned, "I can charge you with everything from aiding a fugitive to complicity in first-degree murder. And, son, I will."

"I'm telling you the *truth*," Barry said tearfully.

"Take him inside," Pinchus told Sam. "Get names, addresses, phone numbers from him. Any place David might be. And toss the place, see what you can find. I'm going to check the basement."

Pinchus went to the first floor. He drew his gun, started down the basement stairs. He was breathing too hard . . . excitement, the climb up. When he reached the bottom, he paused, listening, trying to let his breathing stabilize and his pulse rate fall. He heard a little noise from the game room, but he couldn't tell if someone was in there playing one of the games.

He moved forward cautiously, reached the entrance, and peered around the corner into the room. The video games were chattering and *boink*ing, the pinball machines clicking, lights flashing. But no one was there.

Pinchus walked into the room, gun in hand, and looked around. He noted the last scores that had been registered on the games. Three were phenomenally high, including Rocket Express.

Pinchus did not doubt that David had been here, and recently. The question was, How recently?

Pinchus cleared his mind—emptied it—as best he could. Then he began to walk slowly around the room, trying to be a tabula rasa, trying simply to notice.

Nothing seemed out of the ordinary. There were two small windows in the room, set high, but they were both locked. In midcircuit, directly across from one of the windows, Pinchus stopped. He looked at the grille of a wall vent. The vent was at floor level, between two pinball machines. Something was not quite right about the grille. He stepped over to it, knelt, down, and examined it. The grille wasn't sitting quite flush into its housing. He grasped it, shifted it without resistance.

The vent opening was large enough for a man to climb into. Pinchus shined his Mini-Mag into it. The ducting branched right and left. To the right, the dust on the walls and floor had been heavily disturbed for the few feet Pinchus could see before the ducting slanted away. To the left, the dust was unmarked.

Pinchus took off his jacket and shoulder holster and hung them on the joy stick of a video game. He went to his hands and knees and inserted his head and shoulders into the duct. Then he crawled in, angling to the right.

He held his gun and the Mini-Mag out in front of himself, but kept the flashlight off for now. He didn't want to give away his position. He would flick it on again after he rounded the bend that was only a few feet ahead, the gun in his right hand beside it, the weapon's hammer cocked back, his finger on the trigger ready to fire.

The duct was barely large enough to accommodate him. He pulled himself forward with his elbows, pushed with his knees. The sheet-metal panels made popping noises as he strained forward. He didn't like that. He began to sweat. He could feel dust caking onto his damp face and hands. Displaced particles of dust swirled in the air. They stung his eyes, tickled his nose and throat; he had to fight the need to sneeze. He was sweating heavily now. It seemed that the duct work was growing tighter. Imagination, he told himself. Nevertheless, it was harder and harder for him to move forward. His breath was coming with difficulty. Explosively, he coughed. Then again, and again.

Fear seized him. He couldn't move forward, he couldn't move backward. He grew claustrophobic. With effort, he took hold of himself. He throttled his panic; but knew he had only tentative control over it.

He was partway into the bend. He had no idea how far it stretched out before him, but he needed to know, needed to be able to see. He held his weapon tighter, took in a breath, exhaled half of it, paused an infinitesimal moment, then flicked on the Mini-Mag. The duct stretched ahead perhaps a dozen feet before it turned again. It was empty. But there was something more that Pinchus saw that astonished him: The dust on the floor and walls ahead of him was undisturbed.

He lay there, confused. Then it hit him: Either David had run into the same difficulty he had, and had turned back—or the sonofabitch had set him up. Pinchus shuddered as he imagined a gloating David poking his head and arm into the vent behind him, a gun in David's hand, and anticipated the shock of a bullet striking him from behind.

Not gonna happen, Pinchus told himself. That's not what he wants.

Keeping a careful grip on his panic, breathing with great painful gasps, Pinchus began squeezing backward. He flexed muscles, pushed with his elbows, tried to pull with the toes of his shoes. He gained precious little inches and half inches at a time, then had to rest, then forced his nearly exhausted body into one more effort. Blood was pounding in his ears. Dust-laden sweat stung his eyes, ran down his cheeks. His breathing was ragged, hoarse.

The flood of sweat from his body began to act as

a lubricant. He struggled backward. And then his feet were free . . . his calves . . . and he pushed, gasping . . . and his lower torso was out . . . and he scraped wildly with his shoes, pushed with his elbows, ground his teeth against each other . . . and then he was out completely.

Gasping, he rolled onto his back. He stared up at the ceiling, fighting for breath. The floor tiles were cool against the wetness of his back. Slowly, he pushed himself to a half sit. He was weak. His arms were trembling.

"Jesus Christ!" said Sam Milano, appearing at the entrance to the room. He rushed forward and dropped to one knee, propped Pinchus up. "Jesus, Seymour! What happened? You look like shit!"

"You make . . . a fine . . . detective," Pinchus managed. "Because I feel . . . like . . . shi—"

And then he slumped back in Sam's arms, unconscious.

33

Thursday morning, Peter
Roberts woke at dawn. He felt as good as he'd ever
felt. Beside him, Diane slept. The children weren't up
yet. Peter got out of bed carefully, so as not to waken
Diane. He stood looking down at her, love for her
welling up so strongly in him that tears filled his eyes.

He slipped on jeans and a sweatshirt and went
downstairs. He brewed coffee. He mixed orange juice
and set bacon and eggs out, ready to start making
breakfast for his family when they awoke. He sat in
the breakfast nook sipping coffee and looking out at
the way the early morning sun lit up the trees outside.

He was completely happy.

Last night, he had called Diane to say that
Seymour was pressing him to remain in the office until
he made models of the suspects' teeth from the impressions he'd taken and compared them with the bite
marks on Alice Schaeffer. He had apologized profusely,
said he would be home as soon as he could.

Diane had listened in silence. She had said only,
"Good night, Peter," and then hung up.

When Peter had finally called Seymour and given
him David Harper's name, he had felt powerful,
unconquerable—*he*, Peter Roberts, had done this; *he*
had told them who the murderer was; *he* would give
them proof. And David Harper would stand trial for
the murder of Alice Schaeffer, be found guilty, sen-
tenced to prison, and the case would be closed.

Peter had felt exalted.

He had hurried home. His spirits were soaring

despite the anxiety he felt about Diane. Actually, the threat of losing her had sparked great desire for her in him. Which, coupled with his elation over the night's work, made him feel aroused: He wanted Diane. He wanted her more than he had ever wanted her.

But he did not know how she would react. For the first time in thirteen years, he was unsure of her.

And because of that, the thrill was back.

The house was dark when Peter pulled into his driveway. The night-lights on either side of the front door were lit but nothing else was. Peter parked in front of the garage, didn't bother putting the car into it. Inside the house, he locked the door behind himself, then went quietly upstairs. He undressed in the quasi-darkness of his bedroom, got into bed next to Diane. She was sleeping on her side, facing away from him.

Propped on one elbow, he leaned over and kissed her lightly on the cheek. "I'm home," he whispered.

"Congratulations," she said.

"Diane, I love you."

"You bastard." She sat up. "How dare you just come in here like nothing happened. You've got some goddamn nerve."

"I'll make it up to you. I promise."

She spit into his face. "Bastard."

He flinched.

She raised her arm, swung her hand down, and slapped him hard. He caught her wrist before she could hit him again, caught her other wrist when she tried with that hand. She spit at him again.

"Diane!" he shouted. "Stop it!"

She spat a third time.

"Please," he cried. "I love you."

He tried to kiss her. She twisted her head away. He was very aroused. For an instant, he considered taking her by force. But he didn't.

"All right." He released her. "Do whatever you want."

She hit him with her palm, hit him with a backswing on the other cheek. She kept hitting him, saying, "Bastard . . . bastard" with each blow. And kept hitting him, and cursing him, until her arm grew too weary for her to use anymore.

She collapsed against his chest and began to weep. He held her as she sobbed, saying nothing. In time, she stopped crying. They remained that way, neither speaking.

Suddenly she lunged up. She pushed Peter backward onto the bed. She flung herself atop him, hands holding his face, a thigh going between his legs, her mouth crushing down on his, her tongue thrusting into his mouth.

They made ferocious love.

Afterward, they lay in silence, she holding his hand. In a while, looking up at the ceiling rather than at him, she said, "You're really very sure of yourself, aren't you?"

"No. Not really."

"You hurt me badly, Peter."

"I know. I'm so sorry. I was afraid today that I was going to lose you."

She said nothing.

"Why didn't I?" he asked.

"Let's just say that I didn't want to lose by default."

"I don't understand that."

"You don't have to." She let go of his hand, reached down and took his penis gently into her hand. "I love you, Peter," she said.

He hugged her. "I love you."

"And if you ever do that again, I'll cut your dick off."

And now it was morning. Peter Roberts had a beautiful wife. He had two terrific children. He had a wonderful house. He was a happy man.

Peter glanced at his watch, went and got the paper from the front porch. He brought it back to the kitchen, poured another cup of coffee, and started to sit down with the paper in the breakfast nook. The phone rang, startling him. He went to the counter and answered.

"Hello," he said cheerfully.

"Hello, is this Dr. Roberts?"

"Yes, it is. Who is this, please?"

"Dr. Roberts, this is David Harper."

Peter nearly dropped the phone. He thought David Harper would have been arrested last night.

"Hello?" said the voice at the other end. "I said, this is David Harper. You know—the guy you identified as killing Alice Schaeffer."

Peter's mouth was suddenly dry. He'd become short of breath. "What do you want?"

"You made a mistake," David said with irritation. "You simply made a fucking mistake. And I'd like to know how you could goddamn do that."

"David," Peter said, keeping his voice as even as he could, "there was no mistake. I was extremely careful in making the comparisons."

"Well, something went wrong. Maybe you mixed up your impressions. I can't see how you could have matched my teeth to the bite marks on Alice Schaeffer. I didn't *touch* that woman. I *swear* to you." David's voice turned almost pleading. "Please, will you look over everything again? Somehow you've made a mistake!"

"There was no mistake, David. I'm sorry, but there wasn't. David, I'm not the person you should be talking to. Call Lieutenant Seymour Pinchus. He's the detective in charge of this case. I'm sure the police are looking for you even right now while we're talking."

"I'm sure they are, too," David said dryly. "But it's not your ass on the line, it's mine. And there is no way I am turning myself in so long as you're standing by what you told them."

"Look. Maybe I did make a mistake. Where are you? I'll come over and talk to you about it."

"What do you take me for?" David shouted. "A fucking idiot?"

"No. Not at all," Peter quickly answered. "I'm sorry. I know you're upset. I just think that if we could all sit down together—you, me, the police—we could sort this out. If for some reason a mistake was made, we'll discover what that is and how it was made."

There was a moment of silence. Then David screamed, "Dr. Roberts, go fuck yourself!"

The connection was broken. A dial tone sounded in Peter's ear. His hand was shaking when he replaced the receiver. Peter was certain that the impressions he'd taken and the comparisons he'd made would convince anyone of David Harper's guilt. Still, David was convincing. He sounded credible. Peter became nervous. Would David be able to persuade others? Would Peter's work now be questioned? He had checked and re-checked. The match was perfect; he'd made certain of that. But as sure as he'd been of himself, he now felt an inkling of doubt—an experience that was unfamiliar to him.

"Hi, Dad." Melanie appeared in the kitchen. She was wearing slippers and a bathrobe.

"Hi, cutie pie."

"Wow, you're up early today."

"Yes, I am."

For the first time this morning, Peter wished that he was not. He wished that he was asleep and that David Harper was behind bars.

"Morning, love," Diane called from the top of the stairs. "If that was Seymour wanting you to do something, I'm going to kill him myself."

"No," Peter called back. "It wasn't. It was a wrong number."

34

"Seymour," Sam Milano bellowed when Pinchus walked into the squad room Thursday morning, "what the hell are you doing here? The doctor told you to rest. Man, we thought you'd had a heart attack last night."

"Aha, but I did not," Pinchus said. "And it's eleven o'clock. I've rested enough. Anyway, he said rest, not retire. David Harper is still loose, and they're holding a service for Alice Schaeffer tomorrow. You think I can just sit at home?"

"I guess not," Sam said with resignation. "But promise—no more crawling into air ducts."

"I am capable of learning from experience."

"Good. Listen: Remember you asked me to tell you if I thought you were getting out of line on this case?"

"Don't say it, Sam."

"I have to. You're emotionally involved, Seymour."

"Bullshit. Nothing I've done or said has tainted the facts."

"I know. But I think what's happening is that it's affecting your judgment."

"Show me."

Sam shrugged.

"It's just another case."

"Are you sure?"

"Positive."

"If you say so. You got three calls from Peter Roberts this morning."

"What'd he want?"

"I don't know. Said he'd only speak to you. The

last time, I told him you might not be in today. He said he'd stop by around lunchtime. If you weren't here, he'd talk to me."

"Shit, I hope it's nothing that screws us up."

"I don't know," Sam said. "Oh, by the way ... Mark Donaldson's alibi checks out. He called earlier and came clean with me, not that it matters much now. I think you really scared him. Seems he spent the time with a Fran Carter."

"Does she substantiate that?"

"*He* does. Fran's a guy. Turns out Mark Donaldson is a closet bisexual."

"Jesus."

"No, just Mark and Fran, so far as I know."

"No wonder he was reluctant. Anything else happen?"

"Barry Harper's coming in at one-thirty for additional questioning. Schwenk wants you in his office as soon as you get in. That is, if you get in today."

"Fuck Schwenk. I solve ten cases and he never wants to speak to me. We go for a simple arrest and come up empty-handed, and all of a sudden he wants to talk to his Jew."

"Take it easy, Seymour. The doctor—"

"Fuck the doctor *and* Schwenk," Pinchus fired back. He breathed. After a few moments, he said, "Sorry. It's been a long couple of days."

"No problem. Where do we go from here?"

Pinchus sat down. He put his feet up.

"We're dealing with what some people call a genius or near-genius mentality," he said. "That bothers me—that David Harper might be smarter than we are. If he is, what we need in order to level the playing field is information about him, a lot of it. We know some things, but not enough. Get in touch with the police in his hometown. Tell them what's happening. Tell them David might try to go back there. And tell 'em we need everything about him they can get—school records, if he was ever institutionalized, stuff like that. Anything, everything."

"Right." Sam wrote in his notebook.

"Talk to his mother. Also, I want all the facts associated with his father's death and with the murder of Barry's parents. Maybe we can learn something useful. Get the newspaper clips. So far as right now goes, we know David is a compulsive video- and pinball-game player. Get people out to the arcades, bars, hangout joints, anyplace there's more than one or two of those things."

Sam nodded. "I sent people to the university to canvass friends, instructors, anyone who was in a class with him."

"Good."

"Got one more thing: Collins turned up two witnesses who claim they saw David on Alice's block within an hour of her murder."

"Nice. We have him in another lie—he said he was at Market Square. How'd Collins find the witnesses?"

"She got a list of names of people who'd been in the laundromat that night from the owner. She's been showing them David's picture."

"Good cop, that Collins," Pinchus admitted. "Very nice work."

"I told her that."

"Good."

"I think she'd like to hear it from you, too."

"Right." Pinchus wrote himself a note. Then he said, "I want everything we've got collected into a master file. Everything: autopsy report, evidence list, suspects' statements, the whole *schmear*."

"Already done. You know, this guy may be a genius, Seymour, but he's still a *goyisher kop*. Don't worry. You'll get him."

Pinchus laughed. "What is this? The older people get, the more Jewish they become. I'm convinced of it." He stretched. "Except for Schwenk. Maybe it's time to see him now."

"Don't lose your cool," Sam warned.

Pinchus nodded. He went out of the squad room and down the hall to the captain's office, knocked on the glass window of the door.

Schwenk looked up. Through the open blinds, he motioned Pinchus in.

Pinchus opened the door. "You wanted to see me, Captain?"

"Yes. Come in. Have a seat." Schwenk waited for Pinchus to close the door and sit. "I understand things went pretty wrong last night."

"I wouldn't put it that way," Pinchus disagreed.

"I would. You go cowboying for glory without backup, crawl into an air duct, and nearly kill yourself. You're not getting any younger. You need to lose weight, get in shape."

"You're right. I'll start a diet tomorrow and work out an exercise plan."

Schwenk examined Pinchus's face to see if the detective was putting him on. He couldn't tell. "Fine. Do that. Meanwhile, you still lost a suspect."

"Not because I got stuck."

"How else?"

"I don't know. But I do know he didn't get out through the duct. His trail stopped just about where I did. I don't think he even tried to get out that way. I think he was fucking with me."

"And doing a good job of it."

"Look, Alex—"

"*Captain.* Captain Schwenk."

"Look, *Captain.* We went to pick up a suspect and he wasn't there. It happens all the time. We handled the situation just like we handle every other situation like that."

"So you say."

"So I say."

"Why didn't you put someone on Harper the minute you suspected him?"

"We had five other suspects as well. Trailing six

suspects twenty-four hours a day would require eighteen men working continuous eight-hour shifts. We don't have the manpower for that."

"It didn't take more than half a brain to see that David Harper was the most likely candidate. You could have at least kept *him* under surveillance. I don't know why you didn't see that. It was obvious."

"I guess I'm just not the fucking whiz you are," Pinchus snapped.

"I'm going to overlook that remark, Lieutenant. I know it was said out of frustration. It's hard to take criticism well. But the truth is, you've muffed this one from the start. I'm watching you. One more blunder like this, I'm afraid I'll have to take you off the case."

Never in his entire career had Pinchus been removed from a case. Schwenk had seen an opportunity to embarrass him and was taking it. Pinchus had to get out of Schwenk's office before he lost control.

"Will that be all . . . Captain?"

"For now," Schwenk replied sharply.

Pinchus got out of his chair, fantasizing about picking it up and throwing it at Schwenk, and went back to his desk.

Sam raised his eyebrows.

"You really want to know?" Pinchus said. "Fine, it went simply fine. Schwenk wanted to compliment us on the wonderful job we're doing on the Schaeffer case. He is amazed at the progress we have made. He wanted to know if he could follow us around and pick up a few tips. I told him we were much too busy to have him standing over our shoulders, but, so he wouldn't feel bad, I invited him for lunch on Tuesday. I hope you don't mind."

"That bad, huh?"

"That bad."

For the next half-hour, Pinchus engrossed himself in the master file Sam had created.

Peter Roberts appeared a little after twelve-thirty.

He looked relieved to see Seymour. "Can we go somewhere private?" he asked.

Pinchus took him into an empty interrogation room. They sat at the table.

"I'm glad you're here. I would have told this to Sam if I'd had to, but I'm more comfortable telling it to you."

"Go ahead."

"David Harper called me this morning."

Pinchus took out a notebook and pen. "This morning?"

"Yes. About seven. He said I made a mistake with the comparisons. He said he never touched Alice Schaeffer."

"And?"

"That was about it. He was angry at first, then kind of hysterical at the end."

"Did he say where he was calling from?"

"No."

"Could you hear anything in the background? Noises? Bells? Conversation? Anything like that?"

"No. I tried to get him to tell me where he was, but he wouldn't." Peter fidgeted.

Pinchus waited.

"He was pretty convincing. He *insisted* that I had made a mistake, that I'd mixed up the models or something. And . . ."

"And now you wonder if he was right," Pinchus said.

"Yes. I went to the office this morning and checked everything. It comes out the same way. But maybe I *did* mess up somehow."

"Peter, it's natural to second-guess yourself in something this important. Were you careful with all your procedures? Did you base your conclusion on fact that was unprejudiced and dependent on scientific knowledge?"

"Yes."

"Then don't let this guy get to you. Prisons are full

of people who swear they never committed the crime they were put away for. Hang on to your confidence. Your evaluation was correct. Believe me, I know."

"How? Don't get me wrong—I still think I did everything right—but he was *so* convincing. I can't help but feel some doubt."

"If it helps you to know this, there's other evidence pointing to him, too, including two eyewitnesses who place him near Alice Schaeffer's apartment the night she was killed. He's lied before, he's lying now. What I'm *more* concerned about is the fact that he called you. If he contacts you again, call me immediately. Day or night. I mean that." Pinchus thought for a moment. "If it's late, and I'm not home, try me at Kate's." He wrote down Kate's number.

"Do you think he will?" Peter said, alarmed. "He hung up on me this morning."

"Probably not. But get to me right away if he does."

"I will. Thank you, Seymour."

"Thank *you*, Peter."

They shook hands. Pinchus saw Peter out.

Back at his desk, Pinchus filled Sam in.

"Why would he call Peter?" Sam wondered. "I don't get it."

"Me neither."

"Unless he *isn't* the killer?"

"What do you think?" Pinchus asked.

"I don't know what I think right now. Why's he running if he didn't do her?"

"It doesn't make a lot of sense," Pinchus said.

"He's probably still in town. He could have called long distance, but I don't think he did."

"Feels that way to me, too."

Pinchus turned back to the folder. But he couldn't keep his attention on it. He was thinking of Peter Roberts. Sam had said yesterday that Peter was in an awfully powerful position. Peter claimed not to have remembered that Alice had been a patient. Leaning on his elbow, chin resting on his palm, Pinchus looked down at the evidence file on his desk without really seeing it. He was replaying comments, scenes, memories of Peter Roberts from the thirteen years he had known him.

35

Barry Harper arrived late for his appointment. He was lethargic, depressed. Sam got him a cup of coffee. Then Pinchus and Sam took him into an interrogation room.

As soon as they sat down, Pinchus leaned forward, put his elbows on the table, and said, "When did you talk to him, Barry?"

Barry was startled. "What? Who?"

"David."

"This morning. He called early." Barry sank back into his malaise.

"What did he say?"

"He wanted to know what happened last night, what you said to me."

"And you told him."

"Yes."

"What did he say to that?"

"That he hadn't had anything to do with Alice Schaeffer's murder."

"Where was he calling from?"

"I don't know."

"Where he is now?"

Barry shook his head, slowly. "I don't know."

"Where is he going?"

"I don't know."

"Barry, why the fuck didn't you call us?"

Barry blinked a couple of times. "I fell back to sleep. I only woke up about forty minutes ago. I was going to tell you now."

Pinchus asked Barry to go over again his activities

and David's on Monday night. Barry seemed to have difficulty concentrating, but point for point, what he said matched his original statement.

"That's not how David tells it," Pinchus said. He read David's statement to Barry.

Barry shook his head. "No. I never gave David any message about someone finding his wallet and meeting him at Market Square. I never *got* a message like that." He reasserted that he had stayed in his room to study, hadn't left it even once, and that he had fallen asleep over his books and hadn't seen David until later, when David had awakened him.

"Did you and David discuss Alice Schaeffer's murder after you learned of it?" Pinchus asked.

"No. Well, a little."

"What did David say about it?"

"Just something like, it was too bad."

"That's it? Nothing else?"

Barry knitted his brows. "He asked if I thought the police would catch the guy who did it."

"And what did you say?"

"I said I didn't know. Then I asked him what he thought. And he said, 'No. The police are stupid.' Or something like that. Then he said . . . he said, 'But maybe they'll get lucky after the next one.' "

Pinchus and Sam glanced at each other.

"'After the next one?' Those were his exact words?" Pinchus asked.

"Yes. He said murders like that were always part of a chain."

"Barry," Pinchus said pointedly, "do *you* think David killed Alice Schaeffer?"

Barry's lips trembled. He began to cry. He hung his head down.

Pinchus put a hand on his shoulder. "It's okay, Barry. It's okay to cry. This is hard stuff for everybody. I'll call someone to take you home."

A uniform came and escorted Barry out of the station house.

When Barry was gone, Pinchus declared: "We better find this motherfucker fast, Sam."

Working with phone books, Pinchus and Sam drew up a list of arcades and places like the Kensington Mall that had video games and pinball machines. There weren't many. It was the *bars* that were the unknown quantity and that would consume the time. No way to tell which bars had them, which didn't. They got another detective and two uniforms to help. Pinchus reasoned that the farther from the school a site was, the more likely David would be to chance showing his face. So he directed his team to start on the very outskirts of town and work their way in toward the center, where the university was. It was a long shot, but all there was for now.

By four o'clock, Pinchus was exhausted. The strain of the previous night had caught up with him. He'd been working the Boundary Street neighborhood on foot, his car parked four blocks away. Boundary Street was an old warehouse and shipping area near the river that had been gentrified a dozen years ago. Signs taped up on streetlights announced that the sixth annual Festival of Clowns would be held over the weekend, commencing Friday at noon. He wanted to stop at Lincoln Dorm before he went home, so he decided to make the bar at the end of this block, the Slaughtered Lamb, the last one of the day

The Slaughtered Lamb had a kind of mock old English decor. Although it was only midafternoon, there were already a couple of singles at the bar bantering with each other.

A bartender with freckles and a riot of natural red hair came over to him. "What can I do you for?" she asked.

Pinchus identified himself. "Do you have a game room here or any video games or pinball machines?"

She cocked her head toward her left. "Half a dozen

of 'em. In a little room past the booths there. None of them are gambling games, though."

"Not interested in that." Pinchus showed her a picture of David. "Have you seen this person? Yesterday, maybe today?"

"Nope. But he's kind of cute. What'd he do?"

"Let's just say I don't think he's your type."

"What is my type?"

"Me. I think maybe I'm your type. Around the station, they call me the Tiger."

The bartender winked. "You think you have what it takes to leave me breathless, Tiger?"

"Sadly, probably not."

She laughed. "I don't know, you look pretty deep to me. Listen, I just came on, but Norm is one of our regulars. He was here late last night, and I think he's been here again since noon. Norm?"

A thirtyish man with carefully cut hair and tinted aviator-frame glasses detached himself from a leggy woman down the bar and came over to them.

"Ever see this guy in here?" Pinchus asked. "Maybe in the game room?"

Norm studied the picture. "Sorry. Can't say that I have. Then again, I don't go in there much. I'm usually at the bar."

"You spend a lot of time here?" Pinchus asked.

"Pretty much."

Pinchus gave Norm and the bartender a card. "If you spot him, I'd appreciate your giving me a call."

Before he left, Pinchus went into the game room. Two games showed exceptionally high scores—Rocket Express and Mind Freaker. He made a mental note to stop by this bar again.

Pinchus went back to his car. He drove to the university. He parked in front of Lincoln Dorm and sat looking at the building, studying it. A portion of the basement windows, which were reinforced with wiremesh, projected above grade level. Pinchus got out of his car. He walked over to one of the windows and squatted on his heels in front of the wall. He leaned forward, bracing himself with a hand, and looked in. From a certain angle he could see the grille covering the ventilating duct he'd crawled into last night. He shifted back around and followed that line of sight up to the roof of the four-story dormitory building across the street.

There was someone on the roof. The figure moved. Pinchus saw then that it was not one person, but a couple who had been embracing.

Pinchus stood up. His knees cracked and popped. He went across the street, entered the dorm and started up the stairs to the roof. Between the third and fourth floors, the couple he had seen passed him on their way down, laughing and holding hands. The girl looked a little like Alice Schaeffer. She was spirited too, as Alice had been. Pinchus smiled at them. They smiled back.

There were lawn chairs and lounges on the roof, a redwood table with attached benches, a charcoal grill. Pinchus had the roof to himself. He walked parallel to the wall until he was directly opposite the game room. Across the street, the window. He crouched, squinted. In the gathering twilight, someone had turned the lights on in the room. Two girls were standing at one of the games, one of them playing. To the side of her, Pinchus could see the grille that covered the ventilation duct at the base of the wall.

Had David Harper been standing here last night, he would have had a clear view of Pinchus making a fool of himself. Pinchus became embarrassed, angry. He didn't *know* that was what had happened, but he felt it was possible, maybe even likely: David would have wanted to find a way to enjoy his little triumph.

Pinchus got out his Mini-Mag and played the light over the surface of the roof around himself; a gum wrapper, a penny, a burnt match, and something else—a little circular brass pin. Pinchus bent and retrieved it. It was a tie tack. On its face were the initials *DH*.

36

On the drive home, Pinchus concluded that David had not left the tie tack as a goad to him, but rather had lost it there—if indeed the tack *was* his, which was by no means certain. The possibility that Pinchus would have found the tack was remote; the possibility that David would have anticipated him finding it, even more so.

Pinchus decided to put the case out of mind until tomorrow. He wasn't thinking well now. He just wanted to get home, eat something, call Kate, then soak in a tub of hot water and go to sleep.

Turning onto Elmont Street, where he lived, Pinchus spied a tan Dodge parked in his driveway. There were also lights on behind the living room curtains. Pinchus drove by his house without slowing, pulled to the curb two hundred feet beyond, cut the lights, and shut off the engine.

He got out and walked back to his house, keeping to the shadows. He drew his pistol, stepped quietly to the porch and edged toward the door. He listened. Nothing. He tried the knob. The door wasn't locked.

Pinchus readied himself. He was about to fling the door open and burst in when he heard a voice he recognized and an answering female laugh. He checked himself, took a breath, then another. He put his gun back in its holster. He opened the door and went in. Daniel was emerging from the kitchen, with a cup of coffee in his hand. A young woman in tan jeans and a black cotton sweater was sitting on the couch.

"Daniel!" Pinchus roared. "I thought you weren't coming until tomorrow."

The girl stood up, offering a tentative smile. Daniel went to her side and took her hand. She was pretty, had short hair, dimples, and big brown eyes.

"Dad, I want you to meet Susan."

"A pleasure, Susan."

"I'm pleased to meet you, Mr. Pinchus."

Susan reached out her hand. Pinchus didn't think he would ever get used to women offering to shake hands with men when they were introduced. But he took her hand and shook it warmly anyway.

"Seymour," he said.

"Seymour."

"So, Daniel, to what do I owe the pleasure of your early arrival?"

"We just felt like it," Daniel replied. "I hope you don't mind."

"Bullshit, you felt like it."

"My father tends to be blunt," Daniel told Susan.

Daniel was Pinchus's height, but leaner, had his father's strong jaw.

"I prefer the word *direct*," Pinchus corrected.

"Okay. I was worried about you," Daniel admitted. "I heard what happened last night."

"Sam. He called you."

"He did the right thing."

"He should mind his own business."

"Well, Dad, bluntly—or directly, to use your word—you do look pretty run-down."

"I am fine. The doctor said I am fine." Pinchus went to the sideboard, poured himself a bourbon neat. "And speaking of doctors . . ." He gestured in the direction of Susan's belly.

Susan blushed, but then, before Daniel could speak, she said, "You're going to be a grandfather . . . Seymour."

"*Mazel tov!*" Pinchus walked over to the girl, took

her face in his hands, and kissed her on the forehead. "That means congratulations."

"I know."

"You don't look Jewish."

"I'm not."

"So is this son of mine treating you all right?"

"I'm going to make an honest woman out of her," Daniel announced.

"That's nice. It would certainly be something if she remained a dishonest woman, involved with two cops."

Susan laughed.

"When?" Pinchus asked.

"End of next month," Daniel answered. "We figured we'd pick the exact date while we were down here with you."

"Good boy. Good imminent daughter-in-law. So tell me, have you told your mother yet?"

"Not really," Daniel said tentatively.

"What does that mean, 'not really?'"

"It means she doesn't even know I've been seeing Susan. We decided we'd practice on you, as a kind of test."

"I guess I passed. But when your mother hears, *oy vey*!"

"You don't think she'll take it so well, huh?"

"I think she'll take it this way: When she finds out that you've been living with a girl, she'll bite down hard on her lower lip but say, 'All right, Daniel's a big boy now.' When she finds out you got this girl pregnant, she'll collapse into a chair and moan, 'I can't believe you did this to me.' And when you tell her Susan isn't Jewish, she'll stick her head in the oven."

"But will she come to the wedding?" Daniel asked seriously.

"Hey, she survived your cousin Diane marrying Peter," Pinchus pointed out. "Sure she will. You're her only son. I'll talk to her. It'll be fine."

Susan gave a sigh of relief. "Thank you."

"Daniel and I," Pinchus said to her, "we're not going to let you get away."

Susan kissed him on the cheek.

Pinchus grinned. "You're smart, Daniel, *and* you have good taste. Listen. I'm hungry. Let me take you out to dinner to celebrate."

"We came down for your birthday," Daniel protested. "We want to take *you* out."

"So you do it tomorrow. Or Saturday. Tonight is my treat. But first I want to go over to the drugstore and get a prescription filled."

"We can stop on the way to the restaurant," Daniel suggested.

"I'd rather walk. It's only a couple of blocks. And I'd like to take the walk with Susan. It would give us a chance to become a little better acquainted. Susan?"

"I'd be delighted."

Pinchus went into his bedroom and changed clothes. He put on a jacket. Susan did too. They left the house.

The evening was cool and clear. There was a breeze rustling the leaves of the trees along the street. Above, some stars were visible, even against the glow of the city.

"These next few weeks are my favorite time of year," Pinchus said as they walked. "Just the right amount of chill in the air. Beautiful fall colors. Everything slowing down for winter."

"I think springtime is my favorite," Susan commented.

"That's appropriate. You're young, right on the brink of your own summer. Me, I'm like the fall, getting ready for winter."

"Early fall," Susan said.

"Bless you for not denying that it's fall at all. I'll take early fall."

"Good."

"We turn left here." Pinchus pointed. "At the end of this block there's a little park. We can sit and talk."

"What about your prescription?"

"A little white lie. There isn't any prescription. I just used that as an excuse to lure you out here alone. I didn't want to make you feel self-conscious. I hope you don't mind."

"No."

"Good."

The park was lit by old-fashioned streetlights—illuminated globes set on cast-iron stanchions. There was an empty wading pool, a little cinder-block field house. Pinchus led them to a wooden bench that overlooked the wading pool. They sat down.

"So, tell me about yourself," Pinchus asked.

"Short form or long form?"

"Whatever you want."

"Well, I'm twenty-two, I'm Irish and Italian. I come from a family of five in the Bronx, I graduated from City College, and I work in a bank. As a teller. I want to make a career out of banking. I like bike riding. I like Thai food. I like Anthony Hopkins movies better than I like Arnold Schwarzenegger movies, but I do like the Schwarzeneggers, too. Daniel won't go to see them with me. I'm Roman Catholic, but obviously not a very good one. I love Daniel. If he hadn't asked me to marry him, I would have asked him to marry me. Getting pregnant was an accident, but we both want the baby. Is that the kind of stuff you wanted to know?"

"Yup. I'm satisfied. I'm happy. I think you're going to be good for each other."

"I'm glad. Now you tell me: Does it bother you that Daniel's going to marry and have children with someone who isn't Jewish?"

"It's natural to want your child to marry in the faith. You're not such a good Catholic? Well, I'm not such a good Jew, either. So to me it's not so important."

"Thank you. Tell me some more."

"Long form or short?"

"Whatever you want."

"Okay, I will." Pinchus grew serious. "You probably know, Daniel's mother and I have been divorced for a long time."

Susan nodded.

"Through most of Daniel's childhood, I wasn't a very good father. Please," he raised a hand when she started to protest. "I want to explain. It will make *me* feel better. Daniel told you about his sister?"

"He told me that she died when she was five."

"Yes. Melissa. She was my life. I was totally devoted to her. When she died, I was shattered. I felt as if the world had ended. Daniel was just an infant then. My wife and I loved each other, but not enough to see us through. Or maybe I just wasn't strong enough. I don't know."

"It must have been difficult," Susan said carefully.

"Yeah. But after the shock had passed and it was time to get back to normal life, I couldn't. I was afraid. I didn't want responsibility anymore. I couldn't face it. It took a long time. It wasn't until a few years ago that Daniel and I became close. I'm not proud of what I did. In fact, I'm deeply ashamed of it. But I love my son, who is a wonderful person, and I am happy for you both."

Susan took one of Pinchus's hands between hers. "You're a dear man," she said. "Daniel loves you very much. I know that. He's even following in your footsteps."

"You think he wants to become a detective because I'm one?"

"I think that's part of it."

Pinchus cocked his head. "Do I hear disappointment there?"

"No . . . fear. I worry about whether I'll still have a husband, whether our baby will still have a father a few years down the road. I'm afraid of him getting . . . hurt."

Pinchus squeezed her hand. "Susan, look at me.

Nothing will happen to Daniel. He's a smart boy. Much smarter than me, and look . . . I'm still here. Sure, there's a little danger, but it's overstated, not like you see on television or in the movies. All my years on the force, I've never been shot at. Not even once. I've only had to draw my gun three times, and only once did I have to pull the trigger."

"What happened?"

"Ah," Pinchus said dismissively. "I hit what I was aiming at." He put an arm around Susan's shoulders, gave her a hug. "Most of what we do is paperwork, leg work, and a lot of sitting on our butts thinking. That's ninety-nine percent of it. Honest." He wasn't exactly lying; he was just shading things. "Don't worry, nothing will happen to Daniel. I promise."

Susan smiled. "And just how can you do that?"

"'Cause that's the kind of guy I am. Hey, you hungry?"

"Yes. Very."

"Good. I'm starved. Let's go get Daniel and head out."

"Deal," said Susan, linking her arm through his as they rose and started off.

Pinchus liked that, her arm in his. He liked this girl. He was going to enjoy being a grandfather.

37

Peter Roberts was happy. He and his family were finishing dinner. Peter was at the head of the table, Diane opposite him. Midway between them, to Peter's right, was Melanie; to his left, Paul. Peter beamed at his wife.

"It's very nice to have you eating with us," Diane said.

"Yeah, what's the occasion, Dad?" Melanie asked.

"I wouldn't be such a wiseguy after what you pulled today," Diane warned.

Peter looked inquiringly at Melanie. "Oh?"

"Uh-oh," Melanie murmured.

"Melanie almost got hit by a car," Paul volunteered.

"What!"

"Over Snowball," Diane said. "Your daughter ran right out into the street after him. Thank God, there was someone there."

"Who was there? What happened, for Christ's sake."

"It was getting dark," Diane explained. "Snowball ran out into the street. Melanie went after him. I saw it from the bedroom window. My heart was in my mouth. A van was coming. She didn't look at all, she just ran right out after the cat. Thank God this man was there. He grabbed Melanie and yanked her back. The van's tires were squealing. The driver was skidding. He wouldn't have been able to stop in time."

"Oh, Mel!"

Peter was devastated. He saw in his mind the

bloody, shattered body of a girl Melanie's age who'd been hit by a car near his office last year. He'd pulled over to help just as the paramedics were arriving. But the paramedics had waved him off. He'd become sick to his stomach seeing the child broken like that. "Never, never, *ever* do anything like that again."

"I'm sorry, Daddy." Melanie said it in her most effective I-love-you-to-pieces voice.

It worked. Peter reached out, grabbed her hand, and smiled.

"Who was the guy?" he asked Diane. He needed to embrace the man; at the least, shake his hand.

"I don't know. Someone visiting one of the neighbors. He was out for a walk, I guess. He must have been between the oak tree and the road when it happened. A young man. I thanked him profusely. He told Melanie, 'Cats just aren't worth it, kid. Anyway, they can look out for themselves.'"

"He was right about that last part," Melanie said. "Snowball got out of the way by himself."

"And he always will," Diane assured her. "Anyway, I think it's best for you to stay in the backyard if you want to take him out, okay?"

"Okay," Melanie answered.

While Peter cleared the table, Diane served up ice cream for dessert: strawberry ripple for the kids, chocolate-swirl vanilla for Peter and her. Afterward, Diane ordered the children upstairs to finish their homework. She went up with them, to help Paul, who'd been having trouble with math.

Peter loaded the dishwasher and got it going. He started to wipe down the countertop but was interrupted by a loud knock at the front door. He dried his hands on a dish towel and went to answer the door. He opened it with a smile, expecting one of his neighbors. It was David Harper.

David's right hand was thrust deep into the pocket of the red windbreaker he was wearing. The stubby barrel of a gun pushed the fabric out. David pointed it at Peter's belly. David's face was expressionless.

"We have to talk," he demanded. He placed a foot against the jamb.

For an instant, Peter considered slamming the door. It would break David's foot, give Peter a chance to lock the door when David pulled his foot back, allow him to spin to the phone on the foyer table and call the police. It could also, he realized almost immediately, get him killed.

Peter tried bluffing. "What the hell are you doing here?"

"I just want to talk. Let me in, no one gets hurt. I swear that. I need to talk to you. Alone."

"Go ahead, talk," Peter shot back. "I'm not letting you in here."

David thrust the gun forward. "You're fucking with the wrong person," he said angrily. "This is not the time to act brave, I assure you."

Reluctantly, Peter stepped aside.

David entered, closed the door. "Your family doesn't need to be involved. Where can we do this in private?"

Peter nodded. "In there. The study."

"Go ahead," David said.

Peter went to the study door and opened it, fearing the shock of a bullet in his back.

"Inside," David ordered. "Turn the lights on. Pull the curtains."

Peter did as he was told.

"Sit down."

Peter sat in the morris chair. David came in. He shut the door behind himself, sat down on the small matching couch across from Peter. His eyes were bloodshot. He needed a shave. He looked desperate.

Peter was frightened. But he didn't know what to do except to tell David the truth. "I don't know why you want to talk to me. I didn't make a mistake. I checked again after I spoke with you. Anyone would come up with the same results. I'm sorry; the models of your teeth match the bite marks that were on Alice Schaeffer."

"I know," David replied calmly, surprising Peter. "I figured they must. That's why I have to talk to you. I think I can trust you. Even though I'm scaring the shit out of you right now, you're sticking to your story. You're not trying to lie to pacify me. I like that." David nodded. "Yes, I like it a lot. I think I made a good decision. As I said, the models of my mouth *had* to match. You know why?"

Peter couldn't think of anything to say.

"Because I'm being set up. Somebody is trying to frame me for Alice Schaeffer's murder."

Forthrightness seemed to be the key with David. "I find that hard to believe," Peter said slowly. "In fact, almost impossible. Your bite marks were on that body."

"So you say."

"So would *anyone*."

"I believe you," David insisted. He leaned closer to Peter. "What *I'm* saying is that things aren't always what they appear to be. I'm going to take a chance with you. I trust you. I want you to trust me."

David removed his hand from his pocket. All he was holding was a thick, stubby marking pen.

"Five seconds ago, you would have sworn I had a gun pointed at you. Things aren't always what they appear to be. I'm risking a lot to prove that. You can get up and run. Call the police. Warn the rest of your family about the killer in the house. I probably couldn't stop you. But I'm asking you not to. I need your help. Desperately. Will you give me a chance?"

Peter felt rage, fear. He felt sudden power, and, barely recognizable, compassion. "Go on."

"I'm sorry I forced my way in like I did. But you have to admit, if I hadn't, we wouldn't be talking now, right?"

Peter nodded. In his mind, he was picturing the

brass tools next to the living room fireplace: tongs, a poker. He was almost certain he could make it to the living room a step ahead of David, if it came to that, grab the poker and crack his skull with it.

"I'm not a very patient person," David acknowledged. "That gets me into trouble. People resent me because of my intelligence. I try not to appear arrogant or condescending, but I have a hard time suffering fools, and yes, I admit it, much about people rubs me the wrong way. I haven't had the easiest of lives. Maybe that accounts for my attitude. I don't know. I'm trying to be very honest here, Dr. Roberts. Probably more honest than I've ever been with anybody. I'm in deep trouble and I don't see that I have any choice. Somebody is framing me. I might know who, and maybe even why, but I can't figure out how."

"That's where you come in. You have to figure out how my bite marks got on that body. I could reason through fingerprints, hair, even blood traces, but this—my teeth marks?—no way. Do you have any idea how a copy of a bite could be put on a body? Could you tell if it was done after she was dead?"

"Be–be–fore death," Peter stammered. "Definitely before. There was a great deal of bruising around each one. Dead tissue doesn't bruise. As to how . . . maybe. I'll have to run some tests to see if it can be done. Frankly, I doubt it, especially since Alice was alive, which would have made things more difficult. The medical examiner took saliva samples too. I don't know the results, but if they're a match to you . . ."

"How about semen samples?"

"I don't think there was any semen present."

"Shit."

"Who would try to frame you. Why?" Peter asked cautiously, trying to keep the skepticism from his voice.

"I don't want to say without proof, but it's the only explanation I can think of. That's why I have to know how someone else could have put my bite mark on that body."

"David," Peter said carefully, "have you considered the possibility that . . . well, that you might be unbalanced, that there might be something wrong with your brain? I mean, even organically? David, maybe you *did* do it, but don't know that you did."

"That is a statistical possibility," David said icily. "So is the earth veering out of orbit and plunging into the sun tomorrow. But you would be well advised not to bet in favor of either."

"The police have other evidence too, David."

"Like what?"

"You told them you were nowhere near Alice's apartment that night. Yet two witnesses saw you less than two blocks from it around the time she was murdered."

"Christ, does everyone think I'm some kind of dumb, fucking asshole!" David struggled to calm himself. "I'm sorry. I shouldn't have said that. Can you see that I'm at least *trying* not to alienate you. I know you don't believe me, but I can explain the witnesses and probably any other evidence the police have—everything but the bite marks. Look, when they asked where I was the night Alice was killed, I wasn't about to tell them I just happened to be on her damn street. I *had* to lie. Somebody had left a message telling me to meet him on Sixth and Vine to get back a wallet I lost. But nobody ever showed up. I waited nearly an hour. I couldn't tell that to the police—it sounded too suspicious. So I told them I was waiting at Market Square. I didn't think they would actually find witnesses. Whoever left that message for me is the person who is framing me."

"And who is that?"

"I can't tell you till I've got the proof."

"Go to the police, David. Tell them. If you're right, they'll help you prove it. In the meantime, I'll work on figuring out how the bite marks could have gotten there."

"I can't," David said desperately. "Not yet. I need

to work on this myself. The police are fools. I don't trust them. If *you* have trouble believing me, how do you think *they'll* feel? They won't listen to anything I say."

"David—"

"No!"

Peter made a placating gesture with his hands. "Okay," he said. "Okay."

"I don't want you to tell them I came here today either."

"David, I'll have to. And for me to tell them what you said can only help you. Can't you see that?"

"You honestly think they'll believe what I'm saying?"

"Probably not. But at least they'll check it out."

"Bullshit."

"Can you give me anything else for them? The name of who you suspect."

"Goddamn it, I told you . . . not now."

"Can you tell me at least if it's one of the other suspects?"

"I don't know who the other suspects are, except for Barry. He's the only other person I know you took an impression of. Who else is on the list?"

"I can't tell you. For some reason, I just assumed you knew."

"I don't," David replied. "So we're at an impasse. You won't tell me, I won't tell you. Look, I want your help, and I need you not to go to the police. I'm willing to give you something in return—if you wait twenty-four hours, I'll turn myself in."

"Why twenty-four hours?"

"I think I can get proof of what I'm telling you in that time. And you can figure out how the bite marks were done."

"I can't guarantee that I can."

"You'll do your best. I trust you. You give me this time, I'll surrender myself in a public place. I'll want you there when I do."

"Why me?"

"You're my guarantee. They won't pull any shit on me in front of you. I want that lieutenant there too. That older, gray-haired guy."

"Lieutenant Pinchus?"

"Yeah, him. You can tell them about me tomorrow night. You know Harry's Seafood Market, Fourteenth and Delancey?"

"Yes."

"I'll do it there. Saturday morning. There's a nice open parking lot. You be there with Pinchus at nine o'clock Saturday morning, and I'll give myself up to him. I should be set by then."

"I have office hours Saturday morning, starting at nine. Oh. Well, I guess I can change them."

"Jesus, Doc. You're something else. What the hell. Make it seven. You can still keep your appointments."

"David, I'd like to believe you, but I can't withhold the fact that you were here. Not from the police for a whole day. I have an obligation to tell them."

"And blow me turning myself in? Twenty-four hours," David said with a trace of anger. "That's all I'm asking. I'm pleading with you: Just keep quiet until tomorrow night, just give me that much, and Saturday morning I'll turn myself in. If you don't give me the time, then I won't show up on Saturday. And believe me, I'll know whether you waited or not."

"All I can tell you is that I'll consider it," Peter promised.

"I trust you. You'll do the right thing. I'd better go now. I have a lot to do by Saturday."

David stood. Peter stood with him.

"Good luck," Peter said, trying to sound completely sincere.

David offered his hand. Peter hesitated, then shook it. They were out of the study toward the front door.

Diane was coming down the stairs. "Peter! I didn't know you two knew each other! This is the young man I was telling you about, who saved Melanie."

Peter was startled. David had a half smile on his lips.

"How *do* you know each other?"

"David's the, uh, son of an ophthalmologist in my building. His family is thinking of moving into the neighborhood. When I saw him outside, I invited him in. I didn't realize how much I owed him." He clasped David's hand. "Thank you, from the bottom of my heart."

"You're welcome," David said.

"I hope you do move here," Diane commented. "If there's anything we can do to help, any questions we can answer, please call."

"I appreciate that."

"I'll walk out with David," Peter told Diane. He opened the door.

"Bye," Diane waved. "Thank you again."

When they were outside, David turned toward Peter. "My car is just down the block. You don't have to walk me there."

"Why didn't you tell me what you did for Melanie?"

"You didn't ask. Besides, would it have made a difference?"

"I guess not," Peter admitted. "Were you waiting here all afternoon?"

"No. Just a couple of hours. I was out stretching my legs when it happened."

Peter looked into the street. "I owe you one," he said earnestly. "You want twenty-four hours, you've got it. But I *will* inform the police tomorrow night. So, you'll be there Saturday morning?"

"I give you my word. Thank you, Dr. Roberts. It'd probably be best to tell them we spoke on the phone. Otherwise you'll have cops crawling all over your house till Saturday when I'm in custody."

"I suppose that's all right."

"You're a lucky man, Dr. Roberts: great house,

pretty wife, nice kids. I'd like a shot at getting those things for myself."

Peter made an indefinite gesture.

"Yeah, I know. Maybe I'll have them, maybe I won't."

"None of us knows. I hope you do get them."

They shook hands again, and then David turned and walked off into the night.

38

Pinchus had the squad room to himself early Friday morning. He'd had a delightful time at dinner last night with Daniel and Susan, then a satisfying talk with Kate afterward on the phone—Kate was going to come in and have brunch with them on Sunday—and then he'd said good night to Daniel and Susan, gone into his room, washed up, laid down, and fallen immediately to sleep.

He had slept deeply, and more peacefully than he had on any other night since Alice Schaeffer was murdered. He had wakened early, just before dawn, feeling completely refreshed. So he'd gotten up, made himself breakfast, left a note for Daniel and Susan, and then had driven to the office.

Waiting on his desk when he arrived were faxes from the *Ridgefield Secretary* and the *Filmore County Record* that had come in during the night. They contained copies of stories about the murder of Alan and Wanda Harper four years ago.

Pinchus had read them all, was now reading through them a third time, as the station house hummed with the activity of the arriving day shift. He had a story from the *Filmore County Record* in hand:

FILMORE COUNTY SHERIFF EDGAR DYKSTROM ANNOUNCED TODAY THAT ROBBERY WAS THE APPARENT MOTIVE IN THE GRUESOME SLAYING OF BUSINESSMAN AND FINANCIER ALAN HARPER, 46 YEARS OLD, AND HIS WIFE WANDA, 43,

ON TUESDAY NIGHT IN THEIR EXPENSIVE HOME IN RIDGEFIELD LAKE ESTATES.

THE POSH EAST END AREA WAS STUNNED BY THE WEDNESDAY EARLY MORNING DISCOVERY OF THE BRUTALLY MURDERED BODIES OF ALAN AND WANDA HARPER BY THEIR SON, BARRY, 20, AND THEIR NEPHEW, DAVID HARPER, 16, BOTH OF WHOM ALSO RESIDED IN THE HOME.

"WHAT'S ESPECIALLY FRIGHTENING," SAID ALICE SCHERMERHORN, A RESIDENT OF RIDGEFIELD LAKE ESTATES, "IS THAT ALAN AND WANDA'S HOME WAS EQUIPPED WITH A SOPHISTICATED SECURITY SYSTEM—LIKE NEARLY ALL THE HOMES OUT HERE—BUT THAT DIDN'T HELP THEM AT ALL."

THE FILMORE COUNTY SHERIFF'S DEPARTMENT AND THE RIDGEFIELD CITY POLICE DEPARTMENT BELIEVE THAT THE PERPETRATOR OR PERPETRATORS GAINED ACCESS TO THE HOUSE DURING THE DAY THROUGH AN ATTACHED GARAGE THAT WAS OFTEN LEFT UNLOCKED, ACCORDING TO BARRY HARPER, AND HID IN THE BASEMENT UNTIL AFTER NIGHTFALL.

AN UNDISCLOSED AMOUNT OF JEWELRY AND CASH WAS TAKEN FROM THE HOME. IT IS BELIEVED THAT THE VICTIMS AWAKENED WHEN THE BURGLAR OR BURGLARS ENTERED THEIR BEDROOM DURING THE COURSE OF THE CRIME. BOTH VICTIMS WERE BLUDGEONED TO DEATH, APPARENTLY WITH A BASEBALL BAT.

A SPOKESMAN FOR THE COMBINED TASK FORCE FROM THE FILMORE COUNTY SHERIFF'S DEPARTMENT AND THE RIDGEFIELD CITY POLICE DEPARTMENT SAID LAW ENFORCEMENT OFFICIALS HAVE NO IDEA WHY THE YOUNGER

HARPERS WERE LEFT UNHARMED OR WHY THEY
DID NOT HEAR THE ASSAULT. THE YOUTHS
WERE QUESTIONED YESTERDAY BY AUTHORITIES
AND RELEASED LATE IN THE AFTERNOON. THE
TASK FORCE SPOKESMAN SAID THAT AT THIS
POINT THE BOYS ARE NOT CONSIDERED SUS-
PECTS IN THE CASE.

MONICA FIELDS, A NEIGHBOR WHO HAD IN-
SOMNIA THE NIGHT OF THE MURDERS,
REPORTED SEEING A DARK-COLORED, LATE-
MODEL SEDAN RACING AWAY FROM THE AREA
AT ABOUT 2 A.M. (CONTINUED ON PAGE 7. SEE:
"KILLINGS".)

Pinchus sat back in his chair and stretched. He got
up, went for another cup of coffee. Sam arrived as he
was pouring it.

"You're here early," Sam noted. "Schwenk throw a
scare into you?"

"I never pay attention to the babblings of a fool.
Unless, of course, I'm talking to myself."

"Been here awhile, I see."

"How do you see that?"

"The coffeepot's almost empty. You always make a
fresh one when you get here."

"You're good."

"One of the best. So how long?"

"A couple of hours. I want to knock off early.
Daniel and his girlfriend showed up last night. I'd like
to spend some time with them."

"*Is* she pregnant?"

"She is."

"Congratulations."

"They're going to get married."

"I figured."

"Yeah?"

"When he said he was bringing her down, and that
she might be pregnant."

"I guess you don't see it when it's your own kids. I like this girl, Sam. I like her very much."

"Good."

"You want the last cup?" Pinchus asked.

"Please."

Pinchus poured the last cup of coffee for Sam, put on another pot. He sat down across from Sam. "I've been going over news stories about the murder of Barry Harper's parents."

"Find anything?"

"More questions than answers."

"Maybe the police reports will help. They're coming by courier. They should be here this afternoon."

"It's a crime when the papers are more efficient than we are. Did you get anything on David's mental history?"

"Not yet. A sergeant Nicolaides is supposed to call me. I couldn't reach David's mother. Nicolaides is going to track her down and talk to her for me. What's the story on the parents?"

"They were beaten to death with a baseball bat. What bothers me is that both Barry and David were in the house when it happened—yet neither was touched, and both slept right through it. Their rooms were at the opposite end of the house, but still, it makes you wonder. The house was wired with an alarm system, but that only tripped when the murderer, or murderers, left. The alarm woke the boys up. That's when they discovered the killings."

Pinchus stood up and started to pace the room as he thought out loud.

"The parents were well off. Robbery was the supposed motive, but that doesn't click. I'd like to know who stood to benefit the most from their deaths. I think the local authorities suspected one of the boys. At least for a while."

"Papers suggest that?"

"Just the opposite. But when you make a point of

saying that someone is *not* considered a suspect at this time, you can bet that at one time he was."

"So what made them change their minds?"

"Evidence. A trail of blood was found leading away from the house across the yard to the street. The blood matched the victims'. A neighbor saw a car racing away from the scene. The alarm was tied into the local police station. When it went off, the police responded immediately. It was a messy killing. The Harper boys were still in their pajamas, no sign of any importance on them."

"Why not a robbery that went wrong?"

"Because it looks like careful planning, right up to where the Harpers wake up in their bedroom and get whacked. That shouldn't have happened. Then the perp or perps grab whatever they've already got and run, triggering the alarm. It doesn't scan. You case a place, know enough about it to get in past the alarm, you either wait till it's empty and ransack it or you immobilize the occupants and do it."

"Do you really think one of the Harper boys killed them?"

"Not one of the Harper boys—David." Pinchus sat down again at his desk. "I'm giving odds he gained something big from the deaths. I think maybe we have ourselves a psychopath here."

"There's evidence that says he didn't do it—a blood trail, a getaway car."

"Could be faked."

"How old was he then? Seventeen?"

"Sixteen."

"Pretty young for that kind of thing."

"The kid is smart."

"I don't know, Seymour. It's a stretch."

Pinchus showed Sam the tie tack he'd found, told him where he'd found it.

"It does indeed say *DH*," Sam said. "And if David is indeed what you say he is, he probably would have enjoyed watching you play plug the duct."

Pinchus shuffled through a case folder, pulled out the piece of paper with Barry Harper's name, number, and address that had been in Alice Schaeffer's bag. "Remember this?"

"Sure. Barry told Alice where she could get in touch with him. She wrote it down."

"It's not her handwriting. Not Barry's either. It's David's."

"How do you know?"

"I compared it to the writing in one of Alice's notebooks, then to the signatures we got on the consent forms so Peter Roberts could take impressions. I'm not an expert, but I'll bet a month's pay the experts come to the same conclusion I did: *David* Harper wrote this. My guess is that he wrote it to implicate Barry, slipped it into her bag after the killing. I think we need to talk to Barry again."

"Want me to send someone for him?"

"Let's keep a low profile. Give him a call and tell him to come in."

Sam picked up his phone, checked his notebook, then started to press numbers. Pinchus's own phone rang. Pinchus answered. It was Peter Roberts.

"What's up?" Pinchus asked. "Still feeling funny about David's call?"

"No," Peter said. "But I have to talk to you again. Why don't you come to dinner? Diane would love to have you, and the kids would like to see you."

"That's nice of you, but tonight's no good. Give me a rain check. Why don't you just drop by here? Or if you'd like, I can stop at your office on my way home."

"No. It has to be tonight," Peter insisted. "It's important."

"Peter, I've got Daniel and his girlfriend—his fiancée—at my house. They're down visiting. It's my birthday tomorrow."

"Perfect! Bring them with you. Diane will be thrilled. I didn't know Daniel was engaged."

"I just found out myself."

"We'll have a birthday cake for you and an engagement cake for them. Seven-thirty. Good? Good."

Pinchus relented. Daniel hadn't seen Diane and the kids in nearly a year.

"Just one thing," Peter added. "Please don't say anything about David or his call to me while you're here, okay? I don't want Diane to get upset. I appreciate your coming, Seymour. I do need to talk to you. And it has to be tonight. Sorry I can't be more specific."

"That's all right, Peter. Sounds like you plan not to disappoint on any level."

"I don't."

They said good-bye. Pinchus hung up, shaking his head.

"Anything wrong?" Sam asked.

"I hope not. Did you get Barry?"

"His machine. I left a message. Then I got in touch with Junior Gibney. We've got Junior and two guys we borrowed from robbery watching the building. He said Barry was sitting outside the dorm on the steps. Barry's been doing that a lot, sometimes for hours. Junior thinks he's not going to classes, thinks maybe he's stoned or something."

"Barry doesn't strike me as a druggie. But I wouldn't be surprised if he was on medication, given what he's been through. Want to take a ride over there with me?"

"Nicolaides is supposed to call this morning with that information I wanted."

"Okay, I'll run over by myself. Then I'm going to hit an arcade, check on a couple of other game rooms. See you in a couple of hours."

"I think that game stuff is a waste of time, Seymour."

"You didn't see the guy play. He's a real junkie."

"Maybe you'll get lucky."

"Be a nice change of pace."

39

Pinchus was at the university in twenty minutes. He spotted Junior Gibney parked in an unmarked car, but didn't acknowledge him. Nor did Gibney acknowledge Pinchus. Pinchus pulled over in front of the dorm. Barry was sitting on the steps, staring at the concrete walkway. It was chilly, but Barry was wearing only khakis and a cotton shirt, the sleeves rolled up his forearms.

Pinchus got out of his car. Barry did not stir as he approached.

"Barry, are you all right?"

Barry looked up slowly.

"Lieutenant Pinchus," Pinchus said.

"I know," Barry responded. "Yes. I'm all right. Just kind of depressed, I guess."

Pinchus sat down next to him. "I can believe it, with all you've been through lately. Barry, we have to talk some more. Do you think you're up to it?"

"Why not? I'm pretty much numbed out, so now's as good a time as any. Have you found David?"

"Not yet. What do you say we go inside? It'll be easier to talk there."

"Okay," Barry replied.

They got up and went into the dorm, walked up to the fourth floor. Barry moved slowly, as if he were exhausted. It took him awhile to fit the key into the lock and get the door to his suite opened. Once inside, Barry cleared away a bunch of books that were occupying a couch. Pinchus helped him.

When they were seated, Pinchus began. "Barry, I'm

concerned about you. From what I see and what I'm told, you're not in good shape. What's going on?"

Barry had trouble focusing. "What's going? Well, it's been a hell of a week, Lieutenant. Alice Schaeffer gets killed, David and I get called in as suspects, Wednesday you and your cops jump me in the middle of the night, then you say my cousin is the killer. Hell of a week."

"You on drugs, Barry?"

Barry shook his head. Then he smiled a little. "Well, maybe you could say that. Thorazine. I called my doctor. Needed to calm down. Got a three-day prescription. It's a tranquilizer. Heavy-duty."

"I know what Thorazine is." Thorazine was an unusually potent drug, often used in mental institutions. "You clear enough to answer some questions?"

Barry nodded. "I'm slowed down, not unconscious. Go ahead."

"Okay. First, Barry, I have to ask: Has David tried to contact you at all since Wednesday? Visited, called, got a message to you in any way?"

"Uh-uh. Not with that cop you have outside watching me. Guy isn't hard to spot, you know. And I imagine you've got my phone tapped too. So you must know he hasn't."

"Actually, we stopped short of bugging your phone."

"I hope nothing has happened to David." Barry's eyes glistened with tears. "To be honest, I thought he would get in touch with me somehow by now. Maybe he's hurt. Maybe something happened and he can't. We're very close, you know."

"I know. I wouldn't worry. David is all right. He called Dr. Roberts yesterday."

"The dentist?"

"He thinks Dr. Roberts may have made a mistake."

Barry's disposition brightened for a moment. "Maybe he did. I still don't believe David did it."

Pinchus showed Barry the tie tack he had found. "Does this look familiar?"

"Kind of familiar, but I can't place it. Those are David's initials. It's not his tack, though. David owns maybe three pieces of jewelry and that isn't one of them."

"Barry, you said David exhibited some psychological problems after the death of his father and your parents. Could you be a bit more detailed?"

"I think you're blowing what I said out of proportion. David was very upset. As I was. That is perfectly understandable, given the circumstances. It was also some time ago. Right now, Lieutenant, I'd say that David is saner than you or I."

"Maybe. Maybe not. I have to ask you some potentially disturbing questions about David and your parents' death. You think you can handle them?"

"We'll find out, won't we?"

"I guess we will. I understand that your parents were quite wealthy."

"The estate was worth three million. Is that 'quite' wealthy?"

"I assume the will provided something for David?"

Barry looked at Pinchus for several moments. "I hope you're not going where I think you might be."

"Was David provided for?"

"Seventy-five percent of my parents' estate went to me, or at least it will when I turn twenty-five next month. Right now it's in a trust fund. The other twenty-five percent went to my father's sister-in-law, temporarily."

"David's mother."

"Yes. It will eventually go to David. It's also in a trust, which David's mother draws on for their common needs. David won't see a penny of it until he turns twenty-five. When my parents were killed, David was sixteen. No one plans that far ahead for such a small piece of the pie. You have to admit, you're really reaching for a motive."

"A motive for what, Barry?"

"For David to kill my parents. David may be the genius, but I'm not stupid, Lieutenant. That's what you're implying."

"I'm not implying anything, Barry. I'm looking, that's all. I'd like you to tell me what happened the night your parents were murdered. Beginning from right before you went to sleep up until you realized they had been killed. Take your time. Think carefully. I know it's painful to recreate that night, but I need to hear this from you."

Barry leaned back in his chair, closed his eyes. "All right." After several moments, he said, "Basketball. We were playing basketball. It was early in the evening. We had a backboard and hoop on a pole at the side of the driveway. David and I played a lot of one-on-one." Barry's voice was low, calm. "We played a couple of games that night. It was hot. David kept losing. We were betting on the games. Each time he lost, David insisted on playing another one, double or nothing. We must've played for a couple of hours. It was getting too dark to see the ball, but David refused to quit until he was even. I finally let him win, so we could stop. We went inside, took turns in the shower. We each had our own room, with a connecting bathroom in between. Later we watched some television in the den. There was some thunder, some lightning. I thought it was going to storm, but it didn't. I got really tired, so I went upstairs and went to bed. I was wiped. I remember thinking that we overdid it with the basketball. I went out as soon as my head hit the pillow."

Barry's eyes were still closed. He frowned. "The next thing I remember was David shaking me and yelling my name. He was yelling for me to get up. The alarm was screeching. First I thought there was a fire, but I didn't smell smoke. Then I realized David was crying. He was saying something about my parents. But I couldn't understand him because he was hysterical. I got out of bed and tried to run to my parents' room. I fell down, got up: I was really out of it. The door to my parents' bedroom was open." Barry was speaking more rapidly. His breathing grew shallower. "David yelled, 'Don't go in there, Barry. Don't look! It's horrible.' He caught me and grabbed me by the arm. He was crying. He said, 'Barry, there's nothing you can do for them now. They're dead.' I remember going crazy. I broke away from him and ran into the room. And . . . and . . ."

Barry curled in his lower lip, bit down hard for a long moment, then released it.

"Oh my God, there was blood everywhere. The bed, the carpet. On the furniture. The walls were splattered with it. It was all over the goddamn room." Tears were sliding from Barry's closed eyes and running down his cheeks. He shook his head from side to side. "My father was on the floor at the foot of the bed. He was covered with blood. The side of his head was bashed in. He had this twisted, surprised look on his face. Both his arms were broken. A bone was sticking out from one. I knew he was dead, but I knelt down anyway to touch him. He was so still.

"I realized then I didn't see my mother. I got up and looked around, but I didn't see her right away. The covers were off the bed. They were piled on the floor at the side. I bent over and pulled the blanket up. All I could see was red. At first I thought her face was all covered with blood. Then I saw that she didn't have a face. My God, her face was gone! They whacked off my mother's face! My God, my God!"

Barry's eyes snapped open. He stared at Pinchus. "Look at what the fuck they did! She had no face! She had no face!"

Pinchus moved to Barry quickly, put his arms around him and pulled Barry awkwardly into his chest. "It's okay, Barry, it's okay. It's over."

Barry clung to Pinchus, rocked slowly in place.

"Look what they did to my mother. Look what they did," he said into Pinchus's shoulder.

When Barry was calm, Pinchus released him but kept a hand on his shoulder. "I'm sorry for putting you through this," he said.

Barry nodded. He got up and went into the bathroom. Pinchus heard him blow his nose, heard water running. Barry returned. The tears had been washed from his face. He had a box of tissues. He sat down, blew his nose again. "I'm okay."

"You sure?"

"Yeah. Go ahead."

"Just another question or two. Where was David while you were in your parents' room?"

"Standing in the doorway. He was screaming at me to get out of there. Screaming and crying himself."

"How far were your bedrooms from your parents' room?"

"Our rooms were at the back of the house. Theirs was at the front. Ours were half a flight higher than theirs. It was a good distance, but if there had been screaming, you'd think we would have heard it. I was so out of it even the alarm didn't wake me up."

"Could you have been drugged?"

"By David, you mean."

"You're on a heavy tranquilizer now. Did it feel anything that night like it does now?"

Barry considered. "It's hard to say. Maybe. But you're wrong, Lieutenant. The police found footprints in the dust of the basement that didn't match anyone in the house. And there was a trail of blood leading down the stairs and out of the house to the street."

Pinchus didn't say anything.

"David loved my parents," Barry argued. "You're wrong."

"If David tries to contact you, will you promise to let me know right away? Whether he's guilty or innocent, Barry, it would be best for him if we had him in custody."

"You think maybe he killed Jimmy Hoffa, too?"

"I *am* sorry, Barry. Thank you. I hope you can get some rest."

"Yes. I need to rest," Barry said.

Pinchus said good-bye, and left.

40

When he emerged from the dormitory, Pinchus walked over to where Junior Gibney was parked and exchanged a few words with him. Since Barry had already spotted Junior, there was no reason not to. They made a date to have a beer next week.

From there, Pinchus drove to the first of three arcades he wanted to visit. After the arcades, he went to the gaming center in the Hayward Avenue mall. None of the managers or employees Pinchus spoke with had seen David Harper. Pinchus decided to make one more stop before he returned to the station, even though it would take him out of his way.

Police barricades were blocking off Boundary Street when he got near the Slaughtered Lamb. A banner strung across the street read THE BOUNDARY STREET 6TH ANNUAL FESTIVAL OF CLOWNS. Food vendors and game booth operators were finishing setting up. Some were already open.

Pinchus parked on a side street. He walked over to Boundary and strolled toward the Slaughtered Lamb, enjoying the burgeoning carnival spirit. The smell of sausages and onions was in the air, Cajun chicken. A hawker was inveigling early visitors to knock clown dummies off a shelf with baseballs and win a giant stuffed panda; another offered darts with which to pop balloons on a backboard. Two mimes and a juggler were already out and working. The street was more alive with visitors at this hour than Pinchus would have thought; by nightfall, it would be jammed. A clown in a polka-dot suit and a green fright wig went waddling by, chased by a handful of laughing pre-schoolers who were in turn followed by their watchful mothers. The clown had a sign on his back: CATCH ME IF YOU CAN.

Pinchus smiled. There was only one clown he would like to catch today.

The Slaughtered Lamb's taproom was busy with customers getting an early start on festivities. The juke-box was pounding out something brassy and guitarish; the singer had a wailing voice that Pinchus could not identify as either male or female. The red-haired bar-tender had her face painted with white grease paint and blue stars. She wore a jester's cap. She was busy filling drinks, making change.

Pinchus made his way through the early revelers to the entrance of the game room. Just inside, a couple of young guys in expensive suits stood at each shoulder of a third one who was playing a pinball machine, whooping as he scored. The room was smoky, crowded. All the games were in play. Pinchus surveyed the sea of unfamiliar faces, then his eyes locked on a neatly-combed head of brown hair.

In the rear, playing Mind Freaker, was David Harper.

Pinchus froze, sure he was not seeing correctly.

In that same instant, David's head snapped up, as if his senses were tied directly to Pinchus's. He stared into Pinchus's eyes. Then he whirled, banged open an emergency exit at the rear of the room and plunged through it. The exit's alarm went off.

Pinchus pushed forward, shoving people out of his way. "Police! Move, move!"

He tripped going through the emergency door and half stumbled onto Boundary Street. David was already on the other side. Running, David knocked a man down and sent the woman who had been holding the man's arm reeling. He hurtled down the sidewalk, shouldering people aside. Pinchus went after him.

Halfway down the block, a juggler stepped into Pinchus's way. Pinchus crashed into him and they both went down. The juggler's wooden pins flew into the air. One struck a woman in the chest. She screamed. Another flew into an Italian food truck, knocking over a big jar of tomato sauce. The jar fell to the street and shattered, sending the tomato sauce splattering in an arc. Pinchus gained his feet, looked about wildly.

"Where'd he go?" he shouted. "Goddamn it, where'd he go!"

People were drawing back from him in fear.

"I'm the police!" he roared, flourishing his open wallet to show his badge. "Where did the guy I was chasing go?"

Everyone seemed stunned. No one appeared to know. Finally, a twelve- or thirteen-year-old girl stepped forward and pointed. "I think he went down that alley."

Pinchus ran to the alley. He was breathing heavily. There was a pain in his side. At the end of the short alley, he saw David climbing up a high chain-link fence. David looked back over his shoulder.

Pinchus pulled his gun. "Police!" he shouted. "Freeze!"

He dropped into a half crouch, both arms extended. The thumb of his left hand cocked back the hammer, his right index finger put just a tiny bit of pressure on the trigger. David was caught squarely in his sights.

David had one leg over the top of the fence. He stopped, went motionless.

"Come on back down!" Pinchus ordered.

David swung his other leg over the fence and dropped to the pavement on the other side.

For a suspended instant, Pinchus had a clean, easy shot. He started to pull the trigger. David ran. Pinchus followed him with his gun, wanting to pull the trigger, trying to pull the trigger.

But he didn't.

David rounded a corner and was gone.

Pinchus uncocked his gun, placed it back in its holster.

He didn't know what had happened. He'd had his opportunity and let it slip though his fingers. He was filled with remorse for the act he had not been able to complete. In his soul, he apologized to Alice Schaeffer. He turned dejectedly.

Clustered at the alley's mouth, a bunch of fairgoers were staring at him.

"There's nothing to see," he told them. "Break it up. It's over. It's all over."

He wished it were. He wished David were lying dead in the alley and that it was indeed all over. He was sick with himself.

PART
FOUR

▲

PART
FOUR

41

Units were sent, but Pinchus didn't have much hope that they would find David. He was right. After a fruitless hour, he returned to the station. He wanted Sam to be there; he needed to talk.

Sam was there. "Heard you spotted our boy. Heard you were on the way in. You look kind of shaky. You all right?"

"Yes."

Pinchus recounted the story.

"I'll tell you, Sam. I wanted to pull the trigger. God, I wanted to! But I couldn't." Pinchus banged his fist on his desk. "What the fuck, does someone else have to die in front of me before I can shoot? Like Vince?"

Sam lit a cigarette, even though the squad room was a no-smoking area. He hunched forward, peering at Pinchus. "I don't think that's it, Seymour. I—"

"*You* would have shot the fucker!"

"Maybe I would, maybe I wouldn't have. I don't know. But that's not the point."

"The point *is* if the little slimeball kills again, I'll have blood on my hands. The victim's blood. I don't think I could live with myself if that happens. I can't afford to let that happen."

"No one says it's going to," Sam argued. "I'll tell you why you couldn't shoot: You're not convinced that David is the murderer. It's as simple as that. You couldn't kill a man without being absolutely sure."

"Bullshit. I even think he did Barry's parents, too."

"I'm not saying he didn't. All I *am* saying is: You've gone over all the evidence very carefully. More than once. I think maybe your subconscious has picked up on something that your conscious mind has overlooked—some inconsistency, some detail. Maybe very small, but just enough to cast a shadow of a doubt. And that shadow was enough to prevent you from pulling the trigger."

"Maybe," Pinchus said glumly. "But if that *is* the case, then I think my subconscious is full of shit. David did it."

"How you going to write this up?"

"'Spotted suspect. Gave chase. Suspect escaped.' Lean, clean, and true. Schwenk's just looking for an excuse to cut off my head. No sense giving it to him by putting down the details."

Sam agreed.

"So what did you get?" Pinchus asked.

"The reports still haven't come in, but I did talk with Nicolaides. He says the Harper family wealth was accumulated by William Harper, David and Barry's grandfather. William Harper had two sons: Alan, Barry's father; and George, David's father. George was the younger one. He also had a daughter, Joanna. Nicolaides interviewed an old guy in the area, a doctor who used to play pinochle with William Harper, go fishing with him. This guy says that George was kind of a black sheep. He ran around a lot, even after he was married, got into some situations that embarrassed the family. William was always threatening to cut George out of the will. And finally he did. There weren't any grandchildren then, so no provisions were made for them. Joanna had married someone with even more money than William had. She didn't need anything. So Alan, Barry's father, inherited everything—the money, the prestige, the business. The old guy says that George became embittered and depressed. And here's a kicker for you: Nicolaides tells me George's death wasn't an accident—it was a suicide. He *drove* his car off that cliff."

Pinchus thought. "So David's family gets *bubkes*, his father kills himself, and his mother becomes a drunk. David blames his uncle Alan, who got everything. What about David's mother?"

"I haven't talked to her yet. Nicolaides found her in a hospital in Philadelphia. She's got cancer and she's dying. She has six, seven weeks left. She just came through a procedure. She's sedated. The doctor says we can talk to her tomorrow, day after at the latest."

"Maybe she was sick four years ago," Pinchus suggested. "Maybe David knew it. As I understand it, the way Alan Harper's will was written, David's mother uses the money for her and David's common good until David reaches twenty-five, or until her death, whichever comes sooner. Then the money reverts to him. So for motive, we have revenge for what happened to his family, and greed."

"The problem with greed is that most of the money's gone. David's mother didn't have any medical insurance. He's not going to come into much at all."

"We need a copy of Alan Harper's will. There has to be something in there that changes the way this picture looks."

"It's on the way already," Sam said. "Assuming that David did kill the Harpers—which I don't, but I'll go with you for a minute on this—why does he do Alice Schaeffer?"

"I don't know. Rage, frustration? He wants the money, he's willing to wait for it. He plans and pulls off the murders of his aunt and uncle. Then either his mother gets sick, or if she was already sick, she lives longer than he thought she would. Either way, he has to watch his inheritance shrink down to nothing. It's excruciating. He wants to blame someone, but doesn't know who. He snaps, sees Alice as an oppressor, puts it all on her, takes her down. Or maybe he picked up a taste for killing when he did the Harpers. Or maybe he's just thumbing his nose at the world in general, giving it a big, shove-it-up-your-ass."

"It plays," Sam agreed. "Except for two things that bother me."

"Which are?"

"Remember you asked me to check out Mensa?"

Mensa was an exclusive high-IQ society, most of whose members looked upon themselves as geniuses or at least near-geniuses and were admitted only after extensive testing. Pinchus had a third cousin who taught at MIT who belonged to Mensa and was usually able to work that fact even into the most unlikely of conversations. It had bothered Pinchus that in David Harper he was up against someone smarter than he was. He wanted to know as much about David as he could, including just how intelligent he might be. Because of his arrogance, his pride in his intelligence, Mensa was just the kind of thing that David Harper would be attracted to.

Pinchus nodded. "And?"

"They have a Harper all right—but who they have is a *Barry* Harper. David applied, but didn't score high enough. He's bright, but not as bright as Barry."

"Jesus," Pinchus said.

"The second thing is, Nicolaides told me it was Barry that got treated for mental instability, not David."

"Jesus, Mary, and Joseph."

"Your theory about age and Jewishness notwithstanding, Seymour, I think the older *you* get, the more Catholic you become."

42

Diane Roberts made roast beef for Friday night's dinner because roast beef was Daniel's favorite and Diane dearly loved her younger cousin. She had spent a lot of time with him while he was growing up and she felt more like an older sister to him than a cousin. She made mashed potatoes to go with the roast beef, and a thick, rich gravy with blackened onions, just the way Daniel liked it, glazed carrots and hot rolls.

Pinchus, as he unfolded his napkin and placed it on his lap, announced that this would be absolutely the last meal of such nature and proportion he would eat for months. Then he abandoned any attempts to control his appetite and dug in with gusto.

Diane and Susan hit it off immediately. Before anyone had finished even a first drink, they were knee to knee on a couch whispering and bursting into laughter together. Pinchus was delighted. He knew it was important to Daniel that they get along. After Pinchus met Susan, he hadn't doubted for a moment that they would.

Peter and Diane's children, Melanie and Paul, were even more agreeable than usual tonight, happy to see Daniel, even if Melanie was perhaps a twinge jealous of Susan. Melanie had always been coquettish around Daniel.

"So, who wants dessert?" Diane asked when dinner was finished and the table cleared.

"Why, mother, what could dessert possibly be?"

Melanie asked in a deliberately stagy voice. She winked at Pinchus, at Daniel.

Diane put a finger to her chin. "Oh, I don't know. How about—"

"Homemade apple pie!" Paul cried.

"What a wonderful idea," Diane said.

Melanie smiled. "With a humongous piece of cheddar cheese on top!"

"Perfect," Peter announced.

Diane got up from the table. "Give me a hand, Mel."

Melanie was happy to. "I get to serve Daniel."

Paul jumped up to join them. "I get to serve Uncle Seymour."

"Diane," Pinchus said. "I love you."

"Me too," Daniel stated, whose delight in apple pie with cheddar cheese was only slightly less intense than his father's.

"I know," she commented. "That's why I baked an apple pie from scratch with my very own hands."

"And bought the cheddar cheese from her very own supermarket," Melanie cackled.

"We'll have birthday and engagement cake later," Diane told them.

After dessert and coffee, Peter excused himself and Pinchus. The others were chattering away—Melanie standing next to Daniel's chair with her arm around Daniel's shoulder, Paul sitting on Susan's lap—and quite content to continue.

Peter led Pinchus into the study. He closed the door. They sat. Pinchus waited.

"David called again," Peter revealed.

Pinchus stiffened. "When?"

"Last night."

"Shit, Peter . . . and you're only telling me now? Do you know what you've done? If he hurts someone, it could get nasty."

"Calm down, Seymour. I can explain: He promised

that if I kept quiet until tonight, he'd turn himself in tomorrow morning."

"And you believe him?" Pinchus said incredulously.

Peter told Pinchus what David had said, careful not to indicate that he had seen David in person. "He's going to give himself up tomorrow at 7 A.M., in the parking lot of Harry's Seafood Market. He wants me to be there. He doesn't trust the police."

"That's out of the question. We'll be there, you won't."

"Then he won't show," Peter said in frustration. "Look, I wanted to tell you right away. But he said if I did, he'd know and call the deal off. I couldn't take the chance. Do you want to take it now by going there without me?"

"I'll think about it," Pinchus said. "This theory of his, that he's being set up for Alice Schaeffer's murder . . . I don't get it. You identified the bite marks positively as his, right? And you double-checked, right?"

"Yes. There's no question that the marks match his bite—but that doesn't mean *he* put them there."

Pinchus's jaw dropped as he started to realize what Peter was saying. "A duplicate?"

"Yes."

"Is that possible?"

"I'm not sure. Someone would need to have models of David's mouth, like the ones I made. I was going to test today to see if it would work, but I got called in for an emergency patient. I didn't finish until just in time to make it home for dinner. I'll do the test tomorrow."

"Peter, we've got a lot of circumstantial evidence against this guy, too. He might be jerking you around."

"He says he can explain the stuff like having lied about being at Market Square the night Alice Schaeffer was murdered."

"So why wasn't he there the night we went to pick him up? The only reason for him to have split was that he knew his bite would match the marks on the victim."

"I don't know. He just said he could explain."

"And you believe him."

"I do."

"You *do*? Why?"

"He said he had to work through some things before he could give you a name. That's why he needed time."

"Peter, let me tell you something. I saw David today. I chased him. I had an opportunity to stop him—with a bullet. For some reason, I couldn't pull the trigger and he got away. After listening to you, and having listened to my partner today, I should be glad I didn't kill him. But I'm not. I still curse myself for not having blown him away. That's how much I think he's guilty. I'll tell you something else: I'll be very surprised if he shows up tomorrow. Very surprised."

"I hope you're wrong, Seymour."

"I do too. I hope he's caught before somebody else dies."

"So do I."

"Do you?"

"God, Seymour—of course! What do you think?"

"I think you haven't been totally up front with me. I think you're involved in this in some way other than the one I know about. You were slow to admit that Alice Schaeffer was a patient of yours; when I brought it up again, you got edgy. Now you're trying to argue that David Harper might not have killed Alice, which repudiates the key piece of evidence, the one that you yourself established. Something's going on here, Peter. And I want to know what it is."

Peter looked away.

"How are things between you and Diane?"

Peter jerked his eyes back to Pinchus. He twitched.

"I thought so."

"Why?"

"I sensed a certain tentativeness between you over dinner. Maybe a wound that hasn't quite healed?"

"What are you, clairvoyant?"

"Just perceptive. It comes with the job."

"Okay. Maybe I should tell you the whole story."

"Yes," Pinchus nodded.

Peter gritted his teeth, shook his head. Then he told him. "I was having an affair. Diane just learned about it. It's over now. And we're okay . . . I think. But some other things happened, too. Frankly, I came on to a couple of my patients. One of them was Alice Schaeffer. She was just so incredibly gorgeous."

"How heavy did you come on?" Pinchus asked.

"Actually, it was pretty subtle. She was so beautiful she intimidated me. I thought she probably hadn't even recognized it as a pass."

"Why'd you think that?"

"One, because she didn't respond to it. Two, because she made another appointment, which she probably wouldn't have if she thought anything was out of line. I didn't think any more about it until I found out she'd been murdered. Then I got worried. What if she *had* picked up on it, or realized later what had been going on, and told somebody about it? In a murder investigation, that might come out. My reputation was at stake, maybe even my license. At least that's how I felt. I wanted the investigation to come to a quick conclusion. Don't get me wrong. I still did an honest job on the bite marks. But I felt guilty about the whole thing. And then—wham!—along comes David Harper insisting that I made a mistake."

Pinchus was silent. Then he said, trying to control his mounting anger, "I am happy for you and Diane, that you're working things out. But I am fucking furious that you didn't tell me any of this before. Do you realize what you've done? I now have a primary investigator on a murder case who had more than a passing interest in the victim. I don't doubt the correctness of your comparison work, but when and if the case goes to court, the court may well throw your testimony and this evidence out."

"I swear, Seymour: Any other forensic dentist will come to the same conclusion I did."

"Your Honor," Pinchus said, gesturing toward a lamp, "who is to say that Dr. Peter Roberts did not discard the original impressions he made of the bite marks on Alice Schaeffer's body and replace them with a new set, which he created by using the model he had made of David Harper's teeth?"

"Oh, God."

"Could that be done?" Pinchus asked.

Reluctantly, Peter nodded. "But I have an actual bite mark. One I dissected away from Alice Schaeffer's body."

"Again, evidence that's been in your possession."

"What about exhumation? I'm sure another dentist could match it to the other marks still on the body. It'll prove authenticity."

"Maybe. But Alice was cremated. You didn't know that?"

"No," Peter replied. "No, I didn't."

"Well, she was."

"How big a problem is this?"

"It could be very big. Or if we're lucky, it might not matter at all. I can't make any promises, but if things work out—if, say, David confesses—then what you've told me won't have to go beyond this room."

"Thank you, Seymour. Thank you."

"You're welcome. Remember, though, I can't make any promises."

"I understand."

"You sure David won't show if you're not there?" Pinchus asked pointedly again.

"I'm sure."

"You win. I'll pick you up at six-thirty tomorrow morning. I want to get there early."

Peter nodded. "Six-thirty."

43

At 6:55 A.M. Saturday morning, Lieutenant Seymour Pinchus and Dr. Peter Roberts were sitting in Pinchus's car in the nearly empty parking lot of Harry's Seafood Market. Three cars were parked just behind the market. Lights were on inside as the early arriving employees set up for the day. A delivery truck was backed against the loading dock in the rear of the market. The driver was off-loading boxes of iced fish.

The morning was overcast. There was a nip in the air. Pinchus had turned the heater on briefly on the way over to take the chill out.

A giant red lobster crouched atop the roof of Harry's Seafood Market. Its paint was peeling. The big sign announcing the market-owner's name was missing the second *r*. The parking lot itself was cracked and potholed. Nevertheless, Harry's served the freshest seafood in town and did a thriving business.

A block away, Sam Milano and a uniform waited in another car, in communication with Pinchus by radio.

Peter was nervous.

"Still think he's going to show?" Pinchus asked.

"Yes. He has five minutes still. I never said he'd be early."

"If he does, remember: You stay in the car. Let us handle it."

"Don't worry. I'm not the hero type."

"Good. By the way, What'd you tell Diane we were up to?"

"I said you needed me to classify and authenticate the work I did on the bite mark."

"What's that mean, 'classify and authenticate?' "

"I don't know."

Pinchus laughed for the first time this morning. Peter laughed with him.

Seven o'clock came.

As did 7:05.

Then 7:10.

"Where the hell is he?" Peter moaned.

"Relax," Pinchus responded. "You never said he'd be on time either."

"I don't understand. He looked me right in the eye and said, 'I give you my word.' "

"He looked you in the eye? You *saw* the sonofabitch?" Pinchus exploded. "Where, goddamn it—*where?*"

Peter was shaken. "At—at my house."

"He saw your house, he was *in* your house?"

"Yes."

Pinchus slammed his hand against the steering wheel. "Shit! You told me he called!"

"What difference does that make? I told you everything he said to me."

Pinchus started the car, threw it into gear.

"I didn't tell you because of Diane," Peter explained. "I didn't want her involved. I told her that David was a friend of one of my colleagues."

Pinchus took the car roaring out of the parking lot. He steered with one hand, picked up the radio with the other. "Sam, come in."

Sam's voice came back, tinny. "What's up?"

"Get out to Peter Roberts's place right away. Forest Slope area, 1108 South Aldine. I'm afraid David Harper's there. Get on the horn, see if we've got a unit nearby. Tell 'em it's code red."

The color had drained from Peter's face. He looked at Pinchus with disbelief.

Pinchus said into the radio, "Get another unit to

cover the lot here, in case I'm wrong, in case he does show."

Pinchus sped down Delancey Avenue. He rolled down his window, slapped a red light onto the roof of the car, set it flashing. He flashed his headlights and hit the siren as he ran traffic lights.

"We just decided that I'd say he had called," Peter said weakly.

"*We?*" Pinchus shouted. "You mean David did. He told you what to say! How could you be so fucking stupid?"

"You don't really think he would try to . . ." Peter couldn't finish the question.

Pinchus turned off Delancey onto Elwood with a squeal of tires. He gunned the motor, heading toward Forest Slope.

"You have to understand, Seymour. David saved Melanie from being hit by a car. She ran out into the street after her cat. David was out front, waiting for me. He grabbed Melanie just in time. Diane saw the whole thing. How do you think I felt? I *had* to trust him. I owed him one."

Sam's voice came through the radio. "Right behind you, Seymour. Dispatch says no one's in the Forest Slope area, we'll probably be first on the scene."

Pinchus flicked his eyes up to the rearview mirror, saw the following car. He nodded his head in acknowledgment.

Peter said, "Did you hear me, Seymour? He saved my daughter. Why would he want to hurt my family?"

"I don't know. I don't know anything about this goddamn case anymore."

Pinchus drove fast, with intense concentration. He forced himself to breathe deeply, then again. As they entered the Forest Slope area and raced down Touhy Avenue toward Aldine, he said, "They're probably fine, Peter. It would be stupid for David to do anything to them. I just want to be sure."

Peter had a knuckle in his mouth. He took it out. "Then why are we going so goddamn fast?"

Pinchus didn't answer. Two minutes later, he roared up to Peter's house, stood on the brake pedal and swerved the car up onto the drive and partway onto the lawn.

"Stay here!" he ordered Peter.

But Peter threw open the door and ran toward the house.

Sam pulled to a halt at the curb.

"Take the back!" Pinchus yelled to him. Then he ran after Peter, bounded up the stairs to the porch, and caught up with him at the door, just as Peter banged it open and rushed in.

"Di!" Peter screamed. "Di! Melanie, Paul! Where are you?"

Peter ran through the hall toward the kitchen. Pinchus overtook him and shoved him aside. Pinchus whipped his gun out, burst into the kitchen.

Diane was standing at the counter in a pink nightgown and furry slippers. She was holding a pot in her hand. She looked at Pinchus with a thoroughly perplexed expression.

Melanie and Paul were in the breakfast nook.

"Wow!" said Melanie. "Neat!"

"There's Uncle Seymour's friend and another one outside," Paul happily announced.

He waved through the window at Sergeant Milano and the uniformed officer, who were in the backyard with their own guns drawn.

"So," Diane said, "did you finally decide to come back for a decent breakfast, or what?"

44

It was 1 P.M. The last of Peter Roberts's Saturday patients was gone and Peter had sent Nina home. He was in his lab. He was furious with himself, furious with David. He was grateful that his family had been safe.

"This is the last time that sonofabitch is going to screw us around," Pinchus had said to Sam Milano. He had said it with such vehemence that Peter believed him, believed that it couldn't be any other way.

There was now a patrol car parked outside Peter's house; and there would be one there until David was caught.

Peter was sitting before three separate models of David's teeth—the original, which he was going to keep as reference, and two others he'd made to test. But he was convinced of David's guilt now and had no desire to go through with the tests, even though he had promised Pinchus he would.

The lab door wasn't shut. Peter heard the front door to the office click open.

"Nina?" he called. "Forget something?"

"I don't know," said a low voice, "but I did."

David Harper appeared in the open lab door.

"Is that me?" He pointed to the models on the counter.

Peter was too angry to be frightened. "You've got some goddamn nerve!" he said.

"Take it easy. I'm sorry I didn't show up. I'm here to explain."

"Why should I believe anything you say?"

"I told you I'd turn myself in and I'm going to. I was up late working last night. I simply overslept this morning. I didn't wake up till eight. I knew there wouldn't be any point in going to Harry's so I decided to come here. I called your service and got your Saturday hours from them."

"Bullshit. It's all lies and bullshit, David."

"Bullshit? Call your answering service. Ask them if anyone called around eight-thirty this morning asking about your hours."

Peter didn't say anything.

"Tell you what. I'll call the police right now and tell them to come pick me up. Better yet, *you* dial."

Peter began to waver. "You found what you were looking for?"

"Maybe not total proof yet, but enough for the police to work on. Did you figure out how my bite mark was transferred to Alice Schaeffer's body?"

"I have a theory. It has to do with the models. I haven't been able to test it."

"Jesus Christ, we're talking about my life here! Why not?"

"If you'd been at the market this morning, I would have by now. You get harder to believe all the time."

"Dial the goddamn phone," David shouted. "Get the police here. See if I'm fucking with you."

"I will," Peter shouted back. He picked the receiver from its cradle, started to punch in Pinchus's direct number.

There was a sudden, blurry rush of bodies.

Frightened, Peter dropped the receiver.

Then Pinchus and Sam Milano were in the small lab, with David shoved up against the wall, Pinchus held a gun to David's head.

"David Harper, you're under arrest for the murder of Alice Schaeffer," Pinchus said. "You have the right to remain silent. You have the right to an attorney. . . ."

Sam frisked David down, pulled his arms around

behind him, and handcuffed him. Pinchus finished in-
forming David of his rights.

"How's that for a response time?" Sam said to
Peter.

"Do you understand these rights?" Pinchus asked
David.

"I do," David answered. "Good afternoon, Lieutenant. I understand you've been wanting to speak
to me."

"Do you wish to have an attorney present at the
station when we question you?"

"I can take care of myself."

"Is that a no?"

"That is a no. I don't want an attorney. I don't
need an attorney."

"He was just about to turn himself in," Peter informed them.

"Sure he was," Pinchus replied. "But on the off
chance that he might neglect to do so, we've been
watching you. I had a feeling he'd try to see you
again."

David emitted an exaggerated sigh. "I guess I'm no
match for you brilliant cops. I *was* going to give myself
up, you know."

"You could have done that yesterday, on Boundary
Street."

"Maybe I just wanted to see how fast you could
run."

"And maybe I should have pulled the trigger."

"If you had, you'd hate yourself for having shot an
innocent man."

"Naw," Pinchus said. "My aim is still pretty
good."

David was seated at the table in the interrogation
room, handcuffed. Pinchus sat across from him. Sam
was standing, leaning up against a wall. A technician
was videotaping the session.

"Don't you guys listen?" David moaned. "I have

told you literally six times now that I was standing on the corner of Fourth and Decker Monday night. Fourth and Decker. Not *Sixth* and Decker. Not outside Alice Schaeffer's apartment. And not *in* her apartment. I'm tired of telling you."

"That's a shame you're so tired," Pinchus said. "Because I want you to tell me again. I still have this problem: You told Barry you were going to Faulkner's. You told me you were at Market Square. Now you say you were at Fourth and Decker. Which of these versions am I supposed to believe?"

"Barry and I ate dinner at Faulkner's around six-thirty." David rolled his eyes in resignation. "Then we went back to the dorm. That was around seven-thirty. I played pinball in the basement for an hour. Then I left to pick up my wallet. I never told Barry I'd left it at the pub. *Barry* was the one who gave me the message about this guy finding it and wanting to meet me at nine to return it to me. True: I *didn't* go to Market Square. I went to Fourth and Decker. When you questioned me about Alice Schaeffer's murder, I got scared. I lied because I knew she lived in that area. I didn't think then it was a big deal that I lied—simply because I didn't commit the crime.

"No one ever showed up with my wallet, so I left Decker Street. That was around nine-thirty. I went back to the dorm, to the game room. I played there for a couple of hours, then went upstairs. Barry wasn't home. I went to bed. I woke up about two—I had to go the bathroom. Barry was back. He was asleep at his desk. I woke him up so he could get to bed. I swear to you, that is the absolute truth."

"Barry tells a different story," Pinchus said.

"Of course he does!" David shouted. "He's the one who set me up! *He* was the one who gave me that message. *He* was the one who was out all night. Barry's flaky, you know? And he gets into pills. I didn't bother myself much about the story he told you, because I just figured he went out that night and got stoned, so he wasn't clear about what happened. Can't you see what's going on? Barry's very shrewd. He fooled me, he fooled you. His IQ is almost as high as mine. We *are* blood relatives, you know."

"Actually, his IQ is higher than yours."

"What?"

"Mensa. You know: Barry got in, you didn't."

David smiled. "Lieutenant, on a bad day anyone can test fifteen to twenty points lower than his actual IQ. On a good day, fifteen to twenty points higher. And Mensa has its own, nonstandard tests that were created by existing members, basically to reflect themselves. They're a fairly tautological group. You're familiar with tautology, aren't you? That's using something to define itself. Like: 'The Bible is God's word.' How do we know? 'Because it says it is.' How do we know that what it says is true? 'Because it's God's word.'"

"It's important for you to be intelligent, isn't it, David?"

"What are you getting at, Lieutenant? Are you suggesting I'm a contemporary Nathan Leopold or Richard Loeb? That I would kill someone like they did simply to prove that I'm a superman and can do what I wish with impunity? Since that's been done already, it would hardly be original, would it? If I wanted to prove such a thing, I would find another way. My intelligence is neither important nor unimportant to me, Lieutenant. As a tree is neither important nor unimportant to me. It simply is what it is, that's all."

"Barry tells us you were very distressed after his parents were killed, that you experienced severe psychological difficulties over it. Was he lying again?"

"Not entirely. Was I distressed? Hell, yes. Christ, who wouldn't be? And did I develop psychological problems because of it? I don't know. Probably. What I *do* know is that I told Barry that I did. Barry never had a very stable personality, even as a kid. When his parents were killed, he went over the edge. He lost it.

He was in treatment a long time. I used to tell him that I was pretty fucked up over it too. It made him feel better. The therapy helped, but I think that's when he got hooked on pills. He has not had an easy time in life."

Pinchus remained expressionless. So did Sam.

David looked from one to the other. "What's the point of telling you any of this? You don't believe me. Ask his fucking doctors. Or stuff it up your asses. I don't give a goddamn what you do anymore!"

"Calm down, David," Sam warned.

"Did Barry also write this note?" Pinchus asked. "It was in Alice Schaeffer's bag."

David squinted at the note. "I don't know anything about that. It looks like my writing, but I don't remember writing it. I certainly never gave it to Alice Schaeffer."

"I don't think you did either," Pinchus said. "I think you put it in her bag after you killed her, to implicate Barry."

"Maybe I wrote it out for someone else—*if* I wrote it, which I don't remember doing. Maybe Barry copied my writing and gave it to Alice or put it in her bag himself."

Pinchus clasped his hands together on the table and leaned forward on his elbows. "Nice, David. Real nice. But you killed Alice—and I'm going to make sure you pay for it. Here's how it went down: You found out where Alice lived. You watched her, got her schedule. You broke in, cased the place, worked out the final details. You unscrewed the bulb in the hall so it would be dark and she wouldn't see that the door had been jimmied. When you heard her coming, you concealed yourself in the living room closet."

"This is fascinating, Lieutenant."

"Glad you like it. You cracked the door and watched her strip as she got ready for bed. Probably got you real hot."

"Probably would have if I'd been there. She was a good-looking woman."

"Real hot—so hot that you bit her while you were raping her. You must have liked that. Because you did it three times. Which was actually pretty stupid for a smart guy. And before you left, you put the note with Barry's name into her bag. That was another stupid mistake, never realizing that we would compare the handwriting."

"Lieutenant, you're an asshole."

"That's been suggested before. But you're a killer, David, and if I *am* an asshole, then I am the asshole who's going to put you away."

"Do you really think I would be so stupid as to leave teeth marks on someone I killed? Or try to implicate my cousin by planting a note in my own handwriting? Maybe I'm more intelligent than Barry; maybe he's more intelligent than I. Either way, I am not dumb—and what you've just suggested would be colossally dumb."

"So enlighten me. How did you your teeth marks get on Alice Schaeffer's body?"

David slumped back. For the first time since Pinchus and Sam had begun to question him, he looked uncertain—even frightened. "I don't know," he said. "That's why I went to Dr. Roberts. After I left him Thursday night, I thought of this one thing, and it's the only thing I can think of. I had an impression taken of my mouth last year when I was thinking about having some orthodontic work done. I decided not to go ahead, but the dentist gave me the models he'd made. He told me to keep them in case I changed my mind. They were on some kind of hinged apparatus. I kept them in a shoe box on a shelf in my closet. I was going to try to slip back in to see if they were still there, but you had guys watching the place. They weren't hard to spot."

"We searched your apartment," Sam commented. "We didn't find anything like that."

"Then that's it. Barry must have done something with them to Alice."

"That's pretty far-fetched," Sam answered, although his tone suggested that he wasn't sure.

"I don't see how else," David maintained.

Pinchus said, "Where were you late Wednesday night when we came to the dorm to arrest you? It seems that the only way you could have known we were coming was if you were guilty."

"Yes—if I *had* known you were coming. But I didn't. I was out at a movie."

"At one in the morning?"

"It was an all-night Woody Allen marathon. At Gershwin Hall."

"Anyone see you there?"

"It was dark. They don't turn the lights on when they have a marathon, just show one movie after another."

"Figures," Pinchus scoffed.

"You can check on the marathon," David challenged. "And maybe somebody did see me. I don't know."

"I'm sure there was one," Pinchus said, "but how do we know you were there?"

"I called Barry at a little after two. Originally, he wanted to go with me. But then he said he'd rather stay home and take a nap, come over when *Annie Hall* was shown. He wanted me to call when it was coming up. So I did. That's when he told me the police were looking for me, that they thought my bite matched the killer's. I was scared. I didn't know what to think, what to do. So I ran. I called Dr. Roberts the next day. I figured he had to have made a mistake. Barry must have lied to you Wednesday night. He probably said he didn't know where I was. He assumed I'd disappear after he warned me. Which I did, and which I see now just made me look worse."

"Sam, would you check on what time *Annie Hall*

was being shown? Also, see if those reports are in from the Ridgefield PD yet."

Sam nodded. He left, closing the door behind him.

"I hope they give you the right time. The projectionist is usually stoned. So's half the audience."

"We'll get the right time," Pinchus assured him. "But I know where you were at two A.M., and it wasn't watching Woody Allen movies. It was on the roof of the dorm across the street from Lincoln. Watching me climb into an air duct."

David gaped at Pinchus. "I have no idea what you're talking about."

"Did you find it as funny as a Woody Allen film?" Pinchus took the tie tack he'd found from his pocket and put it on the table. "You lost this on the roof, right at the spot that would have given you the clearest line of sight into Lincoln's game room."

David picked up the tie tack. He examined it. "I can see how things just looked worse and worse. Lieutenant, I don't wear ties. I can't even remember the last time I had one on. And I don't own a tie tack. You see how each of the initials—the *D* and the *H*—are inside a kind of half circle? That's the insignia of Darby House."

"Darby House?"

"It's a house plan. There are fraternities, sororities, and house plans at the university. Darby House is an all-male house plan. Their sister house is Delta House. The two of them give a lot of parties together. Most of the Delta girls live in Hausner, the dorm across from Lincoln, where you found the pin."

Pinchus suddenly felt the weight of his years. He heard the echo of Sam's earlier concern. He *was* personally involved in this case. And it *was* affecting his judgment.

"Let's go back to the day Alice was killed," he continued. "You attended her class that morning."

"Yes."

"Aside from using sexually offensive language—"

"That's a matter of opinion."

"Yes, the opinion of several students who were there. Aside from using sexually offensive language, you objected to having to do a dissection. When you were told you had to, you mutilated a laboratory cat, in the genital area."

"Oh my God. Lieutenant, I could draw out a cat's anatomy for you right now, and I could have drawn it out that morning too. The laboratory work Alice Schaeffer wanted us to do was boring."

"So you mutilated the cat, to make a statement."

"I did not mutilate it. I simply tried to make it look as if I had done the required work. When Ms. Schaeffer came down on me, I lied. I told her I was afraid of cats, that I couldn't stand them. She bought it. Actually, Barry's the one who's afraid of cats. He can't stand them near him. He said that when he saw them dead and pinned down and split open like that in the lab, somehow it made him feel safer, more secure."

Pinchus felt everything slipping away from him. He was not accustomed to self-doubt in an investigation. Not knowing what to do, he threw himself open to impulse. Feeling in nearly as precarious a position as when he had accused Kendall Daniels of killing her husband, he said: "David, let's talk about the murder of your aunt and uncle, about how you benefitted from that."

David looked at him incredulously. "If anyone stood to benefit from their deaths, it was Barry. Not that I think he had anything to do with it. Or not that I thought so until now."

"*Do* you think he killed them?"

"I find that hard to imagine."

"How about you killing them?"

David shook his head. "Lieutenant, this is making me sick."

"Alan and Wanda Harper had a lot of money. They left you twenty-five percent of it, through your mother, to be turned over to you on your twenty-fifth birthday. So we have a possible motive: greed. Further, Alan Harper's good fortune in life came to him partly at the expense of your own father, whom your grandfather disinherited and disowned. Your father later killed himself. You blamed your uncle for that. So now we have an additional motive: revenge.

"After you killed your aunt and uncle, you were satisfied. But then your mother became ill. She didn't have health insurance. Medical bills ate up most of the money she had received in your behalf—your money. You were frustrated, angry. Along comes Alice Schaeffer giving you a hard time, threatening to throw you out of her class and file a harassment complaint against you. As a bonus, she's good-looking too. A perfect target and scapegoat. And—wham!"

David was pale. "I couldn't even conceive of the things you're suggesting, let alone do them. And I don't know where you got your facts about my uncle's will, but they're wrong. My mother received—in trust—*fifty* percent of Alan Harper's estate. The other fifty percent is being held in trust by a bank for Barry. He gets it next month, on his twenty-fifth birthday. When *I* turn twenty-five, *half* of what my mother received will come to me. The other half reverts to Barry. So Barry has to wait until *I'm* twenty-five, too, before he gets his full seventy-five percent of the estate. His part of what my mother received is fully protected. She has been able to use only the interest on it. As for my portion, the bulk of it was stock in Alan Harper's own company, which couldn't be sold.

"What all this means is that when Barry turns twenty-five, he gets half of the original estate, including half the stock in Alan Harper's company. But he can't *control* the company, including liquidate it, until he receives the additional twenty-five percent that goes to him when I turn twenty-five. As I understand it from my mother, my uncle set it up this way so Barry would have to work with the bank for four years and gain some practical experience before taking over.

Also, it was to protect *my* interests for another four years."

"I haven't had a chance to review the will," Pinchus admitted, "but assuming that what you're saying is true, what is the point you are trying to make here?"

"This: That even if my mother spent all the cash from my share of the estate, and liquidated all the assets that *could* be liquidated, and spent those proceeds too, there would still remain the corporate stock. That couldn't be touched. And the value of that stock is now about ten times the value of the cash and all the other assets that were originally my share combined. I haven't watched my inheritance go down the drain— I've watched it increase. I didn't kill Alice Schaeffer to vent anger for having lost my fortune."

Pinchus considered. While Barry had not actually lied to him, he had misled Pinchus by telling him that he would come into seventy-five percent of the estate upon his next birthday.

"Are there any other stipulations in the will?" Pinchus asked.

"If Barry or I die before our twenty-fifth birthday, then our portion of the inheritance reverts back to the estate. So if I had wanted to kill someone, Barry would have been my choice, not Alice. Then I'd get it all."

"No, you wouldn't. If Barry's share reverted to the estate, the courts would decide to whom it would be given. Alan Harper had a sister. She would be in line before you. The appropriate term, I believe, is the law of intestacy."

"That's true, except that under the law of intestacy, a son has precedence over a sibling."

"What are you trying to say, David?"

"Alan Harper was not my uncle. He was my father."

45

"*What?*" Pinchus said.

"Alan Harper was my father," David repeated. "He had an affair with my mother, his brother's wife. And she got pregnant by him. With me. No one ever knew about it. I have a letter written by him to my mother. It's an agreement. She would never reveal the truth about me; he would make certain I would always be provided for. You know he had a sister. Didn't you ever wonder why only my mother, a sister-in-law, participated in the estate? It was my birthright."

"Does Barry know about this?"

"He found the letter a month ago. I think he believed I was going to make a claim for half the estate."

"Were you?"

"No. I couldn't have, even if I'd wanted to. The will stipulates what I was to receive. Son, nephew, it doesn't matter—the will can't be challenged. The only way I could get more is if Barry didn't survive his twenty-fifth birthday, or were declared incompetent."

"Or vice versa. But if one of you was murdered, that would be too obvious."

"Exactly."

"So if you're convicted of Alice Schaeffer's murder, the entire estate belongs to Barry."

"Yes."

"Couldn't you challenge Barry's competency on the grounds of his mental state, and what you say is his drug addiction?"

"Barry is disturbed, but he's far from incompetent. Incompetency is very difficult to prove."

"I suppose Barry might have feared you could make a case anyway," Pinchus said, thinking out loud.

"Shit."

"What?" Pinchus asked.

"I know how this sounds, but I didn't mean it—I told Barry I was going to do that. It was right after he'd found the letter. He was angry at his father, angry at me. We had a bitter fight. Half out of anger, half out of truth, I said it was pretty convenient how his parents were killed, that maybe he did it after all. He went nuts. He swore I wouldn't receive a penny."

Pinchus leaned back in his chair and closed his eyes. He rubbed them with his palms. He didn't like any of this. Then again, he didn't have to. He had faced things he hadn't liked before. It was part of the job, part of life.

This new scenario would explain a great deal. And David was beginning to sound believable. Yet Pinchus had been so sure that he now found it difficult to back away from the thought that David was guilty. And still, no matter what anyone said or felt or did or did not do—there were David Harper's teeth marks on Alice Schaeffer's body.

"You haven't told me yet what happened the night your aunt and uncle were killed," Pinchus reminded him.

"Father," David corrected.

"The night Alan and Wanda Harper were killed."

"There's not much to tell. I remember waking up to the sound of the burglar alarm. I wasn't concerned. It had gone off before without anybody breaking in. Especially when there were thunderheads and lightning, as there were that night. I waited for a while, but no one shut it off. I didn't feel like moving so I yelled to Barry for him to get his ass out of bed and turn it off, but he didn't. Finally I got out of bed and went through the bathroom into his room. He wasn't there. I figured he'd gotten up to stop the alarm, maybe was having some trouble. So I went out into the hall and started toward the front of the house, where the control box was. That's when I saw Barry coming toward me. There was blood on his pajamas and he had this blank look on his face. I yelled at him: 'What happened!' But he didn't say a word. I guess he was in shock. I ran to the master bedroom and . . . and . . . I saw them. Barry appeared in the doorway behind me. He screamed, 'They're dead! They're dead!' I said, 'I know.' Barry started crying hysterically. I did too. That was all. I called the police."

"Are you saying that Barry discovered the bodies, that he was the first to see them?"

"Yeah, why?"

"Barry told me you discovered them."

"And you believe him?" David said angrily. "Can't you see what he's done? He's turned everything around."

The door opened. Sam Milano leaned in but didn't enter. "Seymour, can I see you?"

"Sure." Pinchus exited the room, leaving David with the technician.

He and Sam went into the adjoining room, a small viewing room where they could see David through a one-way mirror.

"I've got bad news in triplets," Sam said. "We've got the wrong guy."

"I'm listening."

"The head of student affairs verifies the Woody Allen marathon Wednesday night. He says *Annie Hall* went on at 2:10 A.M. Since they had a projector breakdown earlier and the schedule was running late, David would have to have been there to know that."

"Maybe he was there at that time, but—"

Sam didn't wait for Pinchus to finish. "This got in half an hour ago." He handed Pinchus a manila folder from the Ridgefield police department. "You're going to want to look at the report from the first officers on the scene, and the ME's report on Wanda. But right now, Schwenk wants us in his office."

"Fuck Schwenk."

"Right *now*," Sam emphasized. "He's got Peter Roberts there. Schwenk and I were both in the hall when Peter came up the stairs, and Peter just started babbling before I could stop him. Schwenk grabbed him and pulled him into his office and said for me to get you, for both of us to get in there pronto. And I think we'd better."

Pinchus glanced at David through the one-way mirror. David was sitting quietly with his hands folded in front of him, looking at them. Pinchus left the viewing room with Sam. On the way to Schwenk's office, passing through the squad room, Pinchus asked another detective to sit with David while they were gone.

"Come in," Schwenk called when Pinchus knocked.

Inside, Peter was excited. "I already told Sergeant Milano and the captain. Now that you're here, I can *show* you all."

Peter set a cardboard box on Schwenk's desk, opened it, and removed a metal frame about six inches high that supported a set of model teeth in its center.

"This is an articulator," Peter explained. "We use it to study a patient's occlusion, his bite. These models are from David Harper. I can open and close them in the same way David Harper's jaw would." Peter demonstrated. Then he raised the articulator up to his neck. "Now watch this."

He opened the models on the articulator, closed them on the side of his lower neck, pinching a section of his skin. Slowly he increased the pressure. His skin turned white.

Pinchus winced at the force Peter was using. Peter grunted.

The edges of the teeth on the stone model began to crumble. Peter released the jaws, freeing his flesh. He turned so that all of them could see his neck.

"Look carefully at the marks. Do you see the fine remnants of stone left behind?"

They leaned forward, peering. Around the slightly bruised area of the bite mark were tiny granules.

Pinchus took his old magnifying glass from his pocket, squinted at the residue. He swiped some onto the tip of his finger and went to the window where he could see it more clearly.

"If you crush it," Peter said. "then wipe it away, you get a little bit of fine yellow powder left, right?" Pinchus experimented. He nodded.

"Remember those grains of what Sam thought might be talcum powder you found on Alice Schaeffer's body?" Peter asked. "I bet they match what we have here."

"I think you're right," Pinchus agreed.

"As far as I'm concerned," Peter continued, "this supports the theory that someone other than David could have put David's teeth marks on Alice Schaeffer's body."

"Hell," said Schwenk, "I'd say this proves it."

"But someone would have had to take an impression of David's mouth and make models beforehand," Peter pointed out. "Frankly, I don't see how that could be done without his knowledge unless he was drugged into unconsciousness."

"He had an impression taken about a year ago," Pinchus recalled. "By an orthodontist. The orthodontist made models. I think he put them on a stand like that."

"An articulator?" Peter asked.

"Yes. David had possession of the models, but they appear to be missing. They could have been stolen. Barry had access to them."

Sam pointed to the folder. "Seymour, I think you better scan the report from the first officers on the scene of the Harper murders."

Halfway down the first page Pinchus went, "Mmmph! It says here that *Barry* discovered the bodies. Barry told me David found them. But his own statement from the night of the murders contradicts that." Pinchus grew angry. "The sonofabitch."

"Check the ME's report on Wanda," Sam suggested quietly.

Pinchus leafed through the file, found the report, read for a few moments. He stopped short. "Oh God."

"What?" Peter asked. "What's it say?"

"Wanda Harper was sodomized before she was killed," Sam stated. "It wasn't considered relevant—so far as the public was concerned—so the authorities held that back from the papers."

"His own *mother*?" Peter looked shaken.

Sam shook his head. "I guess if he could beat her to death with a baseball bat . . ."

Pinchus closed the file. "We have a very sick young man loose out there."

"We've got a fucking mad dog loose out there!" Schwenk said. "What do you have to say for yourself, Pinchus?"

Pinchus shrugged. He felt the burden of his misjudgment heavily. "What's there to say? We made a mistake."

"Hell of a goddamn mistake. What do you intend to do now?"

"Get in touch with Junior Gibney and find out if Barry's still at the dorm."

"Junior was pulled," Sam told Pinchus.

"Who's the stupid shit that pulled him!" Pinchus yelled.

"I did!" Schwenk yelled back. "I called him in yesterday, Friday. And I sent those other two back to robbery. You were going nowhere with that detail. I also pulled the unit from Dr. Roberts's house after you brought David in. We have limited manpower, Pinchus. You've got no one to blame for this but yourself. The investigation was poorly organized and poorly run from the beginning. You had men all over the university and city interviewing people who didn't need to be interviewed and searching locations that didn't need to be searched. I allowed four days of that lunacy. If you had run this as leanly as it should have been, you'd still have a man watching the dorm. You blew it."

"*I* blew it?" Pinchus shouted. "You yourself said David was guilty. When we went for him Wednesday night and came up empty, you claimed you would have figured him for the killer long before we did. You wanted to know why I didn't have a man on him from the start. Now you have the audacity to *blame* me for thinking he was guilty."

"I didn't head the investigation," Schwenk argued. "You did."

"This is fucking pointless," Pinchus said. "Barry's running around loose and we're just standing here. I'm going over to the dorm."

"You're going nowhere," Schwenk announced. "As of now, you're off the case. I'm releasing David and assuming command of this investigation."

Pinchus was speechless. He couldn't believe he had heard Schwenk correctly. But then he saw the inkling of satisfaction on Schwenk's face and knew that he had.

"Fine!" he bellowed.

He threw the Ridgefield folder against the wall, scattering its contents, and stormed from the room.

46

After an embarrassed silence, Sergeant Sam Milano and Dr. Peter Roberts left Schwenk's office. Peter was stunned. He wanted to talk to Pinchus. But Pinchus wasn't in the squad room. No one there had seen him.

"He'll turn up," Sam said confidently. "He probably went off to lick his wounds, or maybe to keep himself from throwing Schwenk through a window, which is what I'd like to do."

Sam walked Peter out to the stairway.

"I feel like an asshole," Peter admitted. "I didn't know any of this was going on. It's just that, when I saw you in the hall, I was excited about what I'd found and I just blurted it out without thinking . . ."

"It's all right," Sam said. "This is between Seymour and Schwenk. It has nothing to do with you." He shook Peter's hand. "Thank you for all your help."

Nearly an hour passed before Pinchus returned. In the squad room, Sam watched him approach, watched him drop heavily into his chair.

"I had to walk it off," Pinchus explained. "I had to keep going until I got rid of all of it. Otherwise, I would have come back and decked the bastard."

"You got a raw deal, Seymour. I'm sorry."

"Thanks."

"Anything I can do?"

"No. I'm okay now. Almost, anyway. I'm not going to let the asshole get to me. What *does* get to me is the way Barry Harper almost stuck it to us."

"It happens," Sam said. "No sense dwelling on it.

Why don't you go home? Weren't Daniel and—what's her name, Susan?—supposed to take you out tonight?"

"I cancelled that when we brought David in. I figured we'd be here late. They went to Chadds Ford to see the Wyeth paintings. They won't be back till about ten. Ironic, huh? I thought I'd be putting this case to rest tonight, but instead, it's put me to rest. Hard to swallow, even if the order did come from an idiot like Schwenk."

"Seymour, what do you say we get out of here? We'll do something together, just you and me. Eat, maybe go bowling. I'll call Helen and tell her to take the kids to a movie. How 'bout it?"

Pinchus smiled. "You're a good friend, Sam. But I think I'll hang around and see if they bring Barry in. I want to see his face."

There was a low rumble of thunder. Lightning flickered.

Pinchus glanced out through the window. "Anyway, it's going to rain."

"Not for a while. Let's get dinner at least. The change of scene will do us both good. We can check back here afterward."

Pinchus was still looking out the window. "It's interesting," he said. "Barry killed his parents during a thunderstorm. It was raining the night Alice died, too."

"You suggesting that he goes on a rampage when the weather is bad? That a storm triggers something in his head?"

"Just an observation. Something's bothering me. Something I can't put my finger on. There's a clue I missed somewhere. One that could have prevented this mess. I'm sure of it. It's gnawing at me."

"Let it go, Seymour."

"Okay," Pinchus nodded. "Let's get dinner."

"Good deal. My treat. I want to pay off my debt. Barry was still one of the three you picked."

Pinchus got into his trench coat. "Not much consolation. He was my third choice."

"Nevertheless."

Pinchus, brightened. "How about Les Trois Amis?"

"Ouch. I thought you were going to go easy on me if you won."

"Well, tomorrow *is* my birthday. I would be delighted to look upon this as a combination of bet payoff and birthday present."

"Le Trois Amis," Sam said. "Happy birthday.

By the time Pinchus and Sam returned, it was raining. Sam dropped Pinchus off at the front of the station, then drove around the back to park. Pinchus mounted the steps. A thin fork of lightning flashed in the distance. Moments later, thunder rumbled.

Inside, the desk sergeant, a man named Vanderhooven, nodded to Pinchus, then glanced about. Seeing no one near, he motioned Pinchus over. Vanderhooven was a tall, thirty-year veteran with gray hair. Most of the station was aware of what had happened between Schwenk and Pinchus that afternoon.

Vanderhooven leaned toward Pinchus. "First thing is, I want to thank you for being the finest cop I've ever had the honor of working with, Detective. . . ."

Then he filled Pinchus in on what happened over the last two hours.

Pinchus went upstairs. He poured coffee for himself and Sam, waited for Sam. Sam arrived, took off his coat and shook it before he hung it up. He sat down, sipped his coffee.

"Not the same as we got at the Le Trois Amis," he said. "But I guess it'll have to do."

"You loved eating there."

"I did. I would have loved it even more if you paid for it." Sam yawned. "Vanderhooven gave me a knowing look when I came in. What's up?"

"Good Captain Schwenk came from Lincoln Dorm empty-handed. It appears that Barry has taken a powder. They did find his car, though, parked right down the street from the dorm. They also found a cardboard box under the front seat."

"And?"

"There was a clasp knife in it with blood on it. And a set of dental models on an articulator. The front teeth were chipped. There was blood on them too. Schwenk sent a unit to pick up Peter Roberts and take him to his office to compare the set in the box with the models he'd made of David. Peter is ninety-five percent certain they match. The lab is checking the blood on the knife and models against Alice's."

"What do you think happened? Did Barry see David? Or did he just sense that his scheme was falling apart?"

"I don't know."

"He probably figured we'd put a bulletin out on his car. Maybe he stole another one."

"They're checking for recent thefts in the area. You know, Barry's car was evidently sitting there all week. Schwenk is screaming that we should have checked it out."

"Is he crazy? We didn't have any reason to. And even if we'd wanted to, on a whim, we had no grounds for a warrant."

"I know," Pinchus agreed. "Still, we blew it. No way around that." He was depressed.

"Seymour. We played it just the way it looked. We didn't blow it."

"Always too late," Pinchus mumbled, turning to look out the window. Heavy raindrops had begun to splatter on it. Then he said, more distinctly, "The bottom line is, there's a killer out there. And he's out there because we fucked up—because *I* fucked up. You were right. I was too involved. I wasn't seeing things clearly."

"*We* made a mistake. And it's not as if we've lost him, as if the damage is irreversible."

Pinchus stared at the falling raindrops, driven

against the window by a slanting wind. They made messy starburst patterns when they struck.

"But we have to accept responsibility for our mistakes. We have to correct them before they lead to damage that *is* irreversible." He swung around and looked at Sam. "Do you know what I'm saying?"

"I think so. You're afraid Barry may kill again. You think you have to get him before he does."

Pinchus nodded.

"You're off the case," reminded Sam.

"I'm missing something, something my subconscious picked up but that I can't bring to the surface. It may tell us where Barry is."

Sam reached for his phone. "Let me call Helen. I want to go bowling. Three games. I'll bet you a dinner on high cumulative score."

Pinchus stopped him. "No. I'm all right, Sam. Seriously."

"You'll go home?"

"I won't stay more than an hour. Promise."

"Might be a nice idea to call Kate."

"Sam," Pinchus said in a pained tone.

Sam raised his hands. "All right. All right. I'm going." He got his coat and put it back on. "Have a happy birthday tomorrow, Seymour. Say hello to everyone for me."

"I will. Thanks, Sam. See you Monday."

"Monday."

Sam left.

Sitting alone, it became even harder for Pinchus to deal with his sense of failure, with his fear that he would be too late once again, and that this time it would be his fault and his alone.

He picked the receiver up from the telephone and pressed in Kate's number.

She answered on the third ring. "Hello?"

Hearing her voice, Pinchus felt some of the darkness begin to leave him.

"Hi, baby," he said tenderly.

"Hi," she answered. "What's up?"

He was glad she sounded pleased to hear from him. "I wanted to talk a bit, if you can."

"Sure. Go ahead."

He told her what had happened, how he felt.

"Yes," she said when he was finished, "that's true. That *is* how you feel. But your feelings aren't *facts*, they are not evidence for the way things are."

He saw immediately what she meant.

She said, "You know, there's a rising—"

"—and a falling away, of everything."

"I say that a lot, huh?"

"It's good you do," he said as a compliment. "I keep forgetting."

"I need to hear it myself."

"Something I read once. To the effect that thirty days ago we were upset about something, but right now, today, we can't remember what it was. We can't even remember what we were upset about seven days ago. A year from now, we're not going to remember how we were feeling today."

"I buy that," Kate said.

"Yeah, I think I do, too."

"Everything okay for brunch tomorrow?"

"Yup. Be at my place at eleven. We'll go in my car."

"Good. See you then."

"I love you," he said.

"I love *you*," she said lightly. "Bye."

       Pinchus stayed at the station awhile, looking back through his notes. But nothing came to him. Nor was there any news of Barry. Pinchus still was not happy, but he was less *unhappy* than he had been before he talked with Kate. He loved Kate. He was grateful for Kate.

He went home.

Daniel and Susan got back shortly after he did. They'd had a good time at Chadds Ford despite a hard drive home in the rain. Pinchus and Daniel had a brandy together. Susan forwent brandy because of her pregnancy and joined them with a glass of juice. Pinchus didn't say much about what had happened today even though he wanted to talk about it with Daniel: This wasn't the right time, not with Susan here, with her newness and uneasiness about police work. And actually, he found it a tonic to leave the case behind and talk about other things, to let Daniel and Susan's youth, their vitality, and their obvious love for each other buoy him.

They called it a night after a single brandy and an hour of talk.

Pinchus fell asleep almost immediately, lulled by the beat of the rain on the roof, on the leaves of the tree outside his window. He slept deeply, peacefully.

But in the morning—a gray, rainy morning—his eyes snapped open and he sat bolt upright. He pulled the phone off the night table and pushed numbers.

Diane answered. "Hello?" She sounded wide awake.

"Hi, pumpkin. It's Seymour. What are you doing up at this hour?"

"Peter had an emergency call. You just missed him."

"Jesus, on Sunday morning?"

"He's becoming a celebrity, I think. What gives me hope is that this time he was annoyed at having to go out. He's on his way to Fairfield County. But he's stopping at the office first. You can reach him—oh, you can't. Sundays, incoming calls are routed directly to the service. The phones don't even ring in the office. I—"

"Thanks pumpkin," Pinchus said, and hung up.

He got out of bed, dressed hurriedly in jeans and a sweatshirt. He pulled on a pair of moccasins over bare feet. He went downstairs, grabbed an apple from a basket in the kitchen to eat on the way. He took a windbreaker from the closet, then was out the door and jogging toward his car, keys in hand.

Peter Roberts was frustrated. He'd cursed the pounding rain on the drive to his office, got drenched on the short run from the parking lot into the building. He wanted to be in bed with Diane. He wanted to be home with the kids. He was pissed off and dripping wet.

The call had come in an hour ago. A coroner in Fairfield County needed his help, was calling because he'd read about Peter in the paper. Last night a car had skidded off the road in Fairfield during the storm, had crashed into a tree, and burst into flames. The driver was too badly burned to identify. The coroner needed Peter for a forensic dental exam. Ordinarily, a trip on Monday would have been good enough. But the car belonged to the son of a county official, and the boy was missing along with another young man, with whom he had been seen earlier. Neither could now be found, and both families were in an agony of uncertainty. The need for identification was urgent.

Acknowledging it was Sunday, the coroner's office instructed Peter to bill them at twice his usual rate.

As if the prospect of a fifty-mile drive through bad weather weren't enough, Peter had to detour to his office first. Normally, he kept his forensic kit in the trunk of his car. But last week he'd brought it to the office to restock and hadn't put it back yet.

Arriving at his office door, Peter unlocked it, reached in, and switched on the waiting room lights. He was grateful that the phone had awakened Diane first and that she had answered. At least she knew the call was legitimate, that he wasn't playing games. He desperately needed her to trust him again. Peter went in and closed the door. He noticed a folded sheet of paper on the floor, which had been slipped beneath the door and which had been dragged in when he'd opened the door. There was a soil line on the paper, an edge had been torn. Peter picked it up and unfolded it.

It was a typewritten piece of doggerel. It read:

> I always pay for services rendered
> I'm grateful for those that you have tendered.
> And when I make a house call,
> I never ask for more, at all.
> That is very good fortune for you.
> So now, good doctor, Adieu, adieu.

Peter could make no sense of it. He assumed it was from a patient who meant it as a joke, but he had no idea who, or what the joke might be. He went into the lab, setting the paper aside on the counter. He got out his forensic bag, checked it. Everything he needed was there.

He looked at the models of David Harper's teeth on the counter, which he'd left out last night after comparing them to the models the police officers had brought him. The two he had tested on his own flesh were slightly damaged. He frowned. He picked one of the models up, turned it over in his hands. He scratched at it with a fingernail.

"Son of a gun," he said to himself.

He turned to the small mirror mounted on the wall behind him. He lifted the model to his throat, positioned the teeth, then applied pressure. He grunted with pain, but increased the pressure until the teeth of the model started to crack. They cracked badly. Peter released the pressure. He looked into the mirror, studying the mark the teeth had left. Then he examined the teeth.

He picked up the phone and called Seymour Pinchus. Seymour's answering machine came on after the second ring.

"Hi, this is Seymour Pinchus. Please leave—"

"Seymour," Peter said. "Are you there? Can you hear this?"

"—your name and number and any message you'd like after the beep, and I'll—"

"Seymour, this is Peter. Please pick up."

"—get back to you soon. Thank you. Good bye."

Beeeeeep.

"Seymour? Are you there? Seymour, this is Peter. Please pick up the phone if you can hear me. It's important. Hello?"

Peter waited. After a few moments Seymour's machine turned itself off and the connection was broken.

Peter searched his pockets for the number of the coroner in Fairfield County. He wanted to call the man and tell him that he'd be late. But he couldn't find the scrap of paper on which he'd written the number. He remembered setting it on the table in the foyer while he got his jacket out of the closet. He couldn't remember putting it into his pocket.

He called home to ask Diane to read it off to him. There was no answer. He hung up and tried again. Again there was no answer. He tried a third time, letting the phone ring and ring. A crack of thunder made him wince. Through the open door of the lab, Peter could see the office lit up by lightning. He set the receiver back down in its cradle, assuming that the storm had knocked out phone service around his home.

48

Diane Roberts put the kitchen phone back on its hook in annoyance. There was still no dial tone. "Damn it."

"Mom said a bad word," Paul observed to Melanie.

"She knows a lot of bad words. You should have heard her last week when she couldn't get the washing machine to work."

"That was a *very* unusual situation," Diane said. "I had to get your stuff washed so you could go to Jenny's party that night."

"Would you say some of them now, Mom?" Paul asked.

"No, I will not. I'm sorry I said that one. Anyway, it looks as if the storm knocked out our phones—and only God knows when your father will get back. So it's just the three of us, gang. Suggestions?"

"How about a movie later?" Melanie proposed.

"Yeah!" screeched Paul. "I want to pick which one we see."

"Okay. But the Sunday paper is scattered all over the lawn from the storm, and I can't call the theaters yet because the phone doesn't work. So I don't know what's playing or when. But it's early, we have plenty of time to worry about that."

"We could look at yesterday's paper," Melanie suggested. "The Saturday guide gives Sunday times, too."

"Wise child. Saturday's paper is in the garage next to the garbage cans."

"I'll get it," Melanie said.

Melanie went into the mud room behind the kitchen and opened the door to the garage.

Meeoooowww. A wet and dripping Snowball shot in from the garage.

"You're back!" Melanie cried. "Oh, poor baby. Did you get all wet?"

Snowball went directly to his food dish and began eating dried kibble. Melanie returned to the kitchen with Saturday's paper and set it on the counter. She got a towel and knelt down next to the cat. She dried him gently as he ate, crooning to him.

"How did Snowball get in the garage?" Diane asked. "And why is he soaking wet?"

"Uh-oh," Melanie said guiltily.

Diane looked at her expectantly.

"Well, see, I kind of forgot to bring him in last night. So he was out all night. And when I called for him this morning, he didn't come. So after Daddy left, I opened the garage door halfway so he could get in out of the rain if he wanted to."

"The garage door has been open since seven-thirty this morning? Oh, Mel. The garage is probably flooded by now. Tons of field mice could have gotten in."

"Uh-uh, Mom. The garage is all dry and Snowball would have caught any mice that tried to get in."

"Did you close the door?"

"Yes."

"Good. Please don't do that again without telling Daddy or me, honey."

"So what's playing at the movies?" Paul asked.

"I'll look after I finish cleaning up. Why don't you two go into the living room and find something to watch until I'm done."

"Come on, Paul." Melanie took Paul's hand and led him into the living room.

Diane stacked the last breakfast dishes into the dishwasher, latched the door closed, and turned the machine on. Nothing happened.

"The TV isn't working," Melanie called from the living room.

"Neither are the lights," Paul said.

They came back into the kitchen.

"That's odd. The power was on when you closed the garage door." The clock on the wall said eight twenty-eight. The second hand wasn't moving. Diane looked at her watch: eight thirty-two. Diane sighed. "I guess the storm knocked out a power line too."

"The Rhodenbarrs's have their lights on." Paul was kneeling on the banquette in the breakfast nook pointing out the window.

Diane looked. "Huh. Must be a circuit breaker then. Damn."

Melanie and Paul exchanged a significant look.

"There are times," Diane said, "when certain language—well, maybe we'll talk about that this afternoon. I have to go down to the basement and flip the breaker. You guys stay here."

Diane opened a drawer and got out the flashlight. She shook it, listening to a single battery sliding up and down in the handle.

"Okay, which one of you took a battery out of here?"

"I borrowed it for the Sega," Melanie confessed. "I'll run upstairs and get it."

"Never mind. There's probably enough light from the windows down there. Back in a minute."

Diane went into the utility room and opened the door to the basement. She made her way down the stairs, one hand against the wall. It was darker than she thought it would be. The small basement windows let in little light from the dreary day outside. Thunder boomed, rattling the house.

She reached the concrete floor and crossed over to the storage closet in which the breaker box board was housed. She turned the knob and pulled, but the door gave only a little. It was stuck. She pulled again, harder. It seemed to give, then spring back. She took hold of the knob with both hands, braced a knee against the jamb and yanked with all her strength. The door gave way suddenly and something came lunging out of the closet at her.

Diane screamed and threw up her arms to protect herself. She stumbled back. There was a thud—and the smell of rising dust—as the ironing board that had fallen forward out of the closet struck the floor.

"Mom?" Melanie called out. "Are you all right?"

"I'm fine, baby," Diane called back. "Something fell out of the closet and took me by surprise, that's all. Everything's all right. I'll be up in just a bit."

Squinting into the closet, Diane located the breaker box. She was about to open it when she noticed that the large metal handle on the side was in the down position. She knew very little of electricity, but that was not the way she remembered seeing the handle the last time she'd had to reset a breaker. She shrugged, took hold of the lever and lifted it.

Above, she heard the dishwasher go on.

"Dishwasher's on!" Melanie yelled.

"TV's on, too!" Paul cried more faintly, from the living room.

"Lights are on! Everything is working, Mom!" Melanie yelled.

"Okay," Diane called back. "Comin' up."

She trotted up the basement steps, closed the door behind her, and went into the kitchen.

"Yay, Mom!" Paul said, clapping.

Melanie whistled.

"Thank you, my dears. What's say we go upstairs and get dressed. We'll meet back down here, figure out what we can do this morning, pick out our movie for later. Okay?"

Melanie and Paul went racing upstairs. Diane followed at a more leisurely pace.

In her bedroom, Diane slipped off her bathrobe, hung it up. She was wearing light blue cotton pajamas. The thermostat wasn't set for winter yet. It had been chilly in the bedroom last night, so she'd gotten up and changed from her nightgown into the pajamas, had slept comfortably then. Now, she toed off her fuzzy pink slippers.

There was a loud hissing outside the window, followed almost instantly by an explosion and a flash of brilliant white light that filled the room. Diane jumped, her heart pounding at how close the lightning had struck.

"Wow!" Paul called from his room.

"Holy Christ!" Melanie yelled from hers.

Both kids appeared suddenly in Diane's room, eyes wide with fright.

"It's okay," Diane assured them. "It was just lightning. Come, let's see if we can find where it hit." She went to the window, gathered them in. Together they peered down the street.

A maple tree by the Scudders's driveway was torn and splintered twenty feet up its trunk; a portion of it lay in the street. The splintered area was smoking.

"Boy, that's something," Melanie remarked.

"Sure is. You two know that our house is grounded, don't you? That means that if lightning ever hit the house—which probably wouldn't happen in a million years—the lightning would be carried to the ground. The house wouldn't be hurt at all and neither would we."

"You sure?" Paul asked.

"Absolutely. Cross my heart. Go finish getting dressed now."

When they left, Diane picked up the remote control for the television. She turned the television on to the weather station. The announcer was talking about the brush fires around Los Angeles.

Abruptly, the television went off. So did the lights.

"Shit!" Diane said, as Paul and Melanie reentered from the hall.

Paul looked at Melanie. "That's worse than damn, isn't it?"

"Uh-huh. Mom, the power's off."

"I know. Thank you, love. There's enough light for both of you to get dressed with. I'll go downstairs again and see what's wrong this time. The power might be out for a while. We may have to use candles."

Diane descended the back stairs to the kitchen barefoot. She went into the utility room—and stopped cold before the basement door. It was slightly ajar. She was certain she had closed it. Well, *almost* certain.

Maybe she hadn't closed it all the way. Maybe Peter had come home, unable to travel in this weather, had seen the power was out, and gone down to the basement to check the box. There had to be a logical explanation. Tentatively, she reached for the knob, began to open the door.

Suddenly the door swung outward, throwing her back. She was pinned between it and the wall, pressed hard. She gasped, sucked in breath to scream.

A hand reached around the edge of the door and grabbed her hair. "You want to stay very quiet," said a harsh voice. "We don't want to alarm the kiddies, do we?"

49

The scream froze in Diane's throat. "Don't touch my babies."

"Give me a reason," the voice said.

"You can have anything you want. I'll *do* anything you want. Just leave them alone. Anything, you can have anything."

"That's good. Good girl. I'm going to let you out now, slow. We'll talk about what you can do for me. Don't try anything stupid. Your kids'll be the ones who pay."

"I won't." Diane struggled to keep herself calm. She had to, for Paul and Melanie's sake.

Slowly the force that had been pressing her against the wall was released. The door swung back. Standing there in jeans and a khaki shirt, with a ski mask over his head that hid his face, and still holding her by the hair, was her attacker. Diane's legs began to tremble. She felt light-headed, sagged back against the wall.

"Mommy!" Melanie was in the doorway of the utility room. Paul was with her, wide-eyed.

Diane rallied. *"Run!"* she screamed. "Get out! *Run!"*

After an instant's paralysis, Melanie grabbed Paul and fled. Diane's attacker turned to look after the children. Diane made a fist. She punched the man as hard as she could in the throat. He choked, and she felt his grip loosen on her hair. Diane ducked around him and ran through the kitchen toward the front of the house, where Melanie was fumbling with the locks on the front door and Paul was pressed into her.

Diane heard her attacker's footfalls pounding a few feet behind her. Bursting into the foyer, she grabbed the children and swept them into the study with her. She slammed the study door, reached for the lock. The door came crushing inward, knocking her backward.

Paul and Melanie screamed.

The attacked lunged forward, grabbed Diane by the hair again, reached for the children. Diane leaped at him, wrapping her arms around him, tangling her legs in his, and brought them both crashing to the floor.

"Run!" she screamed to her children. "Get away! Get *away*!"

"Mommy!" Melanie grabbed a book out of the bookcase and ran forward. She began striking the intruder on the back and shoulders with it. "Leave her alone!" she screamed.

Then Paul was there too, shrieking, pummeling the man with his fists.

The man sent Melanie reeling with a backhanded slap. Paul shied away. Melanie raised the book over her head and prepared to renew the attack.

Diane grappled with the man, trying to keep him from rising off her. She twisted her head to look at her children. "Goddamn you, Melanie! Run! Take Paul and run!"

Melanie hesitated.

"*Run!*" Diane screamed.

Melanie dropped the book, seized Paul's hand, and ran with him out of the study. But to Diane's despair, they ran up the stairs instead of to the still-locked front door.

The attacker hit Diane on the side of her head, then again. The blows stung. Her mind became cloudy. He freed himself from her grasp, stood, took hold of her pajama top and jerked her up to her feet.

"*Real* nice try," he said to her. "I like a girl with spunk."

Holding the throat of her pajama tops, he reached down with his other and took hold of her left breast.

"Spunk and good tits," he said. "A nice combination. How's your pussy?"

Diane blinked, struggling to regain her senses. She felt his fingers probe her vagina through the pajama fabric.

"Fucker!" she screamed. With all her might, she brought her knee up between his legs.

He grunted and released her. She shoved him aside, bolted from the den into the foyer. There, she hesitated in an agony of indecision. Could she unlock the front door in time? Should she run upstairs to be with the children? Should she run in another direction, taking the man away from the children, and look for a weapon?

She heard him coming behind her and opted for the latter. She ran into the living room, seized a vase from a table next to a chair, spun, threw it at him. The vase crashed against the wall without hitting him. She ran for the coffee table in front of the couch, where there was a metal letter opener. Simultaneously, she spied the brass poker by the fireplace. She slowed, not sure which to try for, and her attacker overtook her. He lunged, reaching, and caught her pajama bottoms at the waist. The bottoms were pulled down to her knees. They tripped her. She rolled, kept the man at bay for a moment with kicking feet, screaming, "Bastard! Bastard!" Then she was up, pulling the pajama bottoms back up around her waist, and running for the fireplace.

He caught her from behind, grabbed her with one arm around her throat, the other around her chest. She twisted, tried to kick backward at him, tried to reach his arm to bite it.

"You didn't keep your word," he said into her ear, breathing hard. "You said you'd be nice."

He wrestled her to the aquarium, which stood on a heavy wrought-iron stand at the fireplace. He bent her over the aquarium and forced her head down into the water. She struggled to lift her head, twisted it from side to side, sloshing water out the tank and soaking herself, managing to catch small breaths mixed with water that burned her nostrils and throat.

Laughing, her attacker pulled her head up.

She gasped in air with a loud wheezing sound.

She sensed her attacker shifting his feet. Felt a stronger force at the back of her head. "One more time!" he said gaily, and drove her face back into the water.

Melanie and Paul cowered in the darkness. Snowball was curled in Melanie's lap, oblivious to the children's emotions. Melanie had one arm around Paul, with her other hand was petting Snowball reflexively. She was listening as hard as she could, but all she could hear was Snowball's low purring. Paul pressed into her. He was trembling.

When she'd run from the study with Paul, Melanie had been afraid that she wouldn't be able to open the locks on the front door in time for them get away. So she had turned instead to the stairs and raced up them, dragging Paul behind her.

Without hesitating, she had run directly to her own room. She closed the door. Paul stared at her in terror.

She put her finger to her lips. "Shhhh. Don't make a single sound."

He shook his head, indicating that he wouldn't.

Snowball was lying on Melanie's bed. He had been asleep. Their entry had awakened him. He stretched, rolled over on his back in an invitation to be petted.

"Take Snowball," Melanie said.

Paul picked the cat up and cradled it in his arms. Snowball snuggled in, licked Paul's hand.

Melanie moved a chair from in front of the panel that closed off the sealed stairwell that had once led from the utility room to her room. She had long ago succeeded in opening it, without anyone knowing, but only last year had become sufficiently skillful with tools to fit it with hinges. She gripped the panel on one side and pulled. The long Velcro strip she'd mounted on the other side opened with a tearing sound. Paul stared in amazement. She had never revealed this secret to anyone, not even to Sarah Roy, who was her best friend. Melanie kept treasures in this secret space: an old stuffed bear, a wig Sarah's mother had discarded, forbidden comic books. She knew her father would be angry if he ever discovered what she'd done; worse, he would seal up her sanctuary in a way that she would never be able to get into it again.

"Get inside," she whispered to Paul. "Hurry."

"It's dark there. I'm scared."

"It's perfectly safe. I go in there all the time. Hurry up. I've got some Snickers bars inside. *Hurry, Paul,*" she said urgently.

It was her tone that convinced him. He went inside.

She came in after him. "Sit down. Stay on this landing and don't move. There are stairs behind us."

She pulled the panel closed, secured it with the slide lock she'd mounted when she put the hinges on. She took Snowball onto her lap, put an arm around Paul, and pulled him in close to her. He seized her hand with both of his.

"Not a single sound," she warned Paul.

Diane thought he meant to drown her, and there was nothing, nothing she could do to stop him. He was too strong. She couldn't get her face out of the water, couldn't reach him with her flailing arms. The last of her breath burst from her mouth. She breathed in water, choked—and he pulled her head up by the hair.

She sucked air in hoarsely. Water ran down her face. The water in the aquarium was sloshing from side to side. Fish were flitting about in panic. On the soaked carpet around the wrought-iron were strands of seaweed, a single angelfish flopping about.

Diane's attacker forced her to her knees. She was too weak to resist. He took a pair of handcuffs from his back pocket, closed one of the cuffs around her right wrist, secured the other to a leg and crossbar of the aquarium stand.

He cupped her cheek tenderly with one hand. With his other, he stroked her breasts, squeezed them softly.

"Oh, we are going to have fun," he said. "But first . . ." He stood. "I've got to make sure the kids are asleep."

Diane was shocked into alertness. She clawed for him with her free hand. His image was horrifying. Face cloaked, eyes peering out with a taunting gleam in them. A chill came over Diàne. "Don't you dare touch my babies, you fucking animal!"

"You just won't give up, will you?"

The man swung his foot and kicked Diane in the face. There was the sound of bone cracking. Her head snapped back. Blood gushed from her split lip. Her eyes rolled up in their sockets and she slumped forward to the floor unconscious.

"Back in a jiff," the man said.

He left the living room for the foyer in a slow and calculating manner, then started up the stairs.

Within her sanctuary, Melanie could dimly hear the man looking around the upstairs. He was going from room to room. Paul was huddled against her. Snowball purred quietly in her lap.

Melanie heard the man enter her room. Involuntarily, she held her breath. Paul tensed. Melanie hugged him closer, squeezed his hand.

"Why, this is a charming little girl's room," the man said on the other side of the panel. "Let's see, are you hiding in the closet? . . . No, not there. . . . How about under the bed? ... No, not there either. Where, oh where could you be?

"Children, wherever you are, listen to me. You can come out now. It's all right. I promise that if you do come out, I won't hurt your Mommy. I promise. Come on out now."

Melanie was afraid Snowball's purring was too loud. She stopped petting him.

The cat went, *Meeoww?*

Paul twitched. Melanie bit her lip. She began petting Snowball frantically. The purring resumed.

In a few moments, Melanie heard the man's voice again, from the hall outside her room. "Well, could you have gone down those back stairs there? Are you hiding in the garage? The basement? I guess we'll have to go see. Here I come," he said, "ready or not!"

Melanie waited, breathing shallowly. She strained, listening, but couldn't hear anything. She put her lips next to Paul's ear.

"Here, take Snowball," she whispered. "I'm going to open it up. Stay very quiet. When we get out, we're going to sneak down the front stairs. I'll open the locks on the front door and then we're going to run out and right over to the Rhodenbarrs's house. Okay?"

Paul nodded.

Melanie opened the slide lock, held her breath, then pushed open the panel. Her mouth was dry. Her heart was pounding. She felt like she was going to pee. The room was empty.

"Okay," she whispered. "Let's go."

They crept out, started to tiptoe toward the door.

A hand dropped onto Melanie's shoulder from behind. A voice said, "Tag, you're it."

The man had been pressed up against the wall, concealed by the panel when Melanie opened it.

Paul screamed and threw Snowball upward at the man's face.

Snowball screeched, landed with his claws extended on the man's head and chest.

"Jesus! Shit! Fuck!" The man staggered backward, grabbing at Snowball. Left alone, Snowball would have jumped down to the floor, but now he flattened his ears and wailed and bit and clawed at the hands that grabbed at him.

A heavy crash sounded from downstairs. "Melanie! Paul!" It was their mother's voice.

Melanie and Paul raced from the room. They heard a thumping noise downstairs. They reached the head of the stairs. Their mother was standing bent at the door, opening the locks. Her right arm extended outward and down, chained to the aquarium stand, which she had dragged behind her. The front of her pajamas was soaked. Her hair was wet, plastered to her head and face. There was blood on her mouth.

As Melanie and Paul ran down the stairs, she jerked the door open. "Hurry!" she screamed. "Get out! Run! Run!"

Melanie gritted her teeth. She jumped the last two stairs, pulling Paul after her. Paul stumbled when he hit the foyer floor. Melanie dragged him, half-falling, past her mother, through the door, out onto the porch and down the steps to the yard.

Diane saw the man reach the top of the stairs above her and then the faceless monster came bounding down them. She slammed the door shut after the children, managed to turn one of the locks, then positioned herself as a barricade in front of it.

The man reached the bottom, slapped Diane, and tried to throw her aside.

Diane seized his wrist, jerked it to her mouth, and bit into it as he hard as she could.

He shouted, "Yhhhaaa!"

He clenched his other hand into a fist and hit her, hit her again. She released his hand and fell back against the wall.

He scrabbled at the locks but couldn't find the right one. He slammed a hand against the door. "Shit! Shit!"

He got the right lock finally and turned it. He opened the door, but then stopped and closed it again. He leaned his forehead against it. He stood there, eyes closed, breathing deeply.

"My babies are safe. You can't hurt them. You can't touch them anymore."

He looked at her. His eyes seemed to grow as wide as the holes in the ski mask. "Bitch," he shouted bitterly.

She backed away, toward the living room, dragging the aquarium stand. He followed her.

In the living room, the shattered aquarium lay on the wet carpeting. Fish wriggled on the carpet amid seaweed and gravel and pieces of coral.

Diane kept her eyes on the man, moving backward toward the coffee table.

"You can't hurt them, you sick fuck. I beat you, you scumbag. You bastard. You prickless little piece of shit."

She reached behind her with her left hand, probing for the table, the letter opener.

The man advanced slowly, matching each of Diane's steps with one of his own. "Game's not over yet." Through the mouth opening in the ski mask, she caught a glimpse of his smile.

He drew a knife from his pocket, touched a button on its side. The long blade sprang open with a click.

Diane glanced over her shoulder. Her hand was less than a foot from the letter opener. She threw herself toward it.

The man moved with her, jammed his foot on a leg of the aquarium stand, which was on its side. Diane's fingers missed the letter opener by inches. She crouched, strained toward it.

The man took hold of the aquarium stand, yanked. Diane fell. The man dragged her away from the coffee table. Then he stopped, came around the aquarium stand. Diane was up on her knees.

The man raised the knife. "*Now* the game is over," he said, and brought his arm plunging down.

Diane shrank into herself, eyes squeezed shut.

Booom!

In shock, Diane looked up.

The man was standing above her, knife suspended at shoulder level. He was looking down at his chest. There was a dark hole in his shirt, and and a small circle of blood around it, which began to spread rapidly.

Booom!

A second hole appeared near the first.

The man took a step backward, swayed. The knife fell from his hand. He was looking toward the foyer.

Booom! Booom! Booom!

The man was driven backward as if hit by a sledge-hammer. He struck the wall, bounced off, the front of his shirt soaked in blood now, then turned and fell to the carpet on his back. He lay there, unmoving.

Diane looked toward the foyer where Seymour Pinchus was half crouched, holding his revolver in both hands. Peter was beside him. Pinchus straightened and walked into the living room, his revolver trained on the fallen man.

"It's going to be all right, pumpkin," he told Diane. "I love you."

Peter rushed in to the room and dropped to his knees beside Diane. He wrapped her in his arms. "Oh God, Di!"

"The children," she cried.

"They're with Sadie Rhodenbarr. They're safe."

"Tell them I'm all right."

"Yes," he said, rocking back and forth with her. "Just let me hold you for a moment."

Pinchus squatted next to the fallen figure. He pressed two fingers to the man's carotid artery. There was no pulse.

"For once," he mumbled, "I'm not too late."

Peter said, "What?"

"Nothing. Just talking to myself."

Pinchus put his revolver back into its holster. He grasped the top of the ski mask, pulled the mask up, and gazed down at the face of David Harper.

50

Lieutenant Seymour Pin-
chus didn't get to the station till nearly eleven on Monday morning. He felt good. He felt rested. Actually, he
felt wonderful.

He was coming from Kate's house. They had made
love last night. And again this morning. Which wasn't
bad for a fifty-five-year-old. Then they had sat around
the kitchen table and eaten breakfast. They had
laughed a lot, like schoolkids. Like Pinchus imagined
Daniel and Susan might.

Yesterday, in Peter and Diane Roberts's home, after
he had found the key to the handcuffs in David Harper's pocket, Pinchus had released Diane and got her settled in the study to wait for the ambulance. When
Peter returned from the Rhodenbarrs's where he reas-
sured the kids, Pinchus had sat him down and instructed him carefully on what he wanted Peter to do.
He gave Peter Sam Milano's home phone number.

Pinchus remained till the first uniforms arrived,
which wasn't long. The officers were from another pre-
cinct and didn't recognize Pinchus at first. They gave
him hard looks when they came in, but then the taller
of them nudged his partner and said something to him
and they both became suddenly respectful even before
Pinchus showed them his ID.

"Secure the scene," Pinchus ordered. "Dr. Roberts
will give you a full and accurate statement. If the ambulance doesn't get here in the next five minutes, have
a patrol car take Mrs. Roberts to the hospital. Any
questions you have, direct them to Sergeant Sam Mil-

ano at Rivington Street station, Homicide. Understood?"

"Yes, sir!"

"Good. Carry on."

Pinchus left.

It had been a wonderful birthday brunch with
Daniel and Susan and Kate. He didn't tell them where
he'd been, why he was arriving back at the house just
as Kate was pulling up, or why he was wearing moccasins without socks.

He just winked. "There was something I had to
do," he said. "Business. Not worth discussing now.
Let's go eat. I'm starved."

"Do you want to shower?" Kate asked. "Maybe
change? At least put on socks?"

"Nope. I want to go just like this and I want to go
right now."

The phone rang.

"Let's go." Pinchus waved them onward.

"Don't you want to see who that is?" Kate asked.

"No. Hurry, hurry now. Everybody out and into
my car."

"Well, it *is* your birthday," Daniel said uncertainly.

"Damn straight. Haul ass, son."

It was the best birthday day he had ever had. And
after it was over, and Daniel and Susan were on their
way back to New York, and he had called Rose
Fitapaldi to say he wouldn't be able to visit today but
that he loved her and would be out to see her next
Sunday with Kate, he returned to Kate's house with
her. On the way, he told her what had happened. And
then, after he asked Kate to call the station in response
to the messages Sam Milano, Schwenk, and others had
left on her answering machine about his whereabouts
and tell them she had no idea where he was but would
be certain to inform Seymour that they had called if he
got in touch with her, Pinchus had had the best birthday night he had ever had.

Officers and detectives high-signed Pinchus when he came into the station. He acknowledged them, went up the stairs to the squad room, where he received more smiles and thumbs-up. There was half a pot of coffee left.

"Nice of you to stop by today," Sam said. "Schwenk's going nuts."

"So, *nu*? I'll get to him after we talk. I owe you a talk at least."

"At least," Sam agreed. "I spent most of yesterday putting this together, or as many parts as I could. Helen is not happy with you."

"Flowers?"

"That would help. I suggest a large and costly bouquet."

Pinchus looked in his wallet. "That's doable."

"Good. I told Schwenk that he ought to write you up for a commendation."

Pinchus had poured a cup of coffee and carried it back to his desk. He almost choked on his first mouthful when Sam told him that. "Jesus! What'd the poor bastard say?"

"He mumbled something like, 'Thank you. I'll consider it. Yes. Thank you.' You ever going to let his balls out of the vise?"

"Maybe on Yom Kippur, if he asks."

"How's Diane?"

"They've got her jaw wired. Wasn't as bad as we first thought. A fracture, but she'll be fine."

"Good."

"What about Barry?" Pinchus asked.

"He's gonna be okay, too. David had a rent receipt in his wallet. Little one-room job near the Slaughtered Lamb. He had Barry there, tied up, drugged out of his mind on phenobarbs and a bunch of other stuff. The doctor says he'll be good as new—physically, anyway—in a couple of days."

"Great. So, what'd you get?"

Sam opened a folder, looked into it. "David *was* Alan Harper's son. We found the letter. The deal was like David told us it was. The affair would stay a secret, Alan would see that David was provided for. What it looks like is that George's wife confessed to him one night when she was drunk. So not only did George get disinherited by his father, now he finds out that his wife was fucking his brother, and even worse, that his kid isn't even really his kid. So off a mountain road he goes. David learned the truth a couple of years later, when he uncovered the letter."

"How do we know?" Pinchus asked.

"Nicolaides was able to interview David's mother yesterday."

"So he did kill Alan and Wanda Harper."

"How do you figure?" Sam said.

"He was a smart sonofabitch, even if Mensa didn't let him in. I don't think we can ever prove it, but what I see is this: David figures he can get the whole estate—not just by doing in the Harpers, but by pushing Barry over the edge as well, by convincing him that he, Barry, had killed his own parents. He drugs Barry that night, does the parents, then sets up the scene with the footprints in the basement and the blood trail across the lawn."

"There was a witness, a neighbor, who saw a car speeding away from the street. Remember?"

Pinchus shrugged. "Simple coincidence. Maybe even an excitable imagination. David does something else that night before he sets off the alarm, something he thinks will cause Barry to flip and that also explains why the police reports contradict Barry about who discovered the bodies. Barry told me the truth. David *had* awakened him after supposedly finding the bodies. But Barry lied to the Ridgefield police, said *he* was the one who discovered them."

"Why?"

"I'm guessing. But I'll lay odds it goes something like this: Barry is out like a light. David cleans himself up, then smears Barry's pajamas and bedsheets with his parents' blood. Later, David says, 'My God, Barry. How did your sheets get full of blood?'

"The implication is obvious. David makes Barry think maybe he killed his own parents in some kind of psychotic blackout. Barry has no memory of this, but remember, he's emotionally unstable to begin with, he's been drugged, he's confused. Maybe he doesn't *believe* he killed them, but he's worried. David tells him something like he must have been wakened by the sound of the crime, maybe even have seen the murderers, but gone into shock, blocked it out, and returned to bed without even knowing he'd been up.

"Barry may not be convinced of this either, but it does get him off the hook, so he goes for it. David cooks up a story for him. 'Tell the police that *you* found the bodies,' he says. 'Tell them that you were so upset and terrified that you ran back to your room and threw yourself on your bed sobbing, afraid the killers were still in the house. That explains the blood.' Then they'll both claim that Barry finally screamed out, that they went back to the master bedroom together. David convinces Barry this is the only way to keep the police from thinking that he killed his own parents. After that, I start to draw a blank."

Sam said, "Pass." He held his hands up as if to catch a football.

Pinchus feigned throwing him one.

"From what I got yesterday," Sam told Pinchus, "Barry was in bad shape after the killings. He went steadily downhill. That fits nicely with an attempt by David to push him over the edge. But then something unexpected happens. Barry starts working with a—" Sam looked at his notes, "a Dr. Clare Dunn, who turns out to be a truly dynamite shrink. Barry gets better, so much better in fact, that he even reenrolls at the university here, which he had dropped out of. David follows him. He watches Barry for a year, probably even plays with his head, seeing if he can push him into trouble again. But Barry keeps getting better."

"I like it," Pinchus smiled. "Keep going."

"David realizes Barry is not going to break down, not going to be declared incompetent. Now, it's a year later. November is coming up. Barry's about to turn twenty-five and get half the estate. David's going to lose. The only other provision in the will that would help him is Barry's death, which would be too obvious. However, if Barry's on trial for murder as he turns twenty-five, he can't inherit. Here's where *I* start to get confused. It's like David wanted us to think he, himself, was guilty."

"He *did*," Pinchus said in astonishment. "The little fucker *wanted* us to figure him for the killer. Then he set about demonstrating that he wasn't guilty. He built so many inconsistencies into the evidence against him that it finally looked like it was Barry who was trying to frame *him*. Once you think you've falsely accused someone, it's hard to point the finger at him again. So we crossed David off as a suspect. But he couldn't afford to let Barry be questioned. For this to work, Barry had to die.

"Alice Schaeffer didn't mean anything to him one way or the other. He just needed a victim whose death would throw initial suspicion onto him. David antagonizes Alice in front of witnesses, sets it all up. He makes sure he has contact with her, gets himself seen in her neighborhood the night she's killed; he even puts a note with Barry's name and dorm in *his* handwriting into her bag."

"He's counting on us to discover that it's his writing," Sam said.

Pinchus nodded. "So he can point out to us that he's much too smart to have made such a blunder. The same with the bite marks. How could he, David, have been so stupid as to leave his teeth marks on someone he killed? It begins to look like the only explanation is that he's been framed. By whom? Why? By Barry, the only other suspect whose alibi conflicts with David's, the person who told David he could get his wallet on a corner near where Alice lived, the only one in the world who would have something to gain if David were convicted of murder."

Sam said, "Uh-huh. And when we come to that conclusion, where is Barry? On the run. We go looking and, shit, man, we even find the models of David's teeth Barry used on Alice, along with a knife. We find them in Barry's car. And they're covered with Alice's blood. The little fucker, I'm getting pissed at him all over again."

"I'll tell you," Pinchus continued, "I still think he left that tie tack for me to find, that he *was* watching me get my butt stuck in that ventilator. Anyway, once we let him go, he figures he'll do Peter's family— provide us with Barry's final act of violence. He sets it up as revenge, Barry getting back at Peter for Peter having discovered that Barry used models of David's teeth to frame David.

"He probably plans to kill Barry with an overdose then and dump the body somewhere, make it look like an accident or suicide. Everybody's happy to close out an ugly case. Who's going to ask questions? Yesterday morning, he calls Peter's house, disguises his voice and gets Peter out by saying he's needed in an accident case fifty miles away. With Peter gone, he makes his move. He didn't know Peter would have to go to his office, or that I would finally put my finger on what had been bothering me. Remember when Peter demonstrated how David's bite mark could be duplicated? Some of the tips of the teeth on the models broke. I didn't think anything about it then, but that was what was working in my subconscious.

"When I got to Peter's office, he had just come to the same realization. We tried it. Every time—with *any* of the models he had in the office—the teeth broke before they could cut through the skin. Yet *two* of the bites on Alice Schaeffer had been very deep, deep enough to take impressions from."

Sam snapped his fingers. "He used the models for the first bite, but they broke without marking Alice well enough. So he uses his *own* teeth for the second two bites. . . . The knife cuts on her back were to give him blood to put on the teeth and the knife he was going to leave in Barry's car. The initials, *AS*, were simply to throw us off the real purpose."

"I think so," Pinchus said.

"How did you figure he was going after Peter's family?"

"I saw a poem in Peter's office. Peter said he'd found it under the office door."

"I looked at that in the evidence locker this morning, but I don't get it."

Pinchus remembered the doggerel exactly. He recited it:

"I always pay for services rendered.
I'm grateful for those that you have tendered.
And when I make a house call,
I never ask for more, at all.
That is very good fortune for you.
So now, good doctor: Adieu, adieu."

"Yeah, so?"

"David meant for the poem to be discovered on Monday—Barry's explanation for what he did to Peter's family. 'Services rendered' is Peter's discovery that Barry framed David. 'Grateful' is sarcastic. 'House call' is killing Diane and the kids. 'Good fortune for you' is that Peter was not present in the house and is therefore still alive."

"You got that all at once?"

"No," Pinchus admitted. "But I got it the minute Peter mentioned he'd tried to call home but that the line was dead."

"Nice, Seymour. You never did quite believe that Barry could have done it, did you?"

Pinchus swirled what remained of his coffee around in his cup. He looked down at it. "Just between you and me?" he asked. He looked up.

"You and me."

"As sure as I was in the beginning and nearly all the way through—by this time, with all that went down, when I pulled the mask off the guy I shot, nobody was more surprised than I to see David Harper's face."

"Thank you," Sam said.

"For what?"

"Making me feel less stupid."

"There's something I have to tell you. I don't want it to be a burden, but I need to tell you."

"I'm your partner. We split the load, remember?"

"No. This one's all mine."

"Go ahead."

Pinchus looked into Sam's eyes. "When I came through the front door at Peter's house and saw the guy standing over Diane? I didn't say, 'Police, freeze.' I didn't say, 'Hold it.' I didn't say anything. I just crouched, cocked, and shot him down."

Sam was quiet for a moment, then he spoke. "Second time in your entire career you ever fired your weapon at someone, right?"

"Yes."

"The first time, you did it too late. This time, you didn't."

Pinchus looked away. He swiped a hand across his eyes. "Allergy," he said.

Sam took a packet of tissues from his pocket and gave Pinchus one. "Fall pollen," he said. "Hey, you know what? You lived to see fifty-five. Congratulations on having been wrong again."

"Thank you. Fifty-six, though. I don't know. I got a feeling."

"Next year, not only will I congratulate you on having been wrong once more, but on being a grandfather to boot."

"Grandpa Seymour," Pinchus nodded. "I can probably get used to that."

51

On a cool afternoon in early May, nearly seven months after the Alice Schaeffer case had been closed, Ernest Thompson, an auto mechanic, walked into the Rivington Street station and asked to see Detective Seymour Pinchus. Sergeant Paul Vanderhooven was working the desk. Vanderhooven sent him up to the second floor, to Homicide.

Pinchus was in the squad room, leaning back in his chair. He was idly linking and unlinking a pair of paper clips as he talked with Sam. A nearby window was open a little. The breeze rustled papers slightly on Pinchus's desk. The coming spring smelled wonderful.

Life was good for Seymour Pinchus: He and Kate had just begun talking about living together; he wasn't pushing, she wasn't running. Daniel's new wife, Susan, was delightful. Even Sharon, Daniel's mother, had not only failed to put her head in an oven but had gone so far as to confide in Pinchus that since Daniel had to marry a shiksa, at least he'd picked a good one. And finally, Pinchus was about to become a grandfather.

He could scarcely remember why he'd never thought he would live to be this old—not that fifty-five was that old—or worse, why for so many years he had hardly cared whether he did.

He and Sam were talking about Daniel. Daniel was graduating from John Jay College of Criminal Justice next week. Pinchus was going up to New York for the ceremony.

"He's pretty much made up his mind not to come here, huh?" Sam said.

Pinchus nodded. "The only real question is whether he's going to pick Boston or New York."

"They're both good departments. You disappointed?"

"Sure. But I understand. He thinks he'd always be in my shadow here. He probably would in the beginning. But I know him. He'd carve out his own place. Two, three years from now, it might be different. He'll feel more his own man. Maybe he'll be willing to come then."

"Maybe," Sam agreed.

Pinchus glanced up. A man had come up the stairs and stopped at the rail that separated the squad room from the waiting area. He was big, beefy. He was wearing a green mechanic's uniform with oil stains on it and carrying a brown lunch bag. The man searched the squad room with his eyes, looking for someone. Pinchus knew him, but couldn't place him for a moment.

Pinchus found the name just as their eyes met: Thompson. Ernest Thompson.

Ernest Thompson was the father of Leon Thompson, whom Pinchus had arrested three years earlier for causing the death of a motorist with a .22-caliber rifle. Leon had been convicted of manslaughter. If Pinchus remembered correctly, he was scheduled to be released somewhere about now, on his eighteenth birthday.

Pinchus nodded.

Thompson did not nod back. Instead, he reached into his lunch bag, pulled a gun from it, and swung it up toward Pinchus.

"Gun!" Pinchus shouted.

He sprang up from his chair, jerking open his desk drawer and reaching for his own weapon, which he'd placed there when he came in this morning.

Time, in Pinchus's perception, slowed nearly to a standstill: He saw Thompson let go of the lunch bag and drop into a half crouch. He saw him bring his left hand up to meet his right, holding the gun in both. He saw Thompson's right thumb push the safety lever down. He saw his right finger beginning to tighten on the trigger. He saw the gun itself distinctly, clearly: Desert Eagle, .357 Magnum.

The first shot hit Pinchus in the chest and drove him backward up against the desk behind him. The second caught him in the right shoulder and spun him around. The third slammed into his head and sent him sprawling onto the desk and then falling off it, crashing to the floor.

"The fuck?" Sam screamed.

Sam was out of his own chair, pivoting, jerking his own gun from its holster.

But Junior Gibney, who had been standing closest to Thompson, had already launched himself over the rail. Gibney tackled Thompson high, wrapping both arms around him, and brought him to the floor. The gun discharged again when it fell from Thompson's hand and struck the floor. Officer Lauralee Collins was next to reach Thompson. Others came swarming to help.

"It's all right! We got 'im! We got 'im!" Gibney yelled.

Sam went down on his knees beside Pinchus.

Pinchus was sprawled on the worn brown carpet. His eyes were open wide, surprised. His pupils shifted to focus on Sam. Pinchus's shirt on his right side and chest was sodden with blood. There was an ugly entrance wound on his left temple. Dark blood pulsed from it, ran down his cheek and head, pooled on the carpet.

Pinchus's lips trembled, as if were trying to speak.

"Hang on, Seymour!" Sam pleaded. "Please!" His hands fluttered helplessly above Pinchus, afraid to touch him for fear of hurting him.

Seymour Pinchus gave Sam a pained half smile. Then he coughed up a gout of blood, his eyes closed, and his head rolled to the side.

▼

Pinchus arrived at Hamilton General Hospital in an ambulance with a screaming siren, led by a patrol car with its own siren wailing. Less than twenty minutes had passed after he'd been shot. Other patrol cars with flashing lights, and private and plainclothes cars, carrying detectives and uniformed officers began pulling up at the emergency entrance moments later.

Pinchus was rushed to emergency surgery on the same bloodsoaked gurney on which the paramedics had evacuated him from the Rivington station—after they'd worked desperately to stabilize his vital functions, establish IV lines, after they'd shot him up with adrenalin, trached him so he could breathe.

Sam wouldn't leave the hall outside the operating room. He argued with a nurse, then a senior resident, then finally the assistant administrator. The knees of his pants were wet with Pinchus's blood, where he'd knelt beside him. He had wiped his hands in the ambulance, but there was still dried blood on them, from when he had helped the paramedics take Seymour out. There was blood on the cuffs and forearms of his shirt.

"No," he kept saying to himself, leaning against the wall. "No. No."

Finally Schwenk himself came upstairs to get him. The captain was ashen-faced. He put his hands on Sam's shoulders. "I'm sorry," he said. "I'm sorry, Sam."

Spontaneously, he pulled Sam into him, patted Sam roughly and clumsily on the back. Then he released him.

"Come on downstairs. They've set up a room for us. It's going to be hours."

"I want to stay here."

"You can't, Sam," Schwenk said, not unkindly. "It wouldn't do any good anyway. Besides . . . I need your help."

Sam looked up.

"Someone's got to notify that woman he goes out

with. Someone's got to notify his son. If you want me to, I'll do it—but I thought it might be better if you did, that maybe you'd want to."

"I'll do it," Sam said. "Yes. It's my job." He walked down the hall with Schwenk. "Yes. My job," he said. "Yes."

It was learned, very quickly, that Thompson's son Leon, whom Pinchus had arrested three years earlier, had been scheduled to be released three days hence, on his eighteenth birthday. But that very morning he had either jumped or been thrown to his death from a catwalk over the exercise yard in the juvenile facility where he was incarcerated. No one was comforted by that knowledge.

Daniel Pinchus reached the hospital at seven. It had taken Sam most of the afternoon to track him down— from the John Jay library where he'd been earlier, to a friend's apartment, to a restaurant, to a bookstore, and three or four other places.

Pinchus was still in surgery when Daniel arrived.

Two groups were keeping vigil in two separate areas. The largest was in a section of the lobby that had been cordoned off for that purpose and that was thick with officers and detectives from the Hamilton Police Department, a handful of city officials, friends of Pinchus, and reporters from the papers and radio and television stations. The smaller area was a private lounge used by interns and residents, now given over to Pinchus's family and few intimate friends.

Kate was there, very calm and quiet. Diane was by a silver coffee urn filling a paper cup. Her eyes were red and puffy. Sam Milano and his wife Helen were there. Sam looked grave and tired. He stepped forward to embrace Daniel, his eyes watering. Diane began to cry when she saw Daniel.

Kate waited till Daniel had finished with the others. Then she hugged him softly, and held him that way for several moments. She took his face in her hands. "I'm sorry, Daniel," she said. "I'm so sorry."

Daniel broke down for the first time. He began sobbing, and couldn't stop. The sobs were deep and wracking, tearing painfully from his chest. Tears streamed down his cheeks, dropped from his jaw. Kate led him to a couch and sat down with him. She held him, and he cried into her chest.

"I want to *kill* the sonofabitch that did this," he choked.

"Yes," Kate said. "So do I."

They cried together with their arms around each other, she stroking his hair and rocking him.

A doctor came an hour later. He was middle-aged with silver-gray hair and glasses. He was still in green scrubs, wearing a paper green hat. There were splotches of perspiration on his scrubs.

"I'm Dr. Porter," he said to the anxious group. "I'm a neurosurgeon. Dr. de Mello, our chief of staff, is the overseeing physician. Lieutenant Pinchus is still in surgery. They're finishing up now. Dr. de Mello will give you a more complete report—" Porter glanced at the clock over the door, "that'll be about half an hour. But I wanted to come down now and tell you where we stand.

"Lieutenant Pinchus is still critical. I can't tell you what's going to happen, but he is alive and his vital signs are acceptable.

"He suffered a gunshot wound to the right shoulder that shattered the head of the humerus and ruptured the axillary artery. He was hit a second time in the chest. The bullet pierced the left lung, nicked the aorta, and exited his back. Both these wounds were serious and life threatening, but they were—and are—manageable."

Porter looked at each of them. "The greatest danger is from the third wound, to the left temple. Fortunately, the bullet fragmented. Maybe due to a defect, maybe to the angle at which it struck the skull. I don't know. If it had penetrated directly, and entirely, Lieutenant Pinchus would be dead now. It didn't. However, pieces of it did, which lodged in the brain. We got all but one. The site made that one too dangerous to attempt to remove. We can't tell the extent of the damage yet. I'm sorry. I wish I could give you more. I know it's not much comfort, but we're lucky we have him at all."

Daniel was the one who broke the silence. "Is he going to live?"

"He has a chance."

Kate caught her breath.

Daniel reached for her hand.

"If he does," Daniel said, "will he . . . be all right?"

"That's impossible to say now."

"Can I see him?"

"You're related?"

"I'm his son."

"I would like to see him too," Kate said. She straightened. "I'm a very close friend."

Porter looked at Daniel. "I can arrange for *you* to look in when he's in the recovery room, but—"

"He would want her there, too," Daniel said.

Porter hesitated. "All right. But only for a moment."

Kate squeezed Daniel's hand. He squeezed back.

Two days later, Daniel moved down from New York to Hamilton, into Pinchus's house. Susan came with him, given an early maternity leave by her employer.

"I want to stay here," Daniel told Susan. "Until my father dies or leaves the hospital."

He went to the hospital each day and sat by Seymour Pinchus's bed, holding his hand and talking to him, even though his father—head swathed in bandages, only his nose and part of the right side of his face visible—lay deathly still and unresponsive, in a deep coma.

With Kate's help, Susan persuaded Daniel to attend his graduation ceremony in New York the following week. It's what his father would have wanted, they told him. It's what he would have insisted on, had he been able. Finally Daniel believed them. Susan and Kate went up to New York with him. So did Sam Milano, who took photographs of Daniel in his cap and gown, whooping and hollering when the dean handed Daniel his diploma. Helen Milano stayed back in Hamilton, promising she would get in touch immediately if there were a change in Pinchus's condition. Susan's parents drove down from the Bronx. Daniel's mother took a train in from Connecticut.

After the ceremony, they all went out for a celebratory dinner at a French restaurant on West Forty-sixth Street, Manhattan's Restaurant Row. It was a little after midnight when Daniel and Susan got back to the frame house on Elmont Street on the southern rim of Hamilton. Daniel wanted to go over to the hospital to see Pinchus. Dr. de Mello had arranged liberal access for him so he could go whenever he liked.

"Take your diploma," Susan said.

"That's a nice thought. I will. You sure you'll be all right?"

"Yes." Susan patted her belly. "We both will— though we'll probably be asleep by the time you get back."

Daniel drove to the hospital. He took the elevator up to floor where Pinchus was. When he got off, Barbara, the head nurse, smiled at him. She waggled her fingers hello.

"Did you get it?"

"Yes." He tapped the diploma.

"Congratulations."

"Thank you. How is he?"

"I think he's comfortable. No change."

Daniel went down the hall. He left the door to Pinchus's room ajar, for illumination. He didn't want to turn on the lights. He moved one of the chairs to the side of the bed and sat in the semidarkness, looking at his father.

There were tubes in Pinchus's nose, his throat, his arm. Another disappeared under his hospital gown, near the groin.

"I got my diploma, Pop. I did it."

He held the diploma up, as if Pinchus could see it.

"It was a nice day. Susan was there. Kate was there. Sam took a lot of pictures. You can see them when you're better. He even took one of Kate, Susan, and Mom together—if you can believe that."

Daniel set the diploma down. He took Pinchus's limp left hand between his own.

He laughed. "That was a scene. There was no way around it. I had to introduce everybody. It took Mom about a tenth of a second to figure out who Kate had to be, what her relationship to you was, to me. You could see it play over her face. She was deciding whether she was going to be the Beast of Brooklyn or she was going to make nice. She went with nice. I think now that she's accepted Susan—hell, even *likes* Susan—she's starting to mellow.

"She said for me to tell you that she sends all her prayers and good wishes to you. She said not to tell you that she sends her love because you wouldn't believe it and you'd know she didn't mean it anyway. But she *does* mean the rest of it. . . ."

Daniel talked about the dinner, about the big eight-point buck they'd seen standing by the side of the road next to a field just out of town on the drive home.

It was almost half past one when he said, "Well, it's late, I'd better think about going now, Dad. You . . . take care. You . . ." His lower lip started to tremble. "You . . . Oh, Dad!"

He dropped out of the chair onto his knees beside

the bed. He grasped Pinchus's hand tightly, pressed his cheek to it.

"Dad! Oh, Daddy, please don't die."

He wept. He wept as he had when he was a child and had first understood that his father would not be living with him and his mother anymore.

"Please, Daddy. I love you. Daddy, *Daddy*!"

Daniel usually went to the hospital in the morning and then again in the evening. Kate was there every day, too. Sometimes she stayed until late in the night, sleeping on a rollaway in the staff lounge. Daniel frequently ran into Sam Milano there. If they missed each other for more than two or three days, Sam would usually call to see how things were or to suggest they meet and get a bite to eat together.

On one of the nights Daniel and Sam were out, Sam asked: "What's your situation now with the New York department, with Boston? You got any problems because you came down here? You need someone to make a call for you?"

"No. Everything's okay. I've been in touch. They understand. I mean, neither one knows I'm considering the other one, too, but each says it's okay, I can take the time I need here. They haven't put me under any pressure."

"Good. Susan?"

"The doctor says any day now. Physically, she's great. Psychologically, I'm not so sure. She's holding back. I can't get her to talk about how she feels about my father getting shot, I mean what it does to *her*."

"You mean the possibility of something like this happening to you?"

"Yeah. I think so."

"Let her pick the time. She's got a lot on her plate right now. Anyone married to a cop, sooner or later they *got* to make peace with this. And they all do. Well, most of 'em anyway. You know, it's not just wives—it's husbands too, anyone married to a cop who isn't one herself, himself. Tell you, I'm glad Helen's not a cop."

Daniel smiled. "Well, no danger of Susan being one. I can't picture anyone less likely for the job."

"Count that as luck. But think about it, how you'd feel if she put on a gun and went into all this stuff every day. Then maybe you can get a sense of what it might be like from her point of view."

One night, a little more than three weeks after Pinchus had been shot, Daniel and Susan were lying in bed together. Susan was wearing a light cotton nightgown. She had both hands resting lightly atop her belly. Between them was one of Daniels' hands.

"Forty-five seconds," Daniel said, counting. "Forty-six . . . forty-seven . . . forty-eight—"

The baby kicked.

Susan went, "Ooomph!"

"I told you," Daniel said. "He's not going to settle down tonight. He thinks he's a regular Mighty Power Ranger."

"I wish you wouldn't use the masculine pronoun. We don't know yet."

They had agreed not to ask their doctor, to wait until the baby—either Adrienne or Adam—was born. They had taken Lamaze classes. Daniel was going to be in the delivery room.

"I'll bet you a month of diaper changing on it. If it's *not* a boy, we've got a stomping bull dyke on our hands."

"Daniel!"

"Uh, 'pretty, but unusually assertive'?"

"Reasonably self-respecting."

"Ah."

Susan went quiet. The baby kicked again. Daniel sensed Susan was working something over in her mind.

"You know," she said after several moments. "I've had some talks with Kate on my own."

He hadn't known. "Mm-hmm."

"And Helen and I went to lunch."

"Uh-huh." He had known that.

"We talked. About you and me."

"Us? What about us?"

"You wanting to be a detective."

Daniel became uneasy.

"They're both very strong, Kate and Helen. I'm not as strong they are."

Daniel was reluctant to speak, not wanting to hear any more.

Susan began to cry. "I'm very afraid. I'm afraid you'll get hurt or killed. I don't want to lose you. I want you to be here for our baby."

Daniel held her. He was aching inside.

Susan cried freely. "I'm not as strong as Kate or Helen. But I know you want to do this. I know you just spent four years getting ready for it. I wouldn't want you telling me what to do with my life. So I won't tell you. But I hate what you want to do, that it could take you away from me! It scares me so much sometimes I can't stand it."

"Susan . . ."

"No, goddamn it! Let me finish. I hate it, but I can live with it. I really can. Maybe it'll even be all right some day, like it is for Helen. I wouldn't say this if I didn't mean it. And I'm not going to change my mind and tell you different later."

She wiped the back of her hand across her eyes, got a tissue from the box on the stand by the bed, and blew her nose.

"But I'll tell you this—I will never, *ever* forgive you if you get killed and leave me and the baby!"

The tension, the fear, gave way in Daniel. He cradled Susan in his arms. "I will do my best not to let that happen," he said, promising from his very being. "I don't think it will. It rarely does. But I have heard everything you said. And I love you for it, and I am deeply, deeply grateful."

He didn't tell her that just a minute ago, while he

had felt their child kicking within her—the new life, his life, her life, all their lives—that had she asked him, he would have given it up. He would have given up this choice, this passion, for her and for the baby, though it would have torn him apart to do it; he would have given it up as willingly and honestly as she had just told him that she accepted his choice, and he would have gone forward with her and would have tried very hard never to look back.

But he didn't tell her that. And he knew he never would.

In the weeks that followed, Seymour Pinchus lay deep in a coma. Many people wanted to visit him, but only those with whom he had truly been intimate were allowed to. One of those, though, would not be coming. Rose Fitapaldi had passed away three months earlier and thus was spared the terrible news about her friend.

Scores of others sent cards and letters, baskets of fruit and candies, flowering plants, and bouquets of flowers. Kate gave most of these to other patients in the hospital, to brighten their rooms and keep Pinchus's from being overwhelmed.

Lenore Schaeffer wrote to Pinchus. She expressed her and her husband's deep concern for him and their wishes for his quick and full recovery. She enclosed a photograph of Alice, taken three months before Alice was killed: smiling, vibrant, alive.

I know Alice is in heaven, Lenore wrote, *and I know that she is looking down, watching over you as best she can, and loving you, and holding your hand in hers. God bless you and keep you. Thank you for everything you did for our daughter.*

Kate read the letter to him, though he could not hear her. She got a little frame for the photograph and placed it on the bed stand next to him.

▼

Pinchus's conditioned worsened. It became difficult to maintain his vital functions.

But, in what seemed a blessed kind of symmetry, as one life slowly ebbed, another flowed: Daniel and Susan had a son, six pounds, twelve ounces—Adam Pinchus.

They brought him to Pinchus's bedside, Daniel wheeling Susan down in a chair from the maternity wing, Susan holding Adam in her arms. Adam moved one hand reflexively, worked his mouth with a kind of slurping sound, but was otherwise sleeping serenely.

"Here he is, Pop," Daniel said, with a tremor in his voice. "Your grandson. Isn't he great?"

Susan held Adam up, as if to show him to Pinchus. "You'd really like him, Dad. I don't know who he looks like yet, but he has your eyebrows for sure. They look wonderful on him."

"I love you, Pop," Daniel said.

"I do, too," said Susan. "And so does Adam."

In July, two and a half months after Pinchus had been gunned down, Alex Schwenk returned to his office after an afternoon photo shoot at the deputy mayor's office. He was reflecting—guiltily—on how much simpler, even more pleasant, life had been lately without Pinchus here in the station. Not that Schwenk had ever wished Pinchus any physical harm, certainly, but not that he'd ever wish him any particular good either.

Sergeant Sam Milano buzzed on the intercom. "Captain, I took a call from Chief Foster's office while you were out. They said the new guy's on his way over, should be here in half an hour or so."

"Good, good," said Schwenk. "Listen, Sam, why don't we meet in the lunchroom in fifteen minutes, grab something to eat, and talk a couple of things over."

There was an awkward silence.

"Sam," Schwenk said pointedly, "I want to do that."

"All right, Captain. Fifteen minutes."

The impending arrival of the new man cheered Schwenk. They'd been one short in Homicide since Pinchus was shot, and Schwenk had found himself having to put out more personal effort than he liked to. Milano would be the senior partner in the new team, moving into Pinchus's old position. The new man would train under him.

After ten minutes, Schwenk went downstairs. He told the duty sergeant where he'd be, in case the new man arrived early. Milano joined him in the lunchroom a few minutes later. At the vending machines, Sam insisted on buying. Schwenk offered only a token protest.

Sam dropped coins into the machine. The light came on and Schwenk slapped carelessly at the button for a sugared doughnut. He missed, hit the adjacent one. A plastic-wrapped piece of apple pie fell down into the receiver slot.

"That was always Seymour's favorite," Sam said. "He used to complain about how they were either stale or soggy, but actually, he enjoyed them. I miss Seymour. A lot. I keep waiting for him to walk into the room."

Schwenk made a noncommittal sound. He opened the plastic wrap and looked in disappointment at the pie. "It's soggy," he said.

Suddenly, from the entrance to the small room, a voice called, "You know, Captain, that really tastes a lot better with a hunk of cheddar cheese on it. Trust me, I know."

Schwenk blanched. He turned in disbelief at the familiar voice. It was not Seymour Pinchus—as he had known it couldn't be—but it *was* Daniel Pinchus, holding a personnel envelope with a familiar emblem on it.

"Hi," Daniel said brightly. "I'm your new man."

Schwenk lost what remained of his appetite.

▼

Kate was at the hospital when Daniel arrived that night.

In some ways, it was more difficult for Daniel to see Pinchus as he was now than it had been in the beginning: His father looked so much these days as if he were sleeping rather than in a coma.

The site of the tracheotomy in Pinchus' throat had closed and healed. The bandages were gone from around his head; his hair had grown back and in another month or so would be nearly its normal length. The cast had been removed from around his right shoulder and arm.

But he was not sleeping.

Kate was dabbing Pinchus's face with a washcloth when Daniel entered the room. She had just finished shaving Pinchus. A razor lay next to a can of shaving cream and a bowl of water on a small table.

She smiled. "How was your first day?"

"Good. Funny. Schwenk almost had a cow when I walked in. God, I wish I'd had a camera with me. Also, confusing. It's clear that there's more to this work than I ever suspected." He looked at his father admiringly. "Wow, Pop. I never knew how much you put into it."

They always spoke to Pinchus as if Pinchus could hear them. Dr. Porter said he couldn't. But it didn't hurt anything. And it made *them* feel better, if nothing else.

"I'll take a break," Kate said. "You can tell him about it in private."

"It's all right for you to stay."

"I think this is better between you two. You can tell me later."

Daniel sat down in the chair Kate had vacated, shifted it a little to accommodate for his longer legs. He took Pinchus's hand in his, as he customarily did, and told him all about the day.

"So that's how it went, Pop," he finished. "I'm

going to like it. It's going to work. I'm going to make you proud."

And then Daniel felt a slight pressure from his father's hand.

He looked at Pinchus's placid face. "Dad? Can you hear me?"

His father's grip tightened.

"Nurse!" Daniel shouted. "Nurse! Kate! Hurry, hurry!" He began to weep and holler excitedly.

Over the next few days, Seymour Pinchus came back.

He opened his eyes—and the ophthalmologist found that some shadowy vision still remained in his injured left one.

He could speak—haltingly, and not coherently, but enough to make himself basically understood.

He could hear—unable to comprehend most of what he did hear, but enough so that he could respond.

"Aphasia," Dr. Porter said: the partial loss of the ability to speak and to understand certain words.

It improved quickly.

By the fourth day, Pinchus was demanding, although awkwardly, that his grandson be allowed to stay in his room for more than a few minutes at a time. He didn't remember what had happened to him. He didn't know why he was in the hospital.

After a brief exam on the fifth day, and a few minutes of conversation, Dr. de Mello decided Pinchus was strong enough to be told. With Kate and Daniel on either side of the bed, De Mello began. "It started two-and-a-half months ago," he said, then brought Pinchus all the way up to the present moment.

"So here's the bottom line: You're a tough sonofabitch and you're going to live. Probably longer than a lot of us. But how you do that is up to you. We saved your arm, but you're never going to get much use out of it. You've got one good eye, and about ten percent vision in your other one. You'll probably be able to shake the aphasia completely.

"Now, I am told by Daniel and Kate here and your partner, Sam Milano, that for you, your career and life have been pretty much the same thing. Well, that's over. You've got a life, and you're damn lucky to have it, but your career is over. You won't be able to be a cop anymore. How you handle that, that's up to you. From what everybody tells me, you're tough enough to handle it just fine. Nobody says you have to like it. Just handle it, that's all. Can you do that?"

Pinchus struggled: "I . . . I can nhn ahh . . . I can . . . do it."

"Good!"

Pinchus gave de Mello a baleful look.

De Mello reached down and slapped Pinchus lightly on the foot. "See you tomorrow."

Pinchus rested in silence awhile. He looked neither at Daniel nor at Kate. They didn't press.

"Can do it," he said finally.

Kate kissed him.

"Look forward . . . you . . . nurse me . . . back t' health." He winked suggestively.

Kate batted her eyes in mock coquettishness.

"And . . . turning fifty-six. Now . . . get me apple pie, piece . . . cheddar."

"Right now?"

"Uh-huh."

Kate went out for the pie.

Pinchus turned his head to Daniel. "Adam?"

"Susan will bring him later."

"Good. . . . Daniel?"

"Yes, Pop?"

"Love you. . . . Proud of you."

Daniel wiped his eyes. "I know, Pop. I love you. And I'm proud of you, too."

After a moment, Pinchus said, "One . . . more . . . thing."

Daniel leaned in. "Yes?"

"Tell that . . . son'bitch Schwenk I'll find . . . a way . . . I'll be back!"

Daniel burst out laughing.

The old Fox just might, he thought.

Pinchus had never liked to be told what he could and couldn't do. Someday, he just might look at them deadly, with his one good eye, and make them all eat their words.

"I will," said Daniel. "But for now, can I get you a cup of coffee maybe, to go with that pie Kate is bringing back?"

"Good boy." Pinchus nodded, happy.

ABOUT THE AUTHOR

Dennis Asen was born in Brooklyn, New York. A graduate of Brooklyn College and New York University College of Dentistry, he currently resides in Pennsylvania, and is happily married with three children. DEADLY IMPRESSION is his first novel.